THE

Three complete novels

TRACKERS

TEAM

TRILOGY 1

I0563490

Backtrack: The Scout's Story

Mist: The Bloodhound's Story

Kachina: The Snapshot's Story

Mickey MorningGlory

THE
TRACKERS
TEAM

TRILOGY 1

Books 1, 2, & 3 of
THE TRACKERS SERIES

Backtrack: The Scout's Story

Mist: The Bloodhound's Story

Kachina: The Snapshot's Story

MICKEY MORNINGGLORY

Patent Print Books
Panama City Beach, Florida

This is a work of fiction, and the views expressed herein are the sole responsibility of the author. The characters, places, and incidents portrayed in this book are products of the author's imagination, and any resemblance to actual persons, living or dead, or actual events or locales, is entirely coincidental.

THE TRACKERS TEAM: TRILOGY 1

Published by PATENT PRINT BOOKS www.patentprintbooks.com
PATENT PRINT BOOKS and the fingerprint colophon
are registered trademarks of PATENT PRINT BOOKS

Copyright ©2020 by Mickey MorningGlory
Cover design ©2020 by PATENT PRINT BOOKS
Edited by Ann W. Carns

First Edition: 2020

Printed in the United States of America

ISBN 978-0-9850731-5-2
Library of Congress Control Number: 2020

10   9   8   7   6   5   4   3   2   1

In memory of
Dr. Wilbur A. Middleton ~
My inspiration, my hero, my father.

<u>CONTENTS</u>

PREFACE

The members of the Trackers Team are near and dear to my heart after having them rumble around in my dreams for all these years. This volume combines three of their exciting psychic tracking and romantic adventures and features brothers Noah and Dane Lightfoot and the woman in their lives, Raven Looking Bird. You'll get a chance to meet their families and the rest of the Team. I trust you'll like them; they are some of my favorite people.

~Mickey MorningGlory

FOREWORD

The number seven has always been special in literature and history. What if you discover you are the seventh son of a seventh son? What potential wisdom, force, or power have you inherited from your ancestors? How can you learn to express yourself as a tracker? And will you serve as a force for good or succumb to the selfish lure of evil?

A growing, crowded, exciting society can be found almost anywhere in present-day America. This author produces human characters who live, love, and compete for power and success in the pluralistic State of Florida. Power politics, big-time sports, and mystical dimensions of extra-sensory time travel capture the reader's interest. Unexpected themes drawn from ancient value systems, from Hispanic culture, and from Native American intrigue permeate the more normal local, secular culture in Florida's capital city and its environs. Every reader will identify with the pathos of vicious kidnapping, of fortunes made and lost, and of intimate love so close and yet so far away.

Mickey MorningGlory writes in a crisp, sharp, and brisk tempo. Her compelling characters capture your attention and the suspense of their intricate involvements, both virtuous and vicious, will keep you glued to the page until you arrive at the surprising conclusion. And then you will quickly ask for the next installment in this well-planned series which promises to continue to draw us into the amazing adventures of these exciting trackers.

~ Robert G. Newman, Ph.D.
A.J. Humphreys Professor of Religion
The University of Charleston

BACKTRACK:

THE SCOUT'S STORY

Book 1 of

THE TRACKERS SERIES

MICKEY MORNINGGLORY

Patent Print Books
Panama City Beach, Florida

This is a work of fiction, and the views expressed herein are the sole responsibility of the author. The characters, places, and incidents portrayed in this book are products of the author's imagination, and any resemblance to actual persons, living or dead, or actual events or locales, is entirely coincidental.

BACKTRACK: The Scout's Story
The Trackers Series, Book 1

Published by PATENT PRINT BOOKS www.patentprintbooks.com
PATENT PRINT BOOKS and the fingerprint colophon
are registered trademarks of PATENT PRINT BOOKS

First Edition: 2012
Revised 2020
Printed in the United States of America

ISBN 978-0-9850731-0-7
Library of Congress Control Number: 2012902203

10   9   8   7   6   5   4   3   2

CONTENTS

4 | MICKEY MORNINGGLORY

PREFACE

BACKTRACK came to me in a dream. When I awoke the next morning, I retained total recall of the story—the entire story—and dreamed it again and again. Desperate for an uneventful night's sleep, I finally gave in to the insistence of my nightly dream characters and wrote **BACKTRACK**, and then I slept soundly...for a while.

But the men and women of *The Trackers Series* have many tales to tell, and I am their voice. **BACKTRACK: THE SCOUT'S STORY** is Noah Lightfoot's adventure—the first in the series.

I guess sound sleep will have to wait a while. These Trackers are an active bunch!

~ Mickey MorningGlory

INTRODUCTION

It is my privilege to endorse BACKTRACK. I have read this fine novel and find the facts related to Muskogee Indian customs and rituals to be authentic. Even though this book is fiction, one can learn much about the Creek Indian ways and spirit.

~ Tuskie Mahaya Haco
(Dr. Andrew Boggs Ramsey)
Principal Chief
The Florida Tribe of Eastern Creek Indians
The Apalachicola Band of Creeks

"Legend and history dance together, and sometimes it is difficult to know who leads. But, in all things, there must be truth."

~ Liahona Thistleseed

PROLOGUE

TALLAHASSEE, FL~AUGUST~1990

THE SMOKE WAS THICK, and Dane Lightfoot's nostrils flared as he breathed in the acrid air. Inhaling slowly, he identified burning wood, burning carpet, burning upholstery, burning ... hair?

"Find the origin," he muttered aloud, "Concentrate!"

Dane was a clairscentrist, with an enhanced psychic sensitivity to smells, and tracking fire was his specialty, but he was having difficulty keeping his mind on this journey. He didn't usually have trouble with a routine blaze; however, this time it was different. This time he had an uncomfortable sensation of heat. He made a mental note to tell Lee; then he pulled his thoughts back to the work at hand.

The next breath ended in a choking cough, but not before Dane smelled the cigarette. He recalled the lectures Lee gave him. "Smoking in bed catches up to folks eventually." Dane was glad he finally quit. He smiled as he now detected the faintest wisp of vanilla. He often joked about how that fragrance made his temperature rise. His smile melted abruptly. *I am hot*, he reflected. *I'm really hot! And I can't breathe. It's way too smoky. Better get out now.* "Home," he coughed. Nothing happened. "Home," he called again, but with less intensity. His arms tingled from lack of oxygen, and he was growing weak. He gasped between choking spasms and tensed, waiting for the familiar rush as his mind rejoined his body. "Home!" he croaked again, coughing. *Why doesn't someone send the homing light?*

Dane tried frantically to remember who his beacon was and where he was tracking. Cognition came to him in a flash of blazing light; and as he sucked in a final breath of smoke, Dane Lightfoot realized the stench of roasting skin was his own.

* * *

Four miles away, sixteen-year-old Noah Lightfoot screamed out in his sleep. He woke and jerked upright but did not focus on his surroundings. He coughed out but one word before he fell back on the bed, and that one word was wrought with unbearable grief. "Dane."

* * *

Hundreds of miles away, I saw it all happen through my blind eyes. I had never met them, but I knew them. They were my blood brothers.

I am Luna—short for *Ojos del Luna* (as my village family calls me); *Hvresse Torwv* (as my Creek Indian mother calls me). Both names mean the same—Moon Eyes. I often travel great distances as I play my flute, and in my travels, I can see things that are always dark to me in the waking world of daylight.

The journey tonight is different—not hazy and shadowed, as many of the visions in my travels tend to be, but vivid and colorful, with keen sensory perceptions of sound and smell. I hear my brothers talking, though their mouths are closed. I feel the heat on my face, but I am not on fire. It is the rising sun, already making the dew turn to steam here in the jungle.

My mother says I am a "Keeper." That's why I remember in such detail what I see on my journeys. The stories I tell are not mine, but I keep them in my memory always, as do I keep all the other stories related to my brothers and these people whose lives intersect mine in a strange and unexplainable way. This one is his ... Noah's. It begins the night Dane dies and he awakes.

CHAPTER ONE

FRIDAY, 1992

NOAH LIGHTFOOT SITS MOTIONLESS in a high-backed chair of unfinished pine. His eyes are closed; his breathing, deep and regular. Behind him stands a lanky man of forty-four whose eyes are also closed beneath arched eyebrows. His rugged face is expressionless; his black hair is parted in the center, braided, and wrapped in leather thongs from below his ears to his shoulders. If his lids did not twitch from time to time, he could be mistaken for a drugstore wooden Indian.

Liahona "Lee" Thistleseed is aware of the scrutiny he receives, but he pays little heed to it. He is intent on the young man in the chair. He is listening for one word.

Noah sighs. At least, those in the room think he sighs. But Lee hears something more. He hears the word, "Home." Lee shifts his position. Raising his head slightly, he beacons.

The spectators see no change in the two men, but Noah sees the light—dim at first, then brighter. He moves toward it in his mind's eye as he prepares himself for the rush.

"Home," Noah calls. His conscious mind seems to fly through the light. He opens his eyes. At precisely the same instant, Lee opens his own eyes. Lee relaxes his grip on the chair and smiles down at Noah. Beaconing is a crucial part of tracking. Like a lighthouse on a foggy shore, it lights the way for the mind travelers, and Lee takes pride in his ability to signal. This pride extends to the young man in the chair. Lee had trained Noah and developed his young apprentice's gift. Now, Noah is as good a Tracker as any he has ever seen ... except Dane.

Noah sees Lee frown. The wound is yet tender. Lee loved Dane as his own son; in fact, he trained Dane before any of the others. Noah shakes his head. No matter what anyone says he knows Dane could not have tracked alone that night. It is the first rule of tracking: No one ever tracks without a beacon. The younger Tracker regards his mentor.

"Lee? Where'd you go, buddy? Hey, don't take off without me." Noah laughs, displaying his slightly crossed front teeth and prominent canines in his characteristic arresting smile. When Noah smiles, he is nearly irresistible. Something about his personality seems to hold people hostage. Just barely a man at eighteen and a student at Florida State University, Noah possesses a wisdom far beyond his years. He is strong and dynamic, but he has a spontaneous spirit that allows him to feel at home in any situation, with any group of people. "Charmed and blessed" are the terms Lee often uses about him. It is an unusual combination in one so young ... almost as unusual as his second sight. The Native Americans believe that the psychic gift of second sight is nearly always found in the seventh son of a seventh son. Dane had been the seventh son—the gifted one; Noah is the eighth.

Noah looks across the room at the anxious faces of the two FBI agents. They are look-alike crew cuts in three-piece suits, stock characters in a low budget movie. He has named them "Special Agent Blonde" and "Special Agent Brunette."

"Go, Noles," Noah mugs. This getting no response, he grins and rotates his shoulders. Then, taking a deep breath, he stares fixedly at a thumbtack sticking out of the opposite wall and relates his search.

"The perp's in Atlanta. Ramada Inn. His suitcase contains one pair of black socks and one pair of jockey briefs—with skid marks, I might add. Blue plaid Bermuda shorts—price tag still on 'em—and a Hawaiian print cotton shirt—also with a price tag. On the bed is an open Hush Puppies shoe box—sales slip inside— and a pair of shades—cheap variety, but dark. On the nightstand is a Gideon Bible being used as a coaster for a glass full of pleasing pink Pepto Bismol. There's also an empty box of generic bandage strips." Noah yawns dramatically, the picture of boredom. "Oh yeah, and an airline ticket."

"What airline? What flight?" Special Agent Blonde interjects with a scowl.

Noah pauses and squints. "Delta, flight 419 to L.A., departure time 10:20 AM. One way," he says.

"What about the guy, Lightfoot?" Special Agent Brunette demands, his jaw clenched.

Noah gazes innocently at the two special agents. "Oh, the guy? Let me see if I remember the guy." He mocks them. "The *guy* is in the bathroom, puking his guts out."

"Why?" Special Agent Blonde asks.

"Well, I'd puke, too, if I had that much explosive taped to my pelvis," Noah muses with a snort.

Special Agents Blonde and Brunette jump up and collide, Keystone Cop style, as they grapple for the telephone. Noah smirks at Lee with a familiar, mischievous twinkle in his eyes. Lee raises his shoulders and cocks his head.

"What time? What time is the flight?" Special Agent Blonde calls from across the room.

"10:20 AM, Eastern time," Noah confirms, glancing at his watch. "Just about three hours from now."

Special Agent Blonde repeats the information over the phone. "What does he look like?" the agent asks.

"Aw, Gee Whiz, fellas, Raven does the faces. I don't know how to draw." Noah says, fluttering his eyelashes.

"I knew we should've used the girl instead. They'll just have to pat down all the men who come through the gate." Special Agent Brunette scowls at his partner.

At this point, Lee interrupts. "Gentlemen, do you not realize the man will explode? You must take him unawares, and away from the airport population."

"Right, right! But, we can't. Not if we don't know what he looks like," Special Agent Brunette says. He crosses him arms and clenches his jaw like a petulant little boy.

Lee smiles indulgently, as though the men were simple. "That is true; however, you do know how he will be dressed."

The FBI agents gape at him. Noah hoots at their consternation. *What a couple of goons.*

"Did Mr. Lightfoot not tell you what you should know? Did he not reveal the contents of the man's luggage? It contains some recently purchased clothing, save for the underwear. Look for the man to be dressed as a tourist with brand new shoes that already hurt his feet."

After a moment of fish-mouthing, Special Agent Blonde relays this information rapidly into the telephone.

"Oh, fellas," Noah calls, moving into the kitchen, "This may not be important, but I think it's probably worth mentioning. In his country, the man was once a thief."

"How can you possibly know that? And what do you mean, he was a thief?" Special Agent Brunette is almost panting.

Lee fields this question. "It means that you should look for a Middle-Eastern man with only one hand."

* * *

Earlier that same morning, the Outlaw traveled. The view from the capitol building was breathtaking, but there was no time for sightseeing. There was much work to be done, and only one person could do it. It was nearly delivery time at the distribution center of The Tallahassee Democrat. It was important that the Outlaw's task be completed before the newspapers were released to the general public.

Success. The deed was done; the Outlaw sent the word to the Beacon. In a high velocity *"whoosh"* that no one else heard, the Outlaw's mind returned to its body.

The task completed, there was time for the Outlaw to look out over the skyline. The slight waver in the air would never be noticed. It would only seem like the distortion produced by sleepy eyes taking in the baking pavement in the September heat.

It was a brilliant plan, and it had been working for two years without a hitch. That is, once Dane Lightfoot was out of the way. He should have known that when you get too close to the heat, you get burned.

With a sigh, the Beacon turned and entered the elevator and moments later left the capitol building. The Outlaw watched with satisfaction as the Beacon slowly disappeared down the vacant sidewalk along Monroe Street.

Later, when the newspaper trucks traveled throughout the city, no one would notice the change. In fact, not even the news editor would remember what should have been on those newspaper pages—the pages that had been changed in the twinkling of an eye.

The very perfection of it all made the Outlaw smile again. The rising sun glinted in ice-blue eyes so light they seemed silvery. The Outlaw reached into a pocket and removed a small two-sided vial. Inside each shallow basin, immersed in clear liquid, floated a dark brown contact lens. With a confident, practiced motion, the Outlaw slipped the lenses in place. They covered the silver irises completely, but the Outlaw added light sensitive sunglasses for further disguise.

With great delight, the Outlaw laughed aloud. The sheer genius of it all was the ultimate proof of the Outlaw's superior mind. The two-fold purpose—eliminate one to elevate another—had again been accomplished, and there was no clue, nor trace of any kind, to show that the present had been forever altered by a trip to the past.

CHAPTER TWO
CHIEF OSCEOLA AND THE RAVEN

DRESSED AS CHIEF OSCEOLA, Noah Lightfoot peers at the crowded stadium full of cheering F.S.U. football fans on this Seminole Saturday Night. *There's nothing like this sensation on the whole wide earth,* he says to himself.

The feeling of his cotton britches against the rough wool blanket on Renegade's back defies all attempts at explanation. This is how his ancestors rode; this is a little chunk of the past he is not willing to give up. After two years, the thrill of being Chief Osceola is still so intense, he has decided to go on to graduate school ... just to continue riding this magnificent horse. That he has no idea of a course of study does not concern him. There's plenty of time to decide his major. The first time he mounted this horse, his mind was made up. In fact, the moment he walked onto campus, he knew he would be here a long time. Does the adoration of the home team football fans have anything to do with his decision to stay? Of course, it does.

Despite some criticism by Indian activist groups, Noah feels that dressing as a mascot for this college football team is no shame. At least he isn't a chicken or a dog. Noah is proud to be a symbol of his school and his people.

Tonight, it is no different. Though the open stadium provides no respite from the almost constant drizzle, it is worth anything to ride like a chief. And Noah is the perfect choice for the portrayal of Chief Osceola, one of the most famous Seminole Indian chiefs in history. After all, Noah is a Native American—part Creek, part Seminole—and born and raised on Brighton Reservation in South Florida. But, more importantly—in Noah's mind at least— he doesn't need a wig like most of the other Caucasian Osceolas have used. Noah's own thick, black hair hangs to his shoulders and will never fly off during the celebratory touchdown rides.

Noah looks around at the packed stadium, and then he glances at the scoreboard. The Seminoles are soundly beating the Syracuse Orangemen 32-14. Casey, the first-string quarterback, has been taken out to rest, and second-stringer Brad is at the helm. In Noah's eyes, life just can't get any better. *College is great.*

Noah lets out a high-pitched war cry, and the horse bucks beneath him.

"Whoa, now. Take it easy, Renegade." He croons, trying to rein the horse in, but it keeps shying around. Noah slides off the blanket and walks Renegade around the end zone. Suddenly, the horse's ears prick forward. He whinnies and paws the ground, his head tossing restlessly.

James, the trainer, comes over to help. Noah glances up from the horse briefly and sees ... faintly ... a flicker of light. Quickly putting his arm around Renegade's neck for support, Noah closes his eyes and concentrates in the direction of the light. *It can't be, but there it is again. There is no mistake; it is a beacon ... in the stadium, of all places. Who is tracking tonight?*

Noah listens intently, trying to hear the word. The signal light seems brighter for an instant, and then it begins to die away.

Without a second thought, Noah calls out, "Home!" His mind rushes toward the light. *Faster, faster.* Timing is crucial. He must reach the light before it fades completely away, or he'll be trapped—his mind lost in the darkness while an empty shell of a body remains grounded.

He is almost there. His mind speeds toward what is now just a tiny glow. He closes in rapidly. One more moment, and he is there. His eyes fly open and fall upon James.

"Noah? You O.K., man?" the trainer asks. "You a awfully pale-lookin' redskin," he adds with a toothy grin.

Noah shakes his head to clear his vision, and then he smiles crookedly at James. "You're a pretty light-looking brother, too, my friend," he says. He claps James on the back. "How 'bout them Noles, eh?"

James whoops and makes a scalping motion. "Scalp 'em! Here go your spear, man. Better ride." He hands Noah the long spear that Chief Osceola must plunge into the ground in the end zone after each touchdown.

Noah looks at the scoreboard: 39-14. Somehow, he has missed a touchdown. He jumps on Renegade's back and waves his spear, all the time scanning the crowded stadium for the eyes he glimpsed in that split second before he burst through the light. Those eerie, silver eyes. As his gaze passes over the skyboxes, Noah jerks back so abruptly that Renegade rears. The crowd roars, applauding at the familiar sight of Chief Osceola astride Renegade, its front legs pawing the air, getting ready to make the 100-yard gallop across the field to taunt the opposing team.

"That's wrong. It can't be ..." Noah says aloud. His tortured mind struggles to remember something. *What is it?*

"The stadium. Something's wrong about the stadium. The name is wrong. Dick Camel. Dick? No, not Dick. Dirk. Dirk Camel. Dirk Campbell?" He pauses and stares into the gray sky. "DOAK. DOAK CAMPBELL STADIUM!" he shouts.

The crowd roars again, mistaking his shouts for a war cry. He turns the horse and rides back to the trainer, skidding to a halt just inches from the man. "James, quick, give me a pen."

James obediently fishes a Bic pen from his pocket and hands it to the agitated Indian on the horse. This is nothing new to James. Noah is a quirky dude.

Noah snatches the pen and frantically scribbles "Doak Campbell Stadium" on the back of his hand before he forgets it again. Then, in confusion, he whips his head around to look at the skyboxes. Across the front, written in gold block letters, are the words, **DARRYL KILEY STADIUM.**

*   *   *

Sunday after a home game is a welcome day of rest—or so it should be. But for Noah, the sunrise only marks the passing of a troubled dark into a more troubled light. The vast implications of last night's events weigh heavily on his confused mind, and no amount of thought, conjecture, or logic have been able to bring about the answers he seeks. These things he knows: the one with the silver eyes has the gift and can track—in fact, was tracking with a beacon during the game—but more importantly, somehow, someone has tampered with the past and has changed the present.

Noah is filled with questions. *How long has it been happening? What has been changed? Who is doing it, and why?*

Up until last night, there were only four known Trackers in America—five, when Dane was alive. Noah has been told there are others with the gift, but he knows the gift without training is useless and is usually passed off as intuition or coincidence. The next realization cramps his gut: "Silver Eyes" is what Lee refers to as an "Outlaw," and someone with the right knowledge has trained that Outlaw.

Noah sits swaying gently in his porch swing and lets the myriad colors of the sunrise blur as he concentrates on each member of the elite group of Trackers. Thanks to his highly developed photographic memory, he can see every face quite clearly as he begins a detailed mental character analysis, based on what he knows and what he has been told by Lee and Dane. The first to mind is, of course, a woman ... Raven Looking Bird.

*   *   *

"She walks in beauty, like the night." No phrase had ever been truer. Raven Looking Bird was stunning. She was part Yavapai and part Hopi Indian, but without many of her kinsmen's flatness of face. Her features were finely chiseled into unvarnished cherry wood skin; her small teeth were like perfectly matched pearls.

At twenty-five, her only noticeable imperfection was a fan

of tiny lines at the corner of each hazelnut eye—the result of nearsighted squinting before she finally resorted to contact lenses. That was just one of the holdouts in her stubborn desire to be atypical. Raven liked to play against her looks.

She wore her glossy black hair in a short bob, cropped bluntly at earlobe level, but with bangs cut straight across the top of her eyebrows in the style of her Yavapai-Prescott tribe. Though Tallahassee had a couple of large malls and boasted several fine boutiques, her wardrobe consisted of outdoorsy mail-order clothes from catalogs like Land's End and L.L. Bean; however, no amount of down-dressing and lack of makeup could disguise the fact that Raven Looking Bird was, without a doubt, beauty personified.

Raven was unmarried, but there seemed to be no shortage of potential suitors. She rebuffed any and all advances, but with such style and grace that no man ever felt he had been rejected. Though she had dated many, she confessed to only one true love in her lifetime; nevertheless, that was over, and there would never be another to fill his shoes. The thought of him, yet, saddened her, so she took refuge in her work.

Therein lay her gift. Raven Looking Bird was an artist … not an ordinary run-of-the-mill painter, but an extraordinarily talented portrait artist. Raven was skilled in a variety of media— oils, acrylics, watercolors, charcoal. She had the uncanny ability to create more than a face on a canvas. She could almost capture the soul of her subjects … the very essence of the inner spirit. Most often, this produced satisfied customers, but on occasion, Raven glimpsed some dark malignance within a person. Whenever those times happened, she summarily dismissed the client without explanation and destroyed the likeness. This amazing propensity for melding the inner and outer person into a remarkably life-like visual rendering brought her to the attention of the local law enforcement agency at the young age of twenty-two.

While making preliminary sketches of the police chief's wife, Raven felt a profound sadness coming from the woman. The more she concentrated, the more intense the feeling became. Then, a gentle towheaded child came forward from the doorway and placed his tiny arm across the woman's shoulders. He laid his head against her arm and beamed at Raven. Raven was so taken with the child she painted the two of them in that loving embrace. The boy came with the woman on the two subsequent visits. Raven sensed sublime peacefulness in the woman when the child was with her and knew that this portrait would be one of her very best.

Chief Jack Abernathy and his wife came to pick up the painting a few days later. Raven proudly displayed the finished work on which she had labored late into the previous night. She was not prepared for their reaction.

The man's jaw dropped; his face grew ashen. He stared at the picture without a word. His wife was much more vocal.

"It's Andy!" she cried through a wash of tears. She fixed Raven with a mother's smile. "How did you know? Andy was only four when we lost him in the fire. All our photos burned, too. It's just been a year, but I was afraid I was beginning to forget how he looked." A fresh flood of tears flowed down her already-streaked face. "Thank you. Thank you for giving me back my baby." She embraced Raven and excused herself to the restroom.

The chief finally found his voice. "How did you do that?" he asked, staring at the mother and child in the picture.

Shaken, Raven explained how the little boy appeared to comfort his mother, and how he stood there for her to paint. He never spoke, but he always waved as he followed his mother out the door. She recalled how the light in the studio seemed to brighten while he was there and began to fade as he left.

Three days later, Raven had a visit from Dane Lightfoot and Lee Thistleseed; three weeks later, she was a Tracker; three years later, she was on Noah Lightfoot's mind.

*   *   *

Three hours later, Raven is again on Noah's mind, but now the reason has nothing to do with character analysis. This time, it is business. Lee has called a meeting of all the Trackers. The case is important—one that requires the talents of all four of them.

Noah is to pick up Raven at her apartment and meet the other Trackers at the Governor's Mansion. The news is grim.

Florida's Governor Robert Ramirez's grandchild, Sarah, has been kidnapped. No ransom has yet been demanded. The child was abducted from the front driveway of the mansion while she waited for her grandmother to come out to the car.

There is an added complication to this situation which causes an even greater urgency. Sarah and her grandmother had been preparing to meet her parents at the Mayo Clinic in Jacksonville. Sarah is scheduled for treatments to receive a bone marrow transplant at St. Luke's Hospital the next day. Young Sarah Ramirez has acute lymphoblastic leukemia.

Raven greets Noah at the door with a yawn and a sleepy smile. Even at 8:00 AM, she is breath-taking. Her face is scrubbed clean and free of makeup; she looks more like fifteen than twenty-five. Her hair is pulled back with a turquoise knit headband. She wears a turquoise knit shirt and matching socks. Noah does not have to look at her feet to know what footwear she has.

Moccasins. Raven wears no shoes but moccasins. She has them in all styles and colors of leather—handmade gifts from her mother in Arizona. It is the only Indian custom she permits herself, but it is one she stubbornly maintains from a deep respect for the only other person she has ever loved.

Today, her moccasins are a light doeskin with white beaded fringe, matching her khaki walking shorts. The beads rustle as she breezes past Noah and hops into the front seat of his red Ford Mustang. He turns and follows the lingering scent of her signature cologne like a hungry dog follows a grilled steak. He gazes at her, mesmerized, until she pops open a Diet Coke and breaks the spell.

"Let's go, Chief. We've got work to do," she quips, peering through her trendy, but practical, Oakley sunglasses.

Noah grins, embarrassed, and jumps into the car. "At your service, ma'am," he says and pulls ahead into the traffic just beginning to pick up on Tennessee Street.

Noah and Raven are silent as they ride, absorbed in the task at hand. Nothing is more important to the team than tracking a child … especially one whose diseased body is self-destructing as each minute passes.

CHAPTER THREE

TRACKING SARAH

FIFTEEN MINUTES LATER, RAVEN and Noah park behind Lee's white Volvo on the street outside the Governor's mansion. When they walk into the sitting room, they notice Lee and the other member of their team, Graham Skysong, propped on the sofa. Noah scans the room out of habit. His photographic memory records every detail. It is well-decorated, but simple. There are no big bucks evident here. Noah is pleasantly surprised. He has always thought of these politicians as stuffy rich types who like to throw their money around for show.

A low moan of despair turns Noah's attention to a small plump woman standing at the far end of the room. Mrs. Ramirez is sobbing; her face is buried in the Governor's chest, and he is red-eyed from the strain. Lee nods toward a brocade settee, and Noah makes his way in that direction.

Raven, on the other hand, walks directly over to Governor Ramirez and his wife. She looks Mrs. Ramirez in the eye. "We're here to find Sarah. Please sit quietly so that we may bring her back quickly and safely," she says, in a strong but soothing voice,

Graham and Noah do a double take; Lee holds his breath; but Mrs. Ramirez simply stops crying and slowly sits down with her hands folded in her lap. Raven has that effect on people. Noah carefully assesses the man of the mansion. He is at least ten years older than his wife and has an air about him of pride and dignity. Noah detects no humor in his coffee-colored eyes and heavy brows. He is almost a handsome man; he exudes a kind of strength that could be considered attractive. Noah dislikes him immediately.

The Governor stares at Raven for a long time before he eventually speaks.

"Young lady, I don't know what you propose to do, but we don't have much time. I hope you and the rest of your team of profilers are as good as Jack says you are," he declares. Having set the tone for his household, he sits stoically beside his wife and looks in the direction of the man standing in the doorway.

Raven knows Jack, the police chief whose son was killed in the fire a few years ago. He has grayed around the temples over the past couple of years but is otherwise as she remembered him three years ago: fair, reddish haired, dimpled, and freckled. She smiles at him in greeting.

Chief Jack Abernathy nods in Raven's direction, and then he moves into the room, clears his throat, and speaks in deference to the Governor.

"These people are your only hope, Bob. We ... um ... well, we use them for very complicated cases. I am acquainted with Miss Looking Bird, and I know Mr. Thistleseed personally from my church. He is an honorable man and very trustworthy. If anyone can find Sarah, they can, so let's give them whatever they need to do their work. Time is getting short."

The Governor nods and pulls his wife closer. He sighs. "Do what you have to do."

Lee rises from the couch. Like the leader he was born to be, he directs his team in the tracking process.

"Noah will be first; he is the fastest. Graham will beacon. Find the child and assess her condition. Describe her surroundings. Look for details, Noah. Go now, Son."

Almost before Lee finishes speaking, Noah closes his eyes and is gone. He looks asleep, but Lee and Raven know that neither Noah nor Graham will sleep until Noah's mind is safely guided home.

Lee turns to Raven. "While Noah travels, so shall you. I will beacon. We shall require two pictures—Sarah and her abductor. Begin your preparations."

Raven moves to the Ethan Allen secretary and opens it. On the leaf, she places a 9 x 12 sketch pad. She sits down, pulls a soft graphite pencil from the wire spiral, and holds the point in the center of the pad.

"Let's go," she says. She and Lee close their eyes, slowly inhale, and then exhale simultaneously.

Governor and Mrs. Ramirez blink at each other. Their sitting room is filled with a strange array of guests who are all breathing deeply with their eyes tightly closed.

"Jack?" the Governor questions, "What in God's name is going on here?"

"I'm sorry, Bob. I should have explained it better for you. These guys are really special, but they're not exactly profilers. They've all got these different psychic abilities. We've documented them, and they're genuine. Sounds crazy, I know, but it's true."

"What? Psychics? Please tell me you're kidding."

"I'm telling you, Bob, they get results."

"Psychics, Jack. Are you out of your mind? Since when does the police department use psychics? And how come I've never heard of them?"

"Well, your very reaction is one reason for keeping it quiet. I know how you feel. I was skeptical, too, until I experienced their abilities firsthand. Down at the department, we've got nicknames for each of them, according to what their specialty is. That tall one ... we call him 'The Compass.' He's a remote viewer— good at locations. His 'bird-dog' ability lets him get into the criminal's head. The big guy with the glasses is 'The Echo.' His specialty is clairaudience and direct voice. He can repeat back anything he hears ... in the same voice, no less."

"Oh, good Lord, Jack. They have actual titles. Clairaudience? Direct Voice?" The Governor exhales deeply and rubs his eyes with both hands.

Jack continues quickly. "That cocky young one is 'The

Scout.' He's got a memory like you've never imagined, and he can tell you exactly what he sees, right down to the most minute detail. He's a clairvoyant remote viewer."

"And the woman?" Ramirez says, his tone clipped. "What's her superpower?"

"Raven Looking Bird. We call her *'The Snapshot.'* Most talented sketch artist I've ever used. Just incredible. She's like an automatic writer, but a graphic version called 'hiero-scripting.' You know, like hieroglyphics. Pictures. There used to be another one ... *'The Bloodhound.'* He was a clairscent. He worked on arson cases. He died a couple of years back. That young one is his brother," Jack says.

"What are you, Jack ... a psychic dictionary now instead of the Police Chief? This is a nightmare. Look at them. They look like they're asleep, for crying out loud. How does this thing work?" Ramirez asks.

"Darned if I know, and I don't really care. They call it astral projection or something like that. An out of body experience. But, they get results, like I said, and that's all that matters, isn't it?" Jack is pacing, nervous about his job, his credibility. Bob Ramirez is his friend, but he's also his boss. There was a time when Jack didn't believe in the paranormal, but his experience with Raven has changed his mind.

Ramirez grimaces. "I can see you're really enamored with all this, but it's stupid."

"Just wait, Bob," the chief cautions. "Please, give 'em a chance. You'll see."

The Governor jerks to his feet, fists clenched. "We don't have time to wait! My granddaughter's missing, and we have to find her *now!*"

At that moment, to Jack's obvious relief, Noah comes home from his psychic journey, just before Raven begins to draw.

Graham greets Noah with a "Howdy."

"Howdy," Noah responds. Fixing his gaze on the opposite wall, Noah relates his trip.

"Sarah is pale and very dark around the eyes, but she seems to be holding up pretty well. She's a very frightened little girl, though. Her shoes are off, and she is curled up on a multicolored flowered couch. She is holding a doll. It's a Cabbage Patch Kid with yellow pigtails and green ..."

"Anita gave her that doll to take to the hospital," Mrs. Ramirez cries.

"... eyes. There's a cheap veneer coffee table in front of the couch. She seems to have eaten half a peanut butter and grape jelly sandwich, some tortilla chips, and is sipping an RC Cola. There are no other people in that room, but there is a man in the hallway with his back to her." He stops talking a moment and rubs his eyes before continuing.

"He has rather longish straight black hair, stocky build, and is dressed in baggy-butt jeans and a blue work shirt—kind of like a gas station attendant wears. It's halfway tucked in. His pants are grease-stained on the seat. He has a grimy snuff can ring in his back left pocket and sweat circles under his pits. He's wearing sneakers—gaudy-looking black and orange ones. There's nobody else around."

Noah shifts in his seat and looks around the room. Raven is still traveling, and she is sketching rapidly. The Ramirezes and Jack Abernathy are staring at Noah like he is a television set. He knows this is not the time for cute remarks, so he turns back to face the wall.

"Sarah is flipping through a magazine. She doesn't seem to be reading it, exactly, just looking at it. But she keeps wrinkling up her nose and trying to sound out the words, and then she just shakes her head. There's something about that magazine I didn't get before." He looks at the Governor's wife. "Can Sarah read yet?"

"Why, of course she can read. She's seven years old. She's in second grade. Sarah's been reading for almost two years," Mrs. Ramirez replies.

"Well, she can't read this. Does she know any Spanish?"

"Not really. Just a few words."

Noah clucks his tongue. "That's it, then. Hey, Graham, I think this man is Hispanic, maybe Mexican. His hair is black, but the texture is different from yours and mine. I didn't get a look at his face, but I don't think he's a Native A. When Raven gets back, you should go and listen to him. See if he's speaking Spanish."

"I'm back," Raven says in a voice reminiscent of a popular series of horror movies.

Lee pulls one corner of his mouth up in a crooked half-smile and moves toward Raven. "Now, let us see the child."

Raven hands Lee the sketch pad. He turns to the first of several drawings she has made. It is Sarah. As Noah has already said, she does look peaky. Mrs. Ramirez stifles a cry as Lee shows the picture to her. She nods, and the tears appear again.

While Lee and the Governor examine the picture of Sarah, Raven moves over to the couch and sits next to Graham. They both close their eyes, and Graham starts his journey.

Noah rises and ambles over to Lee. He begins to scrutinize the picture of the man in the doorway. He is, indeed, Hispanic American ... not a Spaniard, by his looks, but likely of Mexican heritage. Raven has drawn him from three angles on her sketch pad: profile, full face, and a full body picture.

The profile shows a broken nose that has never been fixed. Possibly, the man injured it in a street fight, or he could just be accident prone. His hair is cut in a man's shag, one which migrant workers often sport. He has a wide forehead and a few days' worth of stubble on his double chin.

Noah laughs when he sees the full face. Raven has drawn the kidnapper with his mouth open, talking on the telephone.

"Talk about looking down in the mouth." He snorts, but not without reason. It is possible to see nearly every tooth in the man's mouth. One front tooth is capped with a dark metal, and several teeth are missing. "Poor dental hygiene. This guy's mouth labels him as a low socio worker."

Lee is studying the last picture of the full body. He seems to be concentrating on some important detail. "Have you a magnifying glass, Governor?" he asks.

"I don't think so. Mama, do we have one?" He gestures to his wife, to which he receives a puzzled look.

"A heavy crystal glass, perhaps? A juice tumbler would possibly work," Lee says, taking a seat at the secretary.

"Oh, well, yes, we have a set of them. I'll get one. Do you

want juice?" Ever the hostess, Mrs. Ramirez rises and walks toward the kitchen.

"No, my dear lady." Lee smiles at her. "I require only the glass but thank you for offering."

She hurries out of the room and comes back with four different types of glasses. Lee chooses one with a heavy clear base. He holds it over the drawing, slowly raising and lowering it while looking down through the bottom. He moves it up and down several times before he finally holds it steady. Lee gazes through this makeshift magnifying glass for a minute or two.

"Ah," Lee breathes. "I can read the name 'Pedro' on his shirt pocket."

"Pedro!" Noah snorts again. "Oh, yeah. That's gonna be helpful. Shouldn't be too many of those around." He rolls his eyes at Raven.

Lee ignores the comment and continues scanning the picture. "Chief Abernathy, if you would be so kind as to write this down ... 3, 3, 4, 2, 9, 7, E, N, R, I ..." He stops to glance at Raven and Graham. They are watching him intently, impressed with his improvised magnifier. "I think we shall find that information to be a partial telephone number, and quite possibly the name of the accomplice. Is that right, Raven?"

"I just draw what I see," she says.

Lee smiles and nods. "Graham, you have something to share with us, I believe."

Graham recognizes his cue and is quite happy to perform. First, to the surprise of the non-Trackers, he sings in a tiny, whispery, high-pitched voice.

> *"Sunny day, hm-hm-hm hmmm away.*
> *Hm-hm way hm-hm-hm-hm-hm sweet.*
> *Can you hm-hm-hm-hm-hm,*
> *Hm-hm-hm-hm Sesame Street?*
> *Hm-hm-hm-hm Sesame Street?"*

"Oh, *Madre Dios*. Sarah. He sounds just like Sarah." Mrs. Ramirez wails.

"Is this some kind of joke?" her husband demands. His hands and jaw clench.

Lee explains the phenomenon of Graham's ability. "Sir, Mr. Skysong is a Navajo singer and a mimic. He has the gift of being able to duplicate the sounds and voices he hears with perfect accuracy. He sings as the child because he was with the child. She sings because the song makes her happy and less afraid."

"It must be nine o'clock. 'Sesame Street' comes on at nine o'clock," Jack states. Everyone looks at him; he looks down at the floor. "Andy, my son, watched 'Sesame Street' at nine o'clock every morning." Tears well up in the man's eyes as he remembers his little angel who perished in the fire. "Andy loved 'Sesame Street'."

"Shaddup!" Graham shouts.

Taken aback, Jack and the Ramirezes gape at him, but Graham is looking away from them now, and his voice has a strange, guttural quality to it that is lower even than his own natural baritone register.

"Now, he's the kidnapper," Noah observes. "Listen to his phone call, and maybe we can get a lead on the accomplice."

"*Si, si. Pero, tengo mucho hambre, y la Chiquita ... si, si. Pero, no estoy borracho. No. No. Si, es verdad, Enrique. ¿Tu venga aqui? Bueno. Bueno. Si, Enrique. Adios.*" Graham finishes his recitation and looks at Lee. "He's hungry, he's not drunk, and he says the other man is coming. We don't have much time. Where is she, Lee?"

Noah strides to Lee's side and takes a deep breath. "Find her, buddy. I'll light the way."

Lee sits back in the secretary's matching wing chair and reaches into his shirt pocket. He takes out a small notebook and holds it out to Noah, who tears out two pages. Noah gives a page each to Raven and Graham. Then, Noah sits down on the floor beside Lee and closes his eyes. Not a soul says a word; not a soul dares to even breathe. This is the most critical track of all. Breathing slowly, and without further notice, Lee begins to track. As he travels, he speaks; as he speaks, Raven and Graham write.

"Away runs the small, green pony with one eye blind in the hazy dawn. It canters over the rushing water, west to the planted pines. It slows near the home of red cockaded woodpecker; past the dog and the golden spires, to cross yet another water, slower and dark as dusk, beyond the field where the loud yellow bird lands."

Lee's voice is a monotone. He pauses a moment, takes a long, deep breath, and lets it out slowly. Raven and Graham also pause, watching, waiting for the rest of his journey. After another deep breath, he continues in a sing-song chant.

"Green pony rests inside a white stable; light filters through the cracks; the great ball of fire rises in the sky. Again, there is water; the ghosts of empty ships linger yet, and the lapping waves mark the 12-foot spear. The ghost maker's name was Rosco, the child waits nearby, and the Tracker must now come home."

Lee opens his eyes and shivers, his eyelids fluttering slightly as he exhales. Nobody speaks. Raven and Graham compare their notes. At last, Bob Ramirez breaks the silence.

"What is the world was that about?" Bewilderment dominates his rugged face.

"He tracks in poetic metaphor. We decipher it after he finishes," Graham declares.

"What if you can't?" Ramirez barks the question.

"We can," Noah replies. His onyx eyes narrow and flash at the Governor.

Raven steps in before Noah can verbalize a challenge. "You see, Governor, Mr. Thistleseed uses visual images to convey what he sees. It's often a combination of poetic metaphor, simile, and personification. We are familiar with his style and are able to translate ... much as a trained interpreter translates a foreign language. It's a whole team effort when Lee tracks."

"But, how can you tell where Sarah is? He gave no landmarks, no highway or house numbers." Mrs. Ramirez wrings her pudgy hands.

Graham kneels down at her eye level, gently patting her small hand with his beefy one. "Well, Ma'am, *The Compass*'—just like his nickname implies—always gives a direction. This time it's west. And when he mentions animals, they correspond to vehicles. The green pony is a green automobile—probably a Pinto or a Mustang." She nods in understanding.

"Why don't you just ask Mr. Thistleseed what it was? Wouldn't that be faster?" The Governor is used to issuing demands.

"Because he doesn't know ... Bob!" Noah replies so vehemently that he nearly spits the man's name.

"Noah." The word is quiet, but firm. Lee stands and fixes the young man with a reproachful gaze.

"But, Lee ..." Noah's tone is plaintive, like a child's.

Lee is patient, but remains firm. "Noah, there is no need to defend me, and there is no excuse for rudeness."

Ashamed, Noah turns away. Lee lifts his chin and looks at Governor Ramirez pointedly. "As I said, there is no excuse for rudeness ... from anyone. Do you understand? Sarah is at stake here, sir ... not my reputation, nor my colleague's pride, nor your position. I will answer your question, but do not ask any more, or we will waste valuable time."

He pauses for effect, raises his bushy eyebrows slightly, and continues. "I am unable to remember my travels once I return home. For this reason, I carry the notebook—so my team members can record what I see. And now, you must be silent if we are to find Sarah." Turning toward the other Trackers, he dismisses Governor Bob Ramirez and leaves him blinking.

Jack Abernathy's mouth hangs open as he watches this exchange. He cannot remember a time when Robert Ramirez had nothing to say. This Indian, with his rugged face, braided hair, and elegant voice, has effectively dumbfounded a man who uses words as a weapon. Jack, himself, is speechless and, at the same time, he finds himself awed at the immense power Lee wields. It is apparent the dignified older man loves the headstrong young man, and he is obviously embarrassed by his outburst, but he is compassionate as well as just. Protocol is important, but it appears good manners are expected of everyone. Lee draws neither personal nor political distinctions on that point. Jack's admiration is continually growing for this unusual group of second-sighted Indians, and he listens attentively as they decode Lee's cryptic message.

"... has to be a Pinto with a broken headlight. People seem to take better care of Mustangs," Raven states.

"That's for true," Noah confirms. "A Pinto's kind of a

dorky car. It's inexpensive enough for a migrant to pick up a used one for cheap."

"O.K. I agree on the car," Graham says. "Now, let's see. West would take us ... where ... toward Panama City?"

"Definitely. Go over the new bridge. That's the rushing water. You know, by the Jim Woodruff dam," Noah says.

"Planted pines and red cockaded woodpecker. That must be out there in Liberty County. I read about it. Loggers are kicking up a fuss because the Apalachicola Forest is the woodpecker's habitat, but the bird's protected so the loggers can't cut the timber," Raven adds.

"Way to go, Woody Woodpecker," Noah says.

Graham crows a remarkable imitation of the cartoon character. "I have no idea about the dog and the gold spire. How about you guys?"

"Some kind of dog monument?" Raven suggests.

"Mascot. There's a football team over there called 'hound dogs' or 'bulldogs' or something. Golden spires? You got me on that one," Noah says.

"The Church of Jesus Christ of Latter-day Saints," Lee says. "All L.D.S. churches have spires atop them instead of crosses—to point the way to Heaven."

"Anticipated my next question," Noah quips.

"Oh, yeah, the Mormon Church in Bristol. It's always done up in the most wonderful light displays at Christmas time—all different colors and arranged into Nativity scenes. People like to drive through the parking lot at night all month just to view it," Raven says.

"Great. We're on the right track, then. There's a bridge from Liberty County over the Apalachicola River that leads on out to Calhoun County, and that river's usually silty," Noah confirms. "Time changes from Eastern to Central about halfway between Bristol and Blountstown."

"Didn't know that," Graham says.

"Now you do," Noah says.

"There is a small airport right as you get off the bridge." Raven says.

"In Blountstown? Are you serious? That's one of those one stoplight towns, isn't it?" Graham asks.

"Three stoplights, I believe. Light aircraft only. Not a major airport, but maybe the yellow bird is a crop duster. Think we go on to Panama City?" Noah asks.

"No, I don't think so. Lee didn't mention any other landmarks. They must be in Blountstown," Raven says.

"You know, this guy might be a glad picker. Lots of Mexicans work the gladiola fields in the surrounding areas during summer and early fall," Graham says.

"Could be, Gray. They parked in a garage, but not a very well-made one. It's probably connected to a wood frame house painted white. An old one, too, or the sun wouldn't shine through the cracks." Noah grins, proud of his deduction. The others are not particularly impressed.

Graham consults his notes. "More water. Doesn't that same river wind around and go through the county? This place must be near the river, I assume, if he can see the waves lapping at the 12-foot marker."

"Blountstown used to be the site of a large ship-building plant, but it closed down years ago," Lee says.

"Ghosts of ships. Makes sense. But, who's Rosco? Anybody you know?" Noah asks.

Lee smiles. "Rysco was the name of the plant."

"You said 'Rosco,' Lee," Noah points out.

"I guess I must have 'Southernized' it," Lee admits.

"Ah guess yew did." Noah dramatically overemphasizes the colloquial dialect.

Raven jumps to her feet. "Enough, already. Sarah is nearby. Let's go." She is already marching toward the door.

The Governor finally dares to speak up. "Wait. Shouldn't we notify the police in Blountstown?"

Noah responds, this time with more civility. "No way. That might spook 'em. We should go alone ... with Chief Abernathy, of course."

"And right now. The other man is coming. They may leave again, or they may ..." Graham clamps his mouth closed in mid-sentence.

"Or what?" Mrs. Ramirez gulps and nearly strangles.

Lee takes her by the hand. "Or they may harm the child."

Mrs. Ramirez pales and grips her husband's strong arm.

"Go now. Please." Ramirez barely whispers.

"Let's go," Jack says, rushing for the door.

"Gone," Noah says, hurrying to catch up with Raven, who is already buckling up in the back seat of the policeman's SUV.

"I will stay. You must go, Graham. Your talents may be needed. Hurry," Lee says.

Graham Skysong disappears out the door, leaving Lee alone to face Governor and Mrs. Ramirez and their fears. The life of their precious granddaughter is in the hands of a group of the most unusual people they have ever met. They cling to each other like castaways in a raft and move their lips in silent prayers. Lee adds his own prayer to the silence.

CHAPTER FOUR
HIAWATHA'S PROGENY

JACK ABERNATHY AND THE PARTY of Trackers exit the driveway of the Governor's mansion, while Liahona Thistleseed and the two Ramirez grandparents settle down to the difficult business of waiting. They will know, in roughly an hour, whether or not Sarah Ramirez has any chance of being rescued. The tension in the room is tangible. Grief, apprehension, and animosity combine to make the waiting game unbearable. It is Carmine Ramirez who finally breaks the uncomfortable silence.

"Mr. Thistleseed, what you and your friends do confuses and frightens me. I am not a very well-educated woman. What I know, I have learned on my own. My father was an immigrant to Florida. He picked tomatoes in Greensboro and spent most of his wages on liquor ..."

"Carmine!" interrupts her husband, "do not tell him . ."

"*Silencio, Roberto. Por favor. Por favor.*" She begs him, her voice cracking with emotion.

Bob Ramirez knows his wife, and after 30 years of marriage, he understands when she needs to talk to hold herself together, so he acquiesces. He also knows what she needs to tell.

She begins again. "*Mi madre* ... my mother worked as a

laundress for some well-to-do families in Quincy. My four older sisters had married and moved away. I was the youngest of the three remaining girls, but I assumed the responsibilities at home. When I was fourteen, my father left home the same day my mother gave birth to twins, and he never returned. Mama kept the porch light on all day and all night, but he did not come back. Two years later, when my mother died, I turned the light off. My other sisters left soon after. I was a sixteen-year-old girl with two small toddlers to care for. This little family was all I had in the whole world."

She stops to dab at her damp eyes with a white lace handkerchief. Lee notices that her husband is sniffling, but quietly, so as not to attract attention to himself.

Mrs. Ramirez continues. "At seventeen, I met a wonderful man. He was ten years older than I, but he was kind and hardworking, and he loved my sister and brother as much as he loved me. I married this man, and he adopted my family and gave them his name. My little sister Anna died shortly afterwards of influenza. My brother Manuel became our son, and Manuel is Sarah's father. We have five other children, of course, but no sons. So, you see, Sarah is most precious because she is both my grandchild and my niece." She bows her head and weeps openly, comforted by her husband's tender embrace.

"Mr. Thistleseed. You must understand the urgency we feel. Sarah is, indeed, most precious to us. The bone marrow transplant is Sarah's only hope, but she must be well enough to survive the operation. The longer she remains with those ... those people, the more risk she runs of infection to her weakened immune system," Bob Ramirez says.

Lee nods. "I understand completely, sir. I, too, have precious ones whom I would protect at any cost."

"You must also understand that I have never believed in ESP or telepathy or mind reading. I don't mean to insult you, but in my faith as a Catholic, we believe those things come from the adversary ... not God," Ramirez says.

"Yes, I know; however, we neither read minds nor tell the future. We each have a rare gift called 'second sight.' This gift has been passed down through many generations of our people. I must stress to you that it does not originate from evil."

"I have heard of shamans and medicine men. Is that what you are?"

"Some call us that, but I prefer to call us 'gifted.' In the Bible, there are many who possess the ability to know more than what is visible. They were called prophets and seers at that time. We believe it is a trait that falls upon the seventh son of a seventh son, although women are also known to possess the sight."

Carmine Ramirez sucks in her breath. "Women? Really? Do many women have this gift of second sight?" She is wide-eyed.

"A few have been found in the seventh of a series of children born to a seventh child."

Bob squeezes Carmine's hand and looks into her eyes. She drops her gaze and shakes her head. "Does the seventh child of a seventh child always manifest this power?" he asks, still regarding his wife's lowered head.

"We have no way of knowing. We can only ascertain the presence of the gift in those we investigate," Lee replies.

"So many gifted seventh children! I never knew there was such a thing. How can so many be found in one place?" Mrs. Ramirez wonders aloud.

"They say opposites attract, but I find it is more likely that similar people seem to seek each other out," Lee says.

"Birds of a feather flock together?"

"Exactly." Lee laughs at her analogy.

"Speaking of birds ..." the Governor says.

"Ah, yes, Miss Looking Bird is the seventh daughter of a seventh son. She has very powerful sight. We were fortunate to find and train her."

"Train her? Do you mean you can actually train a person to do what it is you do?" Ramirez asks.

"Second sight is a form of clairvoyance. The word comes from French and Latin words meaning 'to see clearly.' We can only train those with a second sight gift already, and not all of them have the ability to become Trackers. Each person manifests the gift differently. Chief Abernathy gave us all nicknames. He refers to me as '*The Compass.*' That is my particular ability—directionality.

Remote viewers see things far away from our immediate location. We call Graham *The Echo* because of his mimicking abilities. He is a clairaudient—the word means 'to hear clearly.' Raven, as an artist, is *The Snapshot,* with an ability to convert what she sees into pictures. And Noah is *The Scout.* He is a powerful remote viewer with a photographic memory. Noah usually goes ahead to see what we're up against."

"Are there more on your team?" Mrs. Ramirez asks.

"That's right. Jack mentioned another guy. He called him *The Bloodhound.* What happened to him?" her husband asks.

"Yes. There were five; there are but four of us left. There was a tragic fire," Lee admits, his voice cracking. "Our Team began with just the two of us. When Dane passed, I trained his younger brother Noah, and he has tracked for two years; Mr. Skysong has tracked for seven; I, myself, have tracked for 32 years. My mentor is long gone. It is different with everyone, but our powers usually surface around our twelfth birthday … near the onset of puberty. Tracking powers cannot be developed fully until we are in our mid-to-late teens. Miss Looking Bird was somewhat of a late starter. She was trained at 22 and has tracked for only three years, but she is very strong and very gifted."

"And very lovely," Carmine observes.

"But not as lovely as you, my *Carminita*." Ramirez purrs to his dainty spouse.

"*Gracias, Roberto*," she says, blushing. She is composed now and interested in the conversation. "*Por favor*, Mr. Thistleseed, tell us more."

"Very well, madam. It will help pass the time," he concedes. A history professor at Florida State University, Lee is always ready to oblige with an impromptu lecture. Squaring his feet in front of him as he sits on the sofa, Lee leans forward and assumes his familiar storytelling posture.

"From the beginning of the ages, among my people there have lived individuals who would seem to become one with the spirits of animals that roamed the countryside. They claimed that they could fly with the birds and run with the buffalo. Some people could imitate the sounds of these creatures with such accuracy that it was believed they had merged with the spirits of the creatures. These people were highly revered and also greatly feared. They were made gods or Holy Ones, and they were consulted about all tribal affairs. Most of them were good people who worked to keep tribal peace, but occasionally there would surface a deceitful and scurrilous person who would use his powers for evil, to incite violence and to terrorize his people. One such person, in the days of my ancestors, was named *Atotarhoh*.

"*Atotarhoh* was an Onodaga leader of great evil and savagery. The Iroquois people were senselessly killing each other all over the land, and *Atotarhoh* was actively involved in keeping the feuds going. According to the legend, he was vile to look upon, with a body bent in seven places and snakes growing from his hair. He had great magic, and no one could dare look upon him without becoming insane.

"There was also a prophetic man who was well-loved by the Creator, *Tharonhiawakon*, because of his goodness. As a reward for his devotion, the Great Peacemaker, *Deganawidah*, was given the power to unite the Five Nations of the Iroquois. These Nations were, from east to west: Seneca, Cayuga, Onondaga, Oneida, and Mohawk. This union was especially important because there were many enemies all around the Iroquois. The Huron and Algonquin were to the north; the Tobacco Nations were to the east; the Susquehanna were to the south; and the fierce Erie 'People of the Panther' were to the southeast. For the Iroquois Nations to survive, they must come together as a unit, thus the immediate importance of either conquering or converting *Atotarhoh* and the Onondaga.

"The Great Peacemaker had a devoted follower ... *Aiontwatha*. You may know him as *Hiawatha*. He and a woman named *Tsikonsaseh*, an elder known for her wise counsel, visited the Five Nations to bring about peace.

"Before they came to the Onondaga, *Hiawatha* was warned in a dream to approach the evil one with care, lest they be driven insane as had others before them. He and *Tsikonsaseh* composed a Hymn of Peace to sing to the man. They sang for hours without stopping, and the song put *Atotarhoh* to sleep. While he slept, *Hiawatha* combed the snakes from his hair. When the snakes were removed, he and *Tsikonsaseh* straightened *Atotarhoh's* body and banished the evil spirit that had invaded his soul. *Atotarhoh* awoke, and he was a good man once again. *Hiawatha* was made head of the League of the Iroquois and bravely led his people in many successful battles against their enemies." Lee proudly regards his audience.

"You are quite the storyteller," the Governor remarks, "But how much of it is true?"

Lee lifts his eyebrows. "Legend and history dance together, and sometimes it is difficult to know who leads. But, in all things, there must be truth. This much is verifiable: The League of the Iroquois was established before the French and Indian war and was organized by a second-sighted prophetic man and a great peacemaker known as *Deganawidah,* the mentor of *Hiawatha.* *Hiawatha* did, indeed, unite the Five Nations and was made a Long Pine Chieftan as a reward. His legacy yet lives."

"Which of the five Indian tribes was he from?" Mrs. Ramirez asks excitedly.

"Mohawk," Lee says, lifting his chin slightly.

"And you are a ...?" the Governor asks.

"Mohawk," Lee answers with the barest trace of pride. "I am the seventh son of generations of seventh sons who originated with *Aiontwatha,* the man called *Hiawatha.*"

Carmine Ramirez claps her pudgy hands with childlike delight and stares at Lee as though she is a fan hoping for an autograph from a movie star. "Mr. Thistleseed, just what did your ancestor's name, *Hiawatha,* mean?"

Liahona Thistleseed winks at her. "He who combs."

The comfortable conversation is abruptly shattered by the jarring trill of the telephone. The Governor leaps to his feet and snatches the receiver off the hook, nearly knocking the handset onto the floor.

"What?" he demands. Then, after listening a moment, he softens his tone. "No. I am sorry, *Chiquita.* I did not mean to shout at you. No, no, everything is fine. Why do you ask?" His eyes widen, and he quickly glances at Lee. Mrs. Ramirez immediately rises to her feet and enters the adjacent room. "Yes, it is true. Manuel called you? No? Wait just a moment. Mama is getting on the phone."

Ramirez waits until his wife closes the door, and then shakily replaces the receiver. He turns to face Lee. "That is my youngest daughter, Maria. She is away at school."

"She knows already." Lee speaks it as an observation, not a question.

"Ah, yes. She is very upset. Maria and Sarah have always been very close."

Robert Ramirez's voice and manner intrigue Liahona Thistleseed. He takes a moment to study the impeccably dressed Governor running his fingers through his now disheveled hair before he probes. "So, Maria is the youngest of your five daughters. How old is she?"

Distracted, the Governor scans the sky outside through the window. "Maria Chiquita is sixteen. She's quite bright. She is already on full academic scholarship at Troy State University."

"That's quite young for college."

"She's very smart," Ramirez says. "She took a double load of high school courses and they let her graduate early. She was Magna Cum Laude, too."

"Impressive. I can tell you are quite proud, And Manuel, he is your only son?"

"Yes, we had another son—twins, actually—but they died at birth. That is why Sarah is so special." Ramirez sighs.

Lee considers that tidbit of information. *Interesting.* But, his objective now is the safety of Sarah. Nearly an hour has elapsed since the others left. He approaches the connecting door. "Mrs. Ramirez," he says, "We must free the telephone line."

Moments later she returns, wiping tears from her cheeks. "Maria wants to know when all is well," she says to her husband.

The Governor nods. The strident telephone summons his attention once again. With trembling hands, he lifts the receiver to his ear. "Yes?"

Turning quickly, Bob Ramirez hands the phone to Lee. "It is Mr. Lightfoot for you."

Lee takes the phone and listens. His eyes sweep the floor, and then he meets the Governor's questioning stare. "Sir, I will require your assistance. I must track again. Mr. Lightfoot will beacon, and Mr. Skysong will take notes. You must hold the telephone so that Mr. Skysong can hear what I say, but under no circumstances must you touch me. Understood?"

The Governor nods. "Yes, of course. But what did he say about Sarah?"

Liahona Thistleseed and Robert Ramirez stand still and solemn; two powerful men united by a common cause. Lee breaks the silence. "The man did not come. Sarah has been moved. Mr. Lightfoot has seen her, and she is weakening. She is not long gone from the location, but we must hurry if we are to catch up to her."

"She's just a child. How can she know where she is going?" Governor Ramirez asks.

"I will not track Sarah. I will track the other man. Mr. Skysong has heard him tell of the place where he will wait for them, but Mr. Lightfoot could not identify it. May we begin, sir?"

Ramirez pulls a chair up beside Lee. "Find him, Hiawatha's progeny. You have my full support and confidence."

Liahona Thistleseed looks into the eyes of Bob Ramirez and sees there the highest honor any man can give another— respect. He settles back in his chair, breathes deeply, and lets his mind travel.

"Nestled near the piney woods, near the scrub oaks where the great Smokey Bear's sky tower hails, he waits toward the waning sun, amid the spiders and snakes where animals of all breeds run the 231 trails. The great black beasts are silent, and the Africans are too thin. The things that once were new are old, the monster waits within, and the Tracker comes home."

Mrs. Ramirez is wringing her hands when Lee finally opens his eyes. Before he can say a word, she rushes him and squeals. "Mr. Thistleseed, I know where he is! I know where that place is!" She snatches the phone away from her slack-jawed husband and speaks rapidly to Graham on the other end of the line. "Go to the junction of Highway 20 and US 231, going towards Panama City. There's an old antique museum there on the corner. It's on the right. It has big African warriors made of plywood and two black animal statues in front. Sarah always waves at them when we go to the beach. Hurry, please hurry! You can be there in twenty minutes if you hurry."

Hanging up the phone, she looks up at the two men in the room, noting the curious expressions of admiration on their faces. "Well," she says, "Sometimes we women have to take matters into our own hands."

Her charming ebullience breaks the tension, and they all give in to relieved laughter. Liahona Thistleseed studies this petite matron. She has appeared decidedly more fragile than she actually is. He detects in her an underlying strength equal to that of her unwavering husband. She is very much like his wife, Wren, in many ways ... except one. But that difference gives her more in common with him than Wren. He peers at Carmine Ramirez through narrowed eyes.

"Mrs. Ramirez. Are you, by any chance, a seventh child?"

Carmine Ramirez stands as tall as her five feet will allow. Her eyes twinkle, and she blushes deeply. "Yes." She says, raising her chin. "I certainly am."

CHAPTER FIVE
VANITY and DIGNITY

ENRIQUE MENDOZA CONTEMPLATES THE CREATURE in his hand as it heroically struggles to escape between his outstretched fingers, only to be squeezed back into his oily palm. Enrique laughs, showing overly white capped teeth, and then he drops the crippled spider onto the dusty counter. It creeps an inch or so before Enrique pulls off its three remaining legs.

"Now I call you 'Daddy NO-legs, eh?" he says, curling his lips in a feral snarl.

Tired of the game, Enrique flicks the almost-dead arachnid across the room with a perfectly manicured fingernail. It is, perhaps, the kindest act the monster has ever performed for one of his victims. That distraction finished, Enrique mulls over the next creature he plans to torture … Sarah Ramirez.

The Political Man promised him plenty, and Enrique intends to collect every penny. As a bonus, the Political Man will throw in the girl. *Not bad for one day's work*, he thinks, *and a play toy comes with it.* He laughs aloud, a mirthless sound from tight lips. "This should fix that *tonto* Governor who has the nerve to call himself Hispanic," he declares.

It is not the ethnic heritage that Enrique objects to, it is the position Ramirez holds. In his own eyes, Enrique Mendoza feels he is *equal to, if not better than,* the man currently in office. But Enrique has *gotten a raw deal* from the *U.S. of A.* He has been *put down* by the *gringos* of America. But Enrique is a man; he never *kisses up* to those who oppress him. He is sure that Bob Ramirez *sold out* to the government. Governor Bob is willing to *lay down and roll over.* Of that, he is sure. But Enrique is a real man; he always *gets going when the going gets tough.*

Enrique Mendoza is a walking cliché. He has learned to use these key phrases and buzz words so he can impress people with his outstanding command of the English language. Men like Governor Ramirez *keep him down.* They are jealous of his ability to converse like an American; consequently, he *has been robbed* of the political career he dreamed of.

Instead, Enrique is a mercenary, a man paid to do others' dirty work. The irony is that Enrique loves it. *Dirty work? Not a chance.* It is a way to realize his true potential as a mastermind of manipulation. The work suits his twisted and sadistic nature. And what can be better than to get paid for what you love to do?

When the Political Man contacted him about the contract, Enrique almost offered to work without pay. The very thought of destroying Robert Ramirez through his precious granddaughter is so delicious. But, of course, *one must pay the bills,* so Enrique named a generous, but entirely fair price, and the Political Man agreed without the slightest hesitation.

He considers the Political Man for a moment. *I wonder if he would like to know what I will do with the child. Nah.* But Enrique thinks of nothing *but* what he will do with the child. He can hardly wait for that moron to bring her. He will pay the low-bred accomplice off with his straight razor, and then he will take the girl, and who knows what will happen next? *Maybe I will marry her. My child bride. Won't the Governor love to have me as a grandson-in law?*

The idea evokes a real laugh from him. "I am so clever. I should have been a comedian," he says, bowing to a non-existent audience. If nothing else, Enrique Mendoza has the highest self-esteem in the world. He is the only true perfection remaining on the earth. *"Vanity—thy name is Enrique."* Of that he is sure.

* * *

Sarah is tired; she is so very tired. If only she can go to sleep and pretend it is all a bad dream. But sleep is impossible. She is hot and beginning to get carsick. The junky car smells of gasoline, exhaust fumes, and something worse ... body odor. It hangs like a pungent curtain in the air all around her. She tries burying her nose in the doll ... the one Mama gave her. That is a little better; it smells a bit like Mama.

Sarah wants her Mama right now. *She and Papa will be so worried, waiting at the hospital for me.* Sarah is sorry they will be waiting; they are always waiting for her, it seems. She thinks about her grandparents. *Mama Mine must be so upset. It isn't Mama Mine's fault, but she will blame herself. She always does. And Papa Berto will stroke her cheek and tell her she is too hard on herself.*

Sarah chokes back a sob. She dares not let the smelly man see her cry. She is much too proud. Even now, she has a deep sense of family honor. A Ramirez has dignity, after all. She has heard Papa Berto remind her father on many occasions. Sarah knows what dignity is; she is determined to set that example, and that means fooling the man who has kidnapped her.

Yes, Sarah knows about kidnappers. She knows they take children from famous people like her Papa Berto and try to get money for them. Sarah has no doubt that her grandparents will pay every cent of money they have for her. But Sarah also knows that sometimes kidnappers kill the children after they get the money. She accepts that possibility as bravely as any seven-year-old can.

Sarah decides that, if it comes down to that, she will die with dignity. She clutches her doll to her face, fights back the tears, and begins to pray.

* * *

"Dear Holy Father up in Heaven. This is Sarah Ramirez.

I think I may die soon, and I want to talk to you first, so you'll remember me when I see you. This bad man is taking me to another bad man, for money, I think. I don't know what made them turn bad, but I am sorry for them. Please, God, if you can, make them not be bad men. I'm kinda scared ... well, a lot scared ... but I'll understand it if you are ready for me now. Before anything does happen, I want to ask you for a couple of things. First, take care of Mama and Papa so they won't be so sad. I know your son died, too, so you understand how they'll feel. And Mama Mine and Papa Berto, too. Please tell them I love them very much. And tell them I kept my dignity. Thank you for listening to me, Our Father, and help me, if you can. *Holy Mary, Mother of God, pray for us sinners now and at the hour of our death. Amen.*" Graham relates her prayer in Sarah's sweet voice. He puts his glasses in his shirt pocket and wipes his tear-filled eyes before he faces the others.

"Faster, Jack. Just floor it, man!" Noah's voice is raspy from breathing through his mouth during Graham's recitation.

Jack Abernathy is already one step ahead of Noah; he jams on the gas pedal, the accelerator climbing toward eighty. Noah looks in the back seat at Raven. She makes no attempt to hide her feelings. Her exquisite face is streaked with tears which she lets fall freely. Noah's heart flutters for an instant as he regards her. Then, he turns his attention to the road and what may lie ahead.

They are close ... very close ... maybe ten minutes at most. *Will we be in time?* Noah agonizes. Sarah seems to think the two men will kill her. *Will they try?* Noah wishes for once that his powers included precognition. If he could foretell the future—but, no—he would never be able to bear it if Sarah is right about her fate.

Noah notices Jack reach across his chest with his right hand. A moment later, Jack lays his service revolver on the seat between them. It is a standard police issue '38 revolver. Its barrel gleams in the early morning sun.

"Glove box," Jack says in a low growl. Noah opens the glove box and sees a 9-mm Luger. "Take it out." Noah does as he is told.

"Know how to use a gun?" Jack asks.

"Nope. Not really. But I do know how to use this." Noah

reaches to his belt and pulls a large Bowie knife from a leather pouch. Jack glances at the knife and back at the young man. Noah grins, but it never reaches the cold black coals of his eyes.

"Be fast, and be accurate, boy."

"You can bet on it, Jack." Noah nods grimly, and then laces his fingers together, cracking his knuckles loudly.

"I know how to shoot." The voice comes from the back seat. "Give me the gun." Raven's tears have stopped; her mouth is a mere slit in her face.

"There's another clip up here ..." Jack offers.

"I won't need another clip."

Jack looks at her in the rear-view mirror. *No,* he decides, *she won't need another clip.*

"Graham?" Noah says, looking over his shoulder at the large man in the back seat.

Graham holds up his beefy fists and smirks. "Never needed anything other than these. But, if it gets hot, I'll let you folks take over."

The carload of Trackers and one law enforcement officer gets quiet. There is a singleness of purpose as they each sight the landmarks—a black bear, a black gorilla, and plywood African warriors ... and a green Pinto with broken headlights.

Inside the dilapidated antique museum, Enrique paces as he looks over his wares. This kid looks sick, and she is scrawny, too. What a waste. She won't be any good as a maid, much less a wife. He doubts she will even put up a fight if or when he gets ready to play with her. *So, this is the product of a Governor's spawn?* Enrique is not impressed. It serves to reinforce his high opinion of himself. Well, *business is business,* and it is *time to get the show on the road.* Of that he is sure.

Enrique Mendoza turns to the grease monkey holding Sarah. *"¿Cuantos dineros?"* he asks the man, careful to stay a safe distance upwind from him.

The man scratches his lice-ridden head, weighing in his simple mind the possibility of asking for more than he has been promised. With a greedy gleam in his eye and a snaggle-toothed grin, he holds up five fingers.

"¿Cinco?" Enrique asks, the picture of innocence. He knows the agreed-upon payment is only $2,500; the imbecile is trying to *jack up the price.*

Pedro nods vigorously. *"Si, cinco."*

Enrique gives the man a brilliant view of his expensive dental work while he reaches slowly into the vest pocket of his Armani suit. As he does so, Pedro releases Sarah, who sinks down to her boney knees with an audible moan. The accomplice advances upon Enrique; Enrique has his hand on the straight edge. Just a little closer, and he will be able to slice him.

At that moment, a vintage Coca-Cola bottle tips over. Enrique jerks at the reverberating sound. The movement is all that is needed to alert Pedro to the concealed razor. He cries out and raises his arm in time to catch the full force of Enrique's slash. He howls as the blood gushes from his cut forearm. Falling to the floor, the man crawls away like the spider Enrique has discarded.

Jack kicks the bottle out of the way and rushes at Enrique. "Drop it," he cries, trying to level the revolver at the man.

With cat-like swiftness, Enrique whirls around to face Jack. Jack sees the blade a second too late to avoid. It catches his hand near the wrist and slices through the meaty flesh almost to his thumb, knocking the gun away at the same time. Jack grunts and ducks in time to keep from losing his chin and nose on the rebound, but Enrique takes him out with a swift kick to the midsection. Jack drops to his knees and vomits.

Enrique seeks his *payload*; she has crawled away from the Mexican, who is now wrestling with Graham. They look evenly matched, so Enrique skirts them and begins to hunt for Sarah.

The dirt floor is covered with mouse poop, but Sarah knows this is her only means of escape. God has sent some angels to distract the bad men, but He still expects a person to help herself as much as she is able. She scoots under the sagging display tables, watching the disembodied legs of the people all around her. She has no idea which feet belong to the bad men and which feet belong to the angels, so she hides from all of them.

Noah will wait no longer. Raven is stationed just outside to cover the exit, but the noise inside indicates a raging battle. He must find Sarah. He slips in the back entrance and creeps ... slowly and stealthily ... the way he has been trained since childhood. He makes no noise; he is aware of every sound and every movement. The melee is mainly in the front of the shop; this part of the museum is quiet. A slight gasp commands his attention. He crouches and looks beneath a decomposing table. His breath catches in his throat when he sees her, frail and diminutive, clasping her abraded knees to her chest.

"Sarah. Sarah, I'm Noah. Your Grampa sent me to find you. Come to me, honey. I'm going to take you home."

Sarah regards Noah with wide frightened doe eyes. She pushes herself farther back against a termite-weakened table leg.

"Don't be afraid of me, Sarah. I'm your friend." He attempts to coax her from under the table.

Sarah stares at the huge blade he holds in his right hand. Noah realizes she views him as another potential kidnapper.

"Look, Sarah, I'm putting it away. Come on out, sweetie. I won't let those guys hurt you." He slowly slides the knife back into the leather pouch.

Sarah studies him suspiciously, but Noah holds out his arms to her and lets his heart show in his expression. Sarah sees truth there and inches out from under the table. She stands up unsteadily, brushing cobwebs and detritus off her doll and her ruined clothing. She looks traumatized, utterly depleted. At that moment, Noah wants nothing more than to enfold the child in his arms and protect her from all the bad guys in the world.

Sarah reads Noah's face, gives a wan smile, and staggers toward his outstretched arms. Before she reaches him, a movement appears in Noah's peripheral vision too late. Enrique Mendoza pounces from behind a fractured cabinet and snatches Sarah. She is so slight; he is able to hoist her off her feet and suspend her with one arm while he brandishes the razor with the other hand.

The weapon suits Enrique's up close and personal predilection for violence, and Noah scrutinizes the way he moves it back and forth like a swaying cobra ready to strike. But Noah is dangerous, too. Snaking his hand to his belt, he grips the hunting knife. He hunkers down in a combat stance, his eyes never leaving those of his enemy. Sarah swoons and drops her doll. Enrique kicks it away impatiently.

"Son of a mangy dog. Do not tempt me, Indian boy. I will cut her before you can take a breath. Now, back away." Enrique actually snarls at him, the razor on Sarah's throat. He no longer looks like the man he believes himself to be. His hair is plastered to his oily forehead; his expensive suit is wrinkled; dirt and blood cake his fingernails.

Noah is stricken. Seeing the wildness in Enrique's eyes, he knows the man has nothing to lose. On the contrary, he will probably enjoy killing Sarah. Noah retreats slowly, his eyes not leaving his adversary for an instant. Enrique advances. As he nears the back entrance, he gives Noah a wide berth and withdraws out the door, his voice keening in victory. Enrique shuffles backwards toward the freshly waxed Mercedes he has parked behind the building, keeping Noah at bay with the blade beneath Sarah's chin.

Graham and Jack approach the rear exit behind Noah and watch in dread as Enrique opens the car door. There is no opening for a shot, yet Jack keeps his gun trained on him, and Graham balances on his toes, ready to spring. Noah turns the knife in his hand, holding the tip of the sharp blade. All he needs is an opening, just a small turn of the man's head or a drop of the shoulder, and he can send the knife into him, but he must clear Sarah. There can be no chance of hitting her. The men wait, watching, ready to strike when the opportunity arises.

Once outside, Enrique grapples with the door handle His uncertainty causes Sarah to slip through his grasp. He roars and faces the building, desperately sweeping his arms, trying to retrieve his captive who lies huddled in the dirt at his feet. Noah seizes his opportunity and flings the knife. At the same instant, an explosion sounds. Enrique Mendoza flies through the air and over the hood of his Mercedes, leaving a slick, red smear of blood behind him.

Raven Looking Bird materializes from behind the building. She strides deliberately over to Sarah and clasps the semi-conscious child to her chest, not giving Mendoza a second look.

"My dolly fell in the room. My dolly. Please, angel," Sarah begs her.

Raven kisses her clammy cheek. "Never you mind, sweet one. The other angels will bring your dolly. Would you like to go home now?"

Sarah nods and lays her head against Raven's shoulder. Raven drops the borrowed weapon in the dirt and carries Sarah to Jack's car. While the others round up the wounded accomplice and call the Sheriff, Raven climbs into the back seat, holds Sarah in her lap, hums an Indian lullaby her mother used to sing, and rocks the little girl to sleep.

Forty minutes later, Sarah Ramirez is airlifted from Calhoun General Hospital in the Lifeflight helicopter and taken to Shand's Hospital in Gainesville where her anxious parents wait. She has weathered the ordeal amazingly well, and the rescheduled bone marrow transplant will take place as soon as her scraped knees are healed, and she is stabilized at that closer location. She has an excellent chance of recovery, thanks to the "angels" who have rescued her.

Pedro Suarez, an illegal alien, is incarcerated at the Leon County Jail after being arrested and charged with kidnapping. His chances of walking any of the fair Florida streets before he is an old man are slim.

Enrique Mendoza's political career is *shut down*. The coroner is not sure exactly what caused the man's death. The long-bladed knife nearly decapitated Enrique, severing the jugular vein and the spinal cord at the same time. The 9-mm bullet blew his heart out of his chest. The coroner finally concludes that both weapons hit simultaneously, killing him instantly.

*   *   *

Jack Abernathy's hand is stitched and bandaged by the time he meets the Trackers back at the Governor's Mansion. There are no reporters. Governor Ramirez has already released a statement to satisfy the curiosity seekers. Family matters are private and have no place in the public eye. Governor Ramirez is just getting off the telephone when Jack arrives.

"The insolence of that man! I do not need his well-wishing. He is a snake, and that advisor of his is an even bigger snake." Ramirez shouts to the walls.

"Kiley?" Jack asks.

"Si, si, si," Ramirez replies, pacing.

"Who told Kiley? Watch out for him, Bob. I think he has his mind set on living in this house," Jack warns.

"Never! Never, as long as I live, shall that—that—man set foot in this house, let alone live here." Ramirez is fuming, his cheeks hot and red.

The telephone rings, and Mrs. Ramirez hurries to answer it. Noah sidles closer to Jack and the Governor to see if he can overhear their heated conversation. He knows it is eavesdropping, but he has heard the name "Kiley." *Darryl Kiley?* Noah has no idea who that is besides the new name of the stadium, but he intends to find out.

"I'm telling you, Bob, the man is gaining support. Heaven only knows how," Jack says.

"I have always stood for the common people. That is how I began. Darryl Kiley is a rich boy, using his money to entice and buy support." He spits these words out with such force that Jack takes a step backward.

"Easy, Bob ..." Jack cautions his friend. Ramirez's face is becoming ruddier.

"He is a snake. He is a blot on this occasion. I have no good words for him. He is ..." Bob Ramirez utters a stream of vehement Spanish, not noticing his wife behind him.

"*Roberto!*" she shrieks.

"Carmine. I am sorry, *Cara Mia*. Those words were not for your ears."

She raises her eyebrows, tilts her graying head, and admonishes him. "Words that are not for my ears should not be for anyone else's ears."

"You are right, as always. Forgive me. I will try to control my temper in the future." Bob acquiesces, kisses her chubby cheek, and bows his head like a chastised little boy. Carmine Ramirez smiles at her husband's eyes peeking from below his thinning hair.

"You are forgiven. Now come. I have news," she says, taking his arm.

They walk toward the others in the room—she with great dignity; he with great sheepishness.

"Sarah is doing well. The doctors have much hope for her. Anita and Manuel are with her. *Dios Mio.* How can we thank you enough?" She is giddy with relief.

"Please, I know you have expenses. I would be most grateful if you would accept a contribution to your organization," the Governor says.

"No, my friend. We do not take compensation for tracking children. That is a duty and a privilege. The safe return of Sarah is payment enough," Lee replies. The statement is sincere, not magnanimous. Among the provisos adopted by their team are that they never seek the cases they work, they always let the police make the first contact, and they rarely accept remuneration.

"Then you will dine with us," Mrs. Ramirez says. She wags her finger at the Trackers. "I do not take kindly to those who refuse my meal invitations." She levels an unspoken challenge to Liahona Thistleseed.

Lee throws his head back and laughs. "How can I argue with a seventh daughter?"

"*Bueno,*" Mrs. Ramirez says. "You will want to excuse me while I prepare the meal." She disappears into the kitchen.

Raven and Noah look at each other with their eyebrows cocked. They have never seen anyone handle Lee Thistleseed so deftly. Jack Abernathy laughs soundly, as does Bob Ramirez, who looks toward the kitchen with unabashed affection.

Graham is puzzled. "The Governor's wife is cooking ... all by herself?"

Jack nods vigorously. "Are you kidding? Carmine wouldn't have it any other way. You folks better go on home and clean up. And don't you dare snack, or you won't have room for the best Spanish meal you have ever set your teeth to. Right, Bob?"

Bob Ramirez rolls his eyes and rubs his stomach dramatically. "Words cannot describe it. Come back at 2:00 and bring your appetites. Don't dress up, though. We like to eat comfortably. When Carmine cooks, Carmine cooks!"

Jack agrees. "Believe me, folks," he remarks as they make their way to their cars, "No amount of money in the world can equal Carmine Ramirez's cooking." He smacks his lips together. "We are in for a treat!"

Jack Abernathy pulls his Ford Bronco out into traffic and waves back at the four Indians. They stare stupidly at each other for a moment, and then race to their cars, whooping in exultation. In little more than one hour, they will be back for a meal, the likes of which they have never known.

If Noah Lightfoot did possess the gift of claircognizance he earlier desired, he would know that they will be joined at that meal by an incredible young woman who will change his life forever ... Maria Ramirez.

CHAPTER SIX
MARIA COMES TO DINNER

MARIA RAMIREZ IS A REMARKABLE TEENAGER. At sixteen, she is somewhat of a child prodigy, on a full academic music scholarship to Troy State University in Alabama. She is gifted, not only with a very high I.Q., but with undeveloped clairvoyant abilities, though she has no knowledge of the unusual nature of her powers. In addition, Maria is uncommonly talented in music; she sings and plays the piano like a professional, after no lessons whatsoever.

Her psychic powers are untrained; however, Maria "feels" things about people. She can pick up emotions, intents, and sometimes catch dreams. Maria is a lucid dreamer and has a literal smorgasbord of "clair" senses: clairvoyance, clairsentience, and clairempathy—seeing what is hidden, picking up senses, and feeling emotions. Knowing her father's insistence that these types of capabilities are evil, Maria keeps them quietly to herself; however, she sometimes slips up. She knows her mother covers for her, and she really believes that her father suspects, but it is a topic that is never, ever discussed openly. Despite being able to objectively tune in to, or subjectively tune out, other people, nothing has prepared Maria for what she will feel about Noah Lightfoot. Of all the feelings she has ever experienced, the one she has never experienced is love at first ... or perhaps second ... sight.

The days after Sarah's abduction crawl by for Maria. She is unable to concentrate on her studies. Of what use are harmonic inversions when a girl's heart aches for something she has not even known existed a week before? Maria looks at the clock. Only a few minutes more and she will be on her way to Tallahassee; on her way to her parents' anniversary dinner; on her way ... to Noah.

During the past week she has carefully gone over each detail of the events during the Sunday dinner her mother prepared.

*　　*　　*

Maria arrived just as the guests were sitting down. In her heart, she already knew Sarah was safe, but by that time she was three-quarters of the way home, so she decided to continue on to visit with her Mama and Papa. She walked in to find her parents with Jack and Betty Abernathy and a room full of Native American Indians, all sitting at tables set up on the veranda.

"*Buenas tardes,*" she said.

Bob Ramirez jumped up. "Maria! What are you doing here?" He hurried over to embrace her.

"Want me to leave?"

"Never. Never, my Chiquita." He kissed her on both cheeks, and then escorted her into the room. "My daughter, Maria," he announced grinning.

Maria bounded over to her mother and hugged her fiercely. "*Mamacita*, I was so frightened. I'm so relieved that Sarah is safe now. Where is she? With Manuel?"

Carmen's eyes widened and flicked nervously to Liahona Thistleseed. "*Si,* she is with them even now, thanks to these wonderful people. Maria, these are the Trackers I told you about. You remember—the ones who found her and rescued her from some terrible men."

Maria had never heard her mother lie before. She tilted her head and wondered what the big secret was all about. This was the first she had heard about any trackers. Knowing her mother, there was good reason for the deception, so Maria kept her lips pressed closed.

Lee rose from his seat. "May I introduce myself? My name is Liahona Thistleseed. You must be the daughter who called earlier today."

Maria smiled politely. "Yes, I was at school when I felt ..." she began.

"... when she felt she should call her Papa like she always does on a Sunday morning. Isn't that right, Maria?" Her father's interruption did not go unnoticed by Lee.

Both her parents were acting peculiar. Maria took in his intense expression. "Yes. I always call on Sunday morning. That's when Mama told me about Sarah."

Graham sauntered closer to Maria. "Well, is that right, Pilgrim? You sound like a dutiful daughter to me." He laughed at her raised eyebrows and cocked head—a typical response to his impression of John Wayne. "I'm Graham Skysong, man of a thousand voices."

"I'm girl of a thousand term papers right now," she countered. "Maybe you can help me find a thousand people to write them for me!"

"Don't look at me," Noah called, giving her the full benefit of his brilliant smile. "I've got term papers of my own to write. I'm Noah Lightfoot—also known as 'Chief Osceola' around F.S.U. campus. And this is Raven Looking Bird. She's our resident artist." He graced the woman on his left with a different, more intimate smile than the one Maria received.

At that moment, Maria surmised Noah's deep feelings for Raven; at that moment, Maria was startled to realize that she was intensely jealous. In fact, from the moment she first registered his presence, Maria fell totally and hopelessly in love with Noah. But when he looked at her, he saw only a cute young girl. He might have been more interested, had it not been for the fact that Noah seemed to be falling totally and hopelessly in love with Raven.

Raven confused Maria. She was such a striking woman, in a different sort of way, and even though Maria thought she was much too old for him, Raven could be the luckiest woman in the world for all the attention Noah devoted to her. But there was an underlying sense of such sadness and loneliness coming from her that Maria's own eyes began to mist from the pain of it. What bothered her more was the feeling that the woman was longing, not for Noah, but for someone else.

Lee broke her concentration. "How did you know Sarah was out of danger?"

"I just felt like she was." Her reply was unguarded.

Carmine rushed to the rescue. "Maria knows we would never have company for dinner if Sarah was still missing or hurt."

"Well, sure." Maria recovered from her blunder. "Mama never cooks when something is wrong."

Governor Ramirez stepped into the middle of the room and threw his arms out wide. "Now that all the introductions are completed, let's get down to what we are gathered here for ... Carmine's cooking!" He bowed his head, as did his family. The guests followed suit while Governor Robert Ramirez of the State of Florida graciously asked a blessing on the food.

The formalities over, the Ramirez family and their guests began dinner. Preoccupied with Raven though he was, Maria was pleased that Noah seemed to appreciate the simple eloquence of Carmine's dinner party. The three tables were arranged in a modified U shape, with her father's table in the center. All were covered with fine white linen tablecloths and decorated with vases of fresh flowers, along with large crystal pitchers of chilled *sangria* in which orange, lemon, and kumquat slices floated. A Spanish dinner was a sensual experience—a leisurely affair meant to feed the senses as well as the belly. Bob explained that, according to their Spanish tradition, all the food is served from the stove, one course at a time, and individual plates are brought to the table. Carmine took pleasure in filling the plates, while Maria served the heaping portions to the seated guests, describing the ingredients, the recipes, and her mother's preparations.

The first course to be served was the soup appetizer. Carmine prepared a delicious *sopa de lentejas Madrilena*—lentil soup, Madrid style. It was a fragrant combination of onions, pimentos, green peppers, tomatoes, carrots, and lentils that were simmered for over an hour until the vegetables were soft, and the broth was thick. Betty Abernathy laughed watching Graham scrape his spoon around the sides and bottom of his bowl, scooping every smudge of soup he could find, but she elbowed her husband when he began to do the same thing. Jack dropped his spoon back into his bowl.

The next course was e*nsalada*—salad. This mixture of lettuce, carrots, bologna, cheese, green olives, and hard-cooked eggs was served on a chilled crystal plate and seasoned with a simple dressing of salt, pepper, vinegar, and olive oil that seemed to please both the men and the women. Raven, particularly, seemed to enjoy the dish.

For the main course, Carmine had cooked her specialty— *paella.* Maria brought a shallow, two-handled black skillet directly from the stove and placed it at her father's table. As custom dictated, the man at the head of the table served the *paella* to each diner at his table. As the head of the family, Bob Ramirez was pleased to perform this honor, almost as much as he was pleased to eat this, his favorite dish.

"There is really no English equivalent for the word *paella,*" he said. "Once you eat it, you will always know it as *paella!*"

He was right, of course. Even the preparation had no English equivalent. The ingredients were fresh; their combination and seasoning were time-consuming and handed down through generations of mothers to daughters. Carmine was well known for this one particular dish, as her mother had been. The first requirement was to soak and rinse fresh clams, as well as shell and devein large, juicy shrimp. Next, a special garlic-seasoned sausage was pan fried and sliced. Serving-sized pieces of chicken were browned in olive oil, along with minced onion, chopped red pepper, and crushed garlic. Then, all the meats were covered and set aside to rest and drain.

The next step involved combining rice, chicken broth, oregano, and saffron in the special *paella* skillet. Carmine never measured; she just knew how much to use from years of experience. When these ingredients came to a boil, the skillet was removed from the heat and left covered until the rice plumped. The chicken, sausage, shrimp, and clams were artfully arranged on top of the rice, and crisp green peas were scattered over the entire dish. Carmine used peas she had harvested from her own garden, blanched, and frozen this past summer. The food-laden skillet was baked in the oven, and then served steaming hot at the table. It was no wonder that *paella* was Bob Ramirez's favorite dish. As if there was not enough food to consume, the guests were also served *pisto manchego*, which was stewed vegetables consisting of onions, zucchinis, tomatoes, and potatoes, seasoned with garlic and fresh parsley, all from Carmine's backyard garden.

Jack Abernathy inhaled his plate, smacked his lips, and looked with puppy dog eyes at his wife. "Forget it," Betty said. "If you want this kind of food, you better get it from Carmine. I can barely get pot roast right!"

"And that's a fact!" Jack laughed through a mouthful of rice and received a sharp kick.

It went without saying that one did not eat quickly in Spain. With so many courses to consume, the midday meal was a relaxed leisurely gathering, usually lasting between one and two hours. Spaniards took their time with their food to relish every morsel and to savor each individual ingredient, as well as the combinations thereof.

This meal was no different, but for those used to eating on the run, it took discipline not to wolf down what was served. By the time the *paella* arrived, Noah had finally caught on, but he was fast becoming quite full. It was apparent that Carmine and Maria heaped extra-large portions onto his plates.

Although most of the guests protested they could eat no more, there was no way to turn down dessert, and they were quite surprised to find they still had room for it. The caramel custard *flan* melted in their mouths. It was not too sweet and was just light enough to eat after a meal of such grand proportions. Its coolness was a welcome balm to their fiery palates, and the caramel sauce seemed to neutralize the garlic so prevalent in the rest of the dishes. No plate was left empty.

When, at last, they pushed themselves away from the tables, there was no question as to their activities for the remainder of the day. After many "thank-yous" and raves over Carmine's cooking,

Jack and Betty Abernathy and the Trackers all went to their homes ... to nap.

* * *

Maria has relived every minute detail of that dinner from the time she was back at school until now. She looks forward to tonight's anniversary party with the anticipation of a bride.

An anniversary is always a time for rejoicing. In the Ramirez household, there is no greater reason for celebration than that of the two people responsible for a large clan of Ramirezes. The party is held in the banquet room of the Radisson Hotel. The entire family is in attendance, with the exception of Manuel, Anita, and Sarah, who must remain in a sterile environment for several months until Sarah's bone marrow transplant stabilizes her condition. The group is augmented by the Trackers: Liahona Thistleseed and his Cherokee wife Wren, Graham Skysong, Noah Lightfoot, and Raven Looking Bird. Other attendees include law enforcement, politicos, local celebrities, and the media.

Raven is more stunning than Maria remembers. She is dressed in a handmade Yavapai outfit of intricately woven white linen, trimmed in turquoise and shell ornaments and soft white rabbit fur, with, of course, matching rabbit fur moccasins. Maria has also dressed especially for the occasion. But even in her black beaded silk dress, Maria feels like a plain child in a homespun smock beside the dazzling brilliance that Raven exudes. That Noah cannot take his eyes off Raven makes Maria more uncomfortable.

Despite her nervous anxiety and disappointment, Maria thinks the evening is going pleasantly, due, in a large part, to Graham's expertise on the Karaoke. The soundtrack machine in the room is usually put to use by patrons in various stages of inebriation, but it is dedicated to the Ramirezes on this occasion. Karaoke performances entertain those who sing and those who listen, and some of the family are actually pretty good singers. But none is as accomplished as Graham Skysong—a one-man revue. He sings song after song as Frank Sinatra, Elton John, Stevie Wonder, and even Barbra Streisand in a rendition of "People" that brings down the house.

After a while, Bob Ramirez takes the microphone and dedicates a song to Carmine, his lovely wife, for 30 years of unequaled joy and companionship. Gazing intently into her eyes, the Governor of the State of Florida begins to sing unaccompanied, his baritone voice somewhat scratchy, but his tender heart fully present in a verse from a Spanish love song titled, *"Momentos en el Tiempo."*

> *"...Me refugió en tu amor,*
> *Y nuestros corazones eran como uno.*
> *Estaba Perdida en tus ojos*
> *Y nuestros sueños eran los mismos.*
> *La vida no es más que un momento en el tiempo ..."*

Overcome with emotion, he cannot finish. Instead, the Governor simply stops and tenderly kisses his wife while the audience applauds. Graham takes the microphone and translates the song *sotto voce*—half voice. "... I took shelter in your love ... and our hearts were as one ... I was lost in your eyes ... and our dreams were the same ... Life is but a moment in time ..." The big man speaks in an interpretation almost as touching as the song itself. Selecting another song, he launches into a Kenny Rogers rendition of "Lady."

Noah takes Raven's hand and leads her to the dance floor, followed by several other couples. Maria's heart flutters; she stops breathing. She watches as Noah holds Raven closely and rubs his cheek against hers. Raven responds by stroking his long black hair.

Again, Maria senses that sadness from Raven. *Why does she mourn so?* Maria tucks a note in her mental file to investigate this woman. She will be sure to spend some quality time with Raven. As she watches, Noah kisses Raven, and Raven returns the kiss. Curiosity changes to anger at that kiss. Maria is suddenly sure that Raven is in love with someone else. As quickly as that emotion appears, it is replaced with another. For the first time this evening, Maria feels ... hope.

Graham ends the song, and the couples leave the floor as Bob again takes the microphone. He catches Maria's eye and beams at her. "*Por favor, Chiquita,*" he asks, "Will you sing a dance for your Mama and me?"

The family calls out their approval and urges her forward. "What shall I sing for you?" Maria asks.

"Anything, *querida*. Whatever your heart desires." He lovingly cradles his daughter's petite hand.

"Just so long as it is slow enough for me to avoid your father's left feet." Carmine teases her husband.

Maria scans the song list and selects a tune she likes. Graham cues up the soundtrack, the intro plays, and Bob escorts Carmine to the floor. Maria sings, and an angel's voice floats through the room.

> "*You say you're the seventh son*
> *of a seventh, seventh son,*
> *I guess that's why I love you, you are my only one...*"

The voice that resonates over the speakers is sweet and powerful, full of a maturity attributed to women with years of training. Her pitch is as true as her tone is clear, and the essence of her presence fills the room more tangibly than her voice. The effect is like E.F. Hutton—total silence.

As Governor and Mrs. Robert Ramirez dance around the floor, two stewards appear at the dining hall door, joined by several couples from other rooms. Carmen and Bob don't notice the onlookers. They see only each other. But the crowd isn't gathered to watch the Governor dance with his wife; they are enthralled by the diminutive young lady with the chocolate eyes and the velvety voice. But she is completely focused on the one person in the room whose eyes are not on her. Noah.

> "*You can take a man into your heart,*
> *And love him every day.*
> *You can give him everything you hold dear,*
> *But you cannot make him stay...*"

Lee witnesses the event, looks at his wife, and reads the

word Wren mouths just as Maria's own voice sings out, "love."

"You can be my first and last love,
Instead of going your own way."

Lee feels the familiar nudge of Wren's ample body next to him and places his hand over hers. He is not surprised to see the knowing gleam in her eye. Wren does not possess her husband's gift of second sight, but she does have the knack of a long-married woman's perception.

"Liahona," she murmurs. "This room is very warm tonight, isn't it?"

"Oh? Is it? I am quite comfortable." Lee loves to toy with his wife.

He winces as she pinches the inside of his leg. "You know what I mean. Look around you. There is love, and passion, and jealousy, and possibly a broken heart. Do you not see?"

"Of course, my little bird. But they do not, so mind your manners. They will find out on their own in time."

He pecks her round cheek, fully aware that Wren will thoroughly enjoy the evening's soap opera.

When Maria finishes singing, the room thunders with applause. Reluctantly, the banquet staff resume their duties while Maria's Uncle Juan and Aunt Rosa sing a duet. Maria watches Noah escort Raven to her seat, then excuse himself to get drinks. Determined to garner some information, Maria makes her way to the table. She stops short when she sees Graham pull up a chair and detours to the restroom to summon up her courage.

Raven regards Graham as he pulls the ashtray close. "You're in great voice tonight, Gray."

He pulls out his hard pack and flips back the top. "Thanks, Bird. I'm having a good time. How 'bout you?"

"Lovely. This is a delightful family. They seem so genuine, and some are really quite talented."

"That's for sure. That Maria is incredible. Did you hear her song? What a voice!" With a practiced flick of the wrist Graham pops two cigarettes up above the rest. "Smoke? They're lights." He offers the pack to her.

Raven shakes her head slightly. "Thank you, but no."

Graham puts the box to his mouth and draws out one cigarette. "Still on the tobacco wagon, huh?"

He flips open the lid of a silver lighter engraved *G.S.* and set with tiny turquoise stones, ignites the end of the cigarette, and inhales deeply, never taking his eyes from Raven's face.

"Sure do love this lighter, Bird," he says. Snapping the lid closed, he exhales, wafting the tendrils of smoke her way and watching her reaction.

Raven looks away from the lighter and blinks her eyes rapidly, fighting the impulse to cough.

"Don't worry; I'll put it out before Chief comes back. We know how he hates smoke." Graham's sardonic tone matches his fixed smirk.

Raven raises her eyes to meet his. Her gaze is kind; her tone is patient, but the message is clearly reproving. "Jealousy does not become you, Graham. Be done with it."

The red fire of shame singes his cheeks. Graham examines the ash of his cigarette as if its smoldering is of great importance. Its heat is mere degrees less than his burning embarrassment. He stubs it out with reverence—the last ember of a memory also snuffed away.

"No," he says, rising. "It does not. Forgive me."

Head held high, Graham turns and walks deliberately toward the bandstand. Noah passes him bringing *sangria* for himself and a Diet Coke for Raven. She smiles at him through stinging eyes as she sips the cola.

"Too much smoke in here for me, Noah. Let's go back to my apartment."

Noah is eager to comply. As they get up to pay their respects to Bob and Carmine Ramirez, they are oblivious to the many sets of eyes following their every movement, nor do they suspect the turn of events playing out.

Noah glances toward the dance floor and sees Graham take Maria's willowy hand in his brawny one and place a tender kiss on her upturned wrist. For some reason, Noah feels a trifle annoyed.

He doesn't know why, but he doesn't like Graham being so interested in Maria. True, there is about a ten- or twelve-year difference, but Graham is essentially a pretty youthful guy. He has a great sense of humor, and even Raven remarks on his good looks. *But Maria is just a girl,* he thinks, forgetting that he is only two years older. Noah does not like the idea of Graham and Maria together. It is like an itch or a tickle in the back of the throat—bothersome and hard to get to. His irritation vanishes, however, when Raven eases her shapely frame against his side.

"Let's say goodnight, Noah. There's Carmine," Raven suggests, making her way toward Mrs. Ramirez. Noah follows obediently. As they come closer to the Governor and his wife, they notice that Ramirez is clenching his fists tightly. Noah glimpses two men leaving the banquet room. They seem to be the objects of Governor Ramirez's anger. One man is of average build, with thick reddish blond hair; the other man is stocky and dark-haired. Seeing them, Raven tenses on Noah's arm.

"What's going on?" Noah asks.

"Governor Ramirez. He looks awfully mad," Raven replies.

They gradually ease closer to the conversation. Maria rushes to her father's side and tries to calm him down, with little success. Jack Abernathy shakes his head as he glances toward the door where the two men disappeared.

"The unmitigated nerve of that ... that ... man!" the Governor sputters, blowing his breath out in ragged puffs.

"Now Papa ..." Maria tries unsuccessfully to soothe him.

"To come here on this night! He had no right ... no right to intrude," Ramirez says.

"Papa, he only wanted to congratulate ..."

"He only wanted to make a showing ... to gain public favor ... to humiliate me. And that trained monkey of his. Odd. He has no business here," her father argues.

"Easy now, Bob." Jack cautions his friend. "Remember your blood pressure."

"He is odd, I tell you. Have you seen him up close? Who wears sunglasses at night?" Ramirez demands. "What is he, a movie star?"

"Oh, c'mon, Papa," Maria says. "I don't really think he ..."

"A trained monkey. A gorilla. And that Kiley, he's a snake." Ramirez hisses his point.

Kiley? Noah edges closer and tries to catch another glimpse of the man whose name now graces the F.S.U. football stadium.

"He didn't seem so bad ... for an old guy." Maria shrugs.

"Old guy? Thank you very much, *Chiquita*. He is at least ten years younger than I am!" Ramirez sounds wounded.

"Oh, Papa. You know what I mean."

"*Si.* I know what you mean." He is inconsolable.

Carmine hurries over to her husband, begging. "Roberto, *por favor* ... dance with me, before your face gets any redder."

"My face is not red."

Carmine takes her husband's hands. Desperately, she eyes Maria, pleading. "Sing, Maria, sing! Graham, please! For Heaven's sake, will somebody please sing?"

Graham hurries to the microphone with Maria in tow. Carmine turns her attention back to her irate husband. "Come, Roberto, dance with me," she insists.

He surprises her by lifting his head and striding toward the dance floor, pulling her with him. "Old guy? I'll show you an old guy. Come, Carmine. We dance. Maria, be a good daughter. Sing *'La Bamba'* and watch your poor 'old' Papa boogie!"

Graham laughs and punches up the song. Maria sings with great gusto but her voice is nothing compared to the gusto with which her father dances. Carmine's eyes roll as she struggles to keep up with him. But the tension is broken, and Bob Ramirez is back to his jovial self. When the song ends, he swings his wife around like a rag doll. After several spins, he dips her and finally kisses her loudly on the lips, to the crowd's obvious enjoyment.

Noah and Raven wave to the celebrants and start to leave as Graham and Maria strike up a duet. Strolling down the hallway with his hand in the curve of Raven's back, Noah can hear Graham's remarkable rendition of Nat King Cole singing, "Smoke Gets in Your Eyes." And just for an irrational instant, Noah is terribly afraid.

CHAPTER SEVEN
DREAMERS AND TRAVELERS

IT IS A NIGHT OF DREAMS: dreams come true and dreams unfulfilled; of power and surrender; of life and death. The dreams of the waking cross into the dreams of the sleeping, and what is dreamed by one is shared by another, as well. Little does she realize, but Maria is the catalyst for this dream projection, and her instant attachment to Noah is what sets the dream in motion.

For Noah, his time with Raven is not at all as he has imagined. The experience is so exquisite, he wonders if the night is a dream, after all. Noah is not a stranger to love but spending time with Raven is like exploring a new and different land. He becomes completely lost in her conversation; he wanders in her presence until she takes the lead. Only then does he travel on familiar ground. But still, the way is distant—as distant as the woman herself. He expected physical pleasures, and he visualized a union worthy of the big screen, but he is surprised to find contentment in simply holding her.

Raven guides his emotions down unfamiliar paths. Yet, there is a familiarity about her that eludes him. He has a sense of knowing what he can have no way of knowing, but sentient, in the tangible here and now. She feels almost like a memory, but she is brand new.

Noah tucks the intrusion away until the talking ends. But, in the quiet that follows, it comes back to taunt him, like forbidden fruit hanging just out of reach, an expectation never to be reached, a marriage never to be consummated.

Raven has fallen asleep against his chest with her feet tucked beneath a sofa cushion. She stirs, and Noah catches her scent. It is fresh and sweet and clean, like her. Pushing the nagging thoughts from his mind, he settles her more comfortably on his side. He brushes a lock of silky hair off her cheek and scoots down to lay his head beside hers on the arm of the couch, breathing in the smell of the dusting powder she has sprinkled on her clothing.

In the seconds just before sleep totally consumes him, Noah's restless synapses forge a dream. As he finally surrenders to the REM state, the dream emerges and travels to the sleeping beauty many miles away.

*   *   *

Sleeping alone in the guest room of the Governor's Mansion, Maria Ramirez receives the dream and makes it her own.

She is airborne and hovering, drifting in that weightless phenomenon one has when dreaming, where the laws of gravity no longer apply. The rooms below are none with which she is familiar. She seems to be above a kitchen. It is simple and unadorned. It is undeniably a bachelor's kitchen.

Maria is surprised to realize she can smell things in this dream. This is something new. In fact, all her senses are heightened. The colors are especially vivid, the sounds are crisp and clear, the dominant smell is ... sugar cookies. Someone dressed in a large man's pajama top is baking. Raven. Raven appears to be baking sugar cookies.

A man sits in the adjacent room. His chest is bare, and he is dressed in the pajama trousers matching Raven's shirt. Noah. No, not Noah. He turns to face her. He is faceless, but Maria recognizes his long black hair. Noah's.

Maria detects an overwhelming acerbic smell. Raven is

burning the cookies. The heat in the oven is set too high. Noah comes into the kitchen, opens the smoking oven, and pulls out a pan. He cries out as the pan burns his hands. Maria sucks in her breath and tries vainly to reach him, but she is powerless to do anything but simply float overhead. Raven lies curled up on the floor, sleeping in a fetal position. Noah covers her with his body. When he rolls over, Raven disappears in a puff of thick grey smoke.

Noah calls, "Come home." The floor loses consistency and becomes soft, spongy. Still, Noah searches for Raven and begs for her to come home. *"Let her go,"* Maria implores, though her words make no sound.

Maria catches a glint of reflected light out the window. She pushes off the wall and drifts in that direction to see what is outside. Sometimes she is able to influence the outcome of her dreams, so she wills herself to see. *Raven? Nope, that's not Raven out there.* Eyes. White eyes. No ... silver eyes. Watching, just watching. Silver eyes watching Noah, who is beginning to give off wispy tendrils of smoke. Suddenly, great clouds of dark smoke billow from his body. The eyes just watch. She wants to scream. *Help him!* The cookies burn. Noah becomes ashes.

Maria gasps for breath and flings the covers off the bed; sweat clings to her body and seals her thin nightgown to her small frame. She looks about the darkened room in fear, sniffing the air for some sign of a fire. Detecting none, she strips off the soaked gown and sits naked in the dark, letting the air cool her sticky skin.

When chill bumps set in, she rummages in her suitcase for an oversized t-shirt to slip into. She dresses quickly and runs her fingers through her hair; then she stealthily tiptoes into the kitchen for a glass of apple juice. Sitting at the moonlit counter, Maria savors the tart coolness of the juice while she analyzes the dream.

Maria has caught dreams before but none as vivid as this one. Perhaps it is her instant attraction to Noah that makes this dream so real. She is sure of the subtext: Raven means trouble for Noah. Maria does not feel Raven intentionally wants to hurt him, but there is a very deadly aura about her.

Maria dissects the symbols from the main body of the dream: sugar cookies, Raven, Noah, silver eyes, smoke. *Where there's smoke, there's fire.* She can place all of them except the silver eyes. She isn't even sure how eyes can be silver. *What does that mean?*

Are Noah and Raven lovers? The thought makes her stomach cramp, but the shared pajamas seemed to suggest they are. The sugar cookies are easy enough to interpret. Raven's cologne, *DeVanille*, is the essence of vanilla. Fire. Other than suggesting passion, i.e. *"hot and heavy,"* she can't think of what else the fire can mean. Neither Noah nor Raven smoke. But Graham does. Silver eyes. Maria tilts her head back and moves her eyes rapidly back and forth. It's a little device she uses to remember things that elude her. Graham's eyes are brown behind his wire-rimmed glasses—silver wire rims.

Maria shudders. That could mean Graham also loves Raven. *But enough to kill Noah over her?* She wonders. Maria thinks back to her first meeting with Raven. There had been another man in Raven's life for whom she still longed. It could have been Graham.

But Graham is so gentle, so entertaining. If Maria was not already in love with Noah, and if Graham was just a teensy bit younger, she would consider dating him. He seemed to be quite interested in her this evening. She remembers how he let his lips linger on her wrist when he kissed it and how he looked so deeply into her eyes when they sang together. Maria isn't a connoisseur of romance, but she is no dummy either. It could be an act, or Graham may be on the rebound. If so, he should just leave her out of it.

Maria grows tired of the "could've-would've-should've" game and rubs her eyes, yawning deeply. She opens the refrigerator and thrusts her arm into the light spilling out. Her watch reads 3:00 AM. She needs rest to figure this out. After breakfast, she will invent some excuse to go to Noah's house, and she will tell him of the dream and her interpretation of it. Tired as she is, her heart races at the thought.

Maria slips beneath the covers with a smile on her face. As she drifts into sleep, she holds the image of Noah's handsome face in her memory. It is not there when she awakens. In fact, very little of Maria Ramirez's memory remains when she awakens.

*   *   *

Noah rouses from a deep sleep to the sound of what he thinks is a fire drill at an elementary school. He pushes himself up to a sitting position on the couch and shakes his head, and then he slams his hand down on the snooze button of a tiny travel alarm clock. He stops in mid-yawn and scans the room for Raven. She is gone, but she has taped a note to the clock telling him there are frozen bagels and cream cheese in the kitchen.

Noah smiles and inhales the sugary fragrance of her that permeates the room. Last night was wonderful, not in a locker room story kind of way, but satisfying nonetheless ... except for that vivid dream. He cannot shake of the feeling of dread it gives him. He has to talk to Lee right away about the alarming elements of the dream.

Noah lies back on the cushions and dials Lee's number. He picks up on the first ring.

"Yes, Noah," he says.

"How'd you know it was me?" Noah asks.

"No other person dares to call my home at 6:45 in the morning," Lee states.

"Aw, gee. I thought maybe you were second-sighted or something like that."

"Perish the thought. Now, what is on your mind, Noah?"

"I had a weird dream, Lee, but I think I know what it meant. I really need to talk to you about it. I think you and I need to track a certain someone. Lee, I know his sounds bizarre, but I believe someone is doing some unauthorized tracking." Noah pauses, waiting for Lee's wisdom.

Liahona Thistleseed is silent.

"Lee?" Noah has a bad feeling about this.

"I will meet you at your house at 7:00, Noah. You can get there by then," Lee says.

"Yeah, it's just down the ... uh. Hey! How'd you know I wasn't at home?"

"Lucky guess," Lee says. "Hurry now, son."

"On my way." Noah smiles to himself. Sometimes Lee lets down that proper veneer, and a downright good sense of humor emerges. He dresses quickly, grabs a partially defrosted bagel, and forces a rectangular chunk of cream cheese into the hole. *"That Raven—what a cook!"* He snickers as he slams the door and jogs to his car, cheese infused bagel sticking prominently from between his front teeth.

In less than fifteen minutes, he is home, and Lee is waiting for him. Lee walks inside and settles onto the couch. Noah pops the bagel into the microwave, cream cheese still intact, and completes the thawing. He splits it in two and offers the half without teeth marks to Lee.

"No, thank you. Wren fed me half an hour ago," Lee says, patting his stomach.

"Lucky man," Noah says, to which Lee nods shrewdly.

"Now, Noah, please be kind enough to explain what is going on. What is this dream, and who is tracking without a beacon?" Lee seems anxious on this point. Noah knows he is thinking of Dane, of course. All the Trackers know Lee's policy about not tracking alone.

"Someone has been tracking without authorization, Lee. Not alone, though. With a beacon."

"Who is it?" Lee's voice is well modulated, but Noah senses the strain lurking at the surface of the question.

"I don't know. Well, I have some ideas, but I'm not entirely sure. I want to track to find out … right now, if you'll signal." Noah is impatient, as usual.

"Whom are you tracking?" Lee is not impatient, as usual.

"I don't want to say just yet. But I really feel like I have to go now, Lee. Please, indulge me. I won't be long."

Lee can see that Noah is teetering on the brink of an anxiety episode. He trusts the young man, just as the young man trusts him. He knows Noah will tell him if his hunch proves correct.

"Very well, Noah. But you must explain everything to me when you return. Agreed?"

"Agreed. Thanks, Lee. Let's go."

Noah closes his eyes. His breathing becomes deep and regular as he tracks his quarry.

*   *   *

At precisely 7:15, the Outlaw takes another trip. The overall objective of the mental business trips is still two-fold: eliminate one man, elevate another. Traveling is becoming second nature to the Outlaw, and each time, the journey goes more smoothly. But the Beacon is beginning to balk. There is more resistance this time, and the Outlaw must resort to the original threat to bring about a radical change of attitude in the Beacon. Once the balance of power is restored, the Outlaw is able to go about the business at hand.

This has been just a short jaunt into the past to clean up some loose ends. But the next journey will be a dangerous and complicated trip. The Outlaw must put trust into the Beacon to give the signal. After some thought, the Outlaw proceeds to raise the stakes. The Beacon objects, at first, but finally agrees to the terms. A time and place are arranged for four days from today at the Opperman Music Hall on the F.S.U. campus.

Their business concluded, the Outlaw and the Beacon go their separate ways, but not without secret plans on the part of both of them. The Outlaw decides to use the Beacon in four days and then terminate the "partnership" permanently. The Beacon intends to do the same.

*   *   *

Noah opens his eyes and looks over at Lee Thistleseed. Lee raises one eyebrow, but he doesn't say a word. Noah shakes his head grimly.

"Dead end. Didn't find a thing," he grumbles.

Patiently, like a father to a son, Lee asks him again, "Whom were you tracking, son?"

Noah looks embarrassed. "Graham."

"Graham?"

"And Raven."

"And Raven," Lee repeats. "Why, Noah?"

"Well, I ..." Noah stops, flustered, and shakes his head. "I'm not really sure, Lee. Something crazy is going on, and I don't quite know what to make of it."

"Between you, Raven, and Graham?"

"Yes. No. I don't know. It's not a personal thing. Well, it is a personal thing, but that's not what I'm talking about."

"What are you talking about?"

"Lee, jeez, this is gonna sound goofy, but I'm pretty sure somebody is tracking into the past!" Noah's eyes are wild as he glares at Lee.

"I see," Lee says.

"You see? You see? Just what do you see?" Noah shouts. Lee's calmness is infuriating, and Noah is losing control; his voice rising in pitch and volume.

"I see that you are upset, and you must calm down." Lee raises his voice a mere notch for emphasis. Once Noah gets cranked up, he is not easily assuaged.

"You don't see jack-diddly, man. You don't see anything. That's the point. You don't see at all!" Noah bounces on his toes, back and forth, like a caged animal.

He is inches away from Lee's face, screaming at him. He has crossed the line, and it takes him completely by surprise when his mentor slaps him on the jaw. Noah shakes his head and gapes at his friend. Lee has eyes of steel, and they never leave Noah's face.

Noah's own eyes spill over. He hasn't cried in years. Not since Dane died. He doesn't realize how much he needs to cry until Lee puts his large hand on Noah's head and pulls it against his shoulder. He sobs like a little boy. Lee never flinches, but two enormous tears course their way down his leathery cheeks and fall onto the young man's hair. A long time passes before Noah lifts his head up from the older man's chest.

Lee gently reestablishes conversation with the young Tracker. "Noah, you must make me understand what is so heavy on your heart and mind. I am here to help you. You must trust me and know that I love you as I loved your brother, like my own sons. Together we are strong, you and I. We have the power between us to right many wrongs. But, I must understand what we are dealing with. Please, tell me of your dream. Then, tell me of this Outlaw."

Noah gratefully relates everything he knows and everything

he suspects. He describes the dream; he confesses his intimate feelings for Raven and his confusing annoyance at Graham's possible relationship with Maria. He explains how he noticed a beacon at the football game and the silver eyes that signaled the end of the track. Noah studies Lee's reaction to the name change of the stadium and thinks he sees—hopes he sees—a flicker of recognition there. After he talks himself out, Noah takes a deep breath and waits for Lee's take on the whole thing.

Lee has heard many insane things in his life, but he has no doubt that Noah is being completely honest with him. He weighs the implications carefully in his mind. Danger is evident in these occurrences. The Outlaw Tracker is powerful. And evil.

Time tracking takes such skill and daring that Lee will not even try to teach his protégés. Rarely is there ever a need to time track. Traveling into the past has been forbidden by every Indian tribe on the American continent since long before the white men "discovered" it. Traveling into the past or the future is against the laws of Father Spirit and Mother Earth. Only traveling in the present is allowed, and even then, it is reserved for honorable gifted persons who are trained by other honorable gifted persons.

The Outlaw is gifted, but not honorable. The Beacon is equally dishonorable. They have broken all the sacred taboos. To track or signal unjustly demands the harshest of punishments— permanent and unconditional removal of any powers and privileges associated with the gift. This consequence can be imposed only by another Tracker of greater power. Liahona Thistleseed's gifted lineage, beginning with Hiawatha, makes him the most powerful Tracker in America. Therefore, it is up to him to impose the penalty. But first, the Beacon and the Outlaw must be identified and located. That will be tricky and potentially dangerous for both Noah and Lee. If Lee underestimates the Outlaw's power, Noah runs the risk of being seriously hurt.

"In my opinion," Lee tells Noah, "we must exercise great care lest we alert the Outlaw and the Beacon of our suspicions. I suggest you contact Raven and tell her I wish for the four of us to dine together so we may discuss upcoming assignments or political candidates. I will get in touch with Graham. Above all, Noah, we must act naturally."

"Right. But, Lee, what if they're both involved?"

"We will deal with it, Noah. But remember, this is 20th century United States of America. Citizens are innocent until proven guilty. Perhaps they know nothing. If that is the case, then good. If not …"

Lee's voice trails off, but Noah well understands the meaning. If the Outlaw and the Beacon are unaware of the suspicions they have aroused, there is a slim chance that he and Lee can safely intervene. He hopes and prays that whatever has happened will not require drastic action. Other innocent people can be hurt. He reads the disquiet behind Lee's compassionate gaze. *Not a good cover up, Buddy.* Noah pressed his lips together and looks at the floor, a deep crevice forming between his eyes. With a deep sigh, he reaches over and picks up the telephone to call Raven.

CHAPTER EIGHT

BEG FOR WATER

GRAHAM, WITH HIS USUAL EXUBERANCE, has already scouted ahead after Lee calls to find a new dining experience for the group.

"Do you like Spanish food? My friend said this place has the best food in town. They've got a Spanish lady who can cook socks and make 'em taste good," Graham says. He smacks his full lips in anticipation.

"Spanish food has become somewhat of a favorite of mine since we tracked and found Sarah," Lee confirms.

"Sarah who?" Graham asks, distracted. "Here it is, folks. Everybody dismount."

The restaurant is named simply *Que Pasa.* The four Trackers walk in and seat themselves as the sign directs. They choose a table near a small bandstand which is outfitted with a microphone, an upright piano, a modest set of drums, and an acoustic guitar. No performers are present. The overhead lights are dim, but it is evident the place is kept clean and orderly. The décor is Southwestern, with a smattering of festive pottery set in recesses along the adobe walls. Tablecloths of bright yellow are accented by woven cloth napkins of green, orange, blue, and red. A tad overstated, but tastefully done. Noah likes the effect.

"I give it eight spoons on ambience," he quips with a kiss-blowing motion of his fingers, "Now, let's rate the service."

Their waitress arrives promptly. She is young, dainty, and adorable in her sensible shoes and peasant skirt. She smiles brilliantly at Noah, but he only stares stupidly at her. Graham seems immediately taken and does his best to make a lasting impression by speaking to her in impeccably accented Spanish.

"*Buenos tardes, Senorita. Me llamo Graham. ¿Como te llamas?*" He rapidly articulates another sentence or two of small talk which makes her laugh. She has a musical, tinkling sort of giggle that is delightful and contagious.

"*Me llamo Maria,*" she answers with a grin. "Would you like to order now?"

Indeed, the name tag on her starched white blouse reads, "Maria." Noah continues to stare at her, making her shift uncomfortably. Raven is annoyed with his impolite behavior and nudges his leg beneath the table.

"Noah," Raven hisses. She leans toward him, spreading her napkin over her knees. "Noah! For heaven's sake. What is the matter with you? Stop staring at the waitress!"

Noah's response is to stare now at Raven.

"Have you lost your mind? What do you want to eat?" she says behind a forced smile.

"Maria?" he asks.

"She's not on the menu, Buddy." Graham laughs nervously at the tense display.

Noah turns to Lee. "Lee?"

"He's not on the menu, either, you dope." Graham snorts, trying to deflect attention away from Noah's peculiar behavior.

Lee looks compassionately into Noah's eyes. Then, very deliberately, he addresses Maria Ramirez.

"My dear Maria. Would you be so kind as to summon the cook? I'd like to speak with her personally about her specialty. I understand she is quite talented in the kitchen," he says.

Maria beams. "My mother is wonderful when it comes to food. I'll go get her. Be right back, y'all." She hurries away, casting a backward glance at Noah who continues to stare.

"Didn't I tell you this is a great place? Man, isn't she a doll? I swear, I'm in love!" Graham rolls his eyes comically, but nobody seems amused.

In a moment, the cook joins them. She is a plump, but handsome woman, except for a careworn look about her eyes.

"Hello, Carmine." Lee greets her warmly.

"Carmine? Do you know her?" Graham asks.

"Why, Graham. Did you not know that I, too, often frequent good restaurants? Besides, I have heard it said, 'when Carmine cooks, Carmine cooks!' Am I right, dear lady?" Lee says.

Carmine grins and blushes. Lee probes gently for any sign of recognition in Carmine Ramirez, Raven, and Graham. There is none. It seems, in all likelihood, that he and Noah are the only Trackers who know the mother and daughter. Lee listens as Carmine describes today's specialty: s*opa de lentejas Madrilèna, ensalada, arroz con pollo, pisto manchego,* and *flan* for dessert.

"My personal favorite is *paella*, but it takes at least an hour to prepare. I usually substitute the chicken and rice dish because many guests are too much in a hurry and they are not accustomed to waiting so long. It is good, too!" she explains.

"I have no doubt," Lee replies.

Graham and Raven both decide on the courses that Carmine recommends; Lee and Noah order the same, painfully aware that Carmine Ramirez cooked almost the same meal for them just two weeks ago in the Governor's Mansion.

Raven is quite put out with him; Noah has no illusions otherwise, but he cannot deal with her now. He concentrates on Maria and Carmine and wonders what has happened in their lives that they are reduced to cook and waitress in a local café. *Why do Lee and I still know them, but they don't know us? And Graham and Raven—are they just acting the part of ignorance? Why doesn't Graham remember Sarah?* Lee provides no help. He is perfectly composed, whereas Noah is a mass of nerves. A jangle of chords on the piano directs his attention to the diminutive stage.

"Ladies and Gentlemen," the pianist announces. "Today you have the outstanding privilege of hearing an angel sing. Our very own Maria Ramirez is having a birthday tomorrow, but today, she is still sweet sixteen, and we make her entertain. Come on up to the stage, *Chiquita*."

Maria bounces up to the microphone to the applause of the customers and staff. "Thank you. Oh, gosh. What should I sing, Jose?" she asks.

Jose takes his place at the piano and tenderly smiles at her. "Sing 'Beg for Water,' Maria. It was your Papa's favorite, y'know," he says.

Immediately, Jose begins the intro to the song. Maria adjusts the microphone stand to suit her five-foot height, and then she sings. The voice is still smooth and sweet as honey, and Noah knows its every nuance. He consumes her with his eyes and ears and, surprisingly, with his heart. The feeling shocks him. After the intense feelings he felt for Raven just last night, he is unnerved that he should experience similar, but slightly different, feelings for Maria. He hopes none of the others notice.

Raven notices and noisily excuses herself to the ladies' room; Graham notices and tenses like an angry wasp about to sting; Maria notices and sings directly to Noah.

> *If we had to beg for water.*
> *I know what I would do.*
> *If our souls were flaming embers,*
> *I would beg for water for you.*
> *I would beg for cool, clear water to sooth your fire,*
> *it's true.*
> *I would burn up in the process,*
> *but I'd beg for water for you.*

Noah groans, and Lee kicks him under the table. Maria keeps singing.

> *We may not last forever, although I hope we do,*
> *For time may change my whole life,*
> *but not as much as you.*

Noah catches Lee's gaze and confirms his thoughts.

Time may change my whole life. Time has been changed again, and this change amounts to murder. It is easy to find who benefits. Check out the current Governor. Noah places his bets on Darryl Kiley. To find the Outlaw will be difficult, at best; to find the Beacon will be nearly impossible.

Noah glances over at Lee and finds him studying Graham. *Can it possibly be Graham?* Graham Skysong is one of the most honorable men Noah has ever known. He is a credit to the Navajo people. He does not live his life to excess, and he is able to balance the Navajo way with the Jesus way. Despite his auditory and verbal gifts, and the fact that he is big and burly, he is basically a quiet man. Only two things really excite him—singing, and a pretty girl; Maria is both in one package. No wonder Graham is so giddy this afternoon. *How can Graham be the Outlaw? But, if not Graham, can it be Raven?* Noah shudders in spite of himself, the cramp twisting in his gut again. The only person he can be sure of is Lee, by virtue of the fact that Lee is also studying him.

When Maria finishes her performance, nobody applauds more vigorously than Graham. But Maria has eyes for Noah alone. Though time has changed her lifestyle, it has not changed her deeply seated feelings. True love is the one thing that can transcend time. Noah reads it in her face, and so does Graham.

"What is it with you Lightfoot boys?" Graham snarls. "First Raven; now Maria. Why don't you leave some women for the rest of us guys?" He gets heavily to his feet and storms out of *Que Pasa.*

Raven returns from the restroom after the song is over and sits stiffly in her chair. In a few minutes, Maria brings their orders.

Raven looks around. "Where's Graham? Having a smoke?"

Noah shrugs his shoulders, looking embarrassed. "Uh, I dunno," he mumbles.

Lee comes to the rescue. "Graham has left. I believe he had some stomach distress."

"Too bad," she says through a mouthful of chicken and rice, "This food is outstanding."

Noah's fork hovers in the air. He knows the food is outstanding, but he can't quite bring himself to eat it. If anyone is experiencing stomach distress, it is he.

Lee, on the other hand, is devouring his meal with obvious relish. He gives Noah a quick glance with raised eyebrows. "Eat, Noah. You need your strength," he says.

The admonishment is not lost on Noah, so he puts fork in mouth and forces himself to chew and swallow, almost gagging in the process. Fortunately, Raven is unaware of his angst.

As soon as dessert is finished, Lee calls for the check. "My treat," he says, to which he receives no protest. Raven and Noah are both accustomed to having their meals paid for.

"Please come back again soon," Maria says, giving Noah a brilliant smile.

"Uh, yeah, O.K. We'll be back," Noah says before being ushered out the door by Raven.

The three remaining Trackers leave the restaurant, and each is lost in thought. Raven is disturbed about her relationship with Noah. But Lee and Noah are tormented about something much greater in scope. In exactly one-half hour, they plan to make the most dangerous track of their lives ... a track backwards in time.

Back at the apartment, Noah knows Raven is annoyed by the way she keeps ruffling her bangs and pushing her hair back behind her ears. She punches up the cushions on her couch, all the while keeping a slight smile pasted on her face.

"Raven," he says. "I'm sorry, but I can't stay. I need to go on home."

"Home? Or back to *Que Pasa,* Noah?" Her voice does not change in timbre, but Noah feels it all in her tone.

"Why would I go back to *Que Pasa,* Raven? I couldn't eat another bite. These two o'clock meals just do me in."

She turns and forces a radiant smile; he feels his breath catch at her loveliness. Although his body wants to stay, his mind is screaming to leave. He doesn't want to anger Raven any more than he already has, but he has to find out what happened to Maria.

"I'm sorry, but I ... um, well ... I really have a splitting headache," he manages. It is a lame excuse, but she seems to buy it. Her features soften.

"I'm sorry, Noah. How insensitive of me not to notice. Go home, pull the shades, and lie quietly until it passes."

"Thanks for the advice. I'll call you later." He is relieved that she doesn't insist he stay with her. She turns and heads toward the kitchen.

"Wait," she calls. "I'll get you something for your eyes. It really helps a lot."

Noah hears her sorting through the vegetable bins. As he turns away, he notices a tiny object on the floor, catching the light. Bending down, he swiftly picks it up and slides it into the pocket of his jeans, just before Raven returns.

"Here," she says, holding out a sandwich bag full of sliced cucumbers. "Put a slice over each eye while you rest. It helps your headache and keeps your eyes from getting puffy."

"Thanks. I'll make this a daily part of my beauty regimen." He forces himself to mosey to the door and steps outside with Raven on his arm. She kisses him lightly on his closed mouth.

"Oh, yeah, and Noah, don't eat them after you use them."

"Why? Will they make my teeth puffy?"

She displays a more relaxed grin as she closes the door. Noah barely manages to keep from racing to his car. Ten minutes later, he pulls into his driveway. Lee is already waiting in the living room. He eyes the bag in Noah's hand.

"I see the food at *Que Pasa* did not fill you," Lee says, his face the picture of seriousness.

"Ha, ha. You're a very funny guy, lately. This is so my eyes won't be puffy."

Lee purses his lips into that peculiar half-smile. "Thank you for sharing your spa secrets. Can we get down to business, now?"

"This is serious stuff, Lee. Now it looks like Governor Bob's been snuffed. It's Kiley. I know it is!" Noah paces the room like a caged panther.

"Kiley is Caucasian, Noah. He cannot track." He pauses to consider another idea. "He can possibly offer political favors in exchange for a Native Tracker's cooperation, though."

"But who's the Outlaw, man? Better yet, who trained him ... or her?"

"Tell me what you know. We'll proceed from that point," Lee suggests.

"Raven and Graham both seem oblivious to the change in status of Carmine and Maria Ramirez," he states.

"So, it would seem," Lee considers that observation for a moment. "But our Trackers are fine actors …"

"Yeah, they're not off the hook yet. Graham was at Raven's this morning when I called. She said he was returning some books he had borrowed." Noah reaches into his jeans pocket. "Look what I found on her floor."

He extends his hand with the tiny object in his palm. Lee touches the elliptical lens with a moistened forefinger.

"A contact lens—hard, not disposable," he says. "Raven does wear contact lenses, does she not?"

"Yeah, she does," says Noah. "But look. This one's brown. Raven's eyes are already brown, so why would she want a colored contact lens?"

Lee frowns. "Curious. Perhaps Graham also wears them when he does not wear his glasses. But why?"

"I don't know, but this is so weird, Lee! I wonder what happened to Governor Bob …"

"We can ask Maria."

"No," says Noah hastily. "I don't want to see any more hurt in her eyes."

"I see," Lee says, eyebrows raised.

"There you go again with that 'I see' business."

"My apologies. Where were we?"

"Governor Bob's dead; so how else does that change things?" Noah asks.

"Maria is not attending college; she and Carmine work in a restaurant for a living; Sarah has probably died of leukemia …"

Noah whirls around. "No! Not Sarah!"

"More than likely, I'm afraid. Noah, exactly how far do you think Mr. Kiley intends to go with his plans?

"Congressman? Senator?"

"President." It is not a question, but a statement of fact. Lee takes a carefully folded newspaper out from under his arm and lays it on the coffee table. "I took the liberty of collecting your newspaper while I waited for you. You need to read this, son."

Noah gawks at the paper—eyes wide, mouth open. There, captured in shades of grey and white, is Darryl Kiley. He photographs well—a somewhat handsome man in his late fifties with regular, even features. His eyes are light, as is his hair. His teeth are large, but straight and very white. His hand is raised as he waves to a crowd of people. The newspaper caption reads, *"Governor Darryl Kiley (D) greets supporters at the airport in Tallahassee after claiming Presidential campaign support in New York, Massachusetts, and New Hampshire."*

Noah pales. "The other Democratic candidates didn't have a chance. I'm sure Kiley managed to come up with the nomination at the Democratic convention, even though he wasn't the front-runner. Something happened to any man that stood in his way."

"Exactly," Lee says. "Kiley emerged victorious and has gone on to challenge—and will most assuredly beat—the incumbent President."

They consider the ramifications with open horror. Lee speaks next, solemnly, quietly, almost reverently. "I'm afraid we must kill him first."

"What? Whoa, whoa, whoa. Are you crazy? I thought killing was against all your beliefs. Didn't that Moses guy put it in stone? 'Don't kill people' or something to that effect?"

"God put it in stone; Moses delivered the message," Lee replies with arched brows.

"Then I think you better get the message. I mean, you can justify killing someone in self-defense, like that creepy guy who kidnapped Sarah. But, just out and out murder? It ain't worth it for eternal damnation or whatever."

"He has doomed Maria and her mother to a life of labor without benefit of a father and husband. He has undoubtedly killed Sarah, despite our previous efforts," Lee reasons.

"O.K. Then I will kill him. I don't think God will punish me like He'd punish you, Lee. I don't think the Man upstairs would take too kindly to an upstanding Mormon Indian breaking a major commandment like that," he says.

"Noah. Let me tell you a story."

"Make it short; I'm in a bad mood."

"Many hundreds of years ago, a man named Lehi was commanded by God to take his family into the wilderness and away from the wickedness of the city. Lehi did as he was told because he was a prophet of God, and he was a righteous man. Once out in the wilderness, God revealed to Lehi a great journey he was to make to a new world across the sea. Lehi was to take with him nothing but his family and a few possessions. He was also to take two very important records which had been carved into plates of brass. These records were in the possession of a man named Laban.

"Laban was wicked and would not give Lehi the plates. Instead, he tried to kill Lehi. One night, Lehi's son, Nephi, went in his father's stead to retrieve the plates. Again, Laban refused and would not relinquish the plates. He tried to kill Nephi.

"Of such importance were these records that God told Nephi that he must kill Laban. Being a righteous man and a prophet himself, Nephi did as he was commanded. The next night, he slew the drunken Laban, disguised himself with Laban's clothing, and escaped from the city undetected. Because of his obedience to God's will, he was able to obtain the brass plates which he and Lehi would take to the new world. The new world was the Americas. Lehi was the father of the Lamanite people who we believe to be the first Indians."

"And the point is ...?"

"The point is, if it is God's will, it is God's will," Lee says.

"Do you believe it is God's will, Lee?"

"Yes, Noah. I believe it is God's will. That is why I will go. Besides, I have many more years of experience than you, but you have youth and vitality. I need you to stay alert and beacon for me."

"But what if you see something important while you are traveling? I can't beacon and take notes at the same time, and we can't trust anyone else."

Lee reaches into his pocket and pulls out a small, voice-activated tape recorder. "Ta-da. I am prepared. Now, shall we go?"

"I reckon so, buddy. But, Lee, be careful. O.K.?"

"I shall. I shall."

In less than a minute, Lee is traveling into the past.

At first, there is only darkness. Lee is aware of sounds

within sounds, somewhat like echoes in a canyon. Next, there is light—flashes, at first, then streaks, then fireworks exploding everywhere in his peripheral vision. All at once, everything is still. It is as if his body has slammed on brakes. He feels queasy and waits for his internal organs to quiet.

Lee looks around. He knows this place, but he has not been here in many years. This is Dane Lightfoot's house before the fire. Lee is surprised to find he can walk throughout the rooms and not simply float above them like in a dream. He wonders if he will see Dane. He feels his heart quicken within his chest. *Yes, I very much want to see Dane.*

He rounds the corner to the kitchen. *I can smell food.* He has never before been a clairscent, so the sensation of smelling during a track is novel to him. He gasps when he looks into the room. Dane stands with his head stuck inside the refrigerator. Tears spring to Lee's eyes. He has missed Dane terribly. And now, here he is, digging through the icebox, as usual.

"Dane," Lee whispers.

Dane turns around. "Lee! Hey, old buddy. What are you doing here?"

Liahona Thistleseed takes a step backward. "Did you hear me speak?"

Dane cocks his head—a familiar habit of his. "Of course, I heard you. I'm not deaf … just dumb." He laughs, and Lee realizes how much he has missed that laugh. "Really, what are you doing? I mean, I didn't know you were coming over. I've got a hot date, Lee, any minute. But, hey, it's about time you know, huh. Want some juice?"

"N-no. Thank you," Lee stutters. "No, wait. Yes, I do." Lee wants to know just what he can and cannot do in this track to the past.

"Make up your mind, Hona."

"I haven't heard that name in such a long time. Nobody calls me that, but you."

"Hona, are you O.K.? You seem a little out of sorts."

"No. I'm fine, now." He reaches forward to take the juice. He closes his hand around—and all the way through—the glass. It falls to the floor and shatters at his feet.

"My gosh, Lee. You sure you're O.K.? I've never known you to be clumsy."

Dane cleans up the mess with a dishtowel. Lee kneels down to help him, but he is dismayed to find that he is unable to grasp anything solid. *I'm a hologram. I can't wait to tell Noah.*

The doorbell rings, and Dane looks at Lee with wide, bright eyes. "There she is, Hona. I'm gonna ask her to marry me tonight. I'm so glad you're here. It makes everything just perfect. You're gonna love her. I can't wait to see your face. Come on. I want to see your expression when I open the door."

Lee follows Dane to the door. The pure joy in the young man's face is worth the controversial trip back in time. He only hopes he can change things back the way they should be. *Can I restore Dane's life in the process?* If at all possible, Lee intends to break all the rules and do just that. He turns his attention to the opening door. Dane is watching him intently. Lee looks toward the woman on the porch and …

… darkness. His head spins. Blackness surrounds him. He calls out, but nobody hears him. He feels as if he is falling into a black pit; a bottomless hole from which he can never emerge. *Noah! Something has happened to Noah.* That is the only explanation.

"Home," he calls. "Home, home, home." But no light comes. His beacon—the silver cord connecting his mind to his body—is gone. Lee knows what that means: his mind is doomed to wander in deep, black nothingness; his body will be mindlessly waiting in a suspended state on earth, with the tiny tape recorder lying idle for lack of sound. Unless Liahona Thistleseed is beaconed home in 50 minutes or less, his body will die, and his mind will exist no longer.

CHAPTER NINE
SILVER EYES

NOAH LIGHTFOOT LIES UNCONSCIOUS on a teal colored Italian leather sofa. His hands and feet are bound; there is a nasty lump protruding from his disheveled hair. His abductor sits across from him. He is a stocky man with short black hair, beginning to gray at the wings swooping back from his temples. He wears a navy-blue Brooks Brothers blazer with khaki slacks and a white shirt open at the collar, barely wrinkled though the days are sweltering this time of year.

The older man, Noah's captor, inhales deeply, and then he removes his wire-rimmed photogray glasses and sets them on a solid oak end table. Reaching in his jacket pocket, he pulls out a small two-sided vial. He unscrews the cap from each side and puts the container on the table next to the glasses. With quick, experienced movements, he pops out his contact lenses and drops the dark brown discs in the wetting solution. The man blinks a few times to accustom his eyes to the air. He shrugs out of the jacket and lays it across the arm of the chair. Running his hands through his hair, he finger-combs the hairspray out, letting it fall loosely around his head.

Now he looks like his Creek Indian name—John Silver

Eyes—given at birth because of his startling blue eyes. Many Indians have blue eyes, the result of intermarrying with Caucasians to lighten their skin and blend in with the white population. John's eyes, though, push the envelope. They are nearly white, with a tinge of blue around the irises. The midwife insisted he looked up at her through circles of silver; hence the name. As a young man, his eyes made him an object of power in a culture that put much significance on oddities, signs, and portents. As an adult, he disguises his peculiar eyes with brown contacts to keep from unwanted attention.

John regards the young man on his sofa. Leaning forward, he examines a goose-egg on the side of Noah's head, but fortunately, the skin has not broken. John regrets having to hit the boy ... his boy. His mouth twists in a smile as he thinks back to a time before Noah was born, when John was not much older than his son is now ... the "make love, not war" era of the 60s.

*   *   *

At twenty-five, John was young to be a Holy Man, but he was quite gifted, so his youth was overlooked. When he was seven, his training began. His father, already an old man and soon to walk with Father Spirit, sat with young John and sang him the secret medicine songs which are guarded from the outside world to be used only in Seminole and Creek *posketv*, or fasting, ceremonies. John learned quickly. He had a good ear for music and was easily able to memorize the lengthy songs. As a child, John was fascinated by the healing magic his father delivered, and he paid close attention to the treatments with their corresponding songs, plants, and rituals. John's father never asked for pay; instead, he was given gifts of chickens, shotgun shells, knives, tobacco, and red, black, and yellow cloth, usually four yards each, out of which John's mother would make patchwork jackets and skirts for the family to wear and to sell.

After only a year of training, his father breathed his last breath and joined his ancestors in the sky. Young John was sent to live with his mother's people in Walton County, Florida, where he received the remainder of his sixteen-year training from a Choctawhatchee *Heles Pocase*—Medicine Man.

Though the roles of doctor and medicine man were usually separate, John was trained as both. Only members of the panther clan were allowed to be the keepers of the sacred medicine bundles used at the Green Corn *Posketv*. John's father was bird clan, but Creek Indians are matrilineal, and the inheritances are passed down through the mother's bloodlines. John's mother was panther clan, so he was qualified for the honor. John's rigorous training included fasting for enlightenment, sweating to cleanse one's body, and purification with emetic black drinks—also called medicine—to rid evil spirits within the soul. These rituals left him open for instruction through dreams in order to receive omens for the tribe.

John Silver Eyes, who the midwife claimed received power through his ice-blue eyes, excelled in his calling, and he was well suited to the high-prestige, respected position he attained at twenty-three. Soon thereafter, he moved to a small Northwest Florida pit stop that had a good-sized population of local Creek Indians. There, in *Blunt-em-tvfolv*—literally "Blunt-his-town" before being renamed by Moravian missionaries as Blountstown, John presided over the fasting ceremonials held at the square grounds on the edge of the woods near a local park. This location proved to be convenient and popular, attracting a large group of visitors from all over Florida and Georgia. John was the youngest doctor and medicine man the small Creek Indian Tribe had ever had. He was the *Heles Hayv Pocase*—Doctor Medicine Man—and he enjoyed the power.

As Medicine Man of the Lower Creek Muskogee Tribe, John was responsible for beginning the *Posketv*, or Busk as the white men called it, by opening the square grounds with song and prayer, along with the *Micco*—the tribal Chief. Though often confused with a pow-wow, which was a celebration and time of dancing and singing, the Busk was a sacred ceremony of many parts: fasting for enlightenment, cleansing the home and body for renewal, thanksgiving for Mother Earth's gifts, and prayer for Father Spirit's continued blessings. In John's Pine Arbor town, the Busk was performed at four times of the year: Berry in the spring,

Green Corn in the mid-summer, Little Green Corn in late summer, and Harvest in fall. This weekend marked the time of the new moon closest to the summer solstice, and the air was already muggy for the season's Green Corn Busk.

The square grounds were only loosely squared; the sandy area was defined with four open arbors situated on the compass points. Each arbor was constructed of four wooden posts, forming a tall open-topped table, and painted with a redwood stain. The roof of the frame was covered with newly cut willow branches, creating a slightly peaked shelter for the two long benches inside the structure. Participants sat on the benches in the shade and waited for their part of the ceremony. The right front corner post of each arbor was adorned with a log and a conch shell. The logs were used to begin the ceremony, and the conch symbolized life near the Gulf of Mexico, the location of this Creek Indian tribal community.

In the center of the square was a mound of ashes, pieces of pottery, silverware, and other items. This was where the bonfire burned during the three days of the ceremony. The ashes were never removed, and the mound grew with each Busk. The fire was believed to be where the Creator's spirit could dwell, and the rising smoke was the method of taking the prayers directly to Him. The ceramic shards and other objects were gifts given to Father Spirit.

After opening the ceremony, John sat in the shade of the Medicine Man's West Arbor under the fresh willow branches and watched. Opposite him, the women's East Arbor was being swept with willow branches, and the turtle carapace was placed in front, symbolizing the time when *Ludjataka*, the Giant Turtle, brought the mud up from the sea. The stories of the ancestors told that all life began on the turtle's back.

The balmy wind kicked up and blew the green willow branches off the roof of the old warriors' North Arbor. Silver Eyes laughed as he watched Porcupine Jim, the fat one, chase the fallen boughs. Sitting beside him, Chief *Vntolv Haco* also laughed. The Creek name meant "Crazy Andrew," but he was anything but. Resplendent in his jacket of circular red, white, black, and yellow patchwork shapes, Chief Drew was an imposing presence on the grounds, reminiscent of Joseph in his coat of many colors.

"This promises to be an amusing Harvest Busk, as always," Drew commented.

"Never a dull moment," John replied.

"And praise God for giving us rain yesterday," Drew said.

John nodded and apprised the man. Drew Boggs, in addition to being the Chief of their Apalachicola Band of Creeks, was the Principal Chief of the Florida Tribe of Eastern Creek Indians. He was a huge bear of a man, with a full moon face, jet black hair, a perpetual grin, and a surprising tenor voice for someone of his stature. He and his wife, Louisa—a somewhat smaller bear of a woman—always attended the Busks. They were conservative Baptists, and though they never voiced the distinction, they were able to incorporate their Christian belief with the fasting ceremonies and the Native religion. In fact, Drew's own Bible had been buried beneath the fire mound. But the Indian spiritualism he left to the tribal Holy Man, and John appreciated Drew Boggs for allowing him this honor.

Drew caught him looking. His mouth split into an enormous smile, and he reached his paw out to John. They clasped hands and exchanged words of the utmost respect.

"*Mvdo, Heles Hayv Pocase.* It is good, Doctor Medicine Man," Drew said.

"*Mvdo, Tuskie Mahaya Haco.* It is good, Brave Warrior Teacher, my friend," John said.

They returned their attention to the ceremony. Four men appeared at the square ground posts. Each man hefted an upturned log to his shoulder and solemnly marched around the ashes counterclockwise several times before placing the logs "nose to nose" on the compass points of the mound. Carefully feeding tinder between the cross of the logs, they encouraged the tiny embers from the lantern of the Keeper-of-the-Flame, creating a roaring blaze. John nodded. *Good.* It was always a favorable sign for the fire to blaze up. That meant Father Spirit was pleased. It would be a successful Busk. The fire starters tossed handfuls of tobacco on the flames to thank Him Who Watches from Above. The Green Corn Busk had begun.

The rest of the men joined the fire starters and began the

feather dance around the "fire that never dies." Old George Otter seemed lively at the stomp dances today, and Rabbit Bob had made a particularly good water drum out of the stretched hide. The baritone voices rang out *"We He Ha O Ne"* with the tempo set by the drummer. After ten counterclockwise circles around the fire, the men rested in the shade of their arbor. George and Bob, their feather-tipped sticks in hand, began the first of the four calls for the Women's ribbon dance.

"*Hokte Opvnkv!* First call for the ribbon dance," they shouted in unison.

John heard the good-natured harassing from the women. This was tradition. They would make the men call three more times before they took their places for the dance. He heard their preparations in the women's hut and knew, without looking, what they were doing. They had removed their slacks and put on full-length, brightly colored patchwork skirts. T-shirts were exchanged for loose-fitting men's shirts or white peasant blouses—favorites of the younger ladies, many of whom wore them regularly, and often braless, with hip-hugger jeans. In the late 1960s, the Busks really seemed to attract the flower children. Footwear was varied: some wore simple moccasins, some wore tennis shoes, yet others wore no shoes at all. Long ribbons in assorted colors, materials, and sizes were pinned to the backs of their blouses, and some were placed in their hair. Each ribbon represented a person to be lifted up to the Creator in prayers. Three calls had been made, and now the preparations were nearly finished. All that remained was for the women to attach the turtle shells to their legs.

John had always liked the sound of the shakers. His mother had owned leg ornaments with an impressive 15 tortoise shells on each. Hers had been filled with seed beads; many of the newer ones were filled with pellets or gravel. In fact, because of the great expense—as much as $500 for a single set of 12 shells—some of the ones used lately weren't turtle shells at all, but juice or snuff cans filled with shot or crushed rocks and attached to fabric instead of hides. John didn't care. The sound was what mattered. The rhythmic rattling, only slightly muffled by the swish of their skirts brushing their ankles, was hypnotic ... heard, but not seen, like the movement of a spirit in their midst.

The fourth call was made, and the women filed into the arbor, using the east entrance reserved just for them. They sat patiently on the benches under the shade of the arbor and waited. So much of the time was spent waiting, cultivating patience. George and Bob readied the square for their dance. As they waited, the Head Woman, Dolores, spoke to them. Though he could not hear her, John knew what she was saying; what she had said for the last who-know-how-many years.

"We dance with humility and humbleness of spirit. Here, in this square, the individual person is no longer important. But the *talwv*—the town—the community is important. We dance to perpetuate the community and its people; to help the community perpetuate itself. Focus on what we do. Free yourselves from the world," she intoned.

At that moment, John caught sight of the new women, and he could not look away.

Mother Dolores continued her age-old instructions to the dancers. "We will ask for Father Spirit to help us fulfill our duty and obligation as women. It is our duty to sustain the men, for they are not as strong as we are. We dance away from the fire, for we need not its strength as the men do. We would not take the strength from the fire, for in doing so, we would become too powerful, and the men would be robbed of their strength and power. We must protect the men always. That is our sacred purpose as women."

George and Bob took their places. Mother Dolores, the matriarch of the dance portraying First Woman, took the lead clutching an ancient flint knife. Behind Dolores stood her daughter Kellie Cow Peas, the Leading-Lady for this dance, holding a sweet gum twig. The rest of the women rose and formed a line behind them. The shakers rattled as they moved out onto the stomp grounds. John flinched as his forgotten cigarette burned his fingers.

The Tribal Mother spoke once again, a little louder so all could hear. "We will dance 16 times for healing. Remember those who are in need, and dance for them."

Dance for me. John licked his lips as he memorized every detail about the new woman.

She was strikingly tall, taller than the other women by several inches, but she was amazingly agile and graceful. Her long hair, caught at the nape of her neck with a carved shell barrette just above the yellow ribbon pinned to her blouse, was so glossy as to be reflective, like a deep well on a sunny day. Her eyes were black onyx in a honey-colored face, free of any imperfections and full of pleasant experiences.

John had known many women in many ways since his coming of age as a teenager. His position in the tribe and his startling eyes gained him more gifts than cloth or tobacco. Never had a woman caused him to react as absurdly as he did now. He tried to be inconspicuous, but he found that he watched her constantly. He watched her dancing; he watched her resting in the arbor after the eighth round; he watched her drinking the mint water and wished he could taste the lips she touched to the metal dipper. He signaled for the mint water immediately, just so he could touch his own lips to the same spot on the dipper. *Ridiculous. This behavior was for schoolboys.* He disgusted himself, but he couldn't help himself. He hoped Drew didn't notice.

Wherever she walked, he watched. Whatever she did, he watched. Even as he made the emetic medicine, he watched for her reaction. He took great pains to show his expertise as he cut and ground the *tolv*—bay leaves, *passv*—button snakeroot, and *tvwv*—bitter winged sumac. He added the herbs to water and "blew" the mixture together with a hollow twig until bubbles formed. He "fed" some medicine to the fire and nearly spilled it trying to watch her from the corner of his eye.

He continued the ritual of touching medicine, washing, and being scratched for all the tribe to imitate, and still he watched her. He was obsessed with every seemingly insignificant detail of her routine. Her obedience to the medicine ritual was no more or no less than anyone else's, but when she performed it, there seemed to be a difference. She dipped her long fingers into the pot and sprinkled the medicine to the cardinal directions—north, south, east, west—and then she touched her fingers to her tongue four times. *Oh, to be those fingers.*

She drank the black drink that purifies the soul, and when

she swallowed, John also swallowed. She laughed happily and chewed a leaf from the mint water, and he heard wind chimes in her voice. And then, she bathed ... Indian style.

As the warm willow bark water was poured from the conch shell into her waiting hands, she washed ... slowly and sensually ... her face, her shoulders, and her arms. She tilted her head back and washed her throat, letting her lips part slightly as the soothing water spilled down the front of her thin blouse, chill bumps forming on her skin.

John stared at her, slack-jawed, stupid, hypnotized. He had no control; he saw nothing on the grounds but her. He watched her present her arms for scratching with the gar fish teeth—the return gift to Mother Earth for the gifts She gives. As the blood appeared, slowly oozing from the raised welts on her upper arms, John heard his own blood rushing inside his head. He imagined the feel of the droplets, sticky on her bare arms; the salty taste of blood mingled with sweat; the pungent smell of smoke and tobacco in her hair.

His vision blurred, and his heart pounded heavily in his chest. He closed his eyes and inhaled deeply, realizing that, for a few delicious moments, he had forgotten to breathe. He saw her through his closed lids dancing, washing, laughing, tossing her head, twisting her hair and fastening it into a bun with a green willow twig. It was too exquisite to endure. He leaped to his feet— nearly knocking Chief Drew off the bench—and announced that it was time for stickball.

While the younger men competed in a rousing game of Indian lacrosse, the women began preparing the meal. John studied the new woman as she sat at the picnic table and patted fry bread into pancake shapes, and he marveled at the strength in her slender tan hands. He wondered when and how to approach her. He could not remember ever being so intimidated by a mere woman. *Could this be love, or an overwhelming lust?* He thought he knew the difference, but maybe not. He decided to call a sweat tonight; he could talk with her when the men were finished in the sweat hut, and the women were just going in.

Spotting Dolores nearby, he motioned for the Head Woman to come over and speak with him. He stubbed out his cigarette and greeted her warmly, "Hello, Mother Dolores. *Mvdo.*"

"*Mvdo,* John Silver Eyes, all is well. Good *pvsketv* today at Pine Arbor, Eh?"

"Um-hmm. Who is that woman making fry bread with Susannah Two Feathers? I haven't seen her before." He tried to sound nonchalant, but his voice cracked. He hoped Dolores didn't suspect his intentions.

"That's Fawn Lightfoot. I think she's a Miccosukee. She might be Muskogee, but she lives with the Seminole. Her husband is Medicine Man at Brighton Reservation."

John's heart beat erratically. "She's married to a Seminole, huh? Got any kids?" The late afternoon heat was suddenly unbearable. He flushed and sweat beaded up on his brow.

"Well, I hear the old man has six sons from two former wives. They have one son together. That's him with the spotted brown dog."

Silver managed to smile through clenched teeth. "Hm. Cute little fella. The seventh son, huh. Does he have the gift?" John was referring to the Native American belief that the seventh child of a seventh child could have psychic abilities.

Dolores shrugged. "He's only ten, so nobody's sure yet. I wouldn't doubt it, though. He comes from pretty strong stock. They'll know in a couple of years." Puberty usually precipitated the onset of a child's second-sighted abilities.

"Well, I hope her association with the Brightons hasn't hampered her ability to make the bread. I'm extra hungry today. This fast has been slow." He tried to make it sound like a joke, but his laugh came out squeaky. To his relief, Dolores appeared not to notice, but instead was looking at another woman nearby.

"Good point. I'd better send Kellie over to make sure. The *Micco* is grilling chicken from his grocery store today. It'll ruin the whole meal if the bread is flat!" Dolores hurried away to oversee the cooking, snatching Kellie Cow Peas by the arm as she passed.

John saw Kellie's irritated expression and shook his head at her. He would meet up with her later at his camper, but for now, all he could think of was Fawn. He turned on his heel and pretended to watch the stickball game.

He cursed under his breath. "Married ... to a Medicine Man, and with a seventh son, of all things. That could make her more difficult to attain." But challenges were irresistible to John, and a conquest was usually a given. He meant to have Fawn Lightfoot, one way or another. He could wait, and wait he did, but not for long.

*   *   *

Little Green Corn Busk began in late summer, and true to Florida weather, the sun was already generating heat by 9:00 in the morning. John looked around anxiously for Fawn. *She must be here, but where could she be?* A muffled sob caught his attention. He saw Fawn mourning at the quicken post, beating it, as custom dictated, before it would be thrown in the fire to be offered up to the One Above. Relief flooded through him, and he stuffed the yellow ribbon he had been holding back into his pocket.

What a pity her husband died so ... unexpectedly. The old man had passed into the land of the spirits painfully, too. Ironically, John Silver Eyes was with him at the end. Fawn and the Holy Man were not suspicious of John's visit just a few days after Green Corn Busk. After all, Creek and Seminole were once a single tribe. And neither Fawn nor old Lightfoot questioned the healing herbs that Silver Eyes administered to the stricken man. *A medicine man knows medicine, doesn't he?* The only speculation was about the serpent that had been found in the bedding of their *chickee.* A thatched-roof, open sided pavilion, the *chickee* had a central raised platform that was used for a bed, table, or what-have-you to keep critters at bay. It was strange behavior for a snake to crawl in such cool weather, and even stranger for it to climb the platform.

John had done his best, but a rattlesnake's bite was often fatal, especially if complications arose. John was well known for his healing powers, but even the most experienced doctor medicine man could do nothing when the patient developed an allergic reaction to the special poultice of herbs—augmented with powdered venom—that John applied to his snakebite wound. In the end, the treatment failed. The old man convulsed, his aorta burst, and Fawn became a very young widow.

It was such a tragic accident. Fortunately, John was there to comfort Fawn, but as he had carefully planned, it was he who received the greatest comfort.

Now, nine weeks later, John was in need of more comfort from Fawn, but she would not even meet his gaze. John knew he had not disappointed her that night; he never disappointed the ladies in the blankets. *So, what could be wrong? Ah, maybe she felt shame.* John knew he could fix that with a few well-chosen words. Looking closer, he noticed that Fawn seemed especially tired and worn; there was no light behind the onyx eyes ... only grief. John was annoyed. After three months, he reasoned that she should have gotten over the old man's death, especially when she had John Silver Eyes to look forward to. He realized how thin she had become the short time they had been apart. He presumed that was due to the Seminole mourning ritual.

She would be drinking medicine mixed with *osafke hvtke*—white grits—four times each morning for four months, followed by a medicine bath and a dose of the black drink. The drink induced vomiting to ensure internal cleansing. For the rest of the day, she could only eat crackers or bread made with plain flour, more grits, and coffee. In another month, Fawn would be eating normally again, and she would fill out to the pleasing proportions John liked.

It was the rest of her behavior that made him edgy. His plan had worked so perfectly. She never suspected John of murder. After all, he had "tried" to save her husband after the snake struck. Fawn had been so compliant that night, so grateful for his methods of consolation in her grief. Women and their moralities amused him; it was so unnecessary.

He knew it was impossible to talk to her until after the ceremonies had concluded. Men and women did not speak until the fast was broken when the food was served. He would just have to wait. He was used to waiting, but Chief Drew Boggs had come down with the flu and was not at this Busk, so John had nobody to talk to in his arbor, and he was bored.

John performed his duties hurriedly, hoping the tribe would not notice. He was anxious to speak with Fawn. Finally, it was time for the tribe to eat. He had concentrated so much on speeding up the ceremonies that he failed to notice she had not participated in any of the rituals. She sat alone with Susannah Two Feathers, another widow from Brighton Reservation, watching the stickball game and the last four dances. He noticed that Susannah never left her side. That was not unusual; Susannah was her mourning helper; however, he would have to figure out a way to get rid of her for a while if he expected to talk to Fawn.

Only after the first foods had been offered to *Hesaketvmese*—Master of Breath—in the fire did he realize Fawn had not touched the food today. He should have thought it odd, especially, that she did not make fry bread. It had been such a hit at Green Corn Busk, even without the help of Kellie Cow Feas. Kellie was also absent from the *busk* today, and John was glad. She was much too clingy.

John noticed Susannah carrying the quicken post to the fire. "Ah," he said aloud to nobody in particular, "Fawn must be on her moon time." Women, during their monthly cycle, were forbidden to dance or touch the food. Nor were they allowed to approach the fire. As the mourning helper, Susannah performed the tasks Fawn was not allowed to do.

John thought of the strict instructions Mother Dolores gave to young girls entering womanhood for the first time. "We are strongest when we are in our moon time and when we are with child. Therefore, we must be careful not to come near the fire during those times lest we take all its power away and leave none for the men," she warned.

Oh, well. No big deal. He could wait for sex, especially at the risk of losing any of his powers. But he was impatient to speak with Fawn to again offer his condolences and maintain his hold over her. When Susannah excused herself to visit the outhouse, John bolted toward the large community *chickee* where Fawn finally sat alone.

"Fawn?" he said, suddenly feeling timid.

"John." It was a statement; she didn't even look up at him.

"Do you still mourn, Fawn?" His heart beat in this throat.

"Yes." The word was simple, yet it held enormous emotion.

He moved closer to her; she moved away. He grasped her hand; she pulled it away.

"What is it, Fawn? I … I love you." The words came tumbling out before he could catch them. He felt like he was losing his grip. Never before had John Silver Eyes ever spoken of love. Never before had he ever felt love. Only lust. Fawn drew away.

"No, John. This can't happen again. You've been so kind. I know you tried to save him; I know you … um … gave me of yourself because you are a compassionate man. It was selfish of me to use you in that way. Forgive me, please. I never meant to lead you on," she said softly.

The world spun before his eyes; hornets droned in his ears. His hand flew to his warrior's gar fish skeleton necklace, but he felt no power there. *She* was apologizing to *him*. She, whom he had seduced after killing her husband, was sorry for him. That's why she was at the quicken post … to ask forgiveness of him. It was too cruel. Never before had John ever lost his conquest, nor his heart. His fingers, gripping the sharp teeth of the gar fish jaw, stung with tiny cuts, but he ignored the blood that appeared. He panicked. His power, his carefully composed plan. All gone, ruined.

"But, Fawn …" he protested, reaching to take her hand.

She put her willowy fingers to his lips to silence him, and he kissed them. "John Silver Eyes. You are such a special man, as was my late husband. But the Master-of-Breath-and-Life came to me in a dream. He has made it known to me that I have a special task ahead. Well … two tasks, in fact. Father Spirit already gave me the responsibility of raising a seventh son. Now, it seems, He is giving me another seventh son to raise." She looked down, breathless, her voice barely a whisper, and fidgeted with the folds of her skirt.

"What? What other seventh son?" He was confused. He wondered if he heard correctly.

Fawn fixed his ice-blue eyes with her onyx ones, and John could see the fire burning deep behind the black pupils. He jerked backward and drew in breath so quickly he nearly choked. "No. You're not. Uh-uh. It can't be." He couldn't put the words together.

"Yes, John, it's true. I carry your son. Your seventh son. *Hesaketvmese* told me in a dream of your six other sons—sons even you did not know of. This child will be your seventh son, John. I am to raise both the boys in the Seminole tradition." Fawn smiled kindly. "You will always be special, my dearest John Silver Eyes, but after today, I will never see you again. I thank you for your gift, and I thank Father Spirit for sending you to me at the time of my husband's death."

Fawn sighed and looked out over the square grounds, bidding the fire farewell in her heart. After what seemed an eternity she said, "I have always loved Little Green Corn. It is truly a time for blessings of life." She leaned toward John and kissed him tenderly on the lips. "Goodbye, John," she whispered, and then she rose and walked away. John scurried behind her like an affectionate little puppy.

"Fawn! No, you can't just leave me. Fawn, come back. Please, Fawn." He whimpered; he had no shame. John didn't care who noticed; he only wanted Fawn. But Fawn Lightfoot never turned back. Susannah appeared and fell in step by her side. Bitter tears fell from John's ice-blue eyes as Fawn took her young son, Dane, by the hand and walked out of his life forever.

*   *   *

Now, 20 years later, John shakes the happy and painful memories from his mind, pushes a worn, faded yellow ribbon back into his pocket, and studies the unconscious young man on his sofa. How like Fawn he is. John is sure that, if Noah smiles, he will have the same crossed front teeth and prominent canines as Fawn. But this is also his son; he sees proof in the boy's strong jaw line. He is a good-looking young man. John Silver Eyes smiles. Noah is most definitely full-blooded Creek. What a pleasure it would have been for John to train him as Medicine Man. The spiritual training takes 16 years; perhaps, after tonight, he will yet have that chance.

Noah groans and painfully opens his eyes. *Yes, they are black onyx ... just like hers.* John puffs with open admiration. Despite his bindings, Noah tries to leap off the couch and attack. He is quick, but John is quicker. Deftly, he covers Noah's face with an ether-soaked rag, and Noah slumps to the floor. John vows he will never hurt him again. He picks him up, as easily as he would a small child, and carefully lays him on the sofa.

It will take time, but John intends to reclaim his son ... and his son's mother. All he needs is time—or the manipulation of time. He will travel back 20 years and visit Fawn Lightfoot in her dreams. *You were wrong, Fawn. Hvtvm cehecares—I WILL see you again.* Soon, John Silver Eyes will be a family man. He sighs and settles into a matching teal leather Lane recliner. He can wait; he is used to waiting. And he will watch; he is also used to watching. After all, time is on his side.

CHAPTER TEN

<u>LIFE, DEATH, LOVE</u>

NOAH COMES BACK TO AWARENESS slowly, eyes fluttering, tongue stuck to the roof of his mouth. The aftertaste of the ether threatens to gag him, and the headache is excruciating. *Where am I? Not in a good place—face down on a sofa, hands tied behind my back.* A cramp is working its way through his calf, but he resists the impulse to flinch or cry out. Keeping his breathing deep and even, he peers through lowered lashes at the man kicked back on the recliner just a few feet away. He knows this man—John Silver, Darryl Kiley's associate. *Of course! John Silver is the Outlaw. It makes sense, now. A rogue Native American with an agenda.* Noah knows the man's eyes will not be brown, but blue—the same blue eyes he saw at the football field and the dream he described to Lee.

Lee! Noah realizes he has left him tracking alone, without a beacon. *For how long now?* He worries. *Has it been 50 minutes?* Any longer and Lee will die, if he is not dead already. Struggling to control his breathing, Noah knows he will have to send a beacon signal, but if the Outlaw notices, he will drug him again, and Lee will surely die. Noah closes his eyes. Despite the excruciating headache that his concentration causes, he prepares to signal.

The pinging of the doorbell renews the pounding in his

head but brings with it a glimmer of hope. He risks barely opening his eyes and glances at the Outlaw. *Good. He's answering the door.* This will be the only chance Noah has. He hears the Outlaw's harsh voice quarreling with someone. *The Beacon.* Sadly, Noah knows that voice, and his stomach lurches. He'll have to deal with that later; Lee is his first concern right now. He sends the mental signal light as brightly as he dares while the traitors are in the foyer; he has no way of knowing if it will work. But, if Lee is still alive, he will find the beaconing light and come home.

The Outlaw and the Beacon enter the room, and Noah stops his signal. The Beacon rushes over and sits beside Noah's inert body. His sadness becomes angry heat, but he wills himself to remain still.

"If you harm him, I will kill you, John Silver," she snarls. Raven ... the Beacon ... glares into the Outlaw's silvery eyes.

"Harm him? Never. He is my son."

Noah's eyes nearly fly open. *Son?*

"What?" Raven asks, looking first at Noah, then at John.

"Noah is my son ... my seventh son, to be precise. I intend to reclaim him with this trip."

"What do you mean?" She snakes her arm around Noah's shoulders and holds him tightly.

"Very simply put, this is what happened: Twenty years ago, I fell in love with his mother and seduced her. She spurned me because of a dream. She said she was told to take my son and raise him as a Seminole." He pauses and loosens his clenched jaw. "That dream robbed me of my gifted son and his irreplaceable mother. So, I will track back and enter Fawn's dream and give her instructions to marry me instead. It is as simple as that."

"Then you would become his father," Raven says.

"I AM his father," John snaps. "But I might be persuaded to adopt his brother ..." He cuts his icy eyes at Raven and puckers his lips prudishly. "... although, I am not sure if Fawn will approve of you romancing both her sons. It seems rather trashy."

Raven gasps, and John laughs at her expression.

"Of course," John says. "As her husband, Fawn will obey me. It is in your best interest, Miss Looking Bird, to appease me. I determine your present and future happiness."

"What about Dane?"

John spits air. "Bah. Why waste your heart on Dane when Noah is the superior man? And, as the son of an up-and-coming political genius, he will have tremendous wealth and power. However, if you have no interest, I can arrange it so Noah will despise you ..."

"No. No," Raven interjects. "Take your trip. I don't wish to lose Noah like I lost Dane."

"Of course not."

"What about Kiley?"

"What about him?"

"What does this backtrack have to do with him?"

"That is none of your concern, Miss Looking Bird. You just do your part, and I'll worry about the rest. All right?"

Raven hangs her head and drapes her arm protectively across Noah's back. She appears resolute, and John grins smugly. He fingers the gar fish skeleton necklace beneath his shirt collar. Its powers are with him now. He considers his power of persuasion one of his greatest assets; his astral projecting ability to travel in time is another. It matters only that Raven will beacon this immediate personal journey. Once Fawn Lightfoot is his wife, he no longer needs Raven. He will have his own son, Noah, to beacon the rest of his travels. *What a pair we will make, my son and I.* He shivers in anticipation of the elegant lifestyle that awaits him.

John scrutinizes the woman hovering over his son. *Pretty bird. What a shame that she will soon lose her wings.* He finds it a bit amusing that she still thinks Darryl Kiley is the threat. Kiley is just a pawn. Darryl Kiley will never appear on the Democratic ticket. In fact, Darryl Kiley will never appear ever again.

John has it all planned. Wealth, fame, power, and recognition will be his, and his alone—to be shared solely with his wife, Fawn, and his son, Noah. His cheeks wrinkle with a broad smile as he sighs and closes his eyes to time travel.

Raven has it all planned, too. She waits until the Outlaw takes the deep breath that always precedes his travels, and then she moves like a movie in quick time. The arm circling Noah's back whips down to his belt. She snatches the Bowie knife from its leather sheath. It takes her exactly two seconds to cut the rope binding Noah's hands, and four seconds to cover the distance from couch to chair and plant the blade up to its hilt beneath the Outlaw's pectoral muscle. It takes less than ten seconds to ensure that John Silver Eyes will track no more.

Noah hears and sees everything hazily from behind his eyelashes, but he wills himself to remain quiet and still, feigning unconsciousness. Now that he is unbound, he can take control of the situation if Raven tries to stab him as well. The pain and confusion in his head are mild compared to the ache in his heart. He never expected anything like this.

Raven has to use both hands to extricate the knife from the Outlaw. She jumps back to avoid getting any blood on her clothing. Gingerly, she rolls Noah onto the floor, grunting as she pulls him near the chair. She wipes the handle of the knife on his pants, and then places it in his open hand. Coming behind the chair, she bumps against the back so the dead man slumps forward. Another push, and his body falls heavily onto the floor beside his son.

Noah is aware of Raven kneeling next to him. The smell of her now repulses him, and he opens his mouth slightly to dispel the cloying sweet scent of her cologne and the metallic odor of blood and death. She kisses him gently on the cheek. He takes quick, shallow breaths. It is all he can do to keep from retching.

"Oh, Noah," whispers Raven near his ear. "You are so much like them both. Thank goodness you will never be as your father. But, sadly, you can never be your brother, either." With that, she pads softly out the door.

A long time passes before Noah is composed enough to call the police. He has so many confused feelings to sort out. The woman he thought he loved has betrayed him and the entire Indian race; the man who engineered it is … was … his biological father. He wipes the moisture from his face when he hears the police cars drive up. Opening the door, he is relieved to see his friend Detective Jack Abernathy.

"Thanks for coming, Jack," Noah says as they walk into the room. Two other officers follow and move to John's body.

"Yeah. You the one who called?" Jack asks.

"Well, yeah. Of course, I did," Noah replies.

"Name?"

"John Silver, I believe."

"I know that. What's your name?"

"Jeez, Jack, it's me." Noah starts to laugh and abruptly thinks better of it.

"My name is Detective Abernathy. You don't know me well enough to call me by my first name, and I don't know you at all. Now, I'll ask you again. What's your name, or don't you know?"

"Noah ... Noah Lightfoot," he says. He studies the man before him and realizes there is no recognition in Jack's face. The Outlaw—his father—did this. When he changed the past at some point, he erased Noah's friendship with the police chief. *Another tragedy*. Noah shakes his head.

"O.K. How about you tell me what happened, Noah Lightfoot," Jack says.

Noah proceeds carefully. "This guy cold-cocked me and brought me here. I woke up; we struggled; he got the wrong end of the knife. And then I called you guys," he lies.

"Now, just why would Mr. Silver want to kidnap you?"

"Maybe he was a Gator fan?"

"Not funny, smart mouth. You better get serious before you find yourself in jail with some guys who aren't Seminole fans. Understand?" Jack hisses disdain through his teeth.

Noah pulls his head back. "I don't know, sir. Really, I don't. Maybe he mistook me for someone else. We all look alike, you know." He shrugs.

"Um hmm. Have business with him?"

"No, I never even knew him." The statement is entirely true, and Noah feels strangely empty when he says it. He has never known this man who was his father. If he had, his life would have been entirely different.

"Excuse me, Detective Abernathy." The voice comes from a sandy-haired man in the doorway. "Gentlemen, could you wait outside?" he says to the officers standing over the deceased. They hurriedly exit the room and mingle with the bodyguards at the door.

Jack Abernathy cranes his neck to see who has dispatched his officers. He is surprised to see Governor Darryl Kiley, the Democratic frontrunner for President.

"Governor Kiley? What are you doing here?" Jack asks.

Kiley saunters over to Jack, regarding Noah with wary eyes. "I have a scanner in the limo, and I heard the address of my associate. I came as fast as I could."

"I'm sorry, sir, but your associate has been killed," Jack says. "This kid says Mr. Silver abducted him, but I don't ..."

"Ah, yes. I think I can help you out," Kiley says, glancing sympathetically at the body on the floor. "Mr. Silver had been obsessed lately with finding his long-lost son. He spoke of it constantly to me, and I was beginning to have serious concerns as to his mental health. In fact, just this morning I mentioned to Mr. Silver that he should consider checking into Goodwood Psychiatric Center for a rest, and I would gladly pay for his leave of absence. I'm afraid I worsened his condition. He became agitated." He puts his hand on Abernathy's shoulder and squeezes slightly. "Isn't it just possible, in his delusional state of mind, that he imagined this boy to be the son he was seeking?"

Jack runs his hand through his hair, considering the possibility of the Governor's story. "Why this guy? And why kidnap him? It seems like a stretch to me."

Kiley presses his point. "Think about it. If the boy denied the association, I daresay Mr. Silver might have attacked him. There is no doubt in my mind that young ... what's his name?"

"Lightfoot," Jack says.

"Young Lightfoot acted—fortunately for him—in self-defense," Kiley emphasizes. He pauses to gauge the effect this has on Jack. "I suggest he be released, and let's get this affair cleaned up quickly ... and quietly. You see my concern, don't you?"

"Sure, but he'll have to come make a statement at ..."

"I don't think we need a statement, Jack," Kiley interjects. His hand on Jack's shoulder becomes heavier, the squeeze stronger. "Mr. Silver had an accident, nothing more. He tripped and fell on a kitchen knife. I'm sure you'll find a suitable one to place in the wound in his chest. Do we understand each other ... ah

…*Chief* Abernathy?" Kiley says, displaying his overly large white teeth in a sleazy grin.

Jack pulls his lower lip back up to meet his lips, then smiles. "Exactly my sentiments, Governor Kiley. Looks pretty cut and dried to me. Thank you, sir," he says.

"No. Thank you, Chief," Kiley says. He turns his head slowly toward Noah and gives him a smirking, steely-eyed stare. "And thanks to you, concerned citizen, for calling the police when you heard Mr. Silver cry out. Tallahassee needs more young men like you."

Jack snaps his head around. "You heard him, boy. Get out and keep your wise-cracking mouth shut. This fine gentleman just saved your red hide." He holds out the knife toward Noah. "And take this back home where it belongs."

Noah pastes a maniacal grin on his face, accepts the knife, and stiff legs out the door. He looks every bit the cocky yuppie as he saunters down the walk. But if the pedestrians he passes could read his mind, they would know that Noah has nearly crossed the line into mania.

He stops nearby at a Suwannee Swifty convenience store and phones for a cab. Then, he calls Lee's house. The rushing blood in his ears subsides when Wren answers.

"Oh, Noah," Wren chirps. "I'm glad you called. Lee has gone to bed with a headache, but he left me strict instructions to tell you to '… be careful and get over here as soon as you can.' That's what he said. What have you boys cooked up? If it involves something fun, I want to come along."

"If it involved something fun, I'd for sure want you to come along," Noah responds. He assures Wren that he will be there soon, but first he has some other business to take care of. The cab arrives sooner than he thought it would, so he hangs up quickly and races to the curb.

"*Que Pasa,*" Noah says scrambling into the backseat, "Not asking you a question, man. Take me to the restaurant with that name. O.K.? Fast."

The cabby nods and does a passable job of negotiating traffic. A few minutes later, he pulls up to *Que Pasa.* "Wait for me.

I'll just be a minute," he instructs the cab driver before he bolts through the restaurant door. He catches Maria's eye and motions her to a side table.

"Please, sit with me for a second. Can you?" he asks.

Her chocolate eyes dance beneath a thick fringe of lashes. *How have I not noticed this before? Oh yeah. I was a bit distracted ... by Raven.*

"I'm glad you came back," Maria says. "You know, when you came in for lunch today, I kinda felt like I must know you from somewhere."

"Yeah. Sorta," Noah says.

She hesitates, chewing the side of her lip. "Um ... that lady you were with earlier ... your girlfriend ... she's very pretty." She is probing, but she doesn't care.

"She's not my girlfriend."

"Oh! *Bueno!*" It comes out as a squeak, but again, she doesn't care.

"Tell me about Sarah," Noah blurts, interrupting her. He needs to know exactly how much damage has been done by the Outlaw's backtracks.

Maria's face darkens. "How do you know about Sarah?"

"I don't really ... just, you know, someone mentioned the name, and I thought you might have a sister I could fix my friend up with," he lies. He's doing a lot of that lately.

"No. Sarah was my niece, my bother Manuel's little girl. She was seven. She died of leukemia. We couldn't afford a bone marrow transplant for her, so she died. I'm sorry. I've got to go." Maria whimpers and shrugs, tears squeezing out of the corners of her lids. She covers her face, embarrassed, scraping the chair against the floor as she tries to leave.

Noah reaches out and grabs one tiny hand. "Maria, I'm sorry to hurt you, but I need to know one more thing. I ... um ... I knew your father a long time ago. What happened to him?"

She sits back down, pulling at the middle of her lower lip with her teeth. "He drowned at Panama City Beach. Mama said he was trying to rescue Sarah, and that the undertow had pulled her out over her head. She was only two, and she sure couldn't swim at that age. Mama said Sarah was screaming and spitting out water. Papa went out farther and farther to get to her. The riptide pulled him under, and he drowned. It still doesn't make any sense," Maria says, rubbing the crease between her brows.

"What is it, Maria? What doesn't make sense?" Noah asks.

Maria studies Noah's handsome face. She squeezes his hand with surprising strength until his fingers throb. "Noah. Tell me how this can be. Sarah was with me on the shore collecting seashells. She was not in the water!"

"Are you sure?"

"Yes!" She releases her grip and lifts her hand up for him to see. "Noah. Sarah was holding my hand."

"Then who was that in the ocean?"

"You tell me," she demands. "And they never found anyone but my Papa. You tell me how that's possible."

"Maria, I promise you everything will be better. I've got something I have to do, but I'll make it right for you from now on. O.K.? Trust me. I'll see you soon," he assures her.

"If you'll see me soon, then I suppose it will be right." Maria's timid, but radient smile promises many things: hope, love, determination, and, dignity.

The information he got from Maria is worse than he thought. Sarah is dead; Ramirez is dead. Somehow, the Outlaw was able to make Ramirez think Sarah was in the water. *How is that possible? No way could a grown man be mistaken for a little girl.*

Noah dreads his next stop; it does not promise to be as pleasant as seeing Maria. He steps out of the cab in front of Raven's apartment building, pays the driver, and gathers up his resolve. In a few moments, he is at her door. His face is calm when she appears, revealing nothing. When the door closes, he faces her.

"Why?" he asks. His voice is soft, but his eyes are hard.

Raven sits down on the couch and pulls her feet beneath her. She is silent a long time. When she does speak, her voice is toneless; she does not apologize. "I did what I had to do, Noah. My mother was in danger and I had to protect her." She tosses her head and looks down at her hands folded in her lap.

"How?"

"John Silver was a very powerful Outlaw. He had tracking abilities I didn't know existed. He was ruthless in his methods. I had no choice but to beacon for him."

"Why, Raven? What hold did he have over your mother?"

"He could track into the past, Noah—I suppose you know that already. And he was a shape shifter—I bet you didn't know that. He could make himself look like any person or animal he wanted. He could materialize in the past as a hologram, and he could even speak."

"It makes a certain amount of sense now. Go on."

"That man killed so many people by luring them into life-threatening situations. He did that to Robert Ramirez, the man that was Governor before Kiley. He could have done that to my mother. I was afraid."

"He killed Dane?"

"No. I killed Dane."

Noah does a double-take. "You did what?"

"I caused the fire that killed Dane," Raven admits with a shudder. "We had dinner, and I brought some wine. Dane didn't want any, but I insisted. He wasn't very comfortable about it because he had been going to church some with Lee." She half-smiles, ruefully. "The Mormon people don't drink and smoke, you know, and Dane wanted to become a Mormon like Lee. He was learning all about their church, and he wanted me to learn about it, too. I'm just not into organized religion. To tell you the truth, I wasn't ready to give up my habits."

Noah waits while she wipes her sweaty hands on her jeans. She takes a ragged breath and continues. "I would have, in time, because I loved him. You knew Dane quit smoking?"

"I guess so. That's why I was so surprised to hear he fell asleep smoking."

"He didn't. I did." She squares her shoulders. "We were sitting on the couch discussing wedding plans. The wine made us sleepy, and I was smoking. My cigarette touched off the rug, I suppose. The next thing I knew, I was outside on the ground ... safe, and Dane was inside the house ... burning." She cries without moving, without bothering to wipe her tears or her running nose.

Noah cries, too, but he has to know more. "John Silver Eyes..." he urges.

Raven's laugh is mirthless. "He carried me out of the house. He'd been watching through the window. I'm sure he was there to kill Dane, but I came over, so he waited around to see what would happen. I did his dirty work."

"Why would he want to kill Dane?"

"Dane told me that somebody tipped him off about John's powers. He went to interview him and recognized him."

Noah shakes his head and lifts his upturned palms, waiting for her to continue.

"When Dane was a little boy, he saw a man put a rattlesnake beneath a blanket in his father's *chickee*. The man had silver eyes. Dane hid behind a post so the man wouldn't see him. When the man left, Dane ran to get help. But before he could get back, his father returned to the hut. The rattlesnake struck his father. When Dane and your mother arrived, the silver-eyed man was right there watching his father and watching him, too. Dane saw his father die. He said the man gave him 'the evil eye.' He was just a child; he was so afraid."

Raven snuffles, and then she wipes her nose with the back of her hand before continuing. "Dane realized the man he interviewed was the same man that killed his father years before, and he was sure the man remembered him, too. Silver Eyes did plan to kill Dane, but I took care of that."

"Accidently."

"Does it matter? That man saved my life so I would be indebted to him. He said he'd tell the police I set the fire if I didn't help him."

"So, you said you would."

"No. I said I *wouldn't*. I did set the fire, even if it was an accident. I loved Dane. So, what if I went to jail? I lost the only man I ever cared about." She sees his startled expression. "Noah, wait, I'm sorry. I do care about you, but not in the way I cared for your brother. Besides, I think your heart is set for ... someone else ... maybe you don't know that yet."

"Fine. So, Raven. Jail didn't change your mind. What did?"

"I told you. He threatened to kill my mother if I didn't beacon for him. I'd already lost Dane; I couldn't lose my mother."

Noah is silent. Decisions must be made, and he desperately needs Lee's wisdom. He moves in slow motion to the door without making eye contact.

"Noah, will you come back later?"

"No. Not later. Not again. Goodbye, Raven," Noah says, risking one more look at her beautiful face. He lets the door swing closed of its own accord; he can still hear her sobbing.

CHAPTER ELEVEN
BACKTRACK

NOAH IS AT LEE'S DOOR ten minutes later. Wren shows him to the bedroom where Lee is resting, and he sits down in a chair beside the bed.

"You two men will excuse me, please. There is a good movie coming on. It's called 'Scruples.' I will be in the den. If you need me ... wait for a commercial," Wren teases. She pulls the door shut behind her.

Noah explains the events of the past few hours to his friend, omitting nothing. Lee sits still, nodding grimly. When Noah tells him about John, he jerks his chin up.

"Your father? This is a surprise. I would never have ..." Lee swings his legs over the side of the bed and arches his back. The popping startles Noah. "I'm sorry. I must be getting old. Don't worry, son. There is no danger of my getting lost again. Wren is here to see to that. She may look soft, but she packs a solid punch."

"That's for sure. But you won't get lost. You won't be going. I will," Noah says.

Lee starts to object, but the set of the boy's jaw changes his mind. "As you wish, son, but there are a few things you must know. You will be a hologram; you will have no tangibility. You can be seen and heard, but not felt. Be careful what you do, as it will have ramifications in this present life. You may travel only one place at a time. After each journey, you must come right back. We will use Wren as our barometer. She will help us gauge the changes that may have occurred. Do you understand?"

"I understand. Let's get started."

"Let me get comfortable." Lee shifts his position to sit up against the headboard. "Go with God, Son,"

"Amen," Noah replies as his eyes close and he begins his backtrack into the past.

*   *   *

Noah's first impression after he closes his eyes is that something has gone seriously wrong; there is nothing but darkness. Gradually, he becomes aware of sounds and light patterns. It is a sensation somewhere between "MTV" and "Fantasia." When the light show stops, so does his body. Noah groans. The headache is back. After a few moments, he has acclimated himself enough to look around. The scenic panorama is of "The World's Most Beautiful Beaches." Panama City Beach. He has been here many times, but never as a hologram.

Noah strips off his shirt, although he feels no heat, but to be fully dressed at the beach, even in September, looks suspicious. He ties the shirt around his waist and kicks off his shoes. Nobody can steal them, at least. He rolls up his pants legs and scans the beach for Maria.

He sees her just a little way down the shoreline, holding a toddler by the hand. Knowing the crucial time is near, he sprints to reach her, amused to note that his feet make no prints in the soft white sand.

"Maria," Noah calls.

She turns around and faces him, wide-eyed. Stranger! He is cute, but he is still a stranger. She pulls a little girl closer to her side. Sarah, as a toddler, is chubby and tan ... nothing like the sickly child they rescued a few weeks ago.

"What do you want? Go away and leave us alone," she says,

zigzagging in her efforts to elude him.

"Oh, hey, I'm sorry. Your grandma said you didn't talk to strangers. Listen, she told me to tell you, 'Mama Mine and Papa Berto are ready to leave, so come on back right now.' She said to call you, 'Chiquita.' Does that make any sense to you?" he asks.

Maria lets out a huge sigh and smiles at him, braces reflecting the sun. "Thanks. That sounds just like them. You really wouldn't know all that if they didn't tell you. Well, bye," she says skipping away—a twelve-year-old version of the young woman he is sure now that he will come to love.

Noah follows at a leisurely pace to assure himself he has achieved his purpose. He hears her up ahead singing a children's song to Sarah. In about four years' time that same voice will melt his heart. He can hardly wait.

A scream jerks him from the daydream. Carmine Ramirez is wringing her hands, screeching, watching her husband head into the water. Noah runs as fast as he can, knowing he must intervene quickly to save Bob Ramirez's life.

"Stop, Bob, stop. That isn't Sarah. That isn't Sarah. She's here," he calls. He sprints to Maria and tries to grab her hand to pull her along. His arm passes right through her. He has forgotten he is a hologram. He passes Maria and changes his course, running toward Carmine.

"Carmine. Look down the beach. Sarah's with Maria. She's not in the water," Noah yells.

Carmine looks in the direction Noah is pointing and sees Maria and Sarah running toward her. She turns and scans the water. Sarah is out there, too. *No*, she decides, *that must be another little girl in distress.*

"Mama, what's happening?" Maria gulps air.

Carmine embraces both girls. "Papa and I ... we thought Sarah was in the water. It is somebody else. Do not worry; your Papa will save her."

"Oh, no. No. No. No," Noah shouts. He rushes into the ocean and goes through the motions of swimming toward Bob Ramirez and the screaming "child." The growing riptide is pulling the man farther out into the gulf.

"No, Mister. Back away. That is not a child," Noah calls. "I'm a lifeguard. I'm trained for this. Go back. You're putting us both in danger. Swim parallel to the shore. Do it now."

He sees relief on Bob's face; the undertow is greater than the man's swimming ability. Only after Bob approaches the shore does Noah look for the shape shifter. *Gone.* Noah makes his way back to the beach.

Bob is draped with one towel, and Carmine is drying him off with another. He scans the water, and then turns on Noah, taking in his street apparel. "You're not a lifeguard," he accuses.

"Right. And that wasn't a child," Noah replies.

"She was screaming," Carmine says, rubbing her husband's wet hair.

"She was a pelican; they do that sometime. Sometimes your eyes and ears play tricks on you. Look, don't try to be a hero anymore. You could be killed," Noah says.

Maria skips up beside him. "Thanks for helping us," she says with a shy smile.

He steps away before she gets close enough to try and touch him. He waves at both the girls before pulling on his shirt and disappearing behind a garden of colorful beach umbrellas.

Maria turns to her mother with a confused expression. "Mama, why didn't that cute boy get wet when he went into the water?" she asks.

*   *   *

When Noah opens his eyes, he is sitting in the very same chair next to Lee's bed. "Whoa. What a rush." He exhales loudly.

Lee looks at Noah's feet. "Son, where are your shoes?"

"Oops. Left them on the beach. Long story," he replies. "Somebody's gonna have a real tough time picking them up!"

Lee pats Noah's shoulder as he walks to the door and opens it. He summons Wren, and then he returns to sit again on the bed.

"What is it, you two? I am missing the good part," Wren says as she sticks her head in the door.

"We will be quick, little bird, so you can return to your story.

Tell us, please, who is the Governor of Florida?" he asks.

"Robert Ramirez, of course," she replies, frowning and pursing her lips.

"And please be so kind as to name the Trackers," her husband prompts.

Wren rolls her eyes. "Really, Liahona? You, Noah, Graham, and Raven."

"Thank you, my dear. Go back to your movie. I will call you if I need anything."

"Please wait for a commercial, if you don't mind. I'm interested in this movie."

Lee raises his eyebrows. "You have done well, Noah. Our Governor is safe," he says.

"But not for long. I think he—Silver—the Outlaw—may have recognized me. I've got to get back fast. I'll have to kill him in the past, too. Get ready, Lee. I'm going," Noah warns before he travels again.

*   *   *

The second time isn't nearly as psychedelic, and he is prepared for the crash landing. Noah looks around. He knows this house well. It belongs to his brother. He hasn't been expecting to see Dane. *Can I save Dane's life, too?* Like Lee, he is willing to break the rules to have his older brother back again. Noah smells the smoke. He has to get him ... them ... out of the house.

As he passes through the door—literally passes right through it—on his way into the house, he sees the flames beginning to consume the carpet, erasing it like a computer backspace key. Smoke billows; Noah begins to panic.

"Wake up, Dane. Raven, wake up," he screams. He tries to pull them; to shake them. He cannot move them in any way. Burning carpet puts off toxic fumes. If they don't die from the flames, they will soon die of smoke inhalation.

John Silver Eyes. Where is he? Noah lashes his head around, looking for the Outlaw. He is nowhere to be seen. *Wait! Outside. I see him!* Noah runs through the wall. There stands his father in the bushes.

John turns toward the hologram of his son, silver eyes wide, terrified. He begins to chant in the Muskogee language to ward off this spirit.

"John Silver Eyes. Save them. You have to get them out or they'll die," Noah says.

John continues to chant, louder now. He falls backward and crabwalks away from the specter advancing upon him.

"Get them out. Please. Father. Do it for me. Let me remember you as someone who once had love in his heart ... for my mother ... for me ... for your son," he begs.

John looks at his son. Noah observes an ache behind those icy blue eyes. "Noah?" Without another word, the man runs into the burning house. After a few agonizing moments, Noah can see him through the smoke, carrying a body over his shoulder. He carries it across the street and drops it gingerly onto the grass. Looking once more at Noah, John Silver Eyes nods his head once, and then runs back into the house.

The explosion blows shards of glass and burning wood through Noah's intangible body. He stands still, head down. He knows there is no need to look up. There is nothing left of Dane or his father. "Home," he murmurs.

*　　*　　*

Noah meets Lee's gaze through the sting of tears. After many minutes, he speaks to the older man.

"He's history, Lee," he says.

"Did you kill him?" Lee asks.

"No. The ... my father killed himself. He finally tried to do the right thing. Too late," he whispers.

"We make our own choices, Noah," Lee says. He walks slowly to the door and calls out. "Wren, my dear, will you tell us please, who is the Governor of the State of Florida?"

"Robert Ramirez," she calls back to him.

"And please be so kind as to name the Trackers Team members," he prompts.

"You, Noah, Graham, and Dane."

Noah's head popped up. "Wait. Dane? Hey, Wren, did you say Dane?"

Wren appears at the door, a mite breathless from rushing. She cocks her head at her husband. You, Noah, Graham, and Dane. That's what I said." She huffs in mock irritation.

"Wren. What about Miss Looking Bird?" Lee asks.

"Liahona, dear. Are you getting senile so soon? Raven has been gone for over two years, now. In the fire. How can you have forgotten about that?"

"What about the other man?" Noah asks.

"He died, sweetie. He got your brother out and went back in for Raven. They say the house exploded before they could get out. He was a brave and unselfish man, whoever he was."

Wren looks sharply at her husband. "I don't know what your boys are doing in here, but you are making me miss the best part of my movie. Please, wait for a commercial before you call me," she admonishes as she breezes out of the room.

"I've got to go back," Noah says as he prepares to track again into the past.

"No," Lee says. He puts his hand on Noah's shoulder.

Noah starts to protest, but Lee silences him with a squeeze.

"Let it be, Noah. Let it be as it is."

"But, Lee. Raven is …"

"Raven is gone, but Dane is back. John Silver Eyes is gone, but the Ramirez family is again intact. In all things there must be sacrifices in order to achieve balance. We have accomplished what we set out to do … restore the course of time and history. Without the Outlaw to track and Raven to beacon, Darryl Kiley will have no political future."

"But suppose he finds another outlaw to track?"

Lee considers this possibility. "Perhaps you are right. He must not find another person to tempt. But this time, I will go. You will signal for me."

"Let me go."

"No." Lee will not negotiate when his mind is made up.

Noah contents himself to sit back and listen for the word.

He has no doubt that Lee will eliminate Kiley. After an eternity, Lee returns. They do not interrupt Wren's movie; they already know what the answers will be.

Lee is right, as usual. Noah knows things will never be quite the same, but he is willing to live with the trade-off. The balance has been restored, and it is necessary that Raven stays in the past. Dane, his off-beat brother, is back. And as he thinks of Maria, with her little pixie face and diva voice, he feels his pulse race. Tomorrow, he will visit her.

She will be at the Governor's Mansion with her parents, Bob and Carmine Ramirez, who recently celebrated their 30th wedding anniversary. Sarah Ramirez will be recovering from a bone marrow transplant in Gainesville. Tomorrow will be business as usual for the Trackers ... Lee, Noah, Graham. And Dane.

CHAPTER TWELVE
AS USUAL

NOAH EMERGES WITH A JOLT from a deep and dreamless sleep. He slaps the clock several times before he surmises that the phone is ringing. Reaching to answer it, he is surprised at how much he aches all over—like the flu or a fistfight or both.

"Wake up, sleepyhead," Dane says.

Noah's heart falls to his toes when he hears his brother's voice. Lee urged him not to visit Dane last night, but to go home and rest so he would be fresh. They are to meet at Lee's house for Sunday dinner. Lee has made all the arrangements.

"Noah? You awake?" Dane's voice is cheery and sounds very much alive.

"Yeah. I'm awake, big brother. What's up?"

"Just calling to remind you to come to Hona's house for lunch today."

"Right. Time?"

"Now? 11:50. Almost noon. Lunch is at 1:00, so get moving."

Noah sits up straighter. "Dane, where are you?"

"Still at church. Got some business to attend to first, but I'll be there. I've got a big surprise for everybody."

"Church business?"

Dane laughs, his deep baritone voice resonating in the receiver. "Blow out the cobwebs, Chief. I've just got a baptism to go to first. Andy Abernathy, a little guy in my primary class, is eight years old today and getting dunked. Get up and get gone, Noah. Don't be late. See you at one," he says before breaking the connection abruptly.

Noah bounces off the bed and dresses, splashes a little water on his face, shakes his hair, and starts to bolt out the door. He stops. *No need to hurry. There is plenty of time.*

He goes back to the bathroom and takes a proper shower, shaves, and brushes his hair and teeth. He even dresses in clean clothes. He wants to look good when he sees Dane again, and he needs to know about Lee's journey. In less than thirty minutes, he finishes his ablutions and covers the distance between his house and Lee's.

Lee is in good humor when Noah arrives. Wren bustles about, setting places and putting the finishing touches on the food. Graham entertains the three youngest Thistleseed children with cartoon character impressions. He waves when he sees Noah. The kids squeal and snort when Graham becomes Porky Pig talking to Daffy Duck.

Wren and her oldest daughter are setting up a couple of card tables in the family room for the younger children. Shinehah Thistleseed is twenty-four and looks very much like her Cherokee mother, with coarse black hair and an adobe-colored complexion. Her name means "Sun," and she is quite bright—a trait inherited from both parents. She is probably Noah's favorite of Lee's children and is like a cousin to him.

From the corner of his eye, he sees Graham jump up to offer his services. Noah can tell by the way they cut their eyes at each other that Graham and "Shine" are kindling a romance. Wren also notices and disappears into the kitchen, giving them space to get more acquainted, thus showing her approval. What a relief. Shine is one woman he has no interest in pursuing.

He desperately wants to talk to Lee, who seems to be avoiding him. He is hiding more than the fact he has saved Andy Abernathy's life. *Why?* Lee is soft-hearted, but saving the boy has no real purpose, unless it is in some way connected with the elimination of Darryl Kiley. Is Kiley dead? Noah doubts that Lee actually killed the man, but he is sure Kiley will never hold a memorable place in history. He will have to temper his impatience for a little while longer.

A car pulls up outside, and Noah's heart leaps. Dane, at last. Noah wipes his eyes quickly with his sleeve and waves at the familiar figure in the doorway.

Wren claps her hands and beams at the young man. "Hello, Dane. Come on in, and bring ..."

Dane holds his finger to Wren's lips. Lee looks at Noah and twitches his mouth into a grin. He waves him over.

Dane enters the room and calls for attention. "Everyone, I want you to meet someone. I want you to meet my fiancé. She's gorgeous, she's talented, and she's gifted. Lee, we should definitely train her. My wife will make a great Tracker," he announces. He proudly ushers the woman into the room.

She is, indeed, beautiful. In fact, one could say she is beauty personified. She is a Native American Indian, part Yavapai, part Hopi. Her features are finely chiseled into unvarnished cherry wood skin. Her glossy black hair is cut in a short bob, cropped bluntly at ear lobe level, with straight bangs to her eyebrows, and on her feet, she wears moccasins.

"Hello," she says, displaying small teeth like perfectly matched pearls. "My name is Raven ... Raven Looking Bird."

EPILOGUE
THE KEEPER

IT IS LATE INTO THE NIGHT by the time I finish collecting the story of Noah—the Scout—my brother. My heart swells with love for him and for Dane, my other brother, brought back through the veil of death. The cicadas are vocalizing in the trees overhead, and the sun no longer warms my face. Though it never really gets cold here in the jungle, I shiver, and Mother wraps my shoulders in a shawl. My flute falls forgotten at my feet. Mother picks it up.

"Luna," Mother says. "*Vamanos*. Let's go. *Enkv?* OK?"

My mother uses Spanish, English, and Muskogee interchangeably, but I'm used to it.

"What do you keep this time?" Mother asks.

"Tomorrow, Mother. I will tell you tomorrow. Tonight, I am so tired," I say.

She presses me. "When you did not play, you *yvhiketv*—you sang. You sang names."

"Did I? Who did I name?"

"Noah. Dane. Fawn. *Hecetv?* Did you see them?" Her voice is anxious.

"I saw them," I say.

"*Bueno*. Good. Let's go home" she says. She leads me

toward our village, just a short walk away compared to the hundreds of miles I have traveled recently. My hands are stiff, my fingertips bruised and dimpled. I am weak, and even my hair is exhausted from this journey.

"Mother," I say as I hold her hand, "I saw someone else." She stops and stands very still. I can tell that she is not looking at me because she has not turned. *She knows.* Taking a breath, I tell her, "I saw you."

"*Si,*" she says. "Yes. I knew you would. *Mvdo.*" She starts walking again.

Tomorrow, I'll tell her everything I saw ... what I'll keep; tonight, I'll sleep serenely. I am happy. My brothers are alive, and I think, someday soon, I will meet them in the flesh. *Mvdo.*

APPENDIX
LANGUAGE TRANSLATIONS

Muskogee Creek Language

The Muskogee Creek language is spoken extensively on the reservations in Oklahoma; however, in the Southeast, there are relatively few native speakers. In the tri-state region of Florida, Georgia, and Alabama, language classes are held in an effort to keep the language from becoming extinct.

The vowels are pronounced as follows:

A=w_A_tch	E=_I_tch	E=s_EE_
I=s_AY_	O=m_OA_n	U=b_OO_k
V=_U_nder	EU=_U_se	UE=b_OY_
VO=n_OW_	Note: vowels are voiced with partially closed, tight mouth.	

Consonants are sounded as follows:

C=ri_CH_	C= ca_TS_	C=_J_am
F=_F_air	H=_H_air	K=bi_K_e
K= _G_o	L=_L_ike	M=_M_an
N=ma_N_	P=_P_ie	P= _B_uy
R=_TLH_ or _HL_ (There is no English equivalent. The sound is much like an attempt to bring forth phlegm)		
S=_S_ee	S= _Z_oo	SK=wi_SH_
SS=wi_SH_	T=_T_ea	T=_D_ie
W=_W_et	Y=_Y_et	
Note: Consonants are voiced with tight mouths, far back in the throat. The sounds are almost "swallowed."		

Muskogee Words, Phrases, and their Meanings
(in order of appearance)

Tuskie Mahaya Haco – Brave Teacher Warrior (proper name)

Hvresse torwv – moon eyes

Pvsktv – fasting celebration
Heles Pocase – medicine Man
Blunt-em-vfolv – *Blountstown (proper name, Blount-his-town)*
Heles haya pocase – doctor medicine man
Micco – chief
Ludjataka – proper name of the sacred turtle
Vntolv Haco – Andrew Warrior (proper name)
Mvdo – it is well; it is good; good; thank- you're welcome
We He Ha O Ne – syllables used in singing; they have no translation
Hokte opvnkv – women, come out (command)
Talwv – town
Tolv – bay leaves (plant)
Passv – button snakeroot (plant)
Trwv – bitter winged sumac (plant)
Chickee – open-sided house with thatched roof
Osafke hvtke – white corn grits (also called soffkee)
Hesaketvmese – The One Above (proper name for God)
Hvtum cehacares – I will see you again
Enkv – O.K., all right
Vhiketv – *you sang*
Hecetv – you see

Muskogee/English Historical Marker in Blountstown

Meske 1815 mahen, Estecate Ocesvlke Vpvlvcekola fullvt.
Tepokv empefatkvtet eyicet tack Kvlhun vpoketv hatyakvtes.

Apalachicola Creek Indians permanently settled Calhoun County in 1815; Wars forced them out of Alabama.

Mimvm, Tvske Hacoketatet talofv empvtakvn hayvtes.

A new Tribal Town was built by Chief Tuski Hajo Cochrane between Old River and Noble Lake.

Tvske Haco Corakko "Cochrane" Wacenv ehocefkvt toyvtes.

Cochrane is an anglicized version of his Creek name Corakko pronounced "Cho'thlakko" which means Horse.

1823 opunvkv-cokv (Motle Temfvtcetv) oc-ofvn, Corakko Talofv "Cochranetown", Plvnt-Tuske Haco okvntacko hahoyves. Mucv nettv, Plunt-en-Talofv tos.

The 1823 Treaty of Moultrie Creek recognized Cochranetown with its 100 families as part of the Blunt-Tuskie Hajo Reservation now called Blountstown.

1832 opunvkv-cokv (Lucuwv Temfvtcetv) oc-ofvn, Teksvke min vpeyvnonstkes kibocen.

The 1832 Treaty of Payne's Landing compelled local Creeks to emigrate to Texas with Chief John Blunt.

Vyepofvn Tuske Haco echuste vyetvn eyacekot. Polly em-estvlken vtelohyet kvn posketv pokkon sohletkvtes. Mucv, Kvlhun Tacko ofvn, Polly enrohonvpvlke fulle emunks.

Tuskie Hajo Cochrane's daughter, Polly Parrot, refused to go. Her clan fled northward to a Calhoun County wilderness called Boska Bokga, "the last fasting place." The Bokga's people became known as the Boggs family. Many Calhoun County citizens descend from Polly's clan.

Ohrolope 1986, Kvnfvske, Vhakv-hayvlke em-nakaftetv oc-ofvn Ocesvlket Florida Tribe kerkueckv emhoyet omvtes.

In 1986, Florida Tribe of Eastern Creek Indians whose members include the Boggs clan was recognized by the State.

Hiyomat, Kvlhun Tacko estecate Mvkokvlket fulle emunks.

Today, they still maintain their ancient traditions.

Emmekkvlket Tvske Haco Corakko 1832, Polly 1833-1898,
Tvske Haco Can Cems Welev Cose Pokkvs 1900, Tvske Haco
Cems Tvnel Pokkvs 1920, Vles Mvklelan Pokkvs 1933-1961,
Tvske Mvhayv Haco Vuntolv Pokkvs Lumse 1962.

Their unbroken line of titled chiefs is Tuskie Hajo Cochrane-1832; Polly Parrot, regent matriarch 1833-1898; Tuski Hajo John James William Joesph Boggs-1900; Tuskie Hajo James Daniel Boggs-1920; Alice McClellan Boggs, regent matriarch 1933-1961; Tuskie Mahaya Hajo Dr. Andres Boggs Ramsey-1962.

Hocefkvulket omvts Pommekkvlke Pollyketate Rohonvpvlket
omes.

The Tuskie Hajo (Zealous Warriors) all descend from Polly.

Spanish Language

Conversational Spanish, in its many forms and dialects, is one of the most widely spoken languages in the world and is prevalent throughout Mexico, Central America, and the United States. Though it varies slightly by regions, it is generally consistent in its pronunciation.

The vowels are pronounced as follows:

A=w_Atch_	E= b_Ed_	I =s_EE_
O=m_OA_n	U=b_OO_k	Y =s_EE_
Note: vowels are voiced with open, relaxed mouth.		

Consonants are sounded as follows:

B =_B_ed	C=_C_ow	C=_S_ow
D=_Th_ink	F=_F_un	G=_G_un
H=silent	J=_Ch_ew	K=_K_ick
L=_L_ick	LL=_Y_ard	M=_M_an
N=_N_ow	Ñ=can_Y_on	P=_P_ark
Q/QU=_K_ick	R=ca_RR_y	RR=as _R_, but trilled
T=_T_ake	V=_B_ed	W=_W_ater
X=e_X_cuse	Y=_Y_es	Z=pin_TS_
Note: consonants are voiced with open, relaxed mouth. Hard consonants are explosively voiced.		

Spanish Words, Phrases, and their Meanings
(in order of appearance)

Ojos del Luna – Eyes of the Moon (proper name)

Madre de Dios – Mother of God

Si – yes

Pero – but

Tengo mucho hambre – I am hungry

Y – and

La – the

Chiquita – little girl
No estoy borracho – I am not drunk
Es verdad – it is true
Viene aqui – you are coming here
Bueno – good
Adios – goodbye
Silencio – be quiet; silence
Por favor – please
Gracias – thank you
Tonto – stupid; foolish
Cuantos dineros – How many dollars?
Cinco – five
Cara Mia – my dear
Dios Mio – my God
Buenas tardes – good afternoon
Mamacita – little Mama
Sangria – a fruity drink
Sopa del lentejas Madrilene – lentil soup, Madrid-style
Ensalada – salad
Paella – a dish with rice and several different meats and seafood
Pisto manchego – a stewed vegetable dish
La vida esta llena de momentos del amor – Life is full of moments of love
Vivimos un sueño – we lived a dream
Perdidos en la noche – lost in the night
Perdidos en el silencio – lost in the silence
Mi novio – my sweetheart
Querida - beloved
Que Pasa – What is happening?
Me llamo... – my name is...
Come te llamas – What is your name?
Vamonos – we will go

MIST:

THE BLOODHOUND'S STORY

Book 2 of

The TRACKERS SERIES

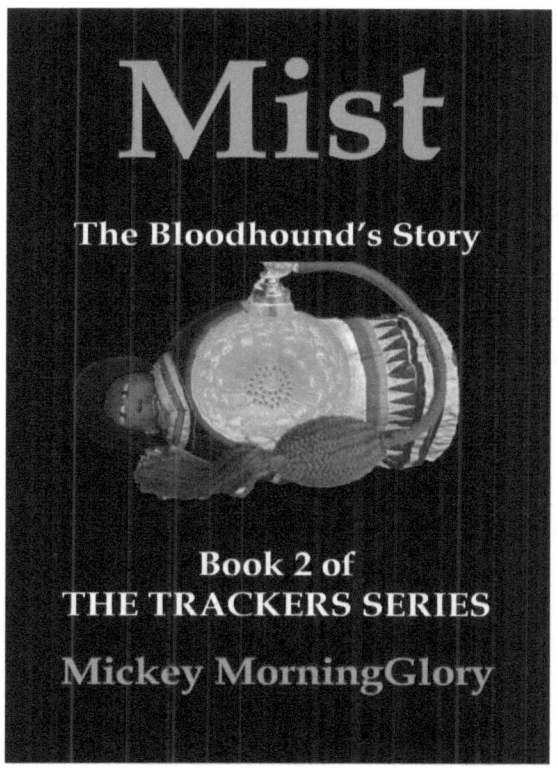

MICKEY MORNINGGLORY

Patent Print Books
Panama City Beach, Florida

MIST: The Bloodhound's Story
The Trackers Series, Book 2

Published by PATENT PRINT BOOKS
www.patentprintbooks.com

PATENT PRINT BOOKS and the fingerprint colophon
are registered trademarks of PATENT PRINT BOOKS

First Edition: 2017
Revised 2020
Printed in the United States of America

ISBN 978-0-9850731-1-4
Library of Congress Control Number: 2017918244

10   9   8   7   6   5   4   3   2

CONTENTS

PREFACE

MIST was not going to be the next book in *The Trackers Series*. It was to be Raven Looking Bird's story. But you know how stubborn those Lightfoot boys are. While I struggled to draft *KACHINA*, Dane Lightfoot kept invading my sleep wanting his tale told. So, Raven agreed to take a back seat until I completed *MIST: THE BLOODHOUND'S STORY*, and now she's glad she did! You'll see why very shortly.

~ Mickey

INTRODUCTION

Ecstasy…the *"Love Drug"*. Even its name invokes thoughts of *euphoria*. Users claim it brings feelings of extreme joy, closeness, trust, exhilaration—emotions that blend well with the "dance-all-night" atmosphere of rave parties.

Unfortunately, this drug-induced "excitement" often causes the user to drop his or her guard, trusting those who cannot *always* be trusted, giving rise to sexual promiscuity, even rape; ingesting other drugs, usually in dangerous or deadly combination; and oftentimes resulting in permanent psychological or physical injury or death.

Over the years, I've found that the use of these dangerous drugs crosses all social divides, all ages, all races…it honors no one. During my thirty-five-year law enforcement career, on too many occasions I've had the unpleasant duty of notifying friends, parents, even spouses, of the arrest, serious injury or death of their loved ones due to illicit drugs. It is a duty that I never wanted and, with each case, *never* forgot.

~ Guy Tunnell
Retired Sheriff, Bay County, FL
Former Commissioner,
Florida Department of Law Enforcement

"Power is its own master; it touches those of its own choosing."

~ Fawn Lightfoot

PROLOGUE

TALLAHASSEE, FL~OCTOBER~1992

SHE COULD NOT HAVE BEEN HAPPIER. Everything was going so well. The music was loud; the beat was strong and pulsating. The lights were incredibly bright and colorful, and they seemed to dance with the tempo of the music. His hands on her bare shoulders gave off heat waves, and it felt good. She gyrated her hips and gave him her best "come-on" look.

He pulled her closer, and they danced as one unit, swaying and bumping to the undulating rhythm of the song. He pushed her hair away from her neck and leaned in close to her, breathing in the intoxicating scent of her perfume as he moved his mouth and licked beneath her ear. Pulling back, he licked his lips. They tingled, but not pleasantly.

She wrapped her arms around his waist. Grasping the back of his shirt, she raised herself up on her toes to meet his kiss. *Hot*, she thought. *So hot*. She giggled at the double entendre, and then she frowned. He was so incredibly attractive, and she was anxious to be with him, but she was burning up. Sweat beaded beneath her nose and dried immediately, leaving a salty, crusty residue; her lips felt parched, chapped.

"I need something to drink." She gasped, pulling away

from him. The room was an oven; she had to cool down.

He agreed, taking hold of her hand and weaving through the dancing throng toward the bar. He suddenly felt he was dragging her—like dead weight. *Why is she hanging back?* Turning around, he felt the room spin, and he shook his head to clear his vision. *Where is she? There.* She seemed yards away, but, looking down, he noticed they still had their hands clasped.

She went to her knees without warning, panting, staring wide-eyed at him. *What's happening?* She panicked. *Help me!* She tried to call out, but her tongue was thick, dry, stuck to her teeth. Her eyes felt like sand in their sockets.

He watched her fall over to her side. It was slow, like a stop-action movie. Her eyes never left his, all the way down to the floor. Then the room tilted away, became dark and quiet, and he was gone, too.

*   *   *

Thirty miles away, Dane Lightfoot came awake slowly, his nose filled with the scents of floral, jasmine, musk, and something he couldn't identify. It was overpowering, and he jammed his index fingers into his nostrils. Pressing on the cartilage between his fingertips, he breathed rapidly in and out through his mouth. He removed one finger, then the other, and took a slow, cautious breath. *Perfume ... very high end, complex, smells expensive.* He took another, deeper breath. S*weat, stale body odor.* Another breath. *What IS that?*

Suddenly, he was overwhelmed with thirst. Flinging back the covers, Dane jumped up from the bed and bounded into the kitchen. Grabbing a plastic cup from the dish drainer, he filled and drank a total of four glasses of tap water before he felt quenched.

The mysterious smell was gone now, and Dane perched on the bar stool, absently running his finger around the top of the cup. *Somebody's dead,* he decided, *and it wasn't pretty.*

*   *   *

Hundreds of miles away, my eyes fly open, and I stare at nothing. I don't know the young couple, but I know Dane, though I've only recently come to learn of him. He is my brother—the one who just returned from beyond the veil of death.

I am Luna—short for *Ojos del Luna* (as my village family calls me); *Hvresse Torwv* (as my Creek Indian mother calls me). Both names mean the same—Moon Eyes. Mother says my eyes are so blue they are almost white, and that is why I am blind. But in my dream travels, I can see everything. I often travel great distances as I play my flute, and in my travels, the world is vivid and colorful, with keen sensory perceptions of sound and smell.

I am a "Story Keeper." I remember in great detail what I see on my journeys. The stories I tell are not mine, but I keep them in my memory always, as do I keep all the other stories related to this group of people whose lives intersect mine in a strange and unexplainable way.

This one is his—the Bloodhound's story. It begins the night my brother Dane awakes smelling death.

CHAPTER ONE
SUNDAY, 1992

LIAHONA "LEE" THISTLESEED'S HOUSE IS BUZZING with
excitement today. The Mohawk leader of the elite clairvoyant
Trackers Team is in his element, with his family and friends all
around him. The three Thistleseed boys—Cy, Bill, and Kenny—
clamor for attention from Graham Skysong, the Navajo clairaudient
who can imitate any voice he hears. Graham entertains them by
doing impressions of Porky Pig, Daffy Duck, and whatever cartoon
characters they call out.

"Nyaaaaahhhh! What's up, Doc," Graham quips in the
voice of Bugs Bunny. In his lap, seven-year-old Shelly—Lee's
youngest child—squeals loudly as he tickles her.

Lee's wife Wren bustles about, setting places and putting
the finishing touches on the food. The oldest daughter, twenty-
four-year-old Shinehah, sets up a couple of card tables in the family
room for the younger kids. Nicknamed "Shine," she looks very
much like her Cherokee mother, with long coarse black hair, an
adobe-colored complexion, and a smile that is as bright as her
name, which means "sun." Selah—four years younger—helps out.
Her name means "to pause," and she does so frequently, much to
Shine's irritation.

This is a day of celebration, different from their usual Sunday dinners. Today, Dane Lightfoot, the Seminole member of the Trackers Team, is bringing a girlfriend. The doorbell sounds. Debby and Zorah—the identical twin girls—scream in unison, "He's here! He's here!"

Dane enters the doorway and calls for attention. "Everyone, I want you to meet someone. I want you to meet my fiancé. She's gorgeous, she's talented, and she's gifted. Lee, we should definitely train her. My wife will make a great Tracker," he announces as he ushers the woman into the room.

She is a year or two older than Shine, and she is breathtaking. Her name is Raven Looking Bird, and she is a Yavapai/Hopi Indian. Her features are finely chiseled into unvarnished cherry wood skin; her small teeth are like perfectly matched pearls. Her glossy black hair is cut in a short bob, cropped at ear lobe level, with straight bangs to her eyebrows, and on her feet, she wears moccasins.

Seeing Lee sitting on the brick fireplace hearth, Noah Lightfoot, Dane's Creek Indian younger brother, walks over and takes a seat beside his mentor. They watch Dane and Raven stroll hand in hand around the room talking to Wren, Graham, and each of the Thistleseed children. Lee smiles as he looks at them … his family … his friends … his Team.

*   *   *

The Trackers Team was Lee's idea, formed out of a need to augment the efforts of local law enforcement to find criminals and missing persons. With the traditional methods hitting roadblocks at every turn, Lee offered his services as a clairvoyant to his friend, Chief Jack Abernathy. Though skeptical, Jack had seen the advantages of Lee's untraditional approach and enlisted his help on a few cases … behind closed doors, of course.

At the time, Lee's beacon—the person who brought his mind back to his body during the astral projection trips—was his friend and mentor, Jimbo Billie, a Seminole from the Lake Okeechobee area. Jimbo was older than Lee and did not travel but he was skilled in mentally sending a signal light that only a clairvoyant could see. Growing weaker by the day from terminal pancreatic cancer, Jimbo had encouraged Lee to seek out and find others to train. The first one they chose was Dane Lightfoot.

Dane was a member of the Leon County Fire Department. He was fairly young—only eighteen—but a valuable member of their department. He seemed to be able to locate the source of a fire when even the arson inspector could not. He said he could "smell" it. That earned him the nickname "Bloodhound," which inevitably drew references to anything related to dogs. But it never seemed to bother Dane. He was good natured and laid back—traits he attributed to his Seminole Indian heritage and the fact that he was raised on a South Florida reservation.

Jimbo Billie had also lived on the reservation. Dane's father, Joe Lightfoot, had been a *Heles Pocase* ... a Medicine Man. When Jimbo's parents and six older siblings were killed in a freak car accident, Joe Lightfoot "adopted" young Jimbo. Jimbo lived with the Lightfoots until Joe's wife died. Old Joe took a second wife shortly after that—a young beauty named Fawn, Jimbo's little sister, also spared in the accident and living with another family on the reservation.

Fawn gave birth to a son, and they named him Dane. According to Fawn, the name meant both "dweller in the valley" and "honorable." Dane was the seventh son of a seventh son. In their Indian beliefs, that meant he was destined to have the gift of second sight. Fawn insisted that he be given a name that insured he would be an honorable man if he was to possess power.

Jimbo had also been a seventh son and had manifested psychic gifts by the time he was twelve, so he knew well the accountability that came with power. When Dane was ten, Joe Lightfoot was killed by a rattlesnake that found its way into their *chickee* hut. According to the matrilineal Seminole tradition, boys were to be raised by the mother's family. As the natural uncle and adopted stepbrother, that task fell to Jimbo Billie. He assumed the responsibility for Dane and Fawn, as well as the child that Fawn gave birth to nine months after Joe's death ... Noah.

Lee Thistleseed's family lived in a neighboring town.

Though he was Mohawk and not Seminole, he was allowed to visit the reservation for their social events. He and Jimbo met and became instant friends. Not only did they both have psychic gifts, they were also young men of integrity. They formed a partnership that included hours and hours of pushing each other to the limits of their clairvoyant abilities. They developed a method of tracking people, places, and things through an out-of-body experience called astral projection. Lee would send his mind on short, and then longer journeys, and Jimbo would concentrate on sending a signal light that brought Lee's mind back to his body. Thus, the Trackers Team began.

When Lee turned eighteen, he left South Florida and moved to Tallahassee to go to college. He and Jimbo kept in touch by mail and phone, and every couple of years they would "meet in the middle" to keep their tracking skills sharp. For 15 years, the two remained devoted friends and maintained their dream of forming a crime-fighting Trackers Team.

When Dane came of age, Lee—a tenured history professor at Florida State University—got him a job in Tallahassee at the fire department, and Jimbo moved north with his nephew. Before he left, Jimbo contacted a friend, who ran the Seminole Village and Culture Center in Tampa and arranged a job for Fawn in the *Coo-Taun Cho-Bee* or "where the big water meets the land" Museum. She and young Noah moved to Tampa to live in a *chickee* house that was reserved in the adjacent village for them.

Lee and Jimbo continued refining their skills and began working cases for the local police department. Six years later, when Jimbo was dying, they brought Dane on board and trained him as Jimbo's replacement. Dane's clairscent abilities were developed, and he left firefighting and joined the fire marshal's organization.

Jimbo Billie died just a year later, but not before he was able to lead Lee to Graham Skysong, a young Navajo singer who had a gift for clairaudience—psychic hearing. Graham was trained as the third member of the Trackers Team. When Noah was sixteen, he received an academic scholarship to F.S.U., and Lee helped him secure two privately funded grants. He moved to Tallahassee and bought a small "fixer-upper" house with the money from the grants.

Shortly afterward, Noah also became a Tracker, bringing the team to its current four members.

*   *   *

Now, three years later, Lee is aware of the fidgeting young man beside him.

"How'd you do it?" Noah asks.

"How did I do what?" Lee asks.

"Bring her back. How'd you get Raven out of the house before it blew?" He turns slightly to catch Lee's eye, but the older man remains motionless on the hearth, hands clasped loosely and elbows on his knees, watching the happy couple as they make their way around his family room and foyer.

"C'mon, Lee. I was there, remember? I saw John Silver Eyes carry Dane out of the burning house. He went back in for Raven, but he didn't come back out before it blew up. You couldn't carry her out. You were a hologram. Right?"

"I was," he replies.

"So..." Noah says.

"So, I had to do something else."

Frustration welling up in his chest, Noah stands and faces his friend. "What, man? What's the problem here? Why don't you just clear it up for me?"

Lee slowly reaches up and takes Noah's hand. "Sit down, Son. Let us not cause a scene. I would rather talk about it in a more private location, but as you are so insistent, I will explain exactly what happened."

Noah resumes his place on the hearth, but he is taut as a piano wire. "You only made one backtrack in time, Lee. How did you get Raven out of Dane's house, and what's the deal with Jack Abernathy's kid?"

"Noah, did you ever read that science fiction story by Ray Bradbury titled 'A Sound of Thunder?' It is about some men who went back in time to hunt a dinosaur."

"Oh, Lee. Please! Not with the stories again."

"Patience, Son. This is a short one. The men went back to the past to 'hunt' a Tyrannosaurus Rex that was already destined to be killed by a falling tree. They were instructed to stay on the path so as not to disturb the surroundings and cause catastrophic changes in the present. When the dinosaur appeared, one of the men became scared and stepped off the path. It was just one step, and he quickly righted himself, returning to the path without incident. It was not until he returned to the present that he realized the implications of his actions. Everything had changed; people, buildings, events, and even language was different. 'I only stepped off into the mud,' he said. But, alas. Looking at his shoe, he saw a tiny butterfly crushed in the sole. The death of that one creature had a ripple effect on time, and nothing was ever again the same."

"So, did you step on a butterfly?" Noah asks.

"Of sorts," Lee replies. "If you recall, our objective was to stop Darryl Kiley from finding a psychic Native American to use as an outlaw or a beacon. That was the only way we could keep him from using a tracker to tamper with the past to raise him to the political status he needed to become the next President."

"Did you kill him?" Noah asks, cocking his eyebrows up.

"No. I scared him. He killed himself."

"Whoa! And…"

"And that was the butterfly. It set in motion the events that bring us to here and now."

"Still lost, Buddy. Help me out."

Lee smiles at Noah indulgently. "Apparently, Darryl Kiley engineered the fire at Police Chief Abernathy's residence, and with Kiley gone, the house never burned …"

"… and four-year-old Andy Abernathy never died!"

"Exactly," Lee says, "ripple number one."

"Then Raven never revealed her automatic heiro-scripting powers by painting the portrait of Mrs. Abernathy and the spirit of her son, Andy."

"Ripple number two. Keep going."

Noah's legs bounce up and down. He shifts sideways on the brick seat, eyes wide as he stares Lee in the face.

"So, you and Dane didn't go to her house to interview her and evaluate her psychic gift?"

"No. As far as anyone knows, today is the first time any of

us have ever met Raven. That includes you, Noah. You have never met her. Do not forget that! See how the ripple grows? We cannot risk causing the butterfly effect."

"This is wild," Noah says. He slumps back against the fireplace, staring at the ceiling.

Noah's excitement is infectious, and Lee laughs at the boy's happiness, clapping him on the knee with his leathery hand. He glances at Dane and Raven talking with Shinehah. Graham is lurking nearby the couple, his eyes on the younger woman. *Good*, Lee thinks. *Graham and Shine will make a fine match.*

"Lee," Noah says, leaning forward again, "I'm still confused. What about the fire at Dane's house? What about my … my father, John Silver Eyes?"

"That fire still happened. I did not see it begin, so I can only speculate as to what really occurred. I believe Dane did, indeed, fall asleep on the sofa—by himself, this time. But judging from the fact that Dane has just come from Andy's baptism at the Mormon church, I am fairly certain that he did not drink any wine, so he was not as impaired as he was when the event took place two years ago as you and I—and only you and I—remember it."

"O.K. I get that. Another ripple. How'd the fire start?"

"Not Raven's cigarette, this time. It was your … um … the Outlaw, I suppose. But Dane was able to get to safety before the fire completely consumed his house."

"Makes sense. What about the Outlaw? He was still there outside, waiting to kill Dane, wasn't he? I saw him—spoke to him when I backtracked to that night," Noah says.

For the first time, Lee shows some discomfort. *How do I tell him what I did—how I lured his father into the house to die?* He looks long and hard at the boy he loves like his own son, and then he does something he has never done before. He lies to him.

"I do not know, Noah. We will have to find out from Dane," Lee says avoiding Noah's eager gaze. "He is, after all, a deputy fire marshal, and I am sure he tracked the arson's origin."

Noah stares at the floor for a long time before he speaks again. "If John Silver Eyes is still alive, we'll have to …"

"No. We will not. If John Silver Eyes is still alive, we will find him and keep track of his activities, so he can never backtrack again." Lee is emphatic.

"What about my mother?"

Lee's heart constricts to see the agony in the young man's eyes. He gently places his hand on Noah's shoulder. "Your mother will never be bothered by him again, Noah. I promise."

"Hey, Hona! Why so serious?" Dane says.

Lee and Noah jump up, startled that Dane has gotten so close to them during this touchy conversation. They are keenly aware of the importance of shielding Dane from this business. *The worst part of keeping a secret is not telling those you love.* Noah Lightfoot and Liahona Thistleseed are the only persons in the world who know of the science fiction story that has played out in the past few days, and that's the way it must stay. *No more ripples*, Lee decides.

"I think it is very serious that you have kept this beautiful lady from us," Lee says. He grins and claps Dane on the back. Snaking an arm around Raven, he gives her a fatherly kiss on the cheek, and then saunters toward the kitchen to mingle with the rest of his family.

"Hona, wait up," calls Dane. Turning to Noah, he grins. "Take care of my woman for a few minutes, little bro. I've got to talk to Lee. Back in a bit, Babe." He leans over and nuzzles Raven, and then hurries after Lee, leaving Noah alone to "get acquainted" with his future sister-in-law.

Raven stands eye to eye with Noah. She is close enough for him to catch a whiff of her signature vanilla-scented perfume, *De Vanille*. He knows it well; indeed, he knows her well. In another reality, just a few days earlier, he was her friend and—almost—her lover. His gut cramps from the memory.

She smiles brilliantly. "Well, Noah. I guess we'll soon be seeing a lot of each other."

"Yeah. Guess so." His attempt at being nonchalant falls short. His hands tremble.

Sensing his nervousness, she makes small talk. "Dane says you're a freshman at F.S.U., and you're 'Chief Osceola' for the football games."

"Go 'Noles' and all that," he says, nodding.

"That's pretty exciting, I bet. What's your major?"

"At this point, I'm just majoring in Renegade, the mascot horse." He laughs slightly.

"What's your gift?" she asks.

Startled at the bluntness of her question, he just stares at her with his mouth hanging open.

"Come on," she says, "Dane's explained all about the Team and how you all have one or more psychic gifts. So, what's yours?"

"Um, it's remote viewing—seeing things that happen far away from where I am. Lee's a remote viewer, too, but his powers manifest differently. I've also got a photographic memory."

"Now that's really neat. How's that work?"

Staring directly into her face, he can't help but show off. "You came in behind Dane. He reached around your back and nudged you forward. Your moccasin caught on the edge of the threshold for an instant, and you looked down to make sure you weren't going to trip. Dane's hand slid to your waist. You reached up and pushed at your bangs, poking your hair behind your ears, and then shook it loose. You bit down on your lower lip, licked at the corner of your mouth, clenched your right fist, and then smiled. Want me to go on?"

Her mouth comes open while he talks. It hangs slack for a moment, and then she lifts the corners into the most radiant smile he has ever seen. It reaches all the way to the corners of her sienna-colored eyes. "You are the bomb!" she exclaims.

"That I am," he confirms. "You look a little thirsty, almost-sister. Let's get you a Diet Coke from the fridge."

Her smile falters a bit. "How'd you know I like to drink Diet Coke?" she asks.

"I must be psychic!" He winks, and then he leads her through the crowded family room.

On the way to the kitchen, they notice Dane and Lee outside on the patio, locked in what looks to be a serious conversation. Dane is pacing and pinching the bridge of his nose, something he does when he detects a smell. He is a clairscent, with psychic sensitivities centered around a heightened sense of smell, and the odors he picked up in the wee hours of the morning have resurfaced. He cocks his head from side to side as if searching for the origin.

"It was a weird smell, Lee. Fruity and floral mixed with pungent and nasty. I even tasted it! Yech. Couldn't get enough water to drink afterwards," he tells his mentor.

"When we finish dinner, we'll try to get away and track it," Lee says.

"Gotta be later on. I've got plans with Raven, if you know what I mean."

"Indeed," Lee says, pulling his mouth up in his well- known half grin.

"Mind in the gutter, Hona! Not what you think. I'm evaluating her psychic gifts, not her physical ones. She looks to be a type of automatic writer, only she manifests with pictures instead of text. Pretty cool, if you ask me. She'll be a tremendous asset to the team."

"I have no doubt. A portrait clairvoyant. Is she amenable to training?"

"She says she is. I want you to do it, though. I'm too close to be objective."

"I will be happy to train her. It will be my honor." Lee opens the patio door and steps into the breakfast room.

"Good deal, then, Hona." Dane twitches his nose and sniffs the air deeply.

"The scent again?" Lee's eyebrow lifts as he turns to look at Dane.

"Yeah. It's really strong, too." He takes another deep breath, holds it, and then he exhales. "Yep. That's exactly what I thought. Pot roast!"

Coming up behind Lee, Wren pokes him in the side. "Pot roast, it is. And it's ready to be served. Shop talk later. Come on to the dining room, and grab your sweetheart, Dane, before your brother charms her away from you. I don't know about you, but I'm hungry. Let's all get ready to eat." She hugs him fiercely before exiting the kitchen.

In the dining room, Dane catches Raven's eye and moves

over to where she and Noah are standing. Lee and Wren move to opposite ends of the large dining table. Graham, Shine, and Cyrus—the oldest son—are to their right, Raven and the Lightfoot brothers assemble on the left. The six other Thistleseed children gather in the doorway between the dining room and the foyer. The room is full of friends and family and much love. Lee takes Wren's hand in his and signals for the children to begin the blessing song from the LDS Primary Song Book that always precedes their meals.

Shine and the five girls begin.

"Thank you, dear Lord, for the things we may need,
So we may serve you in word and by deed,
Let us be faithful in work and in play.
Thank you, Father, for blessing this day."

Lee and Wren sing the second verse.

"Thank you, dear Lord, for the wisdom and might
To teach our children to choose what is right.
Let us be role models—husbands and wives.
Thank you, Father, for blessing our lives."

The three boys—no slackers in the vocal department—finish the song with the last verse.

"Thank you, dear Lord, for our good daily bread.
We know that it is by Your hand we're fed.
Let us be humble and show gratitude.
Thank you, Father, for blessing our food."

At the end of the song, the family and all the guests say, "Amen." The six younger Thistleseeds retire to the card tables in the family room set up especially for them, with Bill and Selah acting as the "adult" table heads. The "over 21" adults sit down at the huge dining room table. In minutes, the entire household can be heard eating and praising Wren's outstanding Southern feast: fork tender pot roast basted in its own juices for hours in the oven, mashed Yukon potatoes whipped with sweet cream butter and sour cream, brown gravy made with a roux from the pot roast juices, fresh field peas and green bean snaps flavored with bacon drippings, buttered corn on the cob, fluffy cat head biscuits, and juicy peach cobbler with heavy cream.

CHAPTER TWO
<u>SCENTS OF LOSS</u>

PROPPED UP AGAINST THE PILLOWS on Dane's bed and still full after eating dinner, Raven yawns for the fourth time. She stretches her arms over her head and rolls to her stomach, lifts up on her elbows, and puts her chin in her hands. Dane stands at the mirror brushing his long black hair. She smiles at the irony this simple act brings. *What a gender reversal we are—long-haired man; short-haired woman.* A slight giggle escapes her lips.

Dane turns to look at her. "What?" he asks.

"Nothing," she says, "just watching you."

"Am I that entertaining?"

"Sometimes."

He puts down the brush and hops onto the bed with her.

"So, what did you think of my extended family?" he asks.

"They're great. I especially love the way all those kids help each other out."

"That's how it is in a big family. I call it 'the trickle-down' method of child-rearing."

"Explain, please," she says, rolling to her back with her hands behind her head. She kicks off her moccasins, rubs her feet together and flexes her toes. She yawns again.

"The 'trickle-down' method—as invented by Mr. Dane Lightfoot. Listen carefully, and learn, my dear. Cy and Shine Thistleseed were the firstborn twins. They were the guinea pigs. They got all the brand-new clothes, wore the cloth diapers, and received the closest supervision. Four years later, here come Bill and Selah. Fortunately, they were the second set of boy/girl twins. The clothing trickled down to them, they wore clean—albeit secondhand—diapers, and they had a little less supervision. After all, now Lee and Wren have four children under the age of five."

"Go on," Raven says.

"Another four years pass, and Lee hangs his pants on the headboard again."

"What's that mean?"

"They joke that every time Lee hangs his pants on the headboard, Wren gets pregnant."

Raven laughs, with an unpretentious Julia Roberts "Pretty Woman" kind of joy. Dane's heart jumps in his chest. *Thank you, God, for this woman!*

"Anyway," he continues, "Wren hits another double, but this time—two girls. Debby and Zorah emerge on the scene, and things get really interesting. Trickle down the clothing, but make some adjustments to the boy stuff, you know. Forget the cloth diapers. Now it's time for the disposable ones. And as for supervision, well, some of that trickled down to Cy and Shine from the folks. You need help when you have six kids! But then, four more years later, Wren finally gets a single. Kenny is the *man*. And by that, I mean he's the seventh child of the seventh son—destined to be the one with second sight like his dad. So, he gets the trickled down boy clothing—minus adjustments—*plus* the girl stuff—with adjustments, of course. Supervision falls to Cy, Shine, Bill, and Selah 'cause Wren's really got her hands full now. But it's all good. And they just keep on trickling down from the oldest to the youngest. Not a bad system, if you ask me. And then, just when it seems that the Thistleseed household is finished with babies— surprise! Shelly arrives, and *everything* trickles down to her! Pretty neat theory, huh?"

Dane looks at Raven for confirmation of his genius, and she

snores—sound asleep. He folds half the bedspread over her legs, kisses her forehead, and goes into the living room, quietly shutting the bedroom door behind him. Plopping down on the couch, he flicks on the television to catch whatever team is happening to play football this afternoon. After a few minutes, his eyes close, and he is also snoring.

*   *   *

The woman studied herself in the mirror. Her hair was perfectly styled and highlighted, her makeup impeccable, her eyes much, much too dilated. She tilted her head, first to one side, then the other. On her dressing table was a vast array of beauty products, expensive satin-lined cases, and crystal bottles. She reached forward and touched the shiny crystal containers that held her perfumes. They sparkled like diamonds, sending off showers of colors that she didn't know existed. She pursed her glossed lips in an "oo" shape, approving of the high color in her cheeks and across her forehead.

For a moment, she looked confused. A tall glass of red wine beckoned her, and she drained it in four swallows before refilling it from the adjacent decanter. She drained that glass just as quickly, and then refilled her glass again. Delicately touching her tongue to each side of her mouth, she studied her lipstick, pleased that there was no smudging.

She shifted her position on the silk-covered stool and was surprised to hear a tinkling sound. At her feet she observed no less than three empty wine bottles. *Curious, but they do make such a lovely sound.* She nudged them against each other again, giggling at the pretty music they made, and then she slipped the alpaca cardigan off her shoulders, letting it lie where it fell beside her stool.

The rainbow lights on the table caught her attention again. She selected a lavender globe-shaped *Lavande* bottle with a jeweled bulb—her most recent favorite. Looking in the mirror, she watched herself grip the bulb and squeeze. The fine mist of fragrance hovered in front of the atomizer in slow motion. She was fascinated with the journey the droplets made from the bottle to her neck. She inhaled deeply, and some of the mist entered her airway, coating her tongue with a bitterness she found unpleasant, so she drank from the wine glass again. *Better ... much, much better,* she thought dreamily. She dropped the wine glass onto the floor. *Oops!*

She squeezed the bulb again, and again, and again, until her hair was damp, and her makeup ran in rivulets down her cheeks. The crystal perfume bottle fell from her grip and broke when it contacted the pile of wine bottles at her feet. *Pretty music,* she thought. She drank directly from the Baccarat decanter until it was empty, then she tipped it over the edge of the table. She clapped her hands at the sound.

Reaching forward, she pulled all the perfume and makeup bottles off the table and let them crash to the floor. The cacophony of sound made her laugh so hard she slipped off the stool, landing on her back atop the shards. Her bare back was deeply lacerated from shoulders to hips, perfume seeping into the wounds. The delicate fragrances combined into a mélange of odors mingled with the coppery aroma of blood. *I don't like this smell.* She moaned. *I don't like it. Don't ... like ...* She whimpered, and then she was still.

*   *   *

"Dane!" Raven shouts, standing over her moaning fiancé on the couch. His eyes are closed tightly, and his hands are clamped over his nose.

"I ... don't ... like ... this ... smell," he says.

She kneels at his head and pats his shoulder. "Wake up, honey. Wake up."

He twitches violently. Raven gently pulls his hands from his nose. He takes a breath and cries out as the malodorous scent fills his sinuses. He pushes his fists against his eye sockets, moaning and rolling face first to the floor. He crawls a few feet, panting like a dog, Raven knee-walking behind him.

"Dane. What's wrong? Is it a dream? A vision? What do I do?" She is frantic.

"Hona." He gasps. "Please ... call ... call ... Hona. Ohh! I ... need ... a ... light. Oh, my guuungh."

Raven snatches the phone from its cradle and begins punching in the number for the Thistleseed house. Selah answers on the third ring.

"Get your dad! Your dad! Something's wrong with Dane. Hurry, please!" Raven cries. In the background, she can hear Selah screaming for her father, then heavy footfalls as Lee Thistleseed runs to the phone.

"Raven. Is he conscious?" Lee asks.

"Yes, but he's … no, I don't know. He said to call you. Please, please help him."

"Keep him talking. Don't let him drift off to sleep. I'll be right there," Lee says, and then he turns and shouts to Wren, who is now at the doorway. "Call Noah! Call him now, little bird. Send him to Dane's."

Lee runs to his car without bothering to put on shoes. He knows what has happened. Dane picked up a scent track without a beacon present, and that's one of the most dangerous things that a Tracker can ever do. It will take both he and Noah to bring Dane back to himself. Timing is critical, so Lee speeds through the streets, hoping to avoid traffic cops. He does not intend to lose Dane again.

As Lee pulls into Dane's driveway, Noah screeches to a halt behind him and jumps out of the red mustang. They don't speak; they don't knock. They burst into the house and find Dane keening on the floor with Raven stroking his hair, rapidly murmuring into his ear.

"Do it, do it," Lee says to Noah.

They both drop to the floor. Lee pushes Raven out of the way and wraps his arms around Dane. Noah slides up against the couch, closes his eyes, and is soon breathing deeply. Lee rocks Dane like a mother holding her child, cooing softly and looking intently at Noah to make sure the young man is in his trance. In Lee's iron embrace, Dane moans, slowly moving his head from side to side. Wet spots appear at Lee's eyes and beneath his nose. *Please, please, God. Let us be in time.*

Dane's movements slow down, and he relaxes, slumping lower to the floor. A few moments later he takes a deep breath, and then lets it out in a shuddering stream. In a voice that is just barely audible, Dane speaks one short little word, "Home," and then he lies still.

"Is he … is he dead?" Raven says. Tears stream from her wide eyes.

"No, he's just sleeping now," Noah says. "He'll be O.K. Just needs rest."

Lee loosens his hold on the sleeping man, grabs a pillow from the sofa, and puts it beneath Dane's head. Reaching into a nearby basket, he pulls a chenille afghan out and covers him. Rising, his knees make popping sounds that draw Noah's attention. Lee shrugs.

The two men sit on the couch, but Raven stays on the floor at Dane's side.

"What happened?" she asks.

"Raven, I hate that you witnessed this, but in a way, it's good that you did. Your training will include ways to avoid 'getting lost' like Dane did today," Lee says.

"Getting lost?"

"Yeah. That's what happens when you track by yourself. Your mind gets lost in darkness while your body is left behind. The first rule of tracking. Never track without a beacon," Noah says. "Lee has the mortality margin fixed at 50 minutes."

"I'm sorry. I really don't understand the beacon part and the mortality margin. What do you mean?" she says.

"The most important person in a psychic track is the beacon," Lee says. "Your beacon is the silver cord that keeps your mind and body connected. When you are journeying in your mind, you must have a lighthouse—a beacon—to get you home, or you will die."

Raven pales visibly. "Die?"

"Uh huh. And that's why you heard Dane say the word 'home' just before he relaxed. He was asking me to bring him home," Noah says.

"But surely Dane knows that. Why would he do such a dangerous thing?" Raven asks.

"Dane is unique," Lee says. "Sometimes the scents find

him before he can search for them. It leaves him very vulnerable to exactly what you saw today. He carries a pager in his pocket for these occurrences. We all do."

At that moment, they hear a rhythmic high-pitched sound coming from the bedroom. Noah holds his own pager in the air.

"I think I found his beeper," he says, looking at Raven.

She blushes slightly but offers no explanation.

Lee leans forward. "Raven," he says, "if you love him as you seem to, it is imperative that you safeguard him. You will be his lifeline. I am sorry to put such responsibility on you, but you will be with Dane more than any of the rest of us. Can I count on you?"

Raven looks at him unwaveringly. "I will never, ever allow anything to happen to Dane."

"Good deal! I'll let you marry him, then." Noah says, laughing at Raven's expression.

Lee shakes his head and rolls his eyes. *How I love these boys*, he thinks. Getting to his feet, he pats Dane carefully on the back, and then heads for the door. Noah follows him.

"Hey, wait. What do I do now?" Raven asks.

"Watch T.V. He'll be out for a while," Noah says. "And when he wakes up, he's gonna be really hungry. If you can't cook— and I know that you can't—better order *Domino's Pizza*."

Where are you going?" Raven asks.

Noah yawns. "Home to finish my nap. These two o'clock meals really do me in."

"What did you say?" she asks, but the door is already closing. *Weird. I swear I've heard him say that before. This Déjà vu is starting to get to me.* Then, taking a place on the couch, she turns up the volume to cover the sound of the snoring from the floor and scans the phone book for the pizza delivery number.

THE TRACKERS TEAM: TRILOGY 1 | 167

CHAPTER THREE
TRAINING

"NO, RAVEN. THE WORD YOU USE to call your beacon is 'home.' You do not say, 'get me outta here' followed by an expletive," Lee says, his brows drawn down to his eyes.

On the couch, Noah, Graham, and Dane convulse with laughter. Raven glares at them, and they shut up—briefly. She twists her mouth into a scowl as she scans the scribbled paper in front of her. Putting down her pencil, she leans back and sighs.

"This is not as easy as I thought it would be," she says.

"Nobody said it would be easy, but I have faith in you, Babe," Dane says. "Just remember, the word is not ..."

"*BLEEP,*" the couch brigade says in unison.

The room erupts in a fresh round of laughter, including Lee who has tried valiantly up to this point to remain objective and neutral. Raven balls up the paper and hurls it at the couch, and then she gives up and joins in the frivolity. After a few minutes of playful teasing, Lee stands and stretches, drains his glass of iced tea, and addresses the young men.

"All right, gentlemen. We have had enough of fun time. Which of you can be serious enough to beacon this time?"

"I'm good to go," Graham says. "I only laughed a little."

His eyes behind the wire-rimmed glasses look innocent, but his tightly pressed mouth gives him away.

Lee surveys the assemblage of male Trackers. "Noah," he says. "You stay. Dane and Graham. You two take a ride to town and bring us back some lunch." When nobody moves, Lee sighs heavily. "My treat."

That sets them all in motion. Noah takes his place at the table. Dane takes the money Lee offers. *Typical.* Graham grabs his jacket and saunters out the door to get the car. The wind catches the door and blows it open wider, filling the room with a decidedly chilly feeling for the first week of October. Lee shivers, catching the door to keep it from hitting the wall. *It is going to be a cold winter,* he observes. And for some reason, it bothers him. He looks back to see Raven gathering the afghan from the basket. She wraps it around her shoulders and returns to her seat. Noah watches her with unguarded eyes. *He is remembering his time with her.* Lee frowns slightly. *We will have to talk about this later—alone, and someday, I will have to tell him about his father's death.* He shakes the dread away and puts a smile on his face.

"All right, you two. Shall we begin again?" Lee says.

Raven tilts her head back and stares at the ceiling, dropping her jaw and sticking out her tongue. "Bleah! Let's do it. I don't know why this is so hard for me, Lee."

Lee sympathizes with her and gives her some more pointers. "It has only been three days, Raven. Training takes a while. You have done well so far."

"I'm doing terrible! I can draw so much better than this. Really, I can."

Noah laughs at her frustration. This is quite different from the confident young woman he brings to mind from just several days ago. *Back then, she was on equal, if not better, footing with the rest of us. Her sketches were spot on, with details so minute they had to be enlarged with a makeshift magnifier made from a juice glass. And her beaconing powers were ...* He stops, and his eidetic memory kicks in, and he remembers. *Her beaconing powers were so good they were used against the Team by the Outlaw, John Silver Eyes.*

*   *   *

Noah had just regained consciousness after being drugged with ether. He struggled to orient himself—to recall where he was and what he had been doing. He remembered. He had been in the middle of beaconing for Lee's track when it happened. Lee was backtracking to find Darryl Kiley, the man who was using a Native American tracker to boost himself to Presidential candidacy. *No, not to find him ... to kill him.* Suddenly he had lost contact with Lee. *Lee!* Noah realized he left him tracking alone, without a beacon. In 50 minutes, Lee would die, if he were not dead already. Noah knew where he was now. He was in the Outlaw's house. The Outlaw was John Silver, Governor Kiley's associate. *Personal thug was more like it.* The man had been watching him. When Noah came to the first time—after the guy coldcocked him—and tried to attack the man, he was put out again with the ether. His head was pounding, but he knew he would have to send a beacon signal without the Outlaw noticing. Noah closed his eyes and prepared to give the signal.

The sound of the doorbell renewed the ache in his head, but it also gave him the opportunity to beacon for Lee without being detected by the Outlaw. He heard the man arguing with someone. The Beacon. Noah knew the voice. It was Raven, and it broke his heart. He sent the signal, hoping Lee would find it and come home.

Raven rushed over and sat beside Noah. He feigned unconsciousness, drawing on all his reserves not to move away from her. He was so angry. *Why would she do this?* She had been a member of the Trackers Team for three years—since before Dane was killed in the house fire. He remained very still and listened to the heated conversation she had with the Outlaw.

"If you harm him, I will kill you, John Silver." She snarled, her eyes narrowed to slits.

"Harm him? Never. He is my son," the Outlaw said. His nostrils flared as he met her glare.

The word evoked confusion in Noah. *Son?*

"Noah is my son—my seventh son, to be precise. Twenty years ago, I fell in love with his mother and seduced her. She spurned me because of a dream. She said she was told to take my son and raise him as a Seminole ..." Silver Eyes said.

What? I'm NOT a Seminole? Noah wondered.

"... and that dream robbed me of my gifted son and his irreplaceable mother. I will track back and enter Fawn's dream and give her instructions to marry me instead," Silver Eyes said.

"Then you would become his father," Raven said.

"I AM his father," he said.

My father? This man is my father? The Outlaw? Noah moaned, barely audible.

"What about Dane?" Raven asked.

The Outlaw spat air. "Bah, why waste your heart on Dane when Noah is the superior man? As the son of an up-and-coming political genius, he will have tremendous wealth and power. However, if you have no interest, I can arrange it so Noah will despise you ..."

As if I ever would or even could, Noah thought with a pain in his heart.

"No. Take your trip. I don't wish to lose Noah like I lost Dane," Raven said.

Noah's heart broke as he put the pieces together. Raven and Dane, his mother and John Silver Eyes. Thereafter, the events occurred rather quickly. The Outlaw prepared to backtrack, and Raven used Noah's own Bowie knife to stab the man, killing him instantly. She cut Noah's bindings and put the knife in his hand, and then rolled the body of his father next to him to make it look like Noah had killed the man. Before she left, she whispered in his ear. Noah remembered the smell of her cologne mixed with the metallic odor of blood and death, and it repulsed him.

"Oh, Noah," she said. "You are so much like them both. Thank goodness you will never be as your father. But, sadly, you can never be your brother, either."

After that, he had called the police. When Jack Abernathy arrived, he did not recognize Noah because his memory had been erased from one of the Outlaw's earlier backtracks. Governor Kiley had been there, too, after hearing his associate's address over the police scanner. Kiley had bribed Abernathy to let Noah go, calling the death an accident, insinuating that Mr. Silver tripped and fell on a large kitchen knife. *Sure. That oughta fly.* But, evidently, Jack bought it because Noah was released without even having to be questioned at police headquarters.

Noah's first order of business was to make sure Lee had found the tracking beacon. With that assurance, he next visited Maria Ramirez. *Oooh. Don't have the energy to think about Maria right now.* Noah winced, the ache in his heart yet fresh from the thought of her. Then he summoned up the next thing that happened in the sequence of events. He confronted Raven at her apartment. She told him that the Outlaw had her on a short leash after threatening to harm her mother in Arizona. She also told him that John Silver Eyes was a shape shifter who could appear as a hologram in the past, and he used that ability to lure people into dangerous situations.

"He killed Dane?" Noah asked.

"No. I killed Dane," Raven said. "I caused the fire that killed Dane. We had dinner, and I brought some wine. Dane didn't want any, but I insisted. You knew Dane quit smoking?"

"I guess so. That's why I was surprised he fell asleep smoking," Noah said.

"He didn't. I did. We were sitting on the couch discussing wedding plans. The wine made us sleepy, and I was smoking. My cigarette touched off the rug. The next thing I knew, I was outside on the ground … safe, and Dane was inside the house … burning."

Raven told him how and why John Silver Eyes had been at the house to kill Dane.

"When Dane was ten, just a little boy, he saw a man put a rattlesnake beneath a blanket in his father's *chickee.* The man had silver eyes. When his father returned to the hut, the rattlesnake struck him. Dane saw his father die. He said John Silver Eyes gave him 'the evil eye.' Dane realized the man he interviewed almost twenty years later was the same man that killed his father, and he was sure the man remembered him, too."

Funny how things get so mixed up, Noah observed. When he backtracked to Dane's house later that evening, he ended up at that very time she spoke of. He saw John Silver outside Dane's house, watching as the fire threatened to burn the two people inside. Seeing Noah, the man had begun chanting in the Muskogee language to ward him off, as if he were an evil spirit.

"John Silver Eyes. Save them. You have to get them out or they'll die," Noah said.

The man continued to chant, backing away from Noah, clutching at the bushes in fear.

"Get them out. Please. Father. Do it for me. Let me remember you as someone who once had love in his heart ... for my mother ... for me ... for your son," Noah begged.

Noah watched as John rushed into the burning building and returned, carrying Dane over his shoulder. When he went back in to save Raven, the house exploded. Noah would never forget the way his father looked at him just before he entered the house.

"Noah?" John Silver Eyes said.

* * *

"Noah?" Lee says. He places his hand on Noah's shoulder and shakes him slightly.

"Earth to Noah," Raven says, meaning to make a joke, but uncomfortable all the same.

Noah's eyes are misted over from dredging up those memories. Aware that his friends are watching him, he gives an exaggerated yawn and rubs his eyes.

"Well, are we gonna do this thing or not?" he asks.

"Where were you?" asks Raven.

"I was in the land of boredom," Noah yawns. "Food here yet? I'm starving."

"Welcome back, Son. We have missed you," Lee says sardonically. "And, no. The food has not arrived. Be patient."

"It's drive-through. They should be back by now. I'm starving," Noah says.

Always starving, Lee observes. "I have an idea. Let us change things up a bit. Noah, you can track, and we can work on Raven's beaconing skills..." Lee begins.

"NO!" Noah shouts. "Let's don't. I … um … I've got to see a man about a dog first."

"What dog?" Raven asks.

Lee shakes his head, drawing the corners of his mouth down sharply.

"Sorry," Noah whispers as he gets up quickly from the chair. He shrugs his shoulders and leans in a little closer to her. "That means I've got to pee." He tiptoes out of the room.

Raven opens her mouth to comment, but finds she has nothing to say. Fortunately, mere moments later, the door swings open. Dane and Graham enter, holding a huge bucket of Kentucky Fried Chicken.

"Braaaackk, pluck, pluck, pluck, pluck." Graham clucks like a chicken. "Dinner is served."

They clear off the table and set the bucket in the center, laying out napkins to serve as plates. Noah returns from the bathroom and grabs a drumstick, cramming it into his mouth.

"Stop!" Dane says. "Bless it first, little bro."

Noah withdraws a partially denuded chicken leg. Bowing his head and looking properly chastised, he looks at the others, waiting for them to bow their heads, too.

"Bless the food on this table … and all that is within. Amen," he says through a mouthful of chicken. Then, laughing, he polishes off the remainder of the leg and reaches in for more.

"So, how'd it go this time?" Dane asks.

"We didn't get anything done. Your little brother had to 'see a man about a dog' first," Raven says.

Chicken spews from several mouths at once as all the men—including Lee—laugh.

Noah lifts his hands in resignation. "A man's gotta do what a man's gotta do."

"That may be, but a man does not need to tell a lady about it," Lee says.

"I'm sorry, Hona. The boy's got no couth. What can I say?" Dane says. He nudges Raven in the side. "Now what were you saying about how you liked my family?"

"I love your family. I do. I really do," she says. "I can't wait to meet your mother."

"She's a keeper. Hey, Noah. When's the last time you saw Mom?" Dane says.

"Before school started. I dunno. Like two months, maybe. It was back in the summer, just after Hurricane Andrew hit down south. I tried to get Mom to leave, but she wouldn't budge and come away from the village."

"That's Mom. Good thing we didn't inherit that stubborn gene of hers."

"Oh, that's for sure. Like it's not the main substance in our blood, bro."

This draws laughter from everyone in the room. It's a well-known fact both the Lightfoot boys are the epitome of mule-headed stubbornness.

"We're going down in a few days. Want to come along?"

"Can't. Got football games, you know, every weekend. When's the wedding planned, by the way?"

Raven and Dane exchange looks. "We were thinking around Thanksgiving," she says.

More spewed chicken. Noah wipes his mouth, figuring up the time frame. "Wow. Short engagement. Well, O.K. Can you do me a favor, though. Don't have it on a Saturday. I really don't want to be the best man in my Chief Osceola getup."

"Who said you were the best man?" Dane quips, receiving a shocked look from his bother. "Nah, don't worry. You will always be my best man, little bro."

"O.K. I've had enough. Who's going to *bleep* for me?" Raven asks.

"I seem to be the only one not still wolfing down the Colonel's finest finger-lickin' chicken, so I will beacon again for you," Lee says smiling. "Men, please try to eat quietly."

Graham and Dane move back to the couch. Noah grabs the bucket of chicken and squeezes in beside them. Though the atmosphere is jovial, they know better than to interrupt a track. All three of them will be sitting on the ready in case something goes wrong. They are the sentries—the watchdogs. Any one of them will jump in and beacon at the slightest hint of trouble. They continue eating, all the while keeping an eye on Lee and Raven as she begins her track.

Her breathing slows, and her chest makes the steady rise and fall they know so well as the body giving way to the mind. Behind her eyelids, the jerky REM movements are very apparent. She takes one short intake of breath, and then her hand starts moving on the table. Clutching a pencil between her fingers, she rapidly sketches on a large piece of blank paper. The three men on the couch lean forward, mesmerized with the phenomenon of automatic portrait clairvoyance—a gift none of them possesses. Her movements are hesitant at first, and then grow more confident.

This time, she's gonna do it! Noah thinks. He is anxious to see what she draws.

Raven's hand moves like a scampering mouse over the paper. She outlines, she adds shading, she stabs at the paper with the point, wearing the pencil down to the wood. Even when the point is completely gone, she continues. Dane quickly, but carefully, pulls the pencil from her grasp and pushes a sharpened one between her fingers. Her hand seems to have its own mind as it travels around the paper. She draws in the middle and all around the sides, the images overlapping, moving from one scene to another, covering the paper completely with graphite.

Suddenly, she stiffens. Her hand clenches around the pencil, and it snaps in half with a loud cracking sound.

"Get me, get me, HOME!" Raven hollers, causing all the seated men to jump back. Her eyes fly open, and she looks wildly around the room. "Yeeoooww!" she cries out. "In my back. Get it out! Get it out now!"

Dane leaps off the couch and grabs her shoulders, raising her t-shirt to look at her back. Seeing nothing there, he looks quizzically at the others and shrugs his shoulders.

"Babe…?" he says to her. But Raven pulls away from him and is staring at the drawing.

"Raven?" Lee says. "Are you all right?"

"I did this? I did this! Look. Look at it! I drew this. I saw it. I did!" Raven says.

She laughs like a child, holding the paper up for all to see as if it is a first-place ribbon.

Noah and Graham clap their hands, applauding her first successful track. Raven drops the paper on the table and dances around the room doing a stereotypical war dance, complete with "whoop, whoop, whoop" sound effects and palm to the mouth, much to the entertainment of her audience.

Lee spreads the paper out on the table to study. Dane joins him, still laughing at his adorable fiancé hopping in place.

The paper is a mass of images from various points of view. A table, a mirrored image of a woman with black streaks below her eyes, a hand holding a goblet. Bottles of different shapes and sizes dominate the drawing. Some are upright, but others are on their sides, with liquid spilling from them. More are broken, shattered, piled up on the floor.

One large bottle fills the center of the page. The word *Lavande* is etched into the base of the bottle. It is globe-shaped with a jeweled bulb atomizer, and a fine mist fans out from its tip.

"Dear God," Dane whispers, just before his knees buckle.

CHAPTER FOUR
AGONY AND ESCSTACY

"KEEP LOOKING, JACK," LEE SAYS into the phone as he paces in a tight circle. "She would have been roughly in her late-thirties or early-forties. Blonde. Found amid a pile of broken wine bottles, perfumes, and cosmetics." He listens for a moment. "Yes. Dane scented her yesterday. One of our team has drawn the scene." Another moment. "Yes. That is correct. We have an artist now. Will you call me immediately if you find something? Thank you."

Raven's mood is decidedly subdued from her earlier excitement. She did, indeed, draw a crime scene, but she failed to realize at the time that the scene was one of death. Dane sits with his arm around her, squeezing her shoulder. At the table, Noah and Graham examine the drawing, hoping to find more clues about the incident and the woman involved.

"Jack will notify us should he discover anything, but he seems pretty sure that nothing of this nature has happened here," Lee says. His pacing slows, and the circle widens.

"Say it," Noah prompts.

Lee stops with his back to them. He turns slowly and regards the young man.

"O.K., I'll say it," Noah says. "She's not anywhere around

here. So, let's find her. I'll go see what I can see."

"I'll light," Graham says.

Sitting in chairs opposite each other with their arms resting on the small maple tabletop, Noah and Graham close their eyes and begin breathing slowly and deeply in sync. They make no other movements and would seem to the uninformed observer to be napping. Raven is rapt with attention. Her eyes flick from one to the other. Dane nudges her, and she sucks in a quick mouthful of air, surprised to realize she has been holding her breath. She takes his hand and squeezes it while she stares at the Trackers before her.

Noah is the first to move. His jaw twitches ever so slightly as he whispers the word, "Home." Then, he opens his eyes. Less than a second later, Graham opens his own eyes, and they stare at one another. Noah grins and winks, making Graham break into a smile. Noah rotates his shoulders and becomes serious. Looking at a spot somewhere over Graham's left shoulder, he begins to relate his journey.

"It's her bedroom. Walls are painted mauve with white crown molding, white baseboards. Curtains are brocade with gold braided tiebacks. Immaculate. Could pass the white glove test. Except for that dressing table. What a mess. Furniture is glossy white French Provincial with pink inserts and gold handles. The stool is covered with silk. It's stained with a red liquid. Not blood. I'm guessing red wine from the looks of the bottles on the floor.

"There are at least three empties there, along with a bunch of perfume bottles—most of them broken, shattered. It looks like someone just swept everything off the table. Black smudges on the tabletop. Police dusted for fingerprints. Dusted the bottles, too. Blood on the glass all over the carpet. That must have been extremely painful, judging from the amount of blood and the large area covered by the stains. Doesn't look like a homicide, though. No struggle—just a mass of broken stuff around that table area.

"Can't tell how she died, unless she bled out from cuts inflicted by the glass shards. She must have just laid there, bleeding to death."

"Did you see anything written? Mail, diary, receipt?" Graham asks.

Noah cocks his head to the side and stares again at the wall. "I see that bottle with the word *Lavande* etched in it. Bunches of labels on the perfumes. *Diamant, Épice d'Asie, Eau de something, Chatoyant No. 2.* Wait. There is a little piece of paper on the floor near the wastebasket. Yes! A credit card receipt. And there's her name. It's—M-a-r..."

"Mary?" Dane asks.

"Marjorie. Marjorie A. Col ... I can't see the rest. Her name is ... her name *was* Marjorie. And she bought something in Tampa," Noah lets out a huff and sits back in his chair. "That's it, guys. That's all I saw. Marjorie from Tampa."

Dane hops up from his seat and hovers over the table, looking at the picture Raven drew. He pushes his long hair behind his ears as he bends closer. Wrinkling his nose, he sniffs.

"I think ...," he says. "I wonder if ..."

"What? What?" Noah asks.

"I've had two episodes involving scents that seem to be perfumes or something. I'm wondering if they're related," he says.

Graham edges closer to his friend. "What other episode, Dane?" he asks.

"Well, the day before I came to Lee's house, I had a dream where two kids died at a nightclub. And the smell was sickly sweet mixed with something pungent. I didn't mention it to you guys in all the excitement of showing off my girl. Maybe Jack can check on it. We can let him know now that the woman—Marjorie—was from Tampa. And in the meantime, I'll track that scent. Noah? How 'bout be my light?"

Lee nods and makes his way back to the telephone, while Noah settles against the chair. Dane takes a seat next to his brother at the table. In seconds, they are both breathing deeply. On the couch, Raven closes her eyes, focusing on the sound of the Lightfoot brothers as they track.

Graham watches Dane's head move slowly from side to side, up and down, and all around as he tracks, trying to trace the odors and smells that are constantly moving through the air. Like a bloodhound following a trail, Dane seems drawn by the scents. Finally, he sits still.

"Home," he whispers. But before he opens his eyes, he shouts, "Whoa!"

Graham nearly falls out of his chair. "What the … ?"

Noah's eyes fly open. They are not on his brother; they are on Raven. "Did you do that?" he asks her.

Raven looks aghast at the men, eyes wide. She bites her bottom lip and nods timidly.

Dane hops out of his chair and whirls around to face her. She cowers against the couch cushions. He rushes to her, leans down, and plants a sloppy kiss on her lips.

"That … was … *intense!*" he says.

Lee runs in from the other room to assess the commotion. Dane is laughing and whooping; Noah is staring at Raven with his chin on his chest; Graham is shaking his head in confusion.

"What has happened?" Lee asks.

Dane turns around with a smile from ear to ear. "Hona, you'll never believe it. My future bride just sent a nuclear bomb of a beacon!" He pulls Raven to her feet for a bear hug that takes her breath away.

Lee regards Raven, then Noah.

"That she did," Noah says with tight lips. "Brightest light I have ever seen. Congratulations Bird. You have officially passed your first beaconing session!"

"Well, before you all get too giddy on me, I need to let you know what Jack found out," Lee says. "There were two kids who died the other night at a local nightclub, just like you said, Dane. The police said they were both high on a drug called 'ecstasy' that compromised their systems."

"Does ecstasy have an odor?" Dane asks.

"Jack said it does not," Lee says.

"Then what did I smell?"

"Most likely, it was the combination of perfumes, lotions, and body odors from all the sweaty people dancing," Noah says.

"How did the kids die?" Raven asks.

"Now that is the perplexing part," Lee says. "According to Jack, they died of dehydration and heat exhaustion. Apparently, the drug inhibited their ability to sweat and cool themselves. When the medical examiner took their temperatures, they were so warm that they were feverish."

"What a horrible way to die," Raven says.

"Take ecstasy and die in agony," Noah says.

"What about Marjorie from Tampa?" Graham asks.

"Jack said he would check on that when he gets a chance, but since it is out of his jurisdiction, it is not going to be one of our cases; nevertheless, he will let the Tampa PD know that we are aware of the occurrence," Lee says.

Just then, Lee's pager sounds. He reads the display, and then he tucks it back on his belt. Sensing that he has stifled the mood, Lee shifts courses. "Well, I understand that there is a party happening tonight."

"A party? When?" Raven asks.

Before she can get an answer, there is a knock at the door. Dane hurries to answer it. He swings the door wide, and in sweeps Wren Thistleseed, followed by the rest of the girls—Shine, Selah, Zorah, Debby, and Shelly. "Surprise!" they shout in unison.

Shelly runs to Raven and puts her arms around her waist. Behind her, the others file in, loaded down with balloons, food, and packages.

"It's for you, Raven. We're having a cagement party for you," Shelly says. "But without a cage, I think."

Raven laughs and hugs the little girl. "Thanks, Sweetie. Where are the boys?"

"Oh, they had to stay home 'cause a cagement party is just for girls."

"That's right," Wren says, "so you men need to take your chicken and go home."

"Hey, this *is* my home," Dane says.

"I guess we will have to join the other males at the Thistleseed home," Lee says, nonchalantly gathering the drawings from the table.

"Well, before we go, can I give the bride-to-be a gift, too?" Dane asks.

Reaching into his pocket, Dane pulls out a small cylindrical object covered in gold filigree and hands it to Raven. She turns it over in her hands, inspecting it with childlike wonder.

"Lipstick?" she asks.

"Not even close. Besides, you don't wear lipstick, Babe. Open it up."

She takes the cap off to reveal a sprayer. Lifting it to her nose, she smiles broadly. "*De Vanille*! My favorite fragrance." She spritzes a little on her wrists and rubs them together. Immediately, the scent of vanilla fills the room.

Graham sniffs the air. "So that's why you always smell like sugar cookies!"

"And since you don't ever carry a purse, you can slip this into your pocket or even carry it in one of your mocs," Dane says.

She throws her arms around his neck and gives him a resounding kiss, much to the delight of the guests. He is slow to pull away, keeping his eyes locked on Raven until Wren pulls on his shirt sleeve.

"And because we're throwing you out of your house, Dane, we got you a present," Wren says. She thrusts a wrapped box into his hands.

"Oh, I get it. We love you, Dane. Here's a gift. Now, get out," he says.

"Something like that," Shine teases. "Open it."

Dane tears the colorful paper off the package. Inside is a handsome square bottle of cologne. He pulls his mouth down in a quizzical expression.

"We know you don't wear cologne, but this one is special. Smell it," Selah says.

He twists open the cap and puts the bottle hesitantly to his nose. Taking a tentative sniff, his eyes widen, his mouth splits into a grin, and he cuts his eyes to Raven.

"Pretty neat," he says.

"It's called *Homme De Vanille*. It means 'Man of Vanilla.' They have similar ingredients, so they smell close to the same," Shine says.

"I can smell that, but this one is way more masculine, right?" Dane says.

"Uh huh. We figured you could wear your 'smell pretty', and

when you have to be away from Raven, you'll still be smelling her," Shelly says.

The room erupts in laughter at her choice of words, and Shelly looks crestfallen, but Dane bends down and kisses her on the cheek. "That is the most wonderful idea I have ever heard, Shell. You are a genius. I'm gonna put some on right now!" He dabs a little on his finger and wipes it on his neck.

Shelly's little face lights up at the compliment, and she skips away to her mother's side. Lee pushes the men—who seem decidedly loathe to go—out the door, leaving the girls to their party. As he pulls the door closed, Dane blows a kiss to Raven, wishing he could shoo everyone away and have her all to himself. *Plenty of time for that later,* he thinks rationally, but his irrational mind nags, *I want her now.*

Watching him leave, Raven feels her face flush. She fans herself with her hand, breathing in the scent of the heavenly fragrance on her tingling wrists.

CHAPTER FIVE

TO TAMPA

THE DAYS SEEM TO BE MOVING so quickly, Raven marvels. She adjusts her seat and leans back just a little. It feels good to relax and take a break from the exhausting training of the past week. She is just beginning to realize what a toll it takes on her—both physically and mentally. She stretches her long legs out before her, pushing the seat back as far as it will go.

"Get comfy, Babe," Dane says. "It's a pretty long ride to Tampa. Let me know when you need a rest stop. There's plenty on the way."

"I'm fine, honey. It's not like I've never taken a long car trip before. I moved here from Arizona, you know," Raven says.

"I know. But, you know, not with me or anything, and I just want you to be comfortable and all, and ..."

"Dane. I'm fine! I have Diet Coke, pretzels, a pillow, a blanket, and a neat book from my mother about Hopi Katsinas to look at. What more do I need?"

"A good driver?" He grins at her.

"You bet. I have the best driver in the world." She leans over and gives him a nuzzling kiss on the cheek. He inhales her sweet aroma and smiles.

"You smell good," he says. "Want to take a short smooch break before we leave?"

She laughs aloud. "I don't know what's with you lately, but you're like a desert nomad who can't get enough water!"

"I'm sorry, but you look and smell so enticing, it takes all my self-control not to attack you every time you're near." He presents his best chastised child look from beneath his lashes.

"Well, keep it in check, Bucko. We've got plenty of time for that. Let's get on the road."

"Your wish is my command." He gives an exaggerated sigh and pulls out onto the street.

Raven snaps her seatbelt in place and reclines against the headrest, her left arm slung lazily across the back of Dane's neck. She wonders about his increase in ardor ever since the engagement party. But then, she has had the same desires. Never before having a steady boyfriend, her love for Dane is unlike any feeling she has ever experienced. She lifts her right hand to push against her bangs, and as she does, her wrist passes close to her nose. She inhales. *I love this scent, and I love this man.* She raises her left knee and reaches into the side of her moccasin, retrieving the lipstick shaped perfume container. She dislodges the cap with her nimble fingers, brings it to the hollow of her neck, and presses the top slightly. Instantly, the essence of vanilla fills the car.

"Babe, I'm gonna have to get you another one of those perfumes before the week is out," Dane says. "I bet you've almost used it up."

"I'm sorry. It smells so good, I can't seem to get enough of it," she says.

"As long as it makes you happy." He reaches over to fondle her knee.

She smiles and replaces the top on the canister. *I better go easy on this. Don't know how much it cost him.*

"New mocs?" he asks, changing the conversation.

She raises her feet to display her most recent footwear. "My mother sent them, along with this book. They're made of yucca plants instead of leather. She thinks they'll be more comfortable in South Florida," she says, admiring the twisted honey-colored fibers laced with soft leather strips. Looking at the shoes makes Raven think about her mother, Robin, one of Prescott, Arizona's finest artisans. She crafts both leather and yucca fiber moccasins and makes decorated pine needle and bark strip baskets so tightly woven that they hold water. Raven is fiercely proud of her mother's talents. Out of respect and to honor her, Raven only wears the many handmade pairs of moccasins her mother sends every few months.

"I can't wait to meet her."

"Soon. And then you'll have a closet full of moccasins, too."

The trip passes relatively quickly, with small talk and an occasional pit stop, and before they know it, they are seeing signs for Tampa on I-4. Raven notices patches of uprooted oaks and broken palm trees along the roadside, as well as some mangled billboards, and she points them out.

"Spinoff from Hurricane Andrew this past August," Dane says. "See that twisted light post? That's from tornado activity. And those trees leaning over … horizontal wind shear. Funny, isn't it? The pine trees don't snap like the hardwoods. They bend. They'll stay bent, too."

"Why didn't your mother evacuate? Isn't it dangerous to be so near a hurricane?"

"She won't leave that village. It's been her home for the past ten years. She doesn't have much family other than us boys. A distant aunt that's a storyteller or something, and maybe an uncle or cousin who wrestles alligators."

"She never remarried after your father died?"

"Nope. Never did. Said nobody interested her, but I sometimes wonder if there was another guy, and she just didn't want us kids to be upset. She won't say. Stubborn, you know."

"Yes, I seem to know someone else like that."

Dane feigns shock and slaps his cheek. "*Moi?* You surely don't mean me, do you?"

"Duh! Oh, look. There's our exit for the Tampa PD." Dane maneuvers the car off the interstate highway, following the signs to lead them to the Tampa Police Department. Lee has already called ahead and spoken with the Chief of Police about the recent death of Marjorie from Tampa. Dane and Raven hope to gather information that may tie her death to that of the two kids in Tallahassee, and to their recent unsettling tracks.

Inside the Chief's office, Raven and Dane sit on round-backed molded plastic chairs, meant to look modern, but feeling much less so. The walls are covered with plaques and framed certificates of commendation, photographs, and dozens of yellow stick-on notes.

Chief Lew Rowan is a large, rotund man with salt-and-pepper hair and narrow squared-off sideburns. His face is tanned and wrinkled, and startling green eyes shine from above high, round cheeks. His frame fills the massive leather office chair which creaks as he rocks it slowly back and forth. At first sight an imposing character, one's intimidation at his appearance fades when he speaks. His voice is soft and pleasant, and his smile is contagious. Raven likes him immediately, and he seems equally charmed by her.

"I got the call from Mr. Thistleseed, and I did some checking," Chief Rowan says, spreading papers from an opened file on his desk. "The lady in question was named Marjorie Alice Collier. And she was quite the Tampa Bay socialite. Came from a wealthy family. You're familiar with Collier County? That's her kin folk. Anyhow, Miss Marjorie was found five days ago in her home by her housekeeper. She had been dead for several hours. Since the night before, apparently. They found her lying on a mess of broken bottles. It appeared she exsanguinated—bled out. Let's see, here."

He rifles through some papers and selects a report. Raven shifts in her uncomfortable seat. The room is hot, and her bangs are beginning to stick to her forehead.

Chief Rowan smiles up at her from the desk. "Here we go. M.E.'s report. Some medical examiner mumbo jumbo ... Blah, blah, blah ... posterior trauma ... length of cuts ... O.K. here it is. Stomach contents. Says she had consumed approximately five liters of wine. Now why don't they say ounces or cups? I hate this metric stuff. How much is five liters?"

"Five of those big bottles, I'd say," Raven offers.

"I'd say that, too, little lady. Now wouldn't that have been easier? To say she drank five bottles of wine? And that would be, like 30 glasses or so. That beats my record! Well, anyway. Let's see. Toxicology. Here's the thing—as if five bottles of wine wouldn't kick your butt—she's dosed up on ecstasy."

"Ecstasy?" Dane says. "Our victims in Tallahassee had taken ecstasy, too."

"Searched her place but couldn't find any evidence. No wrappers, no pills. But it was all in her system. Poor Marjorie. Lookin' for a party but died all by herself." Chief Rowan shakes his head and shrugs.

"Take ecstasy and die in agony," Raven says.

"What's that?" the Chief asks.

"Something my brother said, but it's pretty true. I'd say she died a very painful death," Dane says.

The Chief nods his massive head somberly. "Bad way to die, too."

"But what really killed her? Was it the drug or the alcohol?" Raven asks.

"That's a very good question, young lady. I'd say both, and I'd be right ... and wrong. What do you know about ecstasy?"

"Not much, really. It makes you ... uh ... you get ... I really don't know," Raven admits.

Chief Rowan laughs at her attempt to explain. "It makes you horny. Is that what you meant to say?"

"Yes, I guess," she says, brushing invisible lint from her khaki shorts.

"It does do that, as well as a long list of other things. People say it makes colors vivid, sounds clear, smells, tastes, etc. more psychedelic. Just enhances all your senses. And it makes you feel like you are sexy and alluring. Messes with your inhibitions. Now that, in itself, is not so bad. It's the side effects that get you. Vomiting, paranoia, panic attacks, hallucinations, severe dehydration. Not my idea of a good time."

"So, did the ecstasy kill her?" Dane asks.

"Not according to this report. It says she died from hyponatraemia."

"And that is ..." Dane prompts.

"Liquid poisoning," Chief Rowan replies.

"Liquid poison? You mean like drain cleaner or something?" Raven asks.

"No. Liquid poison-ING. From drinking too much liquid," Chief Rowan says.

"How is that possible? I've never heard of drinking too much liquid, unless it's too much alcohol. Was it alcohol poisoning?" Raven asks.

"You'd think so. I wondered the same thing, so I asked my M.E. He said that drinking excessive water or fluid disturbs the sodium balance in the body and makes the organs swell. And the brain, since it can't expand inside the skull, gets all compressed. That puts pressure on the brain stem and—*boom*—coma leading to death. That's what killed Miss Marjorie. Those five *metric liters* of wine she drank because the ecstasy made her hot and thirsty."

Raven's mouth is dry from all the talk about dehydration and drinking. *What I wouldn't give for a Diet Coke right now,* she thinks. She reaches into her pants pocket and takes out another pack of gum—the third pack of *Juicy Fruit* she's opened today. She puts two sticks into her mouth and chews vigorously, nervously. Seeing the Chief watching her, she extends the pack of gum to him.

"Don't mind if I do," he says, extracting one silver-papered stick from the pack.

For a few moments they sit looking at each other, chewing like two cows in a field. Dane breaks the silence by getting to his feet and reaching out to the Chief.

"Thank you, sir, for your help," he says, grasping the big man's hand.

"Not at all. I'll fax a copy to your department in Tallahassee later today," Chief Rowan replies. He gives Raven a radiant smile. "And thank you for brightening my day."

Raven lets him engulf her slender hand with both of his. "You're very welcome."

"You kids stay clear of the trees while you're here. We've still got limbs falling all over the place," he says as he begins gathering up the mess of papers spread on the desk.

Back at the car, Raven's first order of business is to open the small cooler and take out a can of cold soda for herself and one for Dane. She chugs nearly half the can, then lets out a healthy burp, much to her own surprise.

"Such a lady." Dane snorts, laughing.

"Oh, just shut up and drive," she retorts, anxious to get to the village and meet her future mother-in-law. "All that talk in there made me so thirsty, I thought I was going to dry up in the chair."

Fortunately, the drive is short, and within a few minutes, they see the water tower with a huge arrow through the tank that signals their turn off from I-4. As they arrive in front of the Seminole Village and Culture Center, Raven squirms in her seat.

"Do I look O.K.?" she asks.

"You look perfect," Dane says leaning in for a kiss.

He gets out and rounds the car to open her door. Raven reaches into her moccasin and retrieves the *DeVanille* canister, giving herself another quick spray. Satisfied that she looks and smells presentable, she exits the car and approaches the door on the arm of her handsome sweetheart.

CHAPTER SIX
<u>FAWN LIGHTFOOT</u>

ENTERING THE SEMINOLE INDIAN GIFT SHOP on the way to the Museum is like stepping back in time. Raven marvels at the pictures and the décor, but, most of all, she notices the colors. Patchwork skirts, jackets, and extra-long shirts hang along the walls, their patterns seeming to move like rivers or snakes or running animals. Red, yellow, white, and black dominate the color palate. She is fascinated, and her eyes feel dry from holding them open so wide. Light through the windows catches on racks of earrings and necklaces made of tiny glass seed beads, sending showers of multicolored fireflies dancing about the room. The smell of smoldering sage tickles her nose.

Dane leads her through the room, while smiling and nodding to the woman sitting beside the counter. She is white-haired, dark-skinned, and wrinkled, with row upon row of seed bead necklaces encircling her neck from shoulders to chin. A short translucent cape covers her bodice and bare arms, ending with a ruffle just below her waist. Her skirt is full, with patchwork patterns on different colored backgrounds of horizontal stripes.

Some of the patterns are triangular, some are blocks, and yet others look like the capital letter "T" alternately upright and upside down. The effect is mesmerizing. The old woman's wrinkles bunch together beside her mouth to reveal a broad smile. She waves as they pass through the back door.

Stepping out the door and into the sunlight, Raven's breath catches at the sight of her surroundings. Directly in front of them, in the center of the area, stands the *Coo-Taun Cho-Bee* Museum. It is a massive structure, shaped like an eight-sided star. Around the perimeter runs a wooded pathway, and on the outskirts of the pathway are the most unusual buildings Raven has ever seen. They are open pavilions, like Tiki-huts, but different. The roofs are thatched with palm leaves. Some of the buildings are rounded; some are square. But all are exposed to the elements, with raised platforms in the center and open shelves between the outer posts.

Within the buildings are people—women dressed as the old woman in the shop, men in slacks and long colorful knee-length shirts, and quite a few children, some dressed as the adults, and others shirtless and barefoot, playing with each other or with long-tailed, smooth-haired dogs. Raven laughs aloud.

"What's so funny?" Dane asks.

"Nothing is funny. It's just wonderful!" she says, clapping her hands together.

He hugs her to him. *How like a child she is sometimes.* He wishes he could see things through her eyes. The village is just another village to him, but to her, it's a magical world. Just then, he hears a commotion from beyond the Museum.

"Mom!" he calls.

Fawn Lightfoot appears on the boardwalk. She is tall, perhaps even taller than Raven, and stately, with perfect posture and a relaxed composure. Her face is alight with the afternoon sun as she looks toward them. She walks with her arms outstretched, and Dane runs to embrace her. Raven hangs back, a little unsure of herself, but then Fawn strides forward to throw her arms around her future daughter-in-law. The hug is strong and fierce, as if the women have known each other forever.

"Daughter," Fawn says. "I'm happy you are here, at last."

Raven pulls back and gazes into the older woman's face. Fawn's onyx-colored eyes are so familiar. *Of course. Noah.* There is no mistaking their resemblance, but she also sees Dane in that beautiful face. Fawn's eyebrows pull down in a tiny frown, and then her eyes open wide.

"You smell like cookies!" she says with a huge smile.

The three of them laugh at the statement, and there are no strangers among them anymore. Fawn pulls Dane to one side and Raven to the other, takes their hands, and walks them to her *chickee*—one of the thatched roof houses that surround the Museum. They sit on the platform, and she pours them tall glasses of fresh, cold water with crushed mint leaves. A loud honking noise draws Raven's attention. She looks over Fawn's shoulder and sees a large, grey goose waddling toward the platform. Fawn reaches down and strokes the goose's long neck.

"This is Emma. She thinks I'm her mother, and I guess I am. She follows me everywhere I go. It's a mutually beneficial relationship. I give her treats, and she keeps the bugs away from my *chickee*," she says, throwing a handful of ground corn on the ground for the goose.

"Chickee, like little chickens?" Raven asks.

Fawn laughs brightly. "No, sweetie. A *chickee* is an open-sided house, but sometimes little chickens ... and a big goose ... run through it."

"Is this your home?" Raven asks.

"This is more of a demonstration village, meant to show visitors how the Seminoles live. I do my sewing and basketry here. My *chickee* ... the one I live in ... is much bigger but built the same. There are about 40 of us who live in the village, just behind that fence. I have curtains in mine for privacy, but some of the other families don't use curtains. We just don't look."

"Mom says she doesn't look, but I don't believe her."

"Boy, you hold your tongue. You're not too old to whip." Fawn laughs, reaching up to pat her hair.

"Is that your hair, or is that a hat?" Raven asks.

"Speaks her mind, this one, doesn't she?" Fawn says. "That's a good quality, Raven. Always say what you want to say. I admire that in a man and a woman."

Raven smiles, feeling at ease with the woman, but still

examining the unusual hairdo.

"O.K., I'll give you the short version. Seminole women used to wear their hair long and loose in the beginning, but it was impractical when they moved down south, so they began twisting their hair into buns on the top of their heads. Somewhere along the way, after seeing white women wearing hats and bonnets to shade their faces, someone got the idea to make a hairdo that worked like a hat. It takes two people to fix it. One person leans over while the other one combs the hair forward to the crown of the head and secures it like a ponytail. Then a form is placed either just behind or in front of the ponytail. At first the women used a rolled-up piece of hide, but now we make our own forms in different shapes out of soft wire, fabric, or starched cloth. Once the form is placed, it is pinned to the scalp with bobby pins. Then the ponytail is fanned out and woven into the shape, just like you weave a basket. The ends of the hair are pushed under the form and pinned to keep it tight. *Ta-da*. You now have a hair hat!"

"Can I ..." Raven begins.

"... touch it? Of course. In fact, it's almost closing time, so I'm going to take it down. You can help me," Fawn says.

Dane watches the two women bonding—sharing stories, getting to know each other, becoming mother and daughter without even trying, and his heart swells. As Raven gently unweaves Fawn's hair from the form, he thinks back to a time when his mother was not so happy ... to the time when his father was killed.

*   *   *

Fawn had taken him to the Berry *Pvsktv*—fasting celebration—in North Florida. Dane played with the other children and their dogs and had a great time. There were lots of grownups milling around, but he paid little heed to them. Playing behind the old men's arbor, Dane heard the elders talking about his gift, and he wondered what gift that might be. It was not close to his birthday, and Mom hadn't mentioned anything about a party, so he dismissed it to old people not knowing anything. After all, he was ten years old, and they were ancient.

The ride home the next day was long, but Dane lay on the seat with his bare feet in his mother's lap and listened to her telling stories. She told about the crows that had colorful feathers and sang so wonderfully that everyone else in the forest would be quiet just to listen to them. One day, the crows saw something bright orange on the ground below and a black cloud up above it in the sky. They flew to a blackened tree to investigate, climbing higher and higher until the limb broke. The crows fell to the ground and were burned. Their feathers were turned black by the soot and charcoal, and the smoke hurt their throats so much they could only say, "Caw. Caw."

"That was a fire, Mama," Dane said.

"That's right. Fire is powerful. We respect it, and we never play with it," Fawn said.

She told him the story of the Little People who lived among the trees and came to the bedside of sick people to help them get better. The Little People were afraid of storms and hid in the trees when the thunder sounded. The thunder and lightning chased them all around the trees, but the Little People escaped by disappearing into holes in the trees.

"And that's why you never stand under a tree in a storm," Dane said.

"Or you might get hit by lightning," Fawn said.

His favorite was the story of Possum and his lovely tail. It was so fluffy and full, and he would say to the other animals that his tail was so much better than theirs. One day, the other animals decided to trick him. They told him that his tail could be even more beautiful if he would wrap tree moss around it for a few days. Possum was so vain that he did exactly that. But when he unwrapped the moss, he was so sad. All the hair had fallen off, and it never grew back.

"That's why you don't brag and boast," Dane said. And through the retelling of the old stories, young Dane Lightfoot learned right from wrong.

After the long ride, Dane was glad to get back to his home. It was cold up there at Pine Arbor, and Dane was used to the balmy South Florida weather and his breezy *chickee* home. To tell the truth, he missed his six brothers and sisters, even though they were all much older than he. His father was old, too, but Dane loved to follow him around the village, watching him make medicine and heal sick people. *I will be a heles-pocase medicine man, too, one day*, he decided.

The next afternoon after he returned, Dane was sitting on the ground whittling a stick when he sensed a strange smell from inside the *chickee*. Looking around the pole, he glimpsed a man moving the bedding blankets. The man had his back to him, but Dane could see the four-foot rattlesnake he held behind its triangular-shaped head. The man stuffed the snake head-first into the blankets, and then hurriedly left the hut. Dane knew the danger the snake presented, so he ran to find his mother.

When the two of them ran back to the hut, they saw his father lying on the ground. The snake was still coiled after striking Joe Lightfoot in the neck. Fawn screamed and beat the snake with the mallet she used to grind corn. Dane couldn't move. Eyes wide, he watched his father squirm and twist on the ground. Suddenly, a man came running in with a bag of healing herbs. *What? Another heles-pocase?* Dane recognized him as the medicine man from Pine Arbor. *What was he doing there?* As if he heard him, the man whipped his head around and stared at Dane. Suddenly, his father shook all over and convulsed, then he lay still. Dead.

"Father!" Dane shouted, his cries mingling with the screams of his mother.

The other medicine man put his arms around Dane's mother, but Dane ran forward and pushed him away. He remembered the man's eyes. They were blue—so blue, they were almost white. Silver eyes. Evil eyes.

His mother didn't smile for a long, long time. Not until Noah was born.

* * *

"Dane, I asked you how Noah is," Fawn says.

Dane looks at his mother. Her hair hangs in a long braid down her back, and he realizes he has been daydreaming. "Sorry.

He's good, Mom. Loving his Chief Osceola role at the football games. It suits him, you know. He lives for the roar of the crowd."

"That boy has always been one for attention," Fawn agrees. "Listen, you two. I have to get my supplies put away and tidied up for tomorrow. Why don't you take a tour around the grounds while there's some daylight left? I'll catch up with you in a few minutes."

Dane pulls Raven to her feet. "Good idea, Mom. This one needs some exercise."

"Ha," Raven says, but she is glad to move around. Her muscles are sore from riding, and her arms and legs are stiff. She clasps Dane's hand and listens as he gives her the walking tour.

They stroll on the wooden pathway past the arts and crafts *chickees* and make their way to a large sand-filled pit. Raven leans near the edge to get a better look below.

"Not too close, Babe. That's an alligator pit," Dane says. She pulls back abruptly, and he laughs heartily.

"Don't worry, Honey. It's for the alligator wrestling demonstrations. The real gators are in lairs farther back. The People call them *'Hal Pa Te.'* There's one old snapper back there called 'Big Joe.' He's over ten feet long."

Raven punches him in the arm. "Don't do that again."

"Yes ma'am. Do keep your eyes open, though, because there are animals living in the wild around the village. If you look carefully, you may see bobcats, a Florida panther, deer, giant tortoises, and maybe even a black bear."

"I grew up in the mountains of Arizona. There were a few trees, a little bit of grass, and lots of rocks. It almost feels claustrophobic here. The landscape surrounds you from all sides, and it's so close. And hot. Ye gads, it's hot. How come you aren't sweating like me?"

"I guess I'm used to the heat. We'll get you a drink of water in the Museum."

They enter the *Coo-Taun Cho-Bee* Museum, and Raven instantly relaxes. *Ah, air conditioning!* Locating a water fountain near the door, she drinks deeply at first, but then she remembers what Chief Lew Rowan said about drinking too much. She stops in mid-gulp, and then slowly takes a few more mouthfuls. *Better.*

Fawn is already inside the Museum waiting on them. She puts her arm around Raven's waist and walks her through the Seminole history exhibits.

"Back in 1979, there was a construction crew building a parking garage in this location. While they were excavating, they began to uncover the skeletons of lots of people. When the authorities investigated, they determined the bones to be the remains of 150 Indians who fought and died during the Seminole Wars in the 1800s. The Seminole Nation declared the site a sacred ancestral burial ground and had the construction halted.

"After a lot of heated debate and bargaining, the Seminoles settled for this seven and one-half acre tract of land in which to rebury and consecrate our ancestors' remains. The skeletons are now buried beneath this very Museum. This place became known as Seminole Indian Village. In 1989, we built the Bingo Palace and Smoke Shop. Seminole Medicine Man Bobby Henry runs the village and does alligator wrestling shows sometimes. He's also a rainmaker," Fawn explains.

"He can make it rain?" Raven asks.

"So, they say," Dane says. "I've never seen it, but Mom swears that he can."

"Wow! This is so interesting," Raven says, yawning.

"Yes, it is. But you are tired, and so am I. Let's go to my home, and I will fix you an authentic Seminole supper." Fawn leads Raven out the door. "Come, Emma," she tells the goose, who falls in step behind them.

The walk to Fawn's house is short, just beyond the wooden fence that surrounds the demonstration area. It is exactly as she described it—a larger version of her demo *chickee*. Raven finds it charming and surprisingly cool with the breeze blowing through the open walls. The outer curtains hang about a foot from the ceiling crossbeams and fall all the way to the packed dirt floor. They mimic the patterns in the colorful clothing hanging in the gift shop. The open tops allow the breeze to flow into the partitioned "rooms" and throughout the interior.

Inside the *chickee*, lightweight curtains meet in the center of the structure to form a cross, dividing the area into four quadrants. One section is outfitted with typical kitchen appliances, as well as a large, deep, cast-iron pot on a propane-fed burner. Of the other three sections, one is clearly a bathroom—made private with plywood along the outside. The others are multi-purpose rooms, with raised platforms that can be used as beds or seating areas. Many woven baskets are stacked beneath the platforms and throughout the residence and are filled with bedding, clothing, and other household necessities.

"Son, since I know you two aren't sleeping together, you take the room on the left, and Raven can sleep in my room with me. Why don't you go ahead and get your overnight things, and Raven can help me start cooking," Fawn says, giving Raven a wink.

"Uh, yeah, sure thing, Mom." He grins, knowing Raven's lack of culinary skills. Walking backwards, he waves and blows his fiancé a kiss.

"A wink and a kiss. Aren't I the lucky one?" Raven laughs and rolls her eyes.

Fawn pulls a stool up and directs Raven to sit and watch while she begins the cooking.

"Tonight, we will have Seminole tacos," she says. When Raven makes a confused face, she explains. "Not really tacos. I'm going to teach you to make fry bread. First, we fire up the propane burner. This is vegetable oil. We've got to get it really hot. While it's heating, we mix and pat out the bread."

Into a large bowl Fawn adds flour, salt, and water, mixing the dough with her hand until it pulls away from the sides of the bowl. She uses no measuring cups. This is a technique learned from years of practice. She adds more flour to keep the dough from being too sticky. When it gets to the consistency she likes, she pulls off a handful and begins slapping it back and forth between her floured hands until it is a large, flat pancake the size of a dinner plate and about an inch thick.

Carefully, she slides the bread into the hot oil, and then begins forming another one. She slides another one in the oil and flips the first one over with tongs. When she adds the next one, she removes the first one—now floating on the surface. There is a silent rhythm to her cooking, and Raven is mesmerized, almost hypnotized by her fluid motions. It seems like mere moments have passed, but Fawn has removed all the breads from the oil and transferred them to a brown paper bag to drain the grease and keep them warm.

Dane returns and hands Raven a Diet Coke, then sits on the floor beside her watching his mother cook. This has always been one of his favorite activities. He is totally at peace tonight.

Fawn opens the refrigerator and pulls out a container of precut vegetables—carrots, wild onions, yellow squash, and green pole beans. After adding lard to a cast iron skillet, she dumps all the raw vegetables in and lets them sizzle. In another skillet, she browns up ground venison. The aroma of the food is rich, and Raven's stomach growls. She realizes now how hungry she is.

"Dane. Plates, please," Fawn says.

He jumps up and removes plates, coffee cups, and spoons from a shelf over the oven. He lays them out on the "guest bed," as this is also the table when company visits. Fawn brings the paper sack and a big splatter ware pot over to the platform. She has combined all the vegetables and the meat in the pot and has also added some red beans. In an enamel coffee kettle on another burner, a yellow mixture bubbles. She brings the kettle over and fills their cups with it. Onto each plate, she places a huge piece of fry bread, and then covers it with the meat and vegetable mixture.

"May I bless it?" Dane asks.

Fawn raises her eyebrows, but she says nothing, simply shrugs and nods her head.

"Father, for what we are about to receive, make us truly thankful, and bless us on our journeys and in our daily lives. In Jesus' name. Amen."

"Now?" Fawn asks.

"Dive in," Dane says.

Raven, unsure of how to proceed, watches the others. Seeing Dane fold up the fry bread and topping like a taco, she follows suit. The result is a mouthful of soft, yet crispy bread, succulent meat, and crunchy vegetables. Nearly half of the topping plops onto the plate, and Raven quickly looks up, embarrassed. She is relieved to note that the others have substantial amounts of topping on their plates, too. They take their spoons and scoop it back onto their bread before each bite.

"Delicious," Raven says through a mouthful.

"Try the *sofkee*," Dane says pointing to the mug full of steaming yellow mush.

"What is it?"

"Try it first, then I'll tell you."

"It's not cats or dogs or something weird, is it?"

Fawn drops her fry bread and laughs cheerfully. "It's just ground corn mixed with water, Raven. Try it. If you don't like it, you don't have to finish it."

Raven picks up the mug and sniffs the drink, then she takes a tentative sip. The flavor is deceiving. What looks like thick yellow sludge is actually sweet and hearty.

"This is really good!" she says, taking a bigger gulp. Before she knows it, she has emptied the cup. "May I...?"

Fawn jumps to grab the kettle and refills Raven's mug, delighted that she likes the traditional Seminole drink. The three of them spend the remainder of the time eating, drinking, and becoming a family. After all of the meat and vegetables are finished, the dishes are washed and dried, and the leftover fry bread is rolled up in the bag, they are full and completely talked out.

Fawn scoops out the remainder of the *sofkee* and tosses it outside for her large grey goose, who honks loudly and gratefully.

"Emma will sleep out there and alert us to any animal or human intruders," she assures them.

Raven changes into boxer shorts and a t-shirt and washes her hands and face in the bathroom. She thinks briefly about reapplying her perfume but rejects the idea. It's with her moccasins in a basket in the sleeping area, and she's tired. When she comes out, she sees that Fawn has changed into a cotton nightdress and has covered the platform with several thick blankets, topped by a lightweight quilt. Fawn gives her a quick hug and kiss, and then she climbs up on one side of the platform "bed."

Take your time getting into bed, Raven. We don't follow a clock," she says.

"I won't be long, Fawn. I'm really tired," Raven says.

"Me, too," Dane says behind her.

Raven turns and folds herself into his arms for a kiss. He holds her tightly for a long time before pushing her away. "I love you, Babe," he says.

"I love you, too, Dane."

Turning her around, he pushes her toward her room, and then he draws the curtains around the outside of the *chickee* before entering his own room.

"Mom?" Dane says.

"A story?" Fawn responds.

"Creation," he says, settling himself on the blankets of his platform bed.

Fawn's voice is soft but clear through the hanging curtains as she begins the story. It has always been Dane's favorite. She tells it to him every time he visits, and he never grows tired of it.

"In the beginning of time, the Muskogee People were born out of Mother Earth. Her children crawled up through a hole in the ground like a colony of ants. The People all lived together beside the tall mountains that reached up to the sky in the lands of the west. But there were so many of The People, it was difficult for friends and even families to have alliances with each other.

"One day, *Hesaketvmese*—Master of Breath—sent a thick fog upon the earth, and The People could not see. They called out to each other in fear as they wandered around. They were as the blind. They drifted apart and became lost. Whenever they came upon another person, they would cling to that person, and in this way The People soon began to form small groups for security.

"Finally, Father Spirit took pity on them and began to blow the fog away. He blew His breath first from the eastern edge of the world, where the sun rises. He blew until the world was clear again, and The People could see. The People swore eternal brotherhood within their small groups and promised to be like large families— like brother and sister, mother and daughter, father and son. And then The People sang a hymn of thanksgiving to the Master of Breath for His wisdom.

"Those that were the farthest to the lands of the east were the first group to see the sun. They praised the wind that blew the fog away and called themselves the Wind Clan. The next group called themselves the Bear Clan, for that was the first animal they saw when the fog disappeared.

"Other groups also gave themselves names, choosing the name of the first thing they saw when the fog passed away from them. In this way, their groups came to be known as the clans of Snake and Panther, of Toad and Bird, of Deer and Alligator; Beaver and Otter, Tiger and Wolf, Raccoon, and Sweet Potato ..."

"... but the Wind Clan remained the most important clan of all," Dane says, finishing the story. "Good night, Mom."

"Good night, my son."

Neither of them must bid Raven a good night, for she is already sound asleep. The Florida night is warm, the breeze off the bay is constant, and the family in Fawn Lightfoot's *chickee* is at peace, at last.

CHAPTER SEVEN
CEDAR WOMAN'S GIFTS

DANE AWAKENS TO PLEASANT SMELLS for a change. Food and fresh air. He puts on his jeans and passes through the curtain into the kitchen where Fawn stands stirring a pot of stew. Emma pokes her long neck into the room. Fawn throws her a handful of corn, shooing her out of the house. Dane snickers at them. Seeing him, she smiles and reaches for the coffee pot.

"Coffee?" she asks.

"No thanks, Mom. Don't drink it anymore. How about some *sofkee*, if your goose doesn't mind? I don't get that at home."

"Emma knows her place. *Sofkee*, it is. I'll send some of the ground corn back with Raven with very detailed instructions on how to make it."

"Better show me how to make it. Raven's not much of a cook." He grins broadly.

Fawn fills a mug with the steaming corn and water mixture, and then she pours herself a cup of coffee. They sit facing each other, blowing across the tops of their cups to cool the liquids inside. After a few moments, Fawn puts her mug down and covers Dane's hand with her own.

"Son, your girl is sick," Fawn says.

"What?" Dane frowns at his mother, but he knows she must be right. She's always right about illnesses. Fawn does not have second sight, but she learned from her mother at a young age how to diagnose and treat people using local plants and herbs. It is both her calling and her special gift. Though she has no medical degree, the villagers come to her for advice and herbal cures. She is Cedar Woman, the village healer.

"What's wrong with her?" Dane asks.

"Something poisons her from deep inside. She needs healing," she says.

"What makes you so positive, Mom? Are you sure she's not just overtired from the trip, and from the training?"

"Training? Does she have the gift?" Fawn asks, startled.

"She does. As Noah says, 'she's eat up with it'. But she doesn't know how to use it yet, so we've been training her. You know how taxing that is on your mind and your body."

"Oh, yes. It's been all around me. My dad, your dad, Jimbo, you, Noah, others I know."

"Well, then you certainly understand. Maybe Raven is just overwhelmed."

"Dane, she slept so hot last night that I had to move away. I felt her fever, heard her rapid breathing, smelled the poison coming through her skin. Her eyes are too bright, and her pupils are dilated. She needs cleansing," Fawn insists.

"Mom, I can't just give her black drink or take her out back to the sweat hut. We have to go back to Tallahassee today. She'd puke all the way home."

"And get rid of the sickness ..."

"No. I'll get her to a doctor when we get home." "I can call the *heles-pocase* ..."

"Mom. I love you, but sometimes you push so hard. Please. Let me deal with it," he says, his tone softening.

"You are so stubborn, Dane. You'd think we were bull clan instead of wind!"

"And who do you think I get that from?" He laughs and pats her hand.

"Good morning," Raven says, pushing aside the curtain "I

thought I was in another country for a minute. What language were you speaking?"

Dane jumps up and embraces her, ushering her to a chair at the table.

"Good morning, sweetheart. We were speaking Muskogee. It's the language of the Creeks and some of the Florida Seminole tribes. It's not used much anymore outside the reservation and villages like this one. Did you rest well?" Fawn says.

"I slept like the dead!" Raven says. "I can't remember sleeping that soundly in a long time. I guess I was really tired."

Fawn has already poured a mug of *sofkee* for Raven and begins boiling a pot of water into which she crumbles dried herbs from an assortment of small baskets above the cooking station. She quickly brings the cooking pots from the stove and sets them on the table, along with the warmed fry bread from the previous evening.

"This is breakfast," she says. "Not your typical bacon and eggs, but I think you'll like it."

As before, Raven watches the others to see how to eat the food. Dane loads his plate with a fragrant yellow-orange blend from the large pot.

"This is buttered squash and pumpkin. It's a little like apple butter or jam. Try some," he says. He takes a piece of fry bread and dips it into the pureed mixture, using his spoon to push it up onto the bread. "Do it like this ... like sopping a biscuit in gravy."

Raven tries the technique and finds it relatively simple. The squash and pumpkin are heavenly—sweet and savory at the same time. She is surprised to realize she is still famished.

The next pot contains something that smells similar to spinach or collard greens. Fawn dips it out with a large spoon into a bowl and sets it beside Raven's plate.

"We call this *taal-holelke*. Boiled swamp cabbage. It comes from the bud of the sabal palmetto. In the grocery store, you would call it 'hearts of palm.' We harvest it right here in a garden next to the village," Fawn says.

Raven's eyes roll when she tastes the cabbage. "It's wonderful! I've had hearts of palm, but they were pickled. This is so much better."

Fawn turns back to the pot boiling on the burner. She strains the herbs which have been steeped into the water and pours the tea into another mug, to which she adds a fat chunk of honeycomb. She sets the mug before Raven.

"Try this, Raven. I think you will find it pleasing," she says.

Dane scowls at his mother, but she is nonplussed. Stubborn should be her middle name. This is one of Fawn's special medicinal teas, and she is determined to heal Raven's illness.

Raven takes the mug between her hands and breathes in the fragrant herbal blend. The heat of the water is melting the honeycomb, infusing its sweetness into the tea. She drinks deeply, and then she breathes out and long, "Aaahhhhhh." After few more mouthfuls of food, she drains the mug and smiles. Her face is one of sublime contentment. Color washes across her nose and cheeks. She wipes the moisture from beneath her nose.

Fawn is satisfied with the result. Her healing tea is working, sweating the poison from Raven's body, bringing her internal systems back into harmony.

"I think I will send this recipe home with you. A cup every morning will start your day out right," she says.

"Thank you! Um … how about the *sofkee*, too?"

"Done." Fawn laughs.

"Mom, I hate to say it, but we've got to get on the road. This was a quick pleasure-mixed-with-business trip, but we wanted to see you," Dane says.

Fawn looks down at the floor for a moment, then she lifts her face to the young couple in a radiant smile, nodding. They all exchange hugs, and then Raven leaves the room to get changed.

As soon as Raven is out of earshot, Fawn turns to Dane. "You will give her this tea each morning, Dane. It will cleanse her system. Don't defy me, Son. It may save her life."

A chill tickles the back of Dane's neck. His mother is rarely wrong in matters of life and death. He nods, and then pulls his mother close, holding his lips against her cheek before going into the bedroom.

Fawn busies herself with gathering the ingredients for the *sofkee* and placing them in a large paper bag. She writes preparation instructions on the side of the bag—simple enough that even a non-cook like Raven can understand. Setting that aside, she fills an empty coffee can with the dried herbs for the healing tea—willow, chamomile, sweet grass, and dandelion to calm the system, stinging nettle and spiral orchid to purify the blood, and boneset for fever. In a Mason jar, she packs three long lengths of honeycomb full of honey for sweetening the tea.

Fawn takes the lid off a tiny pine straw basket and removes a dry grayish bundle of sage, wrapped with colored embroidery thread. She lights the tip, and then blows out the flame. Inhaling the smoke from the smoldering sage, she holds it in her lungs. She closes her eyes and asks Father Spirit to bless the tea, and then exhales the smoke into the canister, quickly sealing the medicine with the plastic lid. *It may save her life*, she confirms.

"I love the smell of sage," Dane says behind her. "It's one of the few things that doesn't interfere with my clairscent abilities."

Fawn gives him the basket, the paper bag, the coffee can, the jar, and a stern look. "Never forget the old ways, Dane. They've kept our people going for many years."

"Mmmmm! What's that?" Raven says.

"Sage. It cleanses your home, your body, and your mind. Dane can show you how to use it. If you run out, let me know, and I will send more … and *sofkee* and morning tea. These are things you must have," Fawn says. She reaches down beneath the table platform and retrieves a larger basket, this one made of split palm leaves. "In this basket are things I want you to have. When they heard Dane was getting married, all the ladies in the village made you something."

Raven removes the lid of the basket and pulls out the contents one by one. The first is a tiny box, no larger than a deck of cards, completely covered with seed beads. Inside, Raven finds a set of dangle earrings, a bracelet, and a matching triple strand necklace of red, yellow, white, and black seed beads offset with tiny porcupine quills.

"The jewelry is made by Mary Wilbur. She's the best jewelry maker in the village," Fawn says. "The metal is sterling silver, and the quills came from a porcupine in the woods behind the village."

Seeing Raven's wide eyes, she laughs. "Oh, don't fret, Raven. She didn't kill him. She got them from her curious dog's nose. The beaded box is from Minnie Louie. She's a master in the folk life apprenticeship program."

Raven replaces the jewelry in the small box and reaches back into the basket. Wrapped in a piece of cloth are two dolls, about eighteen inches tall. The male doll is dressed in a long, belted shirt like the ones she saw in the gift shop. On its head is a cloth turban. It has no hands at the end of the long shirt sleeves, and the legs are bare, ending in an indication of moccasins. The eyes and mouth are very simply sewn in colored embroidery floss; the nose, a ridge pulled tightly with thread.

The female doll is dressed in a patchwork skirt and short shawl. It also has no hands, and the facial features are embroidered. Around its neck is a replica of Raven's necklaces, and identical earrings hang from a place where ears should be. It's hair is black cloth, fashioned to look like Fawn's "hair hat." Both dolls are made from a course fiber, giving them a dark reddish-brown skin color.

"Susie Osceola is our doll artist. She uses the traditional palmetto fiber for the bodies."

"I recognize my jewelry and your hair," Raven observes.

"That's right. It's a conspiracy. We all got together to make everything match up. Notice the patterns in your doll's dress. They each have special significance."

Raven looks closer at her doll. She points to each line of patchwork in turn as Fawn explains the symbols. The uppermost patchwork strip is brown with white symbols, each of which looks like upside down "T" with another white line extending from the juncture at an angle running southwest to northeast.

"That is your clan symbol. Dane says your clan is bird."

"Yes. That looks a little like a bird's foot."

The next strip shows a jagged white expanse above a jagged red expanse, giving the appearance of sharp white teeth above blood red ones.

"That one is the symbol for fire," Fawn says.

"Oh. I thought it was teeth," Raven says.

"Fire has been known to bite, it's true, but focus on the red flames instead of the white part overhead. This symbolizes your mate. Since Dane is a fire marshal, we thought this pattern was appropriate. The next one below stands for the four directions—the medicine colors. Black diamonds in the north and south, red diamonds in the east and west, separated by the yellow cross, or 'X' mark, on a white background. This is for protection, health, and to help you find your way in all things."

"And the last pattern?" Raven asks, pointing to a black strip with white vertical lines, cut by two smaller horizontal lines in the upper half of the line.

"That is the symbol for tree—the way the love between you and your mate should grow."

Raven looks at the dolls in wonder, noticing similar patterns on the male doll's shirt. "I recognize fire, four directions, and tree. What's that one?" She indicates a pattern of alternating white and turquoise zig-zags running northwest to southeast on a black background.

"That is lightning—the symbol for power. Lightning is one of the strongest elements in the universe. It gives light and fire, life and death. Dane is the seventh son of a seventh son, and he holds power that has passed down through many generations. You must be a seventh child, too. Dane says you have the gift."

"I draw what is and isn't visible to the naked eye. Dane and the others are training me now. And let me tell you, it isn't as easy as I thought it would be!" Raven laments her lack of skills.

"Don't let her kid you, Mom. She's doing great," Dane says, winking at his sweetheart.

"Fawn. One thing I don't get. You said that Dane is the seventh son. That makes Noah the eighth. How did he get the gift?" Raven asks.

Fawn's smile freezes as she looks at Raven, and then at Dane. "That's a question we have been asked before. Noah would not ordinarily have the second-sight," she admits.

Raven looks at her to complete the explanation.

"Power is its own master; it touches those of its own choosing," Fawn says simply.

"What about you? Do you have the gift?"

"Power also chose me, but I am not gifted like you and the boys are. I learned my arts from my mother. She was Cedar Woman—a healer. And now I am Cedar Woman. But that's a story for another time. You have more presents. The last one I made for you myself."

Raven reaches into her basket now and pulls out a skirt and shawl identical to the one worn by her doll. She jumps to her feet holding the clothing up against her, swinging around so that the skirt fans out from her legs.

"Wow! This is gorgeous! I can't wait to wear it. But not today. It's too pretty for every day. I'm going to save it for a special occasion …" She stands very still and looks up at Fawn. "I'm going to save it for my wedding day, if that's all right with you."

Fawn rushes forward and squeezes the young woman tightly in a fierce embrace. "That is the greatest gift you can ever give me, Raven. I am so honored."

Dane waits as long as he can to separate the two women, but he knows the time is short, and he and Raven need to return to Tallahassee. Work beckons, and the dead cannot rest until The Trackers discover the cause of their passing. Amid kisses and tears, they part ways.

CHAPTER EIGHT
IN SICKNESS

THE RETURN TRIP TO TALLAHASSEE passes much the same way as
the trip to Tampa did. Raven naps most of the way, waking to
guzzle Diet Coke and reapply her perfume. True to Dane's fear, the
canister is emptied before they even get to the town of Perry. Raven
mourns the end of her fragrance with atypical crankiness,
complaining about the heat and the discomfort of the car seat. Dane
pulls into a rest area, so she can walk and stretch her legs a bit.
When she returns from the restroom, he suggests that she draw for
a while.

"With what? On what?" she snaps.

Bringing his hands out from behind his back, he presents
her with a box of sharpened colored pencils and a spiral-bound
sketch pad. Instantly, her mood changes to childish delight.

"You are the best, Dane!"

"Mom's not the only Lightfoot around to bear presents,
m'love," he says.

Raven climbs in the seat and, after a thank-you kiss, flips
the pad open on her lap.

"What'cha gonna draw?" he asks.

"Your mother," she says, busily sketching the face she sees

so clearly in her mind. This is not only her gift, but her talent as well. She hums tunelessly while she draws.

Dane is pleased that she is distracted, at last. *I'll get a new canister of DeVanille for her just as soon as we get back to Tallahassee,* he decides. He glances over at her, and then he settles in for the remainder of the long drive.

Raven takes great care with the portrait of Fawn. She draws her profile, gazing wistfully off into the sky. But the finished picture seems sad, as if Fawn is looking for something she cannot find. That is not the way Raven wants to draw her, but *the pencil is its own master.* She cocks her head to the side. *Funny. That's what Fawn said about Power.*

She flips to the next page and begins again. She decides to sketch a frontal head shot. The image she creates is wonderful. It captures the exquisite lines of Fawn's face and the ubiquitous "hair hat." As she adds contours, color, and shading, it appears that Fawn is right there looking at her. She finishes the picture and looks away out the window.

When she looks back at the image, she is aware that something is not quite right. She studies the face and finds the flaw. The eyes. The eyes are the right shape but the wrong color. Fawn has black onyx eyes in her honey-colored face. The eyes in Raven's picture are light blue—almost silver. The sight of them sends a cramp to her stomach. *I know these eyes, don't I?*

Irritated, she flips to yet another page. This time she draws a full-length picture of Fawn with her hand on the head of her pet goose, Emma. *Oh, yes. This one is going to be special.* Fawn is looking down toward the goose, and she wears a tender smile on her lips. The goose has its head lifted toward the woman, its golden eye shining. Fawn wears her traditional Seminole skirt and shawl, dangling earrings, and seed bead necklaces, and her hair is twisted into a long braid which hangs over her shoulder. Her feet are bare on the swept dirt floor of her *chickee,* and in her other hand she holds the smoldering stick of sage. This is the Fawn she met at the Seminole Village. This is the mother-in-law she already loves.

Satisfied at last, Raven finishes her portrait of Fawn and flips the page over to the next blank. She stares at the paper for a while, waiting for an image to form in her mind. Her vision blurs, and she begins to draw. Her hand moves rapidly and jerkily across the page, and an animal theme emerges. She draws a striped and spotted cat with an elongated muzzle. It stands inside a small cage, its paw lifted, its lips pulled back in a hiss. A tiny long-handled spoon rests in the foreground. Over and over the motif repeats— cat, cage, spoon, cat, cage, spoon. Suddenly she stiffens and groans.

"G-get me ... get me ... ho .... home."

Dane hears Raven moaning and looks at her in alarm. Seeing her stiff posture and closed eyes, he recognizes that she has fallen into a trance. He pulls the car over to the shoulder of the road and closes his eyes, sending a homing beacon for her to follow. In a minute, she opens her eyes to find him staring at her.

"Babe, you were tracking. Are you O.K.?"

"Yeah, I'm fine. I didn't mean to track, Dane. Sheesh! What's wrong with me?" Looking down at the paper in her hands, she gives it her complete attention. "Look at this! What in the world? I can draw better than this."

"Um ... is that a cat? With a really long nose?"

"I don't know what it is. And what does a spoon have to do with a cat? I'm losing it, Dane. I think I'm coming down with the flu or something."

"What feels bad? Do you have to throw up?"

"No, but I ache all over, my throat is so dry, I'm burning up ... and I can't go."

"What are you saying?"

"I keep going into the restrooms, but I can't seem to go. I can't pee!" She gasps, gulping for air. "I'm sick, honey. I'm really sick. Please get me home."

"We're almost there, Babe. Just hang on." Jamming on the accelerator, he fishtails onto the blacktop. Ignoring the unwritten five-miles-over-the-speed-limit rule, he races down the highway, passing cars left and right. Up ahead, he sees the exit that takes them to his house, but looking over at the misery Raven is in, he decides to bypass the turnoff and head to Tallahassee Memorial Hospital. *Mom was right; she is more than sick.*

Dane pulls the car up to the curb of the emergency

entrance, slams it into park, and rushes around the front to open Raven's door. Gathering her in his arms, he carries her inside and up to the desk. Raven is in respiratory distress, so they take her in to a treatment room immediately.

Dane paces in the waiting room, aware that his true love's life hangs on the abilities of the doctors to heal her. Waiting is torture, but waiting alone is worse than torture, so he uses the desk phone to call Lee, asking him to call Noah and Graham.

Less than 15 minutes later, Lee arrives, followed by Noah and Graham.

"Dane, what happened?" Lee asks, hurrying up to the younger man.

"I don't know, Hona. She started getting wiggy on the way home. Then she tracked while she was asleep. After that, it was downhill, and I knew she was in a pretty bad way."

"She tracked?"

"Yeah. Not intentionally. More like she went into a trance. She drew the most gosh-awful picture of a cat. Well, it sorta looked like a cat—a mutated one. I don't know. It was weird. Then, right after that, she got really, really ill."

"What do you think is going on?" Noah asks.

"Noah, Mom said Raven was sick. No, wait … Mom said Raven was poisoned. I don't know how that can be, but I think she was right."

"You know Mom. She knows those things. We have to figure out what poisoned her."

"Sure, don't worry, Dane. We'll find out who or what did this to her," Graham says.

Dane walks to the water fountain and spots the doctor. He sprints over to the door, just as the man enters the waiting room.

"Doctor—uh—Vidjapore, is she O.K.?" Dane asks.

"She will be fine, but I am keeping her for a few days to force fluids and get her temperature down. A high fever is especially dangerous, given her condition," he says gruffly in impeccably accented King's English.

Dane's eyes widen. "Is the … I mean, will she … what about the …"

"You should have thought about that before now, but, yes, everything is all right, so far." He answers with an impatient huff.

His manner puzzles the men waiting in the room. The doctor seems almost angry.

Lee walks up beside Dane. "Doctor, can you tell us what happened to her?"

"Who might you be, her father?" the doctor asks.

"No, I am her friend. This is her fiancé. We are quite worried about her. Perhaps you can explain her condition," Lee says evenly.

"Well, she is very lucky you brought her to the hospital. She is terribly dehydrated, her kidneys have been compromised, and she is on the verge of hypterthermia," he reports.

"What? Like getting frostbite?" Noah asks.

"No, it is the opposite. You are thinking of hypothermia. This girl is quite severely overheated," the doctor says.

"That sounds like ecstasy!" Dane says.

"Yes, young man. You are fortunate she is not dead. She has a considerable quantity of gamma hydroxybutyric acid in her bloodstream. You young people may think that ecstasy is fun and makes your relationship sexier, but it is a dangerous substance," the doctor admonishes. "In large doses, the drug can cause complete system breakdown. Your young lady is seriously ill."

"Whoa, whoa. Wait a minute. We have not taken ecstasy. In fact, we are working with the police department investigating ecstasy-related deaths," Dane insists.

Lee steps forward and puts his hand on Dane's shoulder, glancing back at Noah, who has a reputation for speaking and acting with thinking first. Graham takes the hint and pushes in closer to the young hothead.

"Doctor Vidjapore, we think that someone has been introducing an ecstasy drug into common foods or drinks, and people are having reactions to it. You can check with Chief Rowan of the Tampa Police Department. We've just come from there," Dane explains.

"Yeah, we aren't dope-heads." Noah growls in disgust.

"You may also contact Chief Jack Abernathy of the

Tallahassee Police Department to confirm, Doctor." Lee's tone is emphatic, yet restrained.

Doctor Anjul Vidjapore, a naturalized Indian American, appraises the Native Americans in his waiting room and realizes that he has committed an act he has fought to overcome since he first immigrated to the United States from Bombay. He has judged them on the basis of their ethnic origins, and he is ashamed.

"Please accept my sincerest apologies, gentlemen. I see so many people in here who have abused the social drugs that I jumped to conclusions. But the fact remains, the young lady is suffering from ecstasy poisoning. It is much like a teenage boy and girl I tried to revive just last week. Those kids died, but your lady will recover," he says, lowering his eyes humbly.

"Thank you, sir," Lee says. "We appreciate your candor. Perhaps we may work together to solve this crisis affecting our young people."

"Can I ... can I see her?" Dane asks anxiously.

"Of course, you can. We are not overly busy tonight. We have already been able to move her to a room. You may all go in, if you wish. But try not to overwhelm her. Her condition is fragile, and I have given her a sedative, so she will rest," the doctor says.

The Trackers follow the doctor's directions to Raven's room and stand before the partially closed door, unsure of what to do next. Finally, Noah pushes his way to the front and enters the room, the others following behind him.

Raven lies in the bed, an IV running from her forearm to a bag of clear saline solution overhead. She is pale, and her hair is splayed out on the pillow. Her breathing is shallow, but regular. A white sheet and cotton blanket cover her thin frame.

Dane sits on the rolling stool and walks it to her side, holding her hand. Noah moves to the other side, examining the IV bag, the blood pressure cuff, and everything else in the room. Lee and Graham stand guard at the foot rail. Nobody speaks. They just stare at her, willing her to be well.

A tiny line of spittle escapes the side of Raven's mouth and Dane reaches forward to wipe it away. She wakes and regards the somber faces assembled around her bed. She tries to speak, but her throat is dry. On a nearby wheeled table is a pink cup full of ice chips. She nods in the direction of the tray. Dane grabs the cup and gives her a spoonful of chips. She rolls them around in her mouth, sucking the melting water down her parched throat.

She smiles wanly and clears her throat. They look at her, waiting for her to speak.

"*Bleep,*" she utters.

CHAPTER NINE

TRACKING THE DRUG

THE EMERGENCY CRISIS WITH RAVEN has the entire Trackers Team unnerved. It is one thing to track strangers and casual acquaintances, but it is another when one of the Team is compromised. Now, it has become a personal case. Even though it is late, the men gather at Dane's house to discuss a plan of action, and an argument inevitably ensues.

"No, Graham. She's my fiancé, I'm tracking," Dane insists, clenching his fists.

"Lightfoot, you are the most stubborn man I have ever known." Graham scowls at his friend.

"Guilty as charged."

"Except for your squirrely little brother, that is."

"Ditto," Noah says.

"Gentlemen!" Lee says. "I have heard enough squabbling. I am pulling rank here. Dane, you make the first track. Sniff out the scent you picked up at the night club and compare it to whatever you can smell at Marjorie Collier's home. Noah will beacon for you. Then I want you, Graham, to track to the same nightclub and listen for any references to ecstasy or illegal drug activity. I will beacon for you. Does everybody understand? Under no circumstances are the four of us to be traveling or beaconing at the same time."

Ever since Noah was abducted, leaving Lee without a beacon, this had been a hard and fast rule. At least one person must be fully aware at all times.

All the men nod in agreement. Dane and Noah face each other across the table, while Graham and Lee seat themselves on the couch to wait. In just a short time, the Lightfoot boys are breathing in sync.

In less than ten minutes, Dane returns from his track looking confused and frustrated.

"Nothing. I can't smell anything but sweat and body odor and old flowers at the club tonight. The scent I tracked that first night was heavy and cloying, like rotted oranges covered with mold. And sort of like a damp locker room. You know. Musty, or musky, I guess. I can still smell a little bit of the oranges. It's faint, but it's all over the room."

"What about Marjorie Collier?" Graham asks.

"Same thing. Nothing really jumps out at me. But, then, her place is like going into the mall during Christmas. All the women at the cosmetics counters are spritzing you with perfume samples. Makes me gag."

"It's my turn, then," Graham says. "I'm going clubbing!" He closes his eyes and begins tracking. As his beacon, Lee closes his eyes in turn and listens for the word.

Graham's track is also short—fifteen minutes in all. When he returns and opens his eyes, the team is waiting anxiously for his report. Taking a deep breath, Graham begins speaking in the voices of the people he has just heard.

"Hey, man. I'm looking to score some happy. Got any?" a young man asks, his voice a tremulous tenor.

"Depends on what you're looking for, pal," a deeper baritone-voiced young man says.

"I need Kleenex—for my runny nose. You dig?" the tenor voice says.

"Sorry, but 'The Mister' is already gone," the deep baritone voice says.

"Maaan! That sucks," the tenor whines. "When's 'The

Master' coming back?

The baritone snickers. "He's not the 'Master,' you dweeb. It's 'Mister,' and he won't be back until next week."

The tenor curses. "This kills my buzz. My girl's gonna freak. I promised her I'd X her tonight! Now what am I gonna do?"

"Hey there, handsome. 'The Mister' left some scent samples with me, if you want to surprise her with a tester," a female with a lilting soprano voice says.

"And what's a tester, sweet thing?" the tenor asks.

"All the latest fragrances in spray testers. I've got the perfumes in my bag, but they aren't cheap," the soprano says.

"Why would I want a perfume?" the tenor asks.

"Because 'The Mister' has added some special ingredients to them. And each one comes with a lollipop of your choice," the soprano croons.

"What about X?" the tenor asks.

"Um hm. I bet your girl would like *Chatoyant No. 2* or maybe *VinDoux*," the soprano says.

"*Chatoyant* for sure. How much?" the tenor asks.

"Two bills for a guaranteed rush like you've never known. Your girl will really thank you, if you know what I mean," the soprano says.

"Give me both," the tenor says. "That'll give me two chances at heaven."

Graham stops talking and looks around at his stunned teammates. Each is lost in his own thoughts; the news is more horrific than they even imagined.

Lee breaks the silence. "Tainted perfumes full of narcotics. What kind of person would even dream of doing such a thing?"

Dane bites his lower lip and stares at the floor. Noah reaches over and places his hand on his brother's shoulder, noticing that giant tears are landing on Dane's knees behind the curtain of his long black hair.

"I poisoned her. It was in her perfume all the time, and I didn't even know," he whispers.

"Dane, it has no scent. There was no way you could've picked it up. You couldn't know her perfume was laced with drugs."

"I should have known. Mom was right. Raven was poisoned from the inside. It went through her skin, Noah. Through her skin and into her bloodstream. I almost killed her!" He puts his head in his hands and weeps bitterly.

Noah embraces his stricken brother, not even bothering to stem his own tears. Lee and Graham move back, letting the brothers console each other.

"What do you think, Graham? Is this 'Mister' a local man, or could he be from out of town? Tampa, perhaps?" Lee says.

"I'm betting he's from a larger city. Maybe Tampa. I don't really know. Couldn't get a sense of his location from my track. That's your specialty, Lee. Let's give the boys a little time to get themselves together and then let's see if you can track him," Graham says.

"I'm O.K. Find this guy, Lee. You track him, and I'll go get him," Dane says. His face is damp, and his eyes are swollen, but his demeanor is hard. "I'll beacon."

"No, Dane. You and Noah take notes. You are much too emotional to beacon for me right now. Graham will do it. Go to the table and take notes. I will find him," Lee says.

Dane nods jerkily, knowing that his friend is right. Noah is already at the table with pencil and paper. He pushes a piece to his brother's seat. Pencils in hand, they watch as Lee and Graham settle onto the couch. In just a few minutes, Lee sighs. Eyes closed tightly in his trance, he begins to talk, and the two Lightfoot boys begin transcribing his track.

Lee's voice is monotone as he relates his track. "His steed is black as night, a fearsome cat poised to run. It races north, eyes blazing, reflecting the white and yellow stripes before its paws. It is dark as pitch and cold ... colder ... colder. The ground is brown, dead, covered with crystals. Red and yellow leaves fly away as he passes by. He has run for a long, long time. The sun set hours ago, and the moon is high to his right, and yet he races on and on." He is quiet for a short time, and then he begins speaking again.

"He slows now, his journey nearly ending. The stars before him are everywhere. High, low, right, left. Their colors shimmer and sparkle in circles, rectangles, dancing lines. He rests beneath the bright and brilliant spirits, amid the pulsing stars all around, near the wooded park in the center of the apple. And the Tracker now comes home," Lee says, opening his eyes.

Noah and Dane are already looking at their notes, deciphering the clues that Lee has given them through his cryptic poetic metaphor.

"What'd he say, guys?" Graham asks.

"See for yourself. This is one quirky poem this time!" Noah says, showing Graham his notes.

"I got the car, I think," Dane says. "It's definitely black, and I think it's a Jag. That's the only 'cat' car that I know of."

"I'm with you there," Noah says. "Jaguars have that neat silver figurine on the hood—the cat poised to run."

"Going north, eyes blazing—that's headlights for sure. Reflecting white and yellow stripes on the road," Graham says, looking over Dane's shoulder.

"It's getting colder as he goes farther north. Leaves falling, frost on the ground. Way farther north," Dane says.

"He left before sunset, and it's taking a long time because it's night, and the moon is high," Noah says, checking his notes.

"Still going north. Moon's up in the east, on the right side of the car," Dane agrees.

"Where's he stopped?" Graham asks.

"Stars all around. Colors, shapes, dancing?" Dane says, eyes wide.

"Neon! Big city lights. Signs. He's in a large city in a downtown area," Noah says.

"Good catch, little bro," Dane says.

"A big city with a wooded park in the center of the apples? Wooded park. Apple trees?" Graham says.

"No, he said 'apple.' Singular," Dane says.

"Woodville, Longwood, Parker, Applewood. I can't think of any big cities with wood, park, or apple in their names," Noah says, chewing on his pencil.

"Central Park," Lee says. "It is in the …"

"Big Apple!" the men say in unison.

"He's in New York City," Dane says.

"Exactly," Lee says.

"And that's where I'm going," Dane says, jumping up to grab his coat.

"Not without me, you don't," Noah says, knocking his chair over in his haste to get up.

"Just one minute, you two," Lee says. "Nobody is going anywhere without a plan of action. It is so like you boys to run off half-cocked like this. Dane. Noah. Sit! Now. There is plenty of time to go hunting, but let's know what we're dealing with before you go. Sit, I said."

Like chastised children, Dane and Noah plop down on the couch while Lee casually picks up the telephone and dials Jack Abernathy's home number.

"He's right, you know," Noah says. "We don't even know who we're looking for."

"Someone called 'Mister,' which could be just about anyone," Graham says.

"You said, '*The* Mister,' Gray. That's a little more specific," Noah points out.

"I stand corrected, but that doesn't change the fact that none of us have seen his face or even heard his voice. We need a little more info from Chief Abernathy," Graham says, shrugging his broad shoulders.

"Aaaaagh! You're right. I'm just so ..." Dane says.

"... impulsive ... insane?" Graham offers.

"Oh, step off, Gray," Dane says.

"Step off? Did you really just say, 'step off?' You've been watching *'Seinfeld'* again!" This sends Graham into a giggling fit that passes to the other men when he starts doing impressions of the characters from the TV sitcom. The tension broken by much needed laughter, they all relax and wait for Lee to finish gathering information from the Police Chief.

Lee hangs up the phone and takes a seat at the table. "Jack is checking on the man called 'The Mister' from the club. And he is dispatching a detail to the club to find the girl with the perfume testers. Graham, you may have to go to the station and do a voice I.D. tonight. Is that all right with you?" Lee says.

"Sure thing. I can identify the bartender and the other guy, too, if they round everybody up and if the guy and his girl are still there," Graham says.

"What about us finding this guy in New York?" Dane asks.

"That will be a little tricky since we do not know anything about him. Jack can coordinate with the NYPD to see if there have been any ecstasy-related deaths up there involving tainted perfumes," Lee says.

"I'm still going, Hona. Remember the moldy orange smell I told you about. I know what it is. It's a sickness smell. Jimbo had that smell. I don't know why I didn't recognize it before. Guess I blocked it out," Dane says.

"Jimbo had cancer, Dane. You can smell cancer? Impressive," Noah says.

"I suppose. Anyhow, I'm sure it's the guy. He's covered in the perfume scents, but there's that underlying odor of disease. That's what I've been trying to identify. It was on the kids at the club and the Collier woman...and on Raven. It wasn't the ecstasy, it was the man. He touched the bottles. If I can smell him, I can find him!" Dane insists.

"And if he's going, I'm going," Noah says. "Your rule. Nobody tracks alone."

"Fine," Lee says. "You are both going ... in the morning! Tonight, you two must get some sleep. Graham and I will work things from this end, along with Jack. Pack warm clothes, boys. New York is a very cold city, in more ways than just the weather."

CHAPTER TEN
COUNTRY BOYS IN THE CITY

LEE IS RIGHT ABOUT NEW YORK. It is a very cold city, in many ways. For two young men born and raised in balmy Florida, the temperature difference is extreme, and so is the culture shock. As soon as they step out of the airport at LaGuardia, the Lightfoots know they are in a foreign land.

The taxi ride to the city is less than pleasant, and they are sure that they will die in a horrible traffic accident. The driver speaks a form of English that neither of them can understand, and the fare is more than they anticipated. Fortunately, Lee had the foresight to give them plenty of cash and his own credit card. They lug their bags out of the trunk, thankful to be alive as the car careens back into the sea of vehicles.

After checking into their hotel, Dane and Noah hit the streets to find the New York Police Department. They decide walking may be the safer option, so armed with a map of the "Big Apple" and a subway schedule, they exit the hotel and survey the city's alien surroundings.

Gone are the large expanses of grassy lawns in front of wood framed houses with screened-in porches. Instead, there are endless concrete sidewalks leading to row upon row of apartment buildings, their cracked cement steps framed with iron handrails and heavy front doors covered over in years of reapplied paint. There are no flowers, no yard gnomes, no dog houses in sight. The few trees are segregated by spindly wrought-iron fences surrounding their meager trunks, which jut out from between the sidewalk sections.

Looking up, the gray sky peeks between towering buildings with metal staircases running like rickrack to the roofs. As the clouds move overhead, Noah's sense of balance is confounded. He grips the handrail to steady himself and vows not to look up ever again. Instead, he studies the undulating crowd of bodies.

The people walk with purpose, not stopping to chat or visit with neighbors. Nobody saunters, nobody lopes. Their gate is brisker than the weather. Wrapped in long coats, scarves around their necks, hats on their heads, gloves on their hands, they seem like a marching army advancing on the enemy. They push, they shove, they elbow. They just keep going.

And then there is the smell. Dane spends much of the time shielding his nose from the onslaught of odors. The best scents are those of baking bread, roasting meats, and foods of every ethnic origin. The worst are the stench of the unwashed, the vehicle exhausts, and the combined mix of the expensive fragrances worn by virtually every moving ant in the colony. But of all the odors, Dane's scent identification of New York City is that of roasting chestnuts and urine.

For Noah, the sight of so much activity makes his eyes hurt. He can't stop looking. The movement on the street draws his attention like moving strings draw cats. And as he looks, his eidetic mind stores and catalogs the information until it seems his head will burst. His only solution is to look directly at the ground, at the forward motion of his own two plodding feet, while he presses close to his brother.

Thankfully, the New York Police Department is just up ahead. He relies on Dane to lead the way, relieved when they ascend the stairs and enter the front doors. But, looking up, he realizes that the hubbub continues inside the building. He spots a clock and fixes his gaze on that one solitary object.

The desk Sergeant is a slender, middle-aged man, with

short brown hair and a small mustache. He looks nothing like the television cop stereotype. And, in contrast to their expectations, he is polite and helpful, directing them to an office for a meeting with a detective familiar with their agenda. Once again, Lee and Jack have already paved the way for them.

Detective Michael Ortega shakes their hands and offers them seats across from his desk. He smiles often and has a habit of running his long fingers through his thinning hair. Dane and Noah feel comfortable with him at once.

"We got a call from your Chief Abernathy late last night and were able to pull quite a lot of information about the notorious perp in question. He's called 'The Mister' because of the way he traffics illegal narcotics. In perfumes, of all things. He adds GHB—liquid X—to the perfumes and sells them in their original bottles. They call him 'The Mister' because all the products he moves have spray bulbs or push down atomizers. The drug gets in the system through the skin, and sometimes by inhaling the fine mist. It's hard to detect because ecstasy has no distinguishable odor. It doesn't interfere with the smell of the fragrance," Chief Ortega says.

"Yeah. We found that out," Noah says. "You can't tell if a bottle is tainted or not."

"That's what makes it so hard to catch this guy. You should know that New York has a huge counterfeit fragrance ring, and we can't seem to bust it up. We've had undercover working it for years. Every time we catch a break, another boss takes over and sets up in a different location. We think 'The Mister' was part of this ring, but not anymore. In fact, we think he's gone solo with his own special brand of counterfeiting and tampering. The kids love it because their parents can't tell they're tripping. The laced testers are easier to get their hands on, cheaper, and can be concealed in a purse or a pocket," Ortega says.

Or a moccasin, Dane thinks.

"We've found ecstasy in perfumes as far south as Tampa," Noah says.

"Yeah. We think he's running a line from New York to Tampa and possibly points in between. But mostly in Florida. I think that's where he's establishing his territory. You've discovered three deaths?" Ortega says.

"That's all we know of for now. There could be more, but we haven't been on the case very long," Dane says.

"I understand. And how did you discover the 'smellex' was the cause?" Ortega asks.

"What did you just say?" Noah asks.

Ortega smiles and shrugs. "We call it 'smellex' here. You know … smell ecstasy. Everything has a nickname on the streets."

"Uh huh. I gotcha. My fiancé got terribly sick from it," Dane says.

"Really? How'd she get hold of it?" Ortega asks.

"I bought it from a small boutique in Tallahassee," Dane says. "I didn't know it was laced, and I bet they didn't either. Do you think that guy has a partner? So far, the other victims bought it at a club,"

"No, Dane. What about Marjorie Collier? I bet she didn't get it at a club. She seemed to be wealthy," Noah says

"The wealthy like a good deal as well as the lower class," Ortega says. "Need to check out that boutique. See if it's a chain or franchise or a personally-owned small business."

"Right. I'll have Lee get on it," Noah says.

"What can you tell me about this 'Mister' character? All we know for sure is that he frequents the clubs in Florida and drives a black jaguar," Dane says.

"No kidding? How'd you boys find that out?" Ortega asks, eyebrows raised.

Dane and Noah exchange glances. "Through our investigation. From … uh … a person at a club who saw a guy drive away in a fancy car," Noah says.

"Good work. That's more than we have. Here, he's in the shadows. In the wind. We don't know what he looks like. Nobody has him on the radar, as far as I know, in New York. But we're sure he gets his product here," Ortega says.

"Do you have any idea where? Is it a major fragrance manufacturing house?" Noah asks.

"The perfume I got for my fiancé was a major brand, from Guerlain. I know they are based here in New York," Dane says.

"Look, you guys. I'm all for helping out other departments, but I'm not comfortable with you two nosing around where you don't belong. No offense or anything, but you're not cops. Abnernathy said to give you information. That's it. I don't want you Florida guys turning up dead in my town," Ortega says.

For once, Noah is the level-headed brother. He grasps Dane's forearm and settles him before he can jump up. "We understand, sir. We are just investigating and trying to get a handle on what we're dealing with in Florida. If you can give us any leads that we can take back with us, we really appreciate it."

"No problem. I'm not trying to be a jerk. It's just that you guys could get hurt, you know. I'll make you a copy of the file pertaining to 'The Mister' for your Chief. And if you want to know more about how they make perfumes, check out the Fashion Institute of Technology. They started the Fragrance Foundation. My wife and I visited once. It's an interesting place, but too foo-foo for my taste." Ortega wrinkles his nose.

"Thanks. That sounds like a plan. We'll go there before we leave for home," Noah says.

Michael Ortega takes the file and leaves the office to make a copy. Dane turns angrily to Noah. "I'm not going home until I find this guy."

"Me neither, bro. But I'm not telling that detective. Let's just go along with him thinking we're gonna sightsee a little before we leave. I sure don't want to tick him off and be made to go back before we're ready."

Dane presses his lips together and nods, patting Noah on the shoulder. In just a moment, Ortega returns with a stack of stapled papers. He smiles and remains standing, the cue for the men to end their meeting.

"Thanks again, Detective Ortega. You've been a great help," Dane says.

"No problem. I hope you catch him in Florida and save me the paperwork," he says.

"Yeah, I gotcha. Oh, by the way. We heard that he gives out lollipops with his spray testers. What's up with that?" Noah says.

"That's for the 'clamping' side effect. X users tend to clench their jaws and grind their teeth. Sucking lollipops is one way to relieve that tendency. Also, you might see them wearing big baby pacifiers around their necks for the same reason. The clubs around here keep bubble gum and suckers on the bar. As far as dope goes, ecstasy is one of the milder ones, but deadly just the same."

A chill races down Dane's back as he thinks back to Raven chewing pack after pack of gum. *If I'd only known*, he laments

"Good luck," Ortega says. "Hope you enjoy the tour. Don't buy any perfume while you're here, though. You'll go broke."

Noah and Dane laugh and make their way out to the street and the pandemonium that is New York City. Consulting their map, they locate the street address for the Fashion Institute of Technology, and it necessitates another harrowing taxi ride. This time, their driver is a young Jamaican man with a huge colorful cap of green, orange, and purple barely containing the dreadlocks inside it and a gold front tooth that gleams when he smiles—which he does frequently. Unlike the other cabbie, Jaffey—which he pronounces "jah-Fee"—is chatty and personable.

"You visitin' te city, eh? For te first time, Mon?" Jaffey says to the older Lightfoot brother.

"Yep. First time. Y'all sure have a lot of people."

"Who is Joll?"

"No, not joll. Y'all. It's short for you all."

"Oh, you are from te south? Jaffey know te south. Grits and hounddogs and tings like tat. Tis warm down in te south, eh?"

"By comparison, yeah. Hey Jaffey, what do you know about street dope sold in perfume?" Noah asks.

"You tink all Jamaicans are dopeheads? Jaffey does not take dope. If tat is what you are here for, you get out of tis cab," Jaffey says frowning.

"No, no, no. You misunderstand. We're working with the police from down in Florida," Dane says.

"My brother's fiancé was given some perfume laced with ecstasy, and she's very sick. We're trying to find out where it came from," Noah says.

"If you are narco, ten you better be careful. Te X trafficers are very bad, Mon. Tey will kill you if you cross tem. Don't go talkin' like tis to jus anybody. You already look different, you know!"

"We look different?"

"Yes. You do. Wit tat long black hair and tem dark tans. You 'tract attention. Good lookin' Indian fellows, too. Be careful. Bad people here."

"Thanks, Man. Appreciate the heads up," Dane says.

"Hey, Jaffey. Did you know that your name means 'trickster rabbit' in our language?" Noah says.

"Is tat right?" Jaffey laughs, a deep resonant sound from his chest, before pulling his cab to a stop at the curb.

"Yeah, except we spell it c-v-f-e. It's still pronounced 'Cha-Fee' though."

"Hmm. Maybe it would be good to change te spelling. Jaffey might be a trickster, eh? Here is te place you are going. And here is my card. If you get into any trouble—and Jaffey is afraid tat you might—call tat number and Jaffey will come get you. Keep your money. Jaffey is a big fan of te Seminoles." Jaffey pulls his cab back into the flow of traffic, but Dane and Noah can still hear him singing the Seminole war chant.

In front of them stands the Fashion Institute of Technology, a mid-century structure of metal panels in a harlequin pattern. Inside they hope to find some answers to the counterfeit perfume trade. They nod to each other and begin to climb the stairs. Before they reach the door, a young woman in garish pink fake fur thrusts a pamphlet into their hands.

"Save the civets," she says as they approach. "No more testing on innocent animals."

"Right on," says Noah, pumping his fist as he walks on past the woman.

Dane takes the literature and stuffs it in his back pocket. Together, he and Noah enter the front door, away from the visual and olfactory sensory overload of the streets.

CHAPTER ELEVEN
MAKING SCENTS

INSIDE THE FOYER OF THE INSTITUTE'S C building, also called the Martin Feldman Center, stands a mock-up of the plans for an expansion to the building, boasting Italian marble tile floors and spotless mirrors on the walls. According to the model, glassed-in staircases will flow like rivers all around the interior of the building, inspired by stitching patterns and folded fabric. A North Quad on the fifth floor will connect to the C Building's South Quad, and a decorative glass expanse will replace an existing brick wall. It looks elegant and costly.

"Wow," Noah says. "And I thought the F.S.U. campus was beautiful." Turning back, he notices that Dane is already at the desk, asking questions.

The petite blond receptionist pushes some leaflets across the desk with bright fuchsia manicured fingernails, letting her hand rest on the papers as he tries to pick them up. She stares boldly into Dane's eyes while tapping on the paper in his hand. He looks off to the right, and then back to Noah. He grins and thanks the coquette, not missing the wink of her heavily shadowed eye. Dane hurries to Noah's side, clutching the mass of handouts.

"Gag. I swear I can still taste her cologne," Dane says

rubbing his nose vigorously.

"Growl, meow, meow." Noah purrs like a big cat.

"Yeah, scary. I thought she was going to pounce on me right there."

"Me, too. What'd you get?"

"Nobody here to talk to, but she said we can audit a class down the hall about Michael Edwards and the Fragrance Wheel."

"Who's that?"

"Beats me, but Francine said the class is a 'must go' for fragrance majors."

"Oooo. Francine, huh?"

"Shut up, you doofus. Let's go catch that class and see if we can learn something." Dane heads down the hall.

The double doors to the lecture hall squeak slightly as Dane opens them, and the two brothers wince as they tip toe into the room. Sliding into a couple of seats in the back row, they blink, adjusting their eyes to the darkness. In the front of the room, a large screen is filled with the image of a color wheel, of sorts. Dane counts thirteen different colors around the perimeter of the circle ranging from yellow to blue to green to a variety of pink and red hues. Around the colors are four different word groups categorizing floral notes, oriental notes, woody notes, and fresh notes. At the microphone, the speaker continues her lecture.

"...then, in 1983, Michael Edwards, a European perfumer, attended a fragrance seminar held by one of the largest privately-owned companies in the perfume business. Mr. Edwards was so inspired by the techniques he learned there he developed the Fragrance Wheel you see pictured here. Edwards, as you may well know, had been Halston's international fragrance director for some time until Halston retired and sold his company.

"Edwards then moved to Sydney, Australia, to test market his scent guide. He *completely* revolutionized the fragrance industry when he developed this classification wheel. It took the *'perfumespeak'* out of selecting new fragrances. It takes accords, which you have learned are the foundation stones and base themes of raw material blends, and breaks them down into schemes, showing the relationships between each individual fragrance family. Since 1984, his guide for retailers has become *the* world's most comprehensive fragrance manual. It is updated annually to include all of the *Fragrances of the World."*

The screen image changes to that of a distinguished square-jawed man surrounded by perfume bottles of all shapes and sizes. The lecturer continues.

"Michael Edwards was *truly* a pioneer in the field of fragrances. I consider him a veritable spiritual figure, of sorts. In his own words, he tells us the Koran states, 'perfumes are foods that reawaken the spirit,' and his book is 'a fragrance map to a world of olfactory delights. A great perfume is a work of art. It is silent poetry, invisible body language. It can lift our days, enrich our nights and create the milestones of our memories. Fragrance is liquid emotion.'

"The man is *simply genius!* Thank you for your attention. Class is dismissed."

Students begin leaving the room from doors on the sides and in the back. Dane and Noah find themselves swimming upstream in a river of people as they struggle to reach the lecturer. The woman looks up at them, startled by their appearance, as they introduce themselves.

"We are investigating some deaths in Florida from tainted perfumes, and we were hoping to learn a little about the industry while we are here," Dane says.

"Oh. That's terrible. Well, it didn't happen at this school," the instructor says.

"We weren't suggesting that it did. We, uh, just are wondering how somebody would go about putting an illegal substance in a perfume bottle. A spray bottle," Noah says.

"I'm not really sure that I can help you with that. We just teach the mechanics of fragrance combination, how to be an evaluator trainee, a fragrance architect, a nose ..." she says.

"A nose?" Dane says.

She scoffs. "A nose is a person with a *highly* developed sense of smell who identifies the elements in a perfume."

"Like on the wheel?"

"Exactly. I see you paid attention to my lecture." She seems pleased at the prospect.

"Fascinating stuff. Edwards was a real pioneer."

"You really seem to have a good grasp of the industry, young man. Are you interested in becoming a perfumer?"

"Not me. But my brother ... he's really got a good nose."

"Is that right? Let's test it, shall we? Can you tell what I am wearing?" she asks Dane.

Dane is up to the challenge. He leans closer to the woman and inhales deeply.

"Could you put the slide of the wheel back up so I can refer to it, please?" he asks.

The professor obliges him, smirking slightly.

"O.K. Let me see. You are wearing, um, floral notes of jasmine ... iris ... white roses ... lavender ... daffodil ... and some other flower I can't really identify," he says.

Her mouth hangs open, and she purses her lips. "Very, *very* good, young man. Lily of the valley. That's the one you missed. And the fixative?"

"I don't know what a fixative is," Dane admits.

"A fixative is the base note that holds the fragrances together and gives the scent longevity. It reduces the evaporation rate and improves fragrance stability, so the perfume keeps its original aroma longer. The fixative of *my* perfume is amber. It's *quite* expensive."

"Amber is like a gemstone," Noah says.

"Amber is short for ambergris," she says.

"From whales?"

"Yes. The majority of base note fixatives are animal-based."

"Is that why the animal protection people are at your door?" Dane asks.

"Nuisances. Perfumers don't really harm animals." She huffs. "Nonetheless, I *am* impressed with your ability. Have you ever considered becoming a fragrance architect?"

"No, not really," he says. "I prefer fighting crime."

"Pity. Well, like I said, I can't really help you, but you might try the Sense of Smell Institute. They're the research end of the perfume industry. Good luck." She gathers her papers and flicks off the projector.

"Thanks for your help," Dane says, but she is already walking away.

"Hey!" Noah calls, causing her to turn back. "What's the name of your perfume?"

"*Les Fleurs du Peintre Français*," she says before disappearing out the door.

"*The Flowers of the French Painter?* What a stupid name. C'mon 'Nose,' let's go," Noah says, clapping Dane on the back. They exit the building laughing.

The Sense of Smell Institute is a short walk away, so the two of them amble down the crowded sidewalk, shoving and bumping with the rest of the New York City population. After a brisk trek across the center of the city, they find themselves at the research facility. In contrast to the Fashion Institute, this place is more utilitarian. The men are instantly more comfortable.

The receptionist seems like a normal person. To Dane's relief, she doesn't try to hit on him. Also, he notices that the building has a rather neutral smell, and he is glad. The amalgamation of conflicting scents of the city have given him a pounding headache.

In a couple of minutes, a technician arrives wearing a tie and a plain white lab coat. The man is short and balding, but very obliging. He leads the men through a maze of hallways and into a spotless laboratory full of bottles, beakers, test tubes, and other technicians who smile at the sight of the handsome Native Americans in the lab.

"We are delighted to be of help to the police anytime we can. And especially to Florida police. I went there when I was a little kid, to the beach. It was great," the man says.

"Yeah, yeah. The beach is great. What do y'all do here?" Noah asks.

"I'm a chemist. Part of my job is to perform research on smell-related issues. The Fashion Institute of Technology was the birthplace for The Fragrance Foundation in 1949. A few years ago, in 1982, the Board of the Fragrance Foundation recognized a growing need for more research, so they established the Sense of

Smell Institute. We were originally called the Olfactory Research Fund, but they changed the name. The Institute supports scientific and psychological research around the world in hospitals and universities. Our overarching mission is to unravel the mysteries and the importance of the sense of smell. We also delve into the psychological benefits of fragrance." He gives a tight smile.

"Would that be like aromatherapy?" Dane asks.

The man's smile becomes enormous, revealing a mouthful of large, brilliantly white teeth. "That is exactly right! What can we help you with?"

"Perfume sabotage. We've had deaths in Florida from ecstasy-laced perfumes."

"Oh, dear. We call that 'a fly in the juice.' It's becoming a serious problem, and we're looking for a way to combat it," the chemist says.

"A fly in the juice. Funny," Noah says.

"In the perfume industry, the liquid inside the bottle is called 'juice.' A 'fly' is an unintended substance that mars the product. You know, of course, that ecstasy has no odor. If it did, a 'nose' could detect it."

"We know what a nose is. My brother could be one," Noah says with a chuckle

"Not now, I couldn't. My nose doesn't work right at all. I can't identify anything that I'm smelling," Dane says.

"Oh dear. Sounds like you have Type I Hyposmia. It's an impairment of smell in which scents can still be detected but not recognized," the chemist says.

"Is it serious or permanent?" Dane asks.

"Not really. It originates in your olfactory epithelia area— that's the layer of roughly 15 million sensory cells that are in the upper-rear portion of your nose. It goes away on its own, like hay fever," the man says.

Dane exhales and rolls his eyes. "All I can smell is the city. How do you stand it?"

The chemist laughs. "Pretty rank, isn't it? You know how a coroner copes with autopsies on dead people? I do that, too. My jar of Vicks Vapor Rub® is my best friend some days. I'm sure your nose will be back to normal once you get back to Florida."

"Back to the problem at hand," Noah says. "How can we find this guy who is dosing the perfumes?"

"Ecstasy is a little like human pheromones, which are undetectable to the nose but experienced on a much deeper olfactory level. They have pretty much the same effect on the wearer and the smeller. Generate that animal lust. We've found a way to isolate the presence of pheromones with a color-changing additive. We're hoping that same additive will alert manufacturers and sellers to the presence of other added substances."

"How's that work?"

"Pretty simple, actually. We are urging perfumers to add a small quantity of the colorless, odorless liquid to their juice. If the fragrance is tampered with, the juice turns black. Believe me. Nobody wants black perfume." The chemist smiles broadly, pleased with his explanation.

"Sounds like a great plan for the future, but our problem is the stuff on the street right now. The only lead we have is that the guy selling it has cancer. If he touches the bottle with his bare hands, my brother smells rotten oranges."

The chemist drops his clipboard and stares at the two men. "Your brother can smell cancer?" He looks around at the other technicians in the room, but they are busy at their work.

"If you can smell cancer … wow. Are you interested in staying a little while longer? I'd love to do some tests on your olfactory epithelia."

"Maybe another time. We've really got to get back. My fiancé is sick, and I can't smell anything right now anyway," Dane says as he inches toward the door.

"Will you leave your contact information? I really would like to talk with you more."

"Sure thing. I'll call you, O.K.? C'mon Noah. Gotta go," Dane says.

The chemist has a predatory look in his eye that is frightening. Dane exits the room with Noah in tow. He looks right and left, but the maze of hallways has him confused.

"Noah. I'm lost here." He sucks in air and holds his breath.

"Follow me," Noah says.

Noah runs down the hallways with Dane on his heels. "Stupid, stupid, stupid. I'm sorry, Dane. I'll keep my mouth shut from now on."

"Just don't tell people I can smell cancer. I don't want to be locked up like a lab rat in this stinking city."

Out on the street, the Lightfoot brothers once again join the crush of the citizens. The weather has taken a turn for the worse, and their coats are hardly suitable for the drizzling rain. Shivering, they keep as close to the buildings as the crowd allows. The sun has set, and the lights of the city blaze. To Noah's sensitive eyes, the lights are like a psychedelic acid trip. He clutches at Dane's sleeve to keep from veering off the sidewalk. Noah suddenly turns down a darkened alley for a respite.

"What a pair we are, bro. I can't smell, and you can't see. What good are psychic gifts if you can't use them, huh?" Dane says.

"I'm gonna be sick, Dane. I swear I am." Noah moans, and then he vomits.

Dane puts his arm around his brother protectively, trying to soothe him. "Almost there, Noah. Just a few more blocks, I think,"

A noise back in the alley attracts Dane's attention. A shape emerges. A tall man dressed in a navy-blue pea coat and a ski cap bounces forward, followed by a huskier man in grey sweats and a red hoodie. They eye the brothers while looking side to side, checking for any others in the alley. *Muggers,* Dane realizes.

"Well, lookie here. Two pretty boys having a sweet moment." The pea coat punk makes kissing sounds with his dry, chapped lips.

The hoodie mugger rushes up and grabs Noah's arms, pulling them behind his back painfully. "I've got this one," he says.

Pea coat shakes his hand out, and a knife appears. "I'm gonna get me a new hairdo." He advances on Dane.

Dane hunkers down in a battle stance, but he carries no weapon to use against a knife. His only chance is to circle around and keep clear of the blade. The man continues the kissing sounds and laughs, taunting his prey.

Noah struggles with the larger man, but he is weak from the

nausea. The man slings him around, slamming his head against the brick wall. Noah crumples as all the lights go out.

"Noah!" Dane shouts, seeing his brother lying unconscious on the street.

The big man rushes Dane from behind, knocking him off his feet. Two well-aimed punches in the solar plexus leave him gasping for air. Suddenly, he feels his head jerked back as the man grabs his hair, pulling it tight and forcing him to look up at the mugger with the knife. Dane kicks out, but the man straddles his chest, immobilizing him. Reaching forward, the pea coat thug hacks through the hair held in his partner's hand. He jumps up, holding a long black ponytail and waving it in the air.

"Whoop, whoop, whoop. I scalped me an Indian," the pea coat assailant cries.

Hoodie punches Dane in the jaw and gets to his feet, moving toward Noah. "I'm gonna scalp the other one," he says.

Just then, the alley is bathed in bright light, and a blazing horn sounds. The muggers' startled faces are illuminated as they back away from the light. A tall, lithe man jumps from the car and runs toward the two men. He carries a baseball bat in his right hand. The attackers run, but the man is faster. He swings the bat once, and hoodie falls to the ground. Another swing sends pea coat into the wall. He hits them both again, for good measure, before turning back.

Dane's vision is bleary, but he can see that the man is now coming toward his brother. The man reaches Noah and kneels beside him.

"Leave my brother alone." Dane's voice is weak.

The man puts his arm beneath Noah's arm and helps him into a standing position. Shuffling over to Dane, Noah drops down and embraces his brother.

"You all right? Oh jeez, Dane. They cut off your hair." Noah puts his hand to Dane's head.

"Hair grows back, but if you dead, you dead," the rescuer assures him.

"Thanks, mister. It's a good thing you came by."

"What you mean came by? Been following you all day. Why

didn't you call Jaffey? Got in trouble, just like Jaffey said," the cabbie says.

"Jaffey? Oh, Jaffey. Thank you so much," Noah says.

"Tat's right. You are welcome. Now come, get in te car. Jaffey takin' you back to your hotel, and ten you gettin' outta tis city. New York is not for good Seminole boys like you." Jaffey walks them toward the car parked at the entrance to the alley.

Dane and Noah load up in the cab, and Jaffey drives them back to the hotel. He waits for them while they gather their yet unpacked bags and check out, and then he drives them straight to the airport. After getting their return tickets, he waits with them in the terminal until their flight is called.

There is not much talk. Each of them seems lost in their own thoughts. Noah nurses a bloody split in the side of his head, and Dane mourns the loss of his hair. Jaffey keeps his eyes on them like a strict chaperone. As they prepare to board, Dane reaches out and clasps Jaffey's hand.

"God bless you, brother. You saved our lives," Dane says, smiling weakly.

"Tank you for te blessing. Jaffey would save your life again, if he had to," Jaffey says.

The tall cabby opens Dane's hand and places a hank of long black hair in it. "Tat's all Jaffey could find. Sorry."

Dane regards the hair for a moment, and then he hands it back to the man. "Keep it to remember me by. Hair grows back, like you said."

Without delay, Jaffey pulls out a small pocketknife and slices off one long dreadlock. He holds it out to Dane. "Ten you keep tis to remember Jaffey by."

Dane takes the snakelike piece of hair and clutches it in his fist, nodding, too moved for words.

"I don't have anything to give you, Jaffey, but I'll never be able to thank you enough," Noah says. "Dane says you were great with that baseball bat."

"You gave Jaffey a new name. C-v-f-e. Maybe Jaffey is a trickster rabbit after all, eh?" He gives Noah a strong, slap-on-the-back hug.

The Lightfoot brothers bid Jaffey a bittersweet farewell and board their plane, happy to leave the Big Apple.

CHAPTER TWELVE
AWAKENING

HOURS LATER, DANE AND NOAH LIGHTFOOT disembark their airplane and enter the terminal. They are surprised to see Lee Thistleseed waiting for them. Dane looks at him quizzically, and Lee raises his bushy eyebrows in response. He walks forward and takes their carry-on bags.

"Kenny told me to come pick you up," Lee says. "He did not tell me about the haircut."

"Really?" Dane says, nodding, self-consciously running his fingers through his hacked-up tresses.

"Say what? Kenny told you? No way!" Noah says.

"Yes. It seems that my son may be awakening early," Lee confirms. Seventh children's powers usually begin manifesting around puberty. Lee's young son, Chenaniah is just barely past his twelfth birthday, so the presence of a psychic gift this soon comes as somewhat of a surprise to his father.

"What's his gift? Do you know yet?" Noah asks.

"It appears that Kenny experiences telepathic mind to mind communication," Lee says.

"Really? What makes you think so?" Dane asks.

"Kenny woke me up to tell me that you two were flying

home tonight. When I asked him how he knew, he said that a girl with a funny accent told him to 'send your father to the large bird building to get the brothers.' I took that to mean the airport. I have only been waiting for half an hour, and here you are," Lee says.

"That sounds like Kenny is channeling ... like a medium. Who's this girl with the funny accent? Is she from the spirit world?" Dane asks.

"I have no idea. Kenny says she is not dead, but she lives far away. She can see him, and she talks to him in his head, but he does not see her" Lee says. "Tonight is the first time he has ever heard from her."

"Is that all she said? 'Send your father to the large bird building for the brothers.' That's kindof odd—like she doesn't know what an airport is," Dane says.

"That is all she said. I got up quietly, left a note, and did not wake Wren. I sent Kenny back to bed. I suppose I will have to deal with this in the morning," Lee says.

"A telepath in the family. Now that's exciting," Noah says.

"Exciting? If you say so. If my son is channeling a telepath, then he is the first one I have ever encountered. I am woefully unprepared to train him," Lee says with a frown.

"Life is full of challenges, huh?" Noah says, clapping his mentor on the back.

Distracted by the emergence of Kenny's clairvoyant gift, the Lightfoot men forget their harrowing New York alley experience for the time being and chat amiably while they pile into Lee's car; however, during the ride from the Tallahassee airport to Lee's home, they grow quiet. Dane finds himself reaching for hair that is no longer there, and Noah gently palpates the bruised split on the side of his face. They are both lost in their thoughts, and Lee knows better than to interrupt them. There will be plenty of time when they get back to his house.

Lee pulls into his carport, and the three men silently climb the back steps to the breakfast room. As they enter the house, they are greeted by the sight of Wren, Shine, and Kenny sitting in their pajamas at the picnic-style breakfast table. Shine has an array of antiseptics, cotton balls, butterfly bandages, and antibacterial ointments on the table in front of her. Wren clutches a pair of scissors, a large towel, and a bottle of baby powder. Kenny sits on the bench at the head of the table with his back to the bow window, blowing across a cup of hot chocolate which is piled high with floating marshmallows.

"What is all this?" Lee asks his wife.

Wren shrugs and nods in her son's direction. "After you left to pick up the boys, Kenny told us to gather these things and wait for y'all. I guess he already knew that we'd need them."

Everyone looks at the boy who is innocently sipping from the mug. Young Chenaniah Thistleseed is named for the Biblical Chief of the Levites whose name meant "established by God." Chenaniah, a highly skilled and honorable man, was hand-picked by King David and the elders of Israel to lead the musicians and oversee those who carried the Ark of the Covenant of the Lord from the house of Obed-edom to Jerusalem. Nicknamed Kenny by the other children, the young namesake gives them all a radiant smile, complete with a milk chocolate mustache.

"Yep. The girl told me we needed a 'healer and a shearer' for when you get here. I didn't know what a 'shearer' was, so I asked Shine. She said it was somebody who cuts hair. I figured Mom could do that real good," he says. "Did I do all right?"

"You did great, buddy," Noah says. "A fourth-year vet tech and a mother with sewing scissors work out just fine."

"Well, I guess you two better take a seat and let us women fix you up," Shine says.

Noah straddles the bench Shine offers, and she goes to work cleaning and disinfecting his wound. The split is not deep, but it is long, running in a curved line from his right temple to just in front of his ear. Shine takes great care as she works, and Noah is thankful for her gentle touch. She is truly turning into a great veterinarian with her compassionate spirit and confident manner. Her fingers prod and push the skin together, meeting the edges of the cut smoothly, and then taping them with the butterfly bandages so there is no puckering. When she finishes, she leans back and scrutinizes her work.

"So, tell me. What's the final prognosis, 'Doctor' Shine

Thistleseed?" Noah asks.

"Not a doctor yet but working on it. Won't be much longer. As for your cut—it should heal well with just a tiny scar line. I'll keep checking it to make sure. You keep your hands off your face, and don't pick at it, and it'll be all right. I can't do anything for the ugly, though. You'll just have to live with that face for the rest of your life" she says.

"Ha ha. Thanks, Shine," Noah says. "Hey, Kenny. How about some hot cocoa for the wounded man? Plenty of marshmallows for me."

Kenny is happy to oblige. He hops from his perch and goes to the stove to pour a mug for his friends. In the meantime, Wren does her best to give Dane a haircut that will hide the butchering he received. There is no way to salvage any of the length because of the way the mugger hacked it off at the crown of his head. Her only choice is to clip it close enough all over to make it match.

Dane keeps his eyes closed, not looking at the black locks piling up around his feet. When Wren finishes, she dusts off his neck with talcum powder, and Shine hurriedly sweeps up the cuttings into a dustpan.

"Wow, Dane! You are looking so GQ now." Kenny whistles his approval.

"GQ?" his mother says. "Exactly what do you mean by that, Chenaniah Thistleseed?"

"*Gentlemen's Quarterly Magazine*," Shine says. "It's a magazine featuring fashionably elegant men and women."

"Oh, I know," Wren says. "But how do you know about that, young man?"

Kenny looks embarrassed. "The twins showed me. They said it had 'cute guys' in it. I didn't notice much about the guys, except they all had those short haircuts like Dane's. I looked at *all* the pretty girls, though." Kenny grins and rolls his eyes.

"Kenny's awakening." Noah smirks.

"Oh, no he's not," Wren says. "Kenny's going back to bed. Now, child."

She flicks the towel at his bottom, and the boy runs up the stairs to his bedroom.

While Shine and Wren tidy up the kitchen, the men move into the adjacent family room, each taking his favorite seat. Lee chooses the large wing back chair with its well-worn footstool. Dane piles up on the loveseat, and Noah takes his usual place on the plush rug in front of the fireplace, a balled-up afghan beneath his head.

"Perhaps you feel like talking now," Lee says.

"That was not my favorite trip," Noah says. "Who knew so many things could happen in just one day? I don't even know where to start."

"Let's begin with the most recent events. What happened to your face and your brother's hair?"

Dane and Noah look at each other, and the older brother gets the nod.

"We got mugged," Dane says. "We slipped into an alley to escape the sights and smells of the city ..."

"... I got sick and puked. I've never seen so many lights and colors and people and cars. I thought my eyes were going to pop out ..." Noah says.

"... and what a stench! I swear, I thought I'd never breathe fresh air again."

"Then these characters came out of nowhere. My head was down—because I was barfing, you know—and one of them pinned my arms behind me. The next thing I knew, my head exploded. I don't remember what happened after that."

"The one mugger slammed Noah into the wall. I saw him go down, and I thought he was dead. The other one had a knife, so I was watching him at the same time ..."

"... we had to stash our knives in our luggage before we could get on the plane."

"So anyway, the big guy caught me and wrestled me to the ground. He grabbed my hair, and the other one chopped it off." Dane runs his fingers through his scalp. "Then they said they were gonna scalp Noah."

During the men's tag-team explanation, Wren and Shine move into the room and take their places at each end of the couch. They look from one brother to the other as the story unfolds.

"All of a sudden, this car screeches into the alley, and the driver jumps out swinging a baseball bat. He hits both the muggers and knocks them out, and then he goes over to Noah. I'm thinking he's another mugger, so I come after him, but it turns out he's our Jamaican cab driver from earlier in the day," Dane says.

"And get this. His name is 'Jah-FEE.' He spelled it different but pronounced it the same as our Creek word for …'" Noah says.

"Trickster Rabbit," both brothers say in unison.

"Jaffey had been following us all day because he figured we'd get into trouble. I guess he was like our guardian angel, because if he hadn't come along, I think those punks might have killed us," Dane says.

"Yeah. He took us right then to the airport and made sure we left New York," Noah says. "Oh! And I almost forgot! He gave Dane one of his hairy dreadlocks to remember him by."

During the story, Shine's mouth drops lower and lower. But she's not the only one. Her parents have the same expression. Even the cool-and-calm Lee Thistleseed finds himself speechless and gawking … and afraid. Once again, he has almost lost his adopted sons. A rumbling sound draws his attention. Noah's stomach. Wren also hears the noise.

"Boys, it's late and I know you must be hungry after such an adventure. I've got plenty of leftover vegetable soup and cornbread," she says, pulling Shine up to help her in the kitchen.

With the women out of the room for a while, Lee shifts the conversation to the subject of the tainted perfumes and the reason the men went to New York in the first place.

"What did you boys find out about the ecstasy?" Lee says.

"Evidently, ecstasy is a real problem in New York, but they haven't had any incidences of ecstasy-laced perfumes," Dane says.

Noah sits up and leans his back against the hearth. "They knew about 'The Mister' at the police station—nice people, by the way—but they haven't been able to locate him. They said that he was part of a huge counterfeit fragrance ring, but he's working alone now, peddling his product down here."

"We don't have a name or a face for this 'Mister' character, but we know that his stuff made its way to the boutique in town where I bought Raven's perfume." Suddenly, Dane sits straight up, and his hands immediately go to his head. "Raven! Oh, no. What am I going to tell her?" He jumps up off the couch and begins heading out of the family room.

"And where do you think you're going?" Wren says, stopping him at the doorway.

"I need to go to the hospital," Dane says.

"No, you don't. Raven is fine. She's back at her apartment, and she has ..."

"... she has an in-home nurse tending her around the clock. Sit back down and eat some soup and cornbread. You boys are staying here tonight," Lee says.

"That's right," Shine says, placing a tray on the enormous slice of a cypress stump that serves as the coffee table. "Shelly's sleeping on a pallet in Selah's room, and I'm in Shell's room. Debby and Zorah are having a sleepover out back in my cottage, so you guys get the twin beds upstairs in their room. See! All the sleeping arrangements have been made, thanks to Kenny's heads- up."

Noah slides up to the coffee table and grabs a square of cornbread. "No objections on my end," he says, crumbling it into a huge cup of soup.

Dane sits back down on the couch and resigns himself to letting the Thistleseed women fret over him. The vegetable soup is a welcome balm after a day of unintentional fasting. He leans over the mug and inhales the steam, relieved to note that, although faint, he can detect ham, onion, celery, tomatoes, carrots, basil, oregano, green peppers. *Ahhhh, it smells like home again.*

CHAPTER THIRTEEN

ON THE SCENT TRAIL

THE NEXT MORNING, DANE AND NOAH awake to the intoxicating smell of hickory smoked bacon frying.

"Mmmmm. Smell that? Man's favorite scent," Noah says, bolting from the bed and disappearing into the bathroom. Seconds later, he splashes water on his face and hands and sprints through the bedroom door. His footfalls pound as he descends the stairs two at a time.

Rising from the other bed, Dane ambles to the sink and washes his face. Reaching for the towel, he is shocked at his appearance in the six-foot wide vanity mirror. He has forgotten about his hair. He studies himself in the mirror for a while and wonders irrationally if Raven will still love him without his long, silky mane. Anxious to see her, he quickly finishes his ablutions and wanders down the stairs to the dining room.

Wren has prepared a breakfast of mammoth proportions, but in a household of ten, the addition of two more people doesn't require much change in cooking style. So that everyone can enjoy the visit of the Lightfoot brothers, the youngest children have been given honorary folding chairs at the corners of the table. Nobody minds the extra crowding.

After a sweet blessing on the food by little Shelly, the serving bowls are passed clockwise. The older boys dub this process "he who hesitates is hungry." Needless to say, the bowls pass quickly. At the end of the serving frenzy, Dane's plate is layered with fluffy scrambled eggs, creamy cheese grits, crispy bacon, and fat buttermilk biscuits covered in heavily peppered white sausage gravy.

The dining room is not a place for discussing business; it is a time for family to share their week. This Saturday morning is no different. Shelly is proud of the "A" on her spelling test, Kenny is finally catching on to long division, Debby and Zorah are struggling with driver's education, Selah is sitting by a cute guy in her chemistry class at the junior college, Bill thinks he may change his major to engineering, Cy is working extra hours at his job to save up for his own apartment, and Shine gets to neuter a dog all by herself at work next week.

Long after the serving bowls and plates are scraped, sopped, and some are even licked clean, the family remains at the table, reluctant to leave the company of those they love.

Lee pushes his chair back and stands, and that signals the end of the meal. Wren and the children clear the table and begin the breakfast clean up. Everyone has his or her own chore, and they work like a well-oiled machine.

Lee, Dane, and Noah resume their favorite places in the family room to map out a plan of action. Even though their trip ended suddenly, much was learned in the men's misadventure.

"My first stop is Raven's, if you don't mind. I want to check on her, and she needs to see my new look," Dane says, running his hand across his head.

"It's actually a pretty good haircut, all things considered. Too bad it shows more of your face, though," Noah says.

"It is only hair, Dane. Hair grows back," Lee says.

"Hey, that's what Jaffey said, too," Noah says laughing.

"A wise man, your taxi driver," Lee says. "All right, then. Dane, after you visit Raven, I would like for you to go to the boutique where you purchased her perfume. Ask questions about vendors, employees, purchasers, anyone who may have had contact with 'The Mister.' Try to sniff out more of the tainted fragrances. If you encounter any, do not touch them. Call Jack. He can confiscate the items before they are sold to any other hapless customers."

Dane nods in agreement. Lee turns to Noah. "You and I are going tracking. It is imperative that we locate this man. We need to know where he is today and alert the police in that area—maybe even make a physical trip to the location," he says.

Noah pales. "I ... uh ... I really would prefer not to go back to New York, if you don't mind."

Lee smiles. "Of course not. If we find the man is in New York, I will take Graham."

Noah exhales in relief, and then he lifts his head and looks quizzically at the foyer door.

"Ken, my man. What's up?" he says.

Heads turn as Kenny enters the room frowning. He walks up to his father.

"Dad?" Kenny says. "She says to look south."

"The man is in the south, son?" Lee asks.

"Yes ... with a lady. He's dying."

Lee gives his son a crooked, somewhat sad, smile and gently pats his cheek. "Thank you, son. And thank your friend."

"I already did," Kenny says, walking out of the room.

The three men shake their head, speechless. Finally, Lee breaks the silence.

"Get your bags, boys. We must move quickly. I will call Graham and have him meet us at your house, Noah. Dane, I will drop you at your place, and then you can drive to Raven's."

Dane and Noah race up the stairs while Lee steps into the kitchen to fetch his wife. Wren meets him at the door, drying her hands with a dishtowel, and gives him a quick kiss on the mouth. Lee waves to the rest of the kids and climbs in his vehicle, the Lightfoots on his heels. Ten seconds later, they are on the road.

*   *   *

Ten minutes later, they arrive at Dane's house. Without even bothering to go inside and change clothes, Dane jumps into his car and heads off toward Raven's apartment. His heart pounds like a teenager on his first date all the way there.

Walking up to her door, he summons up his resolve and knocks, pasting a smile on his face. He can smell the sage smoldering from inside, and his smile becomes more relaxed. *She's using my mother's gifts, I bet.* The smile becomes an "O" when the door opens, and he is face to face ... with Fawn.

"Mom? What are you doing here?"

"Why, I'm taking care of my future daughter-in-law. I told you she was sick."

"Yes, you told me so. But who told you? How did you know?" he questions as he enters.

She closes the door and locks it. "Wren Thistleseed is my friend, son. She called me as soon as Lee left for the hospital. I took the bus and got here just in time to take Raven home when she was released. Come, now. You can't have all the fun."

Dane takes his mother in his arms and holds her tightly. "I love you, Mom. You have always, always been there for me."

"And I always, always will." Pulling back, she just now notices his hair. Her eyes widen as she studies his face, but she keeps quiet, knowing he will explain in his own time.

Dane kisses Fawn on the cheek and shrugs, then walks down the hall to Raven's bedroom. He pushes the door open slightly and sees her lying on the bed, propped up against several pillows and covered with a soft patchwork quilt that must have come from Fawn. Raven's eyes are closed, and she is napping.

He scans the room and sees evidence of Fawn's healing remedies everywhere—sage smoking in a large clamshell on the dresser, an intricately woven dream catcher with downy feathers hanging above the head of the bed, a sun-bleached turtle shell bowl filled with fragrant herbs on one nightstand, and an empty cup of what is surely Fawn's blessed healing tea on the other. *Yep. Mom's taking good care of her.*

His gaze goes back to the dresser, and he spots a dozen or more crystal perfume bottles of different shapes and sizes, all labeled *DeVanille*. One is like a round bull's eye target with a red circular label in its center, another is square with a stopper resembling a crown, and one very large bottle is shaped as a deep bowl on a stand with a royal blue semi-circular stopper. A smaller bottle is shaped similarly, but with a more fluted bowl and stand. Tucked here and there are others that are taller, more elongated, ribbed, topped with gold caps, mushroom shaped stoppers, triangular crystal stoppers, and, of course, the gold filigreed atomizer that was her engagement present.

Looking at the bottles, Dane feels the hair on his arms raise. *This is what made her sick.* He quietly walks to the dresser and sniffs deeply in each bottle, trying to detect the rotten orange smell of "The Mister's" cancerous touch.

"Colored water," Raven whispers.

Startled, Dane whirls around to face his fiancé. Even pale and sick in bed, she is breathtakingly beautiful. He rushes to her side and falls on his knees, gently stroking her lovely face with his hands. She smiles, and his heart thumps in his chest. Her hand stretches out and her fingers sift through his short hair. He turns his head and kisses her palm, tears squeezing out from the corners of his eyes.

"Babe, I'm so sorry." He exhales raggedly. "I should've known something was wrong."

Dane looks in Raven's eyes and sees only love there—no blame, no judgment. She reaches up and pulls his head to her chest, her fingers entwined in his short locks. They stay locked in that position for a long time. Then Dane sits back on his haunches.

"What did you say to me a while ago?"

"Colored water. Your mother dumped out all the perfumes and washed the bottles. She filled them with colored water and fragrant herbs. And *Voila*. All-natural perfumes. No unnatural additives. And each one has a different scent. My own personal array of aromatherapies. Go ahead. Sniff them out. I think all the poison is gone."

"If my mother did it, I know it's all gone. She'd make sure of that."

"That's right. You better not doubt me, boy," Fawn says, entering the room. She carries a steaming cup of tea to Raven and also hands one to Dane.

"I'm not sick, Mom," he protests.

"Maybe not, but I see a bruise under your eye, and I don't think you cut your hair on purpose!" She sits on the edge of the bed and looks at him. "We're waiting."

Having no choice but to give his story to the two insistent women, Dane tells them everything, from the sensory overload of the city, to the Fashion Institute of Technology, to the Sense of Smell Institute, to the mugging in the alley. When he finishes, they just stare at him.

Finally, Raven breaks the tension. "Well, I'm disappointed. I wanted you to bring me something from Macy's!"

Laughing, Fawn ruffles Dane's hair and quickly disappears into the kitchen. Moments later, she comes out bringing a tray loaded with mugs of chicken soup, soda crackers, and cheddar cheese cubes for the three of them. They sit around Raven's bedroom eating and chattering like nothing has ever happened. After lunch, Dane explains that he is going to the boutique to search for clues about the perfume saboteur.

"You sleep, Babe. I'll be back pretty soon. I'm not wearing my crime fighting uniform today. I'm only investigating," he says, kissing her forehead.

"If you promise to be careful."

"I will. Sweet dreams."

"No problem with that," Fawn says. "That's a very special dream catcher over her bed."

Dane moves closer to inspect it. Taking a look at the feathers, he laughs. "Emma. Give her my thanks."

"Emma was happy to oblige. She has plenty more feathers." Fawn walks her son to the door and gives him a strong hug. Slipping her hand into his back pocket, she pulls out a folded flyer. "What's this?"

"Oh, that's just some literature this animal activist gave us when we were in New York. You can have it. But what are you doing in my pocket, anyway?"

"Emma sent you a protection totem."

He reaches back and pulls out the totem—a sprig of sage and a long grey goose feather, wrapped together with embroidery floss. He clutches it and embraces his mother.

"I swear, Mom. You and that goose have a peculiar relationship," he says as he leaves.

"That we do," Fawn says walking into the bedroom. "What can I get you, Raven?"

Raven smiles warmly at her future mother-in-law. "One more cup of tea would be super, and then I'm going to take a nap."

Fawn sets the flyer down on the nightstand and picks up the lunch tray. Curious, Raven reaches over and takes the folded paper. She casually reads the back, then opens to the middle and scans the article. It details the endangerment of the African civet—a cat-like animal in the mongoose family used by perfume manufacturers for a base note fixative.

According to the pamphlet, The World Society for the Protection of Animals states the animal's anal glands produce a musky substance. Sometimes, the animals are killed, and the glands are removed. More often, the animals are kept in tiny cages, and their musk is harvested every few days by scraping the substance out of the anal sacs by means of a special tiny silver spoon, a procedure that is painful and inhumane. *Sounds barbaric,* Raven thinks.

Turning the pamphlet to the front, Raven freezes. There, on the front cover, is a picture of an African civet. It is identical to the cat with both stripes and spots and the long muzzle she drew while tracking on the way home from Tampa, complete with the tiny spoon. Raven screams, and Fawn comes running.

*   *   *

Dane's tires screech as he slams on the brakes just in time to keep from rear ending the car in front of him. Pulling his attention back to the road, he locates Connie's Cottage, a quaint boutique housed in a wood-frame building on the banks of Lake Jackson. Its clientele includes up-scale men and women who desire trendy, runway inspired clothing and the fashion industry's latest designs. The atmosphere is hoity-toity, and the wares are expensive, making it *"the"* place to be seen shopping. Dane was referred by another deputy fire marshal, not because the man shops there, but because a friend of a friend of his wife does.

Inside the store, Dane walks slowly up and down   the aisles, trying to pick up the scent of the bottles that have the odor of moldy oranges … and there are several, although the smell is very faint. He is aware of the impeccably made-up saleswoman who begins to follow him. He turns to her.

"Excuse me, ma'am, but I need some help with your fragrances," he says.

The woman smiles broadly, revealing perfectly uniform, braces-straightened teeth behind her glossy red lips. "Of course," she says. "My name is Helene. Are you looking for a gift?"

"Well, not exactly. I came in here a couple of weeks ago and bought a small dispenser of *De Vanille*. I need to know where you got it."

The woman's smile twitches slightly, and she appears puzzled. "We have suppliers that provide us with our fragrance products. Were you wanting to purchase some more?"

"No, I need to know who you purchased it from."

"I'm sorry, but it could have been one of many vendors. I'll be glad to order it for you." Her hand flutters up to the clunky gold necklace around her throat.

"No. I just need to know your source. Was it a company or an individual?"

"I don't know. Why are you asking me? Janie Hiller did our ordering, but she moved away a few days ago. She has a sick family member down south that she was going to care for. Do you want to buy something or not?"

"Ma'am … Helene. I don't want to alarm you, but quite a few of your perfumes have been tampered with. If you don't mind, I'm going to use your phone and call for some help from the police," he says. Seeing her frightened look, he adds, "You aren't in trouble. But I need you to find out where Janie moved. It's very important. We don't want anyone else to die."

"Die? People have died from our perfume? Oh my gosh!"

Dane moves to the phone. "Just get Janie's personnel file and anything else that may help us find her. If you need to phone a supervisor, you can do that after I'm done. And don't touch any of the perfume bottles. They're dangerous."

The saleswoman wrings her hands and nods while Dane calls Jack Abernathy. By the time he finishes the call, she has found a forwarding address for Janie Hiller ... in a Tampa suburb.

*   *   *

Noah, Lee, and Graham sit at the small oak pedestal table in Noah's kitchen deciphering the track from which Lee has just returned. So far, they identify a wooded area in the outskirts of Tampa, with felled branches all around a brown and white cinder block house. Outside the house is the "steed as black as night, a fearsome cat poised to run"—the black jaguar belonging to "The Mister." According to Lee, the "cat is cold, and brown leaves sleep on its head," indicating that the car has not been driven recently, perhaps in the last day or two. This is consistent with the fact that Noah and Dane could not locate the man in New York.

Noah's track of the man reveals a numerical address and a street sign, as well as a glimpse of the man lying on a bed in a darkened room with grayish skin and dark circles ringing his eyes. It is apparent to all of them that "The Mister" is gravely ill from the cancer. Noah also sees several cardboard boxes in the room filled with perfume bottles.

Graham's track gives them more insight about the severity of the man's illness. His voice is raspy and weak, punctuated by frequent deep chest coughing. As to any other occupants of the house, he hears a woman who tends to the man. From their conversation, they are not lovers, but they do seem to be related.

"I bet they're brother and sister," Noah says.

"And I'd take that bet," Graham concurs.

"All right, gentlemen. Let us see what we have. 'The Mister' is on his death bed. He is being cared for by a woman we believe is his sister. They are in a brown block house with white trim at 6475 Lovie Lane in a suburb of Tampa. The woman has a lot of pets, according to Graham," Lee says.

"Yeah. Thanks for the zoo impressions, Gray. Really

entertaining." Noah laughs.

"The presence of the animals indicates that the house is more remote than just being out of the city limits. All the tree limbs lead me to reason that this was an area damaged by Hurricane Andrew," Lee says.

"Downtown Tampa escaped the worst of the storm, but the outlying areas seem to have been hit pretty hard," Noah says.

A car door slamming outside draws their attention to the living room, and in walks Dane.

They quickly bring him up to speed about what they each learned in their tracks, and he gives them the name of the woman, Janie Hiller. The excitement is electric. These are men who love solving puzzles and saving lives. If they had superpowers instead of psychic powers, they would be akin to the Justice League of America. But they are ordinary human beings, subject to mental and physical ills and the fragility of mortality. Nonetheless, they are ersatz superheroes—brave and selfless and determined.

"So, who goes?" Noah asks.

"I'm going," Dane replies.

"Not without me," Noah says.

"Here we go again," Graham moans.

"Boys, I think it will be better if I go alone, this time," Lee says, giving them each a solemn nod.

"No way," Dane argues.

"Dane. You and Noah have just gone through a nerve-wracking experience. I can bring a fresh perspective to this situation, as well as pinpoint the location," Lee explains.

"But Raven ..." Dane says.

"Raven needs you here," Lee states. "I can't risk something happening to you."

"She doesn't need me as long as my mom's with her. I'm going to Tampa," he insists.

"Hey, ya'll. I'm bigger and a better fighter. If there's trouble, I need to be there to help Lee," Graham says holding up his beefy fists.

"Graham makes a good point," Lee says.

The four of them get louder and louder as they each jockey

for position. Through all the noise, they don't even realize that the front door has opened until it slams closed. They instantly stop talking and crowd into the living room, surprised to see Shine standing there.

"Sorry, guys, but there's a change in plans. Dad, you and Graham need to load up in the SUV. It's gassed up and ready to go to Tampa. Dane, go to Raven's and stay with her. You, too, Noah. Your mother's waiting for you," she says.

"Hey! Who died and made you the Queen of the castle, Shine?" Noah says.

"Nobody's dead yet, and that's how it's gonna stay." She bristles, eyebrows raised, ready for a challenge.

"Shinehah. I appreciate you preparing the vehicle. Dane can drive you home," Lee says.

"You're welcome, but I'm not going home, Dad. I'm going with you and Graham."

"Says who?" Graham objects, his eyebrows drawn together. "It's too dangerous for you. I won't allow it."

All heads turn to Graham. "You won't allow it?" Noah snickers at his expression.

"Oh, step off, Noah," Graham says, causing a burst of laughter from the brothers.

"Shinehah. This is not a matter for you, sweetheart," her father says.

"Kenny said I had to go. He even packed my vet-med kit with things he said I'd need," she says. "The girl said for the three of us to go now, before the man dies."

Graham looks confused. "Since when does Kenny tell us what to do?"

"Sorry, Gray. We should've already told you about him. Kenny's waking up, and he's channeling a telepath," Noah says.

Graham pokes out his lower lip, pulls his wire-rimmed glasses down on his nose, and nods. "That's cool. O.K. Let's do what Kenny says. Load up."

Graham and Shine head for the car, leaving the Lightfoot brothers with their hands in their pockets. Lee takes a deep breath. Then he walks over to the men and puts his arms around their shoulders, pulling them both in for a long hug.

"Stay together, boys. Do not separate. Do you understand me? I need you … both of you … to stay together in case we need you to track," Lee says.

"Will do, Hona. You can contact us at Raven's apartment. Find this guy and do whatever you have to. And please, be careful," Dane says.

Lee smiles and releases the men. Walking through the open door, he turns back and waves. Dane and Noah both jerk their chins up in an identical gesture of good-bye. As the SUV drives away from the curb with Graham at the wheel, the Lightfoot brothers pull the front door shut and make their way to Noah's mustang to reunite with Raven and their mother.

CHAPTER FOURTEEN
RAIN AND SHINE

ONE HOUR AFTER MERGING ONTO I-4 the weather suddenly turns bad. The clouds make good on their threat of rain. Lee is glad that Graham is driving, and his oldest daughter is securely buckled into her seat belt in the back. The wind buffets the car, but Graham has an iron grip. To pass the time, Lee fills him in on the powers that Kenny suddenly displays. Quiet and thoughtful in contrast to the Lightfoot brothers, Graham listens carefully and takes it all in before he comments.

"Chenaniah is twelve, now. That is an important time in a boy's life. Were he of Jewish descent, he would be on the verge of manhood. And among my people, he would be ready for a spirit journey," Graham says.

"Among mine, as well; however, we are so-called modern Indians now. We have no rites of passage as in the early days of our people," Lee says.

Graham smiles without turning his eyes on his friend. "I suspect that your son's journey into second-sightedness is more closely geared to your rites of passage than his," Graham says.

"You are very intuitive, Graham. I feel this responsibility quite keenly. I am afraid of making a mistake in his training."

"Mistakes are always possible, Lee, but I seriously doubt you'll err in his training. Besides, you know I'll help you all I can."

Lee reaches over and places his leathery hand on Graham's broad right shoulder. The men seem to have an unspoken understanding, more sophisticated than the father-son relationship he holds with Dane and Noah. *How I would welcome Graham as my son-in-law*, Lee thinks.

The four-hour trip to the Tampa Bay area stretches to five because of the inclement weather. By the time they arrive at their exit, the rain is heavy, and visibility is limited. As the back-seat navigator, Shine scans the street signs for their landmarks.

"There," she says. "Turn right at that street just up ahead. Then we go down four stoplights and take a left."

Graham obediently follows her directions, being careful to avoid limbs on the street. Shine does a masterful job of navigating, and before long they arrive at Lovie Lane. The residential landscape has changed from condos to apartments to neighborhoods to a smattering of homes with large expanses of woods in between.

Lovie Lane is a hard-packed clay road unmaintained by the county. Graham gingerly picks his way between water filled potholes, thankful that Kenny's telepathic partner told him the weather would be bad, and Shine had the presence of mind to drive the rugged SUV.

Thinking of Shine makes his stomach flutter, so he pulls his mind back to negotiating the road. The absence of ruts tells him nobody has left the house since before the rainstorm. He is relieved to see the small block building up ahead. Suddenly, a strong gust of wind rocks the vehicle, and Graham skids to a stop just as a large tree limb falls in front of them, blocking their way.

Having no choice but to go to the house on foot, Lee, Graham, and Shine exit the vehicle, clothed in the clear plastic slickers Kenny has packed in Shine's medical kit. They approach the front door, and Lee knocks heavily. The door opens, and a semi-attractive woman in her late forties blinks at them.

"Yes? Can I help you?" she says. Looking out the door, she sees the limb blocking the road in front of the car. She turns back at the group and surmises that they are travelers who have been stranded. "Oh, my goodness. You're soaked. Please, come on in. You can use my phone."

Taking her lead, the three of them enter the house, taking in the simple hominess of the furnishings. Janie Hiller is a sweet woman, trying hard to do the right thing for a group of strangers. It's hard for them to believe that the brother she harbors is a drug dealer and a killer.

Shine pretends to call a tow service, all the while scanning the rooms around her. Sitting on a chair near the telephone, she feels a tail swipe against her foot. *A kitten*, she decides. Hanging up the phone, she wags her fingers near the floor and is rewarded with a tiny paw darting from under the chair.

"Here, kitty, kitty, kitty," she coos. A tiny animal peeks around the chair leg. Shine flattens her hand on the floor, and the kitten crawls into her open palm. She picks it up and holds it against her chest, scratching behind its rounded, tufted ears. It curls into a ball and rests comfortably in her arms.

In the kitchen, Lee and Graham sit at the modest table talking to their hostess. When Shine enters, Janie's eyes widen, and she stops talking. Shine takes a seat, holding the warm ball of fur on her lap.

"I love your kitten," Shine says. "I've never seen one with this coloring. It's almost like a raccoon with its mask and stripes, but it has spots, too. It's beautiful."

"Thank you. She's a very sweet little thing. A rescue animal," Janie says.

"She's quite an unusual looking kitten. Where did you get her?" Lee says.

Janie stands up nervously. "I found her just wandering around outside."

"Really? She seems to be very young. I wonder where her littermates are," Lee presses. "Did you see a mother cat anywhere?"

"Why are you so interested in a stray cat?" Janie is wary, looking back and forth at the visitors.

Graham has also been studying the animal. Its muzzle is elongated more than normal, and there are other peculiarities about it that bring to mind a drawing he has recently seen. He stares back at Janie Hiller.

"I'm sorry, Ms. Hiller, but this is no ordinary kitten, is it?"

"How do you know my name?" Alarmed, Janie backs away into the living room. Lee and Graham rise and follow her, but Shine stays seated at the table, holding tight to the tiny creature.

"I think you should go back to your car now. My brother is very sick, and I have to give him some medicine. Please. I really want you to leave," she pleads.

"We aren't threatening you, Ms. Hiller. We know about your brother, and we want to help you," Graham says.

"No. No. You'll take him to jail, and he'll die there. He's all I have. I'm taking good care of him. They were going to throw those testers away, so it's not really stealing. He's very ill. We need the money for medicine. Don't arrest him." She begins to cry.

"Ms. Hiller. We are not the police. Your brother has been putting a narcotic into those perfumes. People are sick from it. Some people have died. We just need to get the perfumes off the street so no other people are harmed," Lee says.

"No. Edgar wouldn't hurt anybody. He was putting human pheromones into the perfumes. You know, to make people more attractive ... to make them fall in love, and then they'd want to buy more. They're harmless. I know. I did the research." Janie wrings her hands.

"No, ma'am. He put ecstasy into those fragrances. It's a drug that is dangerous," Graham explains. "Teenagers bought those testers and died."

"I don't believe you. They're pheromones. I would never agree to drugs. I love people. I love animals. I'm against the inhumane testing of products on animals, so why would I let him hurt people?"

"You have other animals here?"

"I ... I have some others. They were lab animals. Dogs, cats, a couple of beavers. They were being tortured so women could have tear-free mascara or use shampoo that wouldn't sting their eyes. Some of them—like the African civet pup that your girl is holding—are kept in cages for years just to get oils and glands that are used in perfumes."

"How did you come by these animals?" Lee asks.

"I went to New York with Edgar once, and he took me to a lab. When I saw those poor animals in the cages, I knew I had to rescue them. We rented a truck and freed them one night after the lab was closed. Edgar had a key. The mother civet had been so traumatized that she died before we got back to Florida, leaving this one pup an orphan. We did a *good* thing by saving them!"

"Ms. Hiller. Where is Edgar? He has cancer. He is dying. He does not have much time. Let us talk to him."

Janie Hiller looks uncertainly at a closed door, and then back at Graham and Lee. Tears streaming down her face, she points at the door.

"Please don't hurt him," she begs.

Lee takes her hand and looks kindly into her eyes. "We are not in the hurting business, dear lady. We are the good guys," he says, helping her to a well-worn club chair.

Graham starts to open the door but stops. "Ms. Hiller? Is your brother armed?"

Janie shakes her head, and Graham tentatively opens the door. Even though his psychic gift is clairaudience, he can smell the impending death coming from the man on the bed. Graham is relieved that Lee ordered Dane to stay home. The odor is wretched. He walks to the bed and looks down at the man.

"Edgar Hiller? My name is Graham Skysong, and I'm here to help you obtain a better place in the land of the spirits. Do you understand me?"

Hiller turns his head toward Graham. He blinks his eyes twice, which Graham takes to mean, "yes." Graham takes his hand. It is dry and papery—the hand of a desiccated corpse.

"Mr. Hiller. The drugs you put in the fragrances have killed people. Have you put any more perfumes out on the streets in the past week?"

Hiller shakes his head ever so slightly. He shifts his eyes to a stack of cardboard boxes against the wall. Lee enters the room and walks to the pile of cartons and opens the top. Inside are decorative boxes of high-end perfumes. He notes their names: *Romarin, Arômes, Céleste, Chatoyant No. 2, Épice d'Asie,*

Séduisant, De Vanille. In the carton at the top of the next stack are smaller boxes—the testers Hiller hands out at the clubs.

"Is that all of them, Mr. Hiller?" Graham asks, to which he receives two blinks. Graham turns to Lee. "Lee, please bring Mr. Hiller's sister in. He's going soon."

Janie Hiller walks slowly over to the bed. Sitting on the edge, she takes her brother's hands in her own. Her tears wet his face. He looks up to her and struggles to speak. Unable to make sound, he mouths the words, "I love you." He exhales his last breath and is gone.

Janie lays her head on Edgar's chest and cries aloud. Quietly, in the background underneath the sound of her weeping, a song emanates from the big Navajo. He sings to guide the spirit to the sky. And silently, Lee adds a prayer.

*   *   *

Twenty minutes later, Lovie Lane is a hub of activity. Chief Lew Rowan, a squad car of officers, and a medical examiner arrive. The tree limb has been removed, and a couple of animal control trucks park near the house. The officers are busy loading the trucks with all manner of animals found behind Janie Hiller's house. Shine clutches tightly to the civet in her arms, watching the animals being rescued, reluctant to give up the tiny civet pup.

The body of Edgar Hiller is placed in a black body bag and removed for autopsy. Officers carefully load the cardboard boxes of tainted perfumes into the trunks of the three squad cars. Oblivious to the steady rain, Lee stands with his arm around Janie Hiller.

"Chief Rowan, Ms. Hiller was unaware of her brother's activities. She thought he was putting pheromones in the perfumes," he says.

"That may be, Mr. Thistleseed, but I still have to arrest her. She did steal all these animals," Chief Rowan says.

"Then may I speak on her behalf?"

"I can give you that, Mr. Thistleseed. Talk to my officer over there. He'll take your statement. Come on, Ms. Hiller, let's get you in the car."

When the Chief reaches for Janie Hiller, she pulls back out of his grasp and runs into the woods, right towards Shine who is standing by the SUV.

"Stop!" Chief Rowan shouts.

At that moment, a streak of lightning flashes over the road. Thunder rumbles, making the ground shake, and then there is a loud crack. Looking up, Shine sees another limb separate from the tree. It begins to fall. She jumps away, shielding the civet with her body, and ends up in Janie's path. The women collide, and the limb lands with a crash on top of them.

The nearby men rush to pull the limb away. Seeing the commotion, Graham races in. His strength is equal to that of two men, and he succeeds in pushing it over to the edge of the road. By this time, Lee has come to his side. With mounting dread, they look at the women.

Janie Hiller lies with her neck at an odd angle, sightless eyes staring up into the rain. The medical examiner checks for a pulse and pronounces her dead. Moving to Shine, he finds a weak pulse. Her right wrist is broken, and her head is bleeding, but she is alive.

"She likely has a concussion and some broken bones. I ... I don't carry medical supplies for living people," the examiner stammers.

"Kenny!" Graham says. He snatches open the car door and finds Shine's medical kit. Sure enough, Kenny has it packed with exactly the right supplies they need to splint Shine's wrist and bandage her head. While the M.E. tends to her wounds, Graham begins to sing a blessing way—a Navajo healing song. His voice is strong and plaintive as he rocks back and forth over the woman he clearly loves. He holds his face and hands up to the sky, letting the rain soak his hair and splatter on his glasses.

The sight of the brawny Indian is a wonder to behold. All around, the other men stop to silently watch and listen. He sings until he hears her voice.

"Oh, Gray. I do love it when you sing," Shine moans.

Graham bends over the woman and tenderly kisses her lips. "And I love it when you speak." Gathering his resolve, he stands up and faces Lee solemnly. "Liahona Thistleseed. I'd like to ask you for the hand of your daughter, Shinehah."

Lee is pleased, but surprised. "This seems rather sudden, Graham. Are you sure?"

"Our existence in this world is fleeting. I don't wish to waste another day of my life without the one I love," Graham whispers, close to tears.

Touched by the suddenness and the formality of his request, Lee simply nods his consent and shakes the man's large hand. Graham kneels beside Shine and gently takes her unbroken left hand.

"Shinehah Thistleseed. Will you please consent to be my wife?" he asks.

"Yes," she says. "I will gladly be your wife."

Graham lets out an uncharacteristic whoop, and the bystanders cheer. Leaning down again, he reaches under the car and pulls out a tiny bundle.

"I don't have a ring, Shine, but I do have an engagement present." Graham winks and gently places the shivering wet bundle in the crook of her arm. "This little 'kitty' is for you."

CHAPTER FIFTEEN

OLD FRIENDS, NEW FAMILY

AFTER SPENDING THE NIGHT IN TAMPA, part of which was at the hospital while Shine was examined and released, the three of them are glad to be on the road for home. This being Sunday, they know Wren will have a huge brunch waiting. The rain has let up, and Graham makes good time on the trip. From their calculations, they should arrive just when everyone else is beginning to sit down. But, of course, they planned it this way.

Shine sleeps much of the way, cradling the rescued civet cub on her lap. "Lovie," as she calls it, is happy to be petted, but it neither purrs nor makes sounds of contentment as other cats do.

"She doesn't purr," Shine says.

"She's not a cat, sweetie. She's a civet. A wild animal," Graham says.

"O.K. I don't have any vet training for a civet. I'll have to do some research when we get home," she says.

"And until you do that, your little 'Lovie' stays in your cottage. If you let her out, I am afraid she may follow her natural instincts and become wild," Lee says.

"I want to show her to the other kids first," Shine says.

"Not until we find out more about her. She must be

inoculated. I do not want any of the children bitten," Lee says.

"Yeah, that's a good idea. She's tame with you, but when she gets a look at that mob of a family, she may get vicious," Graham says.

"Mob of a family?" Lee says. "I can withhold my blessing at any time, you know."

Graham grimaces. "Yes, sir. Point taken. Here we are. Home sweet home."

Graham passes the carport and drives directly to Shine's cottage in the back yard—a barn-style shed with a loft that has been converted into a small house. He reaches into the back seat and takes Lovie from Shine's arms, and then he places the civet on the couch in the little house. After filling a dish with water, he securely closes the door and returns to the car.

"She's all settled until we finish lunch," he says, to which he receives grateful smile from his new fiancé. "Your critter laughed at me, though."

"What?" Shine asks.

"She laughed. Really, I swear she did. You know, like 'ha-ha-ha' laughing."

"Sure, she did. I'm the one with the concussion, and you hear a cat laugh."

"And I'm the clairaudient. Never mind. You'll see when she laughs at you."

"All the more reason for the civet to stay in your house, Shinehah. Your mother can only take so much laughter," Lee says, pulling his mouth into a smirk.

As Graham parks in the carport, he makes a casual observation. "Looks like the Lightfoot crew is here. Hope they leave enough for the rest of us."

When they enter the house, there is an air of excitement. Oddly, the tables are set, but nobody is eating yet. Everyone seems to be crowded into the family room. Lee notices all the furniture has been pushed back against the walls. The two family groups are sitting all around the room, anxiously watching as the trio comes through the doorway.

Police Chief Jack Abernathy stands in front of the fireplace and motions for Lee to join him. As Lee approaches his friend, Kenny passes by him and goes to Shine, gently touching the cast on her hand.

"Did I pack the right stuff?" he asks.

"You did exactly right," Shine says, giving him a hug. "What's going on here?"

Before he can answer, Wren comes over and puts one arm around her daughter's waist and the other around Graham. "Congratulations," she whispers.

Graham and Shine look at Kenny, who shrugs and grins.

"Will you all please stand," Jack says to the guests who are assembled in the room.

From the foyer comes the familiar sound of Bill playing the piano. Because the formal living room was converted to Selah's and Bill's bedrooms, the piano had to be moved next to the stairway. The placement in the high-ceilinged room gives the instrument a music hall sound as it resonates through the open space and up the stairs. The musicians of the family, twins Bill and Selah, often perform together for their family home evenings, usually with Bill playing and Selah singing or playing the cello.

Adjacent to the family room, the door to the master bedroom opens, and out stroll Dane and Noah. Dane is dressed in traditional Seminole clothing, with the long, colorful patchwork shirt over his slacks. He wears a cloth turban on his head. Noah is dressed, ironically, in his Chief Osceola clothing, minus the war paint. They stop and stand in front of the French doors to the right of the fireplace.

Shine's mouth drops open. "Oh! It's a wedding!" She squeals in delight.

The door between the family room and the foyer opens, and Shelly Thistleseed walks out, wearing her blue and white Sunday dress and carefully holding a smoldering stick of sage. She walks down the center of the room, places the sage in a shell bowl on the fireplace, and goes to stand with her mother.

Behind her walks Fawn Lighfoot, also dressed in traditional Seminole clothing of long patchwork skirt, short sheer shawl, and sporting her famous hair hat. She carries a bowl of something liquid, which she also places on the fireplace. She moves over and stands in front of the French doors to the left of the fireplace.

The music changes, and everyone knows who the next to enter will be. Raven Looking Bird walks into the room, and there is an audible intake of breath as they behold her. She is dressed in the outfit that Fawn made for her. The long patchwork skirt swirls around her yucca fiber moccasins, and the sheer shawl floats near her waist as she moves slowly forward.

She wears a matching set of elegant seed bead earrings, bracelet, and necklaces which catch the sunlight shining through the dormer window high above her in the foyer. The effect is like a fairy tale. All the elements of the universe seem to have come together to make this day special.

Dane's eyes mist as he looks at his bride. The word beautiful cannot even come close. She carries no flowers, but instead holds a fan of grey and white goose feathers, again courtesy of Fawn's pet, Emma. As she comes to the front of the room, she hands her "bouquet" to Fawn.

Dane takes her hand, and they face Jack Abernathy and Lee Thistleseed. Jack begins the traditional wedding vows. "Dearly Beloved, we are gathered here in the sight of God to unite this man and this woman in holy matrimony ..."

At the conclusion of his part, Raven and Dane turn to one another and recite their vows, ending with an exchange of rings.

"What God has brought together, let no man put asunder," Lee says.

The next part of the ceremony consists of the bride and groom each taking a drink of the liquid in the bowl—an herbal potion prepared and blessed by Fawn Lightfoot, the Cedar Woman. Then, she takes the feathered fan and the sage and stands before the couple. She uses the fan to direct the smoke over their heads and their bodies, all the way down to their feet. After that, she takes a finger woven sash and wraps the right hands of the bride and groom together.

During these proceedings, Bill plays the music for *"The Lord's Prayer,"* and Selah sings.

"Our Father, who art in Heaven,
hallowed be thy name."

The second phrase is sung by Bill.

"Thy kingdom come,
Thy will be done on earth as it is in Heaven."

The third phrase is sung by a different girl.

"Give us this day our daily bread,
and forgive us our debts as we forgive our debtors."

Noah's head pops up, and he jerks it around to see into the foyer. He knows this voice well, and he knows the girl to which it belongs. Maria Ramirez. He looks back at Lee but sees only amusement in his face. His heart pounds. *Maria is here!* Maria, with whom he fell in love just weeks ago, and whom he thought he may never see again. Maria, whom he will never let out of his life again, is here, and Noah intends to make her his own one day soon.

Selah, Bill, and Maria finish the song together.

"And lead us not into temptation,
but deliver us from evil.
For Thine is the kingdom, and the power,
and the glory, Forever. Amen."

At the song's end, Dane takes Raven in his arms and kisses her for a very long time.

Lee clears his throat. "Family and friends, I give you Dane and Raven Lightfoot."

The room erupts with cheering. Family and friends rush forward to congratulate the bride and groom, as well as Graham and Shine, thanks to Kenny's announcement of their engagement last night. But not Noah. Noah rushes to the foyer to see Maria. He finds her there with Bill and Selah. When he walks up, Bill pulls Maria forward.

"Maria Ramirez. I want you to meet my friend, Noah Lightfoot. He's Chief Osceola at F.S.U. and kinda like my cousin, too," Bill says.

Noah takes her hand and smiles into her eyes, looking for recognition. She gives him a direct stare, turning her head to the side slightly. "Hi there," she says. "Do I know you?"

"Um, maybe. Yeah, well, I don't know," Noah stammers.

"Maria's father is Florida's Governor Robert Ramirez," Selah says. "She sings with us at the junior college sometimes, but she's just transferred to Florida State this semester."

"Maybe we'll see each other around campus," Maria says.

"I'm sure we will. I mean, I hope so," Noah says.

"I'm a music major. I sing and I'm playing the flute in the 'Marching Chiefs' so maybe we can hang out during the games."

"Oh, well, yeah. I'm on the horse, you know. Renegade's the horse, but I don't have to stay on him the whole time. I mean, I can get off the horse and walk around when I'm not actually riding the horse, you know, like during a touchdown or ..."

"My gosh, Noah. I think she gets the picture," Bill says rolling his eyes.

"Right, right. Um, Maria, let's get you something to drink, and you can sit by me at the dinner table, if that's all right with you," Noah takes her hand and walks her toward the dining room.

Selah and Bill watch Noah awkwardly romancing their friend and laugh. They turn to each other and slap their hands in a "high five" gesture, and then begin singing a tune from *"Fiddler on the Roof."*

"Matchmaker, matchmaker, la da da da;
Dum di dum dum; da di da da..."

*   *   *

Early the next morning, the newly wed Dane and Raven Lightfoot check out of their hotel honeymoon suite and point their car west. Their decision to visit Raven's mother in Prescott, Arizona comes out of the suddenness of their wedding. Having no time to fly her mother in for the event, they call her and agree to stay for a couple of weeks as her guests. Raven has carefully packed her Seminole outfit and Dane's, as well, so they can give her mother a reenactment of the ceremony.

Knowing the early winter weather in the mountains can become snowy at any time, she has the foresight to pack them an assortment of socks, gloves, thermal underwear, hats, and coats. Except for his escapade in New York, Dane has spent his entire life in Florida, never having experienced extreme cold. Raven takes anything she thinks her new husband might need. *I hope it snows,* she thinks. *Won't it be fun to see a Seminole playing in the snow?*

For Dane, the anticipation of two weeks in the mountains is exhilarating. *Imagine, two whole weeks of fresh, clean air. That'll really get my nose back into shape.*

Raven turns in her seat and opens the small cooler on the floorboard. Dane hears the familiar pop and fizz.

"Diet Coke already? It's barely past daylight." He laughs, shaking his head.

"Queasy," she replies, bringing the soda can to her lips.

Dane glances at her. "What are you drinking?"

"Ginger Ale. Your mom weaned me off Diet Coke while she was taking care of me. Said a ginger soda without caffeine was better for a girl in my condition."

"Did you tell her about it?"

"Dane, she's your mother, the Cedar Woman. Nobody has to tell her. She just knows."

"You're right about that, thankfully." He leans over and rubs his hand against her cheek, then rests it on the slight protrusion of her belly.

Raven sighs happily, and then she reaches into her moccasin and pulls out the gold filigreed perfume canister that Dane gave her for their engagement. She presses the top and a fine mist of droplets fans out and onto her neck. Instantly, the scent of vanilla fills the car.

Dane jerks the car to the side of the road and slams it into park, facing her.

"What are you doing? That's poison, Babe!"

Raven pats his hand and laughs. "Relax, Bucko. Your mother threw out the bad stuff, remember? This is one of her special herbal blends. It's a mix of lemon, rose, jasmine, patchouli, iris, and vanilla, of course, in extra-virgin olive oil. Fawn is a master of scent combinations. Probably where you got some of your gift, huh?" She caps the bottle and replaces it in her moccasin.

He blows out his breath in relief, and then he pulls back onto the highway. "Babe, you're gonna kill me yet!"

"Nah. But thanks for caring." Searching beneath her seat, she takes out her sketch pad and the box of colored pencils he bought her in Tampa. Turning to a blank page, she starts to draw, humming tunelessly as she outlines and shades her picture. When she finishes, she admires her work.

It is a Hopi Kachina—the Sun god. It is circular, like a target, with an outer rim of thirty-two black scallops. They encircle a ring of white, also divided into thirty-two sections, each with a vertical black line running up and down the centers. These are meant to represent the feathers on the actual Sun god mask.

The central circle is divided into an upper and lower hemisphere with a white dashed line. The upper hemisphere is halved by a white dashed line. To the left of the line the area is colored red with a yellow interior; to the right, it is yellow with a red interior. The lower hemisphere is colored blue. Within it, black lines give the indication of two straight-line eyes and a triangular shaped mouth, also colored black.

Dane glances over at the drawing she holds up for his inspection as she describes it.

"These are feathers, and this is the face. These lines are eyes, and here is the mouth," she says. "The Hopi and some Yavapai Indians believe that the Sun god controls the seasons."

"He looks a little sad, don't you think? He's frowning. Why is that?" Dane says.

Raven looks at her picture, and then compares it to the one in the book her mother gave her. Indeed, the mouth of her Sun god image is inverted, giving it the appearance of unhappiness. "I don't know, Honey. That's just how he wanted to be drawn," she says.

"Well, if the Sun god's unhappy, then we may be in for some

wicked weather," he says.

A chill runs down Raven's back, and she crosses her arms over her stomach protectively.

EPILOGUE
THE KEEPER

BY THE TIME I FINISH collecting the story of Dane, the Bloodhound, the sun is high overhead. It warms my face, and instinctively I close my eyes to keep them from getting damaged. But Mother has already covered my forehead with a cloth. My flute is still clenched between my fingers, and they ache.

Luna," Mother says beside me. "*Que Pasa?* How are you? *Enkv?* OK?"

I am used to the odd mixture of Spanish, English, and Muskogee in her conversation.

"What do you keep?" Mother asks.

"My brother. And now I have a new sister," I say with a trembling smile.

She cocks her head at me, and I can hear her hair brushing against her cotton blouse. "Noah again?"

"Not this time. It was Dane, the one who was brought back from beyond the veil of death when Liahona Thistleseed backtracked to the past."

"And Raven?" Her voice is curious. I can tell that she is smiling, too.

"She has become my sister."

"*Mvdo.* It is good. *Andale.* Let's go" she says. She takes my arm and walks me toward our village. I am weak, as always, and exhausted from such a long journey.

"How long, this time?" I ask.

"Three days, daughter. I fed you while you flew," Mother says. We walk a little more, and then she asks, "How many days did you travel?"

I think about it a minute before I answer her. "Three weeks. I traveled three weeks."

"Hmmph. The last time was only a day. You are gone one day for each week. I am afraid for such long journeys." She pulls me closer.

"Mother," I say as I step lightly beside her, "I spoke to a boy in my journey."

"Did he hear you?"

"Yes. I heard him. I saw him, but he did not see me."

We walk silently for a while. "Mother, I am afraid for my other family," I admit.

"Did you see something else?"

"No. But I know great danger is coming. I feel it, and it is so cold."

Mother drapes a shawl around my shoulders. She continues walking again, slowly. After a few steps she stops and embraces me. She kisses the top of my head, and I feel her lips pull into a smile.

"Do not worry, Luna. You are a *hecetv*—a seer. When it happens, you will see it. And whatever it is, your brothers will overcome it."

"It is not my brothers I am worried about. It is my sister, Raven, and her children."

APPENDIX
LANGUAGE TRANSLATIONS

Muskogee Creek Language

The Muskogee Creek language is spoken extensively on the reservations in Oklahoma; however, in the Southeast, there are relatively few native speakers. In the tri-state region of Florida, Georgia, and Alabama, language classes are held in an effort to keep the language from becoming extinct.

The vowels are pronounced as follows:

A=w_Atch_	E=_I_tch	E=s_EE_
I=s_AY_	O=m_OA_n	U=b_OO_k
V=_U_nder	EU=_U_se	UE=b_OY_
VO=n_OW_	Note: vowels are voiced with partially closed, tight mouth.	

Consonants are sounded as follows:

C=ri_CH_	C= ca_TS_	C=_J_am
F=_F_air	H=_H_air	K=bi_Ke_
K= _G_o	L=_L_ike	M=_M_an
N=ma_N_	P=_P_ie	P= _B_uy
R=_TLH_ or _HL_ (There is no English equivalent. The sound is much like an attempt to bring forth phlegm)		
S=_S_ee	S= _Z_oo	SK=wi_SH_
SS=wi_SH_	T=_T_ea	T=_D_ie
W=_W_et	Y=_Y_et	
Note: Consonants are voiced with tight mouths, far back in the throat. The sounds are almost "swallowed."		

Muskogee Words, Phrases, and their Meanings
(in order of appearance)

Tuskie Mahaya Haco – Brave Teacher Warrior (proper name)

Hvresse torwv – moon eyes

Heles Pocase – medicine man

Chickee – house (an open structure with a thatched roof) *Coo-Taun Cho-Bee* – where the big water meets the land (orig. Hitchiti language)

Pvsktv – fasting celebration

Hal Pa Te – alligator

Sofkee – a corn drink

Hesaketvmese – The One Above (proper name for God) *Taal-holelke* – swamp cabbage or sabal palm

Cvke – trickster coyote

Enkv – O.K., all right

Mvdo – It is well; it is good; good; thank you; you're welcome

Hecetv – you see

Spanish Language

Conversational Spanish, in its many forms and dialects, is one of the most widely spoken languages in the world and is prevalent throughout Mexico, Central America, and the United States. Though it varies slightly by regions, it is generally consistent in its pronunciation.

The vowels are pronounced as follows:

A=w_A_tch	E= b_E_d	I =s_EE_
O=m_OA_n	U=b_OO_k	Y =s_EE_
Note: vowels are voiced with open, relaxed mouth.		

Consonants are sounded as follows:

B =_B_ed	C=_C_ow	C=_S_ow
D=_Th_ink	F=_F_un	G=_G_un
H=silent	J=_Ch_ew	K=_K_ick
L=_L_ick	LL=_Y_ard	M=_M_an
N=_N_ow	Ñ=can_Y_on	P=_P_ark
Q/QU=_K_ick	R=ca_RR_y	RR=as _R_, but trilled
T=_T_ake	V=_B_ed	W=_W_ater
X=e_X_cuse	Y=_Y_es	Z=pin_TS_
Note: consonants are voiced with open, relaxed mouth. Hard consonants are explosively voiced.		

Spanish Words, Phrases, and their Meanings
(in order of appearance)

Ojos del Luna – Eyes of the Moon (proper name)
Que Pasa – what is happening?
Andale – let us go

Fragrances

Many fragrances are given French names that correspond to aspects of their formula, such as flowers, spices, base notes, or fixatives. Other names may be colors, gemstones, or a desirable quality. The names in this book are fictional.

Fragrance Names and their Meanings
(in order of appearance)

Lavande - Lavender

De Vanille - Of Vanilla

Diamant - Diamond

Épice d'Asie - Spice of Asia

Eau de (something) - Water of (something)

Chatoyant No. 2 - Shimmering Number 2

Homme De Vanille - Man of Vanilla

VinDoux - Sweet Wine

Les Fleurs du Peintre Français - The Flowers of the French Painter

Romarin - Rosemary

Arômes - Aromas

Céleste - Heavenly

Séduisant - Enticing

KACHINA:

THE SNAPSHOT'S STORY

Book 3 of

THE TRACKERS SERIES

MICKEY MORNINGGLORY

Patent Print Books
Panama City Beach, Florida

KACHINA: The Snapshot's Story
The Trackers Series, Book 3

Published by **PATENT PRINT BOOKS**
www.patentprintbooks.com

PATENT PRINT BOOKS and the fingerprint colophon are registered trademarks of **PATENT PRINT BOOKS**

First Edition: 2018
Revised 2020
Printed in the United States of America

ISBN 978-0-9850731-2-1
Library of Congress Control Number: 2018947063

10   9   8   7   6   5   4   3   2

CONTENTS

PREFACE

KACHINA, Book 3 of *The Trackers Series,* is Raven's story, set in the mountains of Arizona. When I was about Raven's age, I lived in Prescott—a place incredibly different from the balmy East and Gulf coasts of Florida where I grew up.

While there, I succumbed to my tourist's urge to buy a kachina doll—a misnomer for the intricately carved figurine which is not a doll at all, but a skillful recreation of a religious icon—a *Katsina* deity. Because there exists no "ch" sound in the Hopi language, the word kachina is an Anglicization of *Katsina.*

To establish the distinction between the inanimate objects and the religious icons, I call the doll-like figurines kachinas, and I refer to the Hopi religious ceremonial masks, dancers, and gods as *Katsinam.*

The location of this story is yet vivid in my memory. Though I love Florida, I think fondly of Arizona. I have a sense of how Dane Lightfoot must feel, displaced into a foreign environment that vacillates from paper dry heat, craggy rocks, and misshapen trees to bitter cold and shimmering snow.

I'll say this: Sunrise on the beach is no match for sunset on the mountain. It is a perfect setting for a wedding.

~ Mickey

INTRODUCTION

"In spirit and in ceremony, the Hopis maintain a connection with the center of the earth, for they believe that they are the earth's caretakers, and with the successful performance of their ceremonial cycle, the world will remain in balance, the gods will be appeased, and rain will come."

~ Emily Benedek
The Wind Won't Know Me
New York: Knopf, 1992

"Spirit lives in the seasons, the elements, the outer reaches of the universe, the two- and four-legged creatures, the winged ones, the insects, the trees, the plants, and even the rocks."

~ Jeffrey Wilson, the Apprentice

PROLOGUE

PROVO, UT~NOVEMBER~1992

I STINK, HE THOUGHT. And he did. Sweat circled under his arms and around his collar. From his body emanated the pungent odor of fear. No, not fear. Panic. His lips stuck together, chapped from constant licking, and dried snot whitened the outer edges of his nostrils. Flicking his eyes rapidly left and right, he detected no motion, heard no sounds. Nonetheless, he was not comforted.

He shivered, despite the heat in the building. Taking a step closer to the glass display case, he held his breath and fitted the shiny new key into the lock. The tiny clicking sound did give him some small measure of comfort, and he let his breath out raggedly. He carefully slid the panes apart and took in the contents of the case. Lifting his chin, he acknowledged the spirit captives, and as he grasped each carved wooden figurine, he looked it in the eyes and softly and reverently spoke its name.

"*ANGWUSKATSINA,* Crow.

ANGWUSNUSOMTAQA, Crow Mother.

NATA'ASKA, Big Mouth Ogre.

SO'YOKWUUTI, Ogre Woman.

EWTOTO, Chief.

AHÖLA, Chief's Lieutenant.
LENANGTAQA, Flute Player.
POLIIMANA, Butterfly Maiden.
KWEWU, Wolf.
SOWI'INGKATSINA, Deer Dancer.
TSOPKATSINA, Antelope.
SIKYAQOQLO, Artist.
WUPAMOKATSINA, Guard.
QALETAQA, Warrior.
HEE'E'E, Warrior Maiden.
KOYEMSI, Mudhead Racer.
TUHAVI, Paralyzed Brother.
KIISA, Chicken Hawk Racer.
KWAHU, Eagle.
KOKOPÖLÖ, Humpback.
POOTAWIKKATSINA, Coiled Plaque Carrier.
MUUYAWKATSINA, Moon."
His gloved hand trembled as he reached for the last one.
"*TAWA,* Sun."

The man added it to the other spirit beings safely
ensconced in protective fabric and bubble wrap. With great care
and attention to the photos he had taken of their positions, he
filled their places in the display case with expertly crafted
duplicates, slid the panels closed, and locked the glass. Then,
calm at last, he left the Brigham Young University Museum of
People and Cultures, cradling in his arms the precious cargo
belonging to his people.

The *Katsinam* watched and listened as their mortal
deliverer initiated their escape. They made no noises of
disapproval, for they knew they were going home. Only *Tawa*
knew what was ahead, and he frowned.

*   *   *

Across the country in Florida, Raven Looking Bird
Lightfoot searched beneath her car seat for the sketch pad and the

box of colored pencils her new husband, Dane Lightfoot, bought her in Tampa. Drawing would make the ride to Arizona seem shorter. Although Raven was a legitimately gifted artist, her abilities transcended the ordinary and were influenced by her psychic heiroscripting powers, often without her conscious intention. The term "heiroscripting" was coined by Dane upon their first meeting to reflect her ability to communicate in written symbols. It was not entirely accurate, as Raven's drawings rarely contained written words. She was, in fact, formally categorized as a portrait clairvoyant—one who sees things beyond the normal visual ability to do so and can transfer the images by means of artistic media.

Turning to a blank page, Raven started to sketch, humming tunelessly as she outlined and shaded her picture. When she finished, she admired her work. It was *TAWA*, the Sun god—a Hopi kachina, or *Katsina*, as her people said—a benevolent spirit being. Its face was circular, like a target, with an outer rim of markings meant to represent the feathers on the actual Sun *Katsina* mask. The central circle was divided into three portions--two upper and one lower. To the left of the center line, the upper area was colored red with a yellow interior; to the right, it was yellow with a red interior. The lower hemisphere was colored turquoise blue. Within it, black lines gave the indication of two straight-line eyes and a triangular shaped mouth, also colored black.

Dane glanced over at the drawing, listening as his wife described it.

"These are feathers, and this is the face. These lines are eyes, and here is the mouth," she said. "The Hopi and many of the Yavapai Indians believe that the Sun *Katsina* controls the seasons."

"He looks a little sad, don't you think? He's frowning. Why is that?" Dane said.

Raven looked at her picture, and then she compared it to the one in the book her mother gave her. The mouth of her Sun god image was inverted, giving it a scowl.

"I don't know, honey. That's just how he wanted to be

drawn," she said.

"Well, if the Sun god's unhappy, then we may be in for some wicked weather," he said

A chill ran down Raven's back, and she crossed her arms over her stomach protectively.

* * *

Hundreds of miles away, my eyes fly open, and I stare at nothing. I know the young newlywed couple. Dane is my brother—one who just returned from beyond the veil of death. Raven is my new sister, and she carries my nephews in her belly.

I am Luna—short for *Ojos del Luna* (as my village family calls me); *Hvtesse Totwv* (as my Creek Indian mother calls me). Both names mean the same—Moon Eyes. My eyes are so blue they are almost white, and Mother says that is because I am blind. But when I play my flute, I can see everything in my dream travels. I often travel great distances, and the world is vivid and colorful, and I experience keen sensory perceptions of sound and smell.

I am a "Story Keeper." I remember in detail what I see on my journeys. The stories I tell are not mine, but I keep them in my memory always, as do I keep all the other stories related to this group of people whose lives intersect mine in a strange and unexplainable way.

This one is hers—the Snapshot's story. It begins the first day of my new sister's married life.

CHAPTER ONE

ARIZONA~MARCH 1993

DANE LIGHTFOOT WATCHES RAVEN, his very pregnant wife, as she stirs in her sleep. Lying on her side on the overstuffed sofa, she is a vision of loveliness in the soft red and yellow glow of the fire. She is covered by a heavy wool blanket with a bold pattern of shapes and colors that was handwoven by her Yavapai Indian mother, Robin. Bugle, Robin's fat pet beagle, lies at Raven's feet, his thick tail slowly thumping against the sofa.

Four months ago, the family packed Bugle into the car and moved up into the Bradshaw Mountains to live in one of the four furnished guest houses overlooking the campus of Embry-Riddle Aeronautical University-Prescott in Arizona. Situated almost to the 7,700-foot summit of Spruce Mountain, the houses are owned by the University, but they are used at the discretion of its president, Johnathan Hunter. A consummate bachelor, Hunter is the lone occupant (most of the time) of the largest of the four houses. ERAU's Provost, Dr. Wil Albertson, occupies the other large house, along with his wife and mother-in-law.

Robin Looking Bird is employed as the housekeeper for the "president's residences," and Hunter has arranged for her to live in the smallest of the houses, so she does not have to make a daily drive up the treacherous Forest Road 52A on the mountain. The snows came early this year and, though it is technically spring, the freezing weather has yet to relent.

Dane's Jeep Wrangler, with its jaunty rag top that was so perfectly suited to sunny Florida, quickly became impractical for Prescott's frigid weather conditions. Fortunately, because of his job with the Prescott Fire Department, Dane has the use of a high-clearance four-wheel-drive Chevy truck. Robin's Ford Explorer sits too low to navigate anything but the short trips from driveway to driveway to driveway to driveway of the mountaintop residences. Consequently, the two ladies have been prisoners on the mountain since just before Christmas.

Raven sighs, and Dane pulls the blanket up over her swollen belly, then he grabs his coat and heads for the door to gather more firewood. The cold air and high altitude render him a bit breathless, and he thinks about Florida. It seems like just yesterday that he and Raven made their way from Tallahassee, Florida, to Prescott, Arizona, right after the wedding. He can almost smell the smudge stick of sage she carried as she walked through the Thistleseed's family room toward him, dressed in the traditional Seminole skirt and blouse that Dane's mother, Fawn, had made especially for her future daughter-in-law.

* * *

It was an impromptu family and close friends' affair at the home of Liahona Thistleseed, the Mohawk senior member of the Trackers Team. Fawn Lightfoot and Wren Thistleseed had arranged the ceremony while part of the Team was in South Florida wrapping up their latest case. As soon as they returned to the house, the ceremony began, much to everyone's delight.

Dane Lightfoot was dressed in traditional Seminole clothing. His long colorful shirt was embellished with patchwork squares representing his Wind Clan, fire symbols for his position as a fire marshal, and a jagged lightning bolt pattern that stood for his psychic power. The mid-thigh length shirt was worn loosely belted with a long sash over lightweight cotton slacks. A cloth turban covered his head. Noah, his younger brother, was similarly attired, but his outfit doubled as his football mascot getup as Chief Osceola, minus the war paint. They stood in front of the French doors to the right of the family room fireplace.

The door between the family room and the foyer opened, and eight-year-old Shelly Thistleseed walked out, wearing her blue and white Sunday dress and carefully holding a smoldering stick of sage. She walked down the center of the room, placed the sage in a shell bowl on the fireplace hearth, and went to stand with her mother Wren, a handsome, full-blooded Cherokee.

Behind her walked Dane's mother, Fawn Lightfoot, also dressed in her traditional Seminole clothing of long patchwork skirt and sheer, elbow-length shawl. She was sporting her famous hair hat, an intricate arrangement of her long hair woven over a hat-shaped form and held in place with bobby pins. She carried an earthenware bowl of a dark liquid, which she also placed on the brick hearth.

Musical accompaniment from the foyer was supplied by Bill Thistleseed on piano, with twin sister Selah and Noah's love interest, Maria Ramirez, on vocals. The music changed, and Raven Looking Bird walked into the room, dressed in the handmade outfit that Fawn gave her as an engagement present. The long skirt was adorned in patchwork squares which matched Dane's shirt. It featured a lightning bolt pattern to reflect their shared psychic powers and bird feet symbols for her Bird Clan. The hem of the skirt swirled around cream-colored yucca fiber moccasins her mother had crafted for her, and the sheer shawl floated near her waist as she moved slowly forward. She wore elegant matching earrings, bracelet, and necklaces crafted of red, black, and yellow seed beads and porcupine quills which reflected the sunlight shining through the dormer window high above her in the foyer.

Dane's eyes misted as he gazed lovingly at his bride. She carried no flowers. Instead, she held a fan of grey and white feathers, courtesy of Fawn's pet goose, Emma.

Dane took her hand, and they faced their officiating friends at the fireplace, Police Chief Jack Abernathy and Dane's mentor, Liahona "Lee" Thistleseed. Jack began the traditional wedding vows.

"Dearly Beloved, we are gathered here in the sight of God to unite this man and this woman in holy matrimony ..."

After his part, Raven and Dane turned to one another and recited their vows, ending with an exchange of rings.

"What God has brought together, let no man put asunder," Lee said, as the couple beamed at each other.

Then, the bride and groom each took a drink of the liquid in the bowl—an herbal potion prepared and blessed by Fawn, a Seminole Indian Cedar Woman. Taking the feathered fan and the smoking embers of sage, Fawn stood before the couple. She used the fan to direct the cleansing smoke over their heads and their bodies, all the way down to their feet. After that, Fawn took a finger-woven sash and wrapped the right hands of the bride and groom together to symbolize their union.

"New and old family and friends, I give you Dane and Raven Lightfoot," Lee said, smiling so broadly his eyes almost disappeared beneath his heavy brows.

The following day, the couple loaded up the Wrangler and headed to Prescott for a honeymoon. Thus, Dane and Raven Lightfoot's life began, as typical as most newlyweds, but with two exceptions: both of them had powerful psychic abilities, and Raven was already 12 weeks pregnant ... with twins.

*   *   *

"Hey, Bucko. What's up?" Raven says from the couch.

"Thinking about you, Chubs," Dane says.

"Watch it, watch it! It's your fault, this baby belly." She sits up and stretches catlike, gazing at the fire and rubbing her bulging stomach.

"Wouldn't have it any other way." He sits beside her and strokes her bobbed hair, remembering a time when his hair was longer than hers.

Outside, the sun begins to set, bathing the room in streaks of red, orange, purple, pink, and yellow. Sunsets on the mountain are spectacular, especially when the lights reflect off the snow. They sit close to one another, watching the flames dance in the huge fireplace. The hearth is enormous, filling one entire wall of the room with stacked flagstone and topped with a massive mantle of local wood. Above the mantle is a row of thick, glass blocks which allows ambient light to fill the space without sacrificing heat. The family has taken to spending most of the time in this room since the snows began.

A huge sectional sofa forms a U-shape in front of the fireplace, and each section is large enough for an adult to sleep comfortably. The farther along Raven's pregnancy progresses, the more she takes up residence on "her" section of the couches. At 32 weeks, she has little energy. Her doctor has confirmed that she is carrying twins, and he recommends as much rest as possible, given her medical history. Raven is a good patient and follows his instructions willingly. These babies are important to her, and she has no intention of risking them. She lays her head upon Dane's shoulder and thinks back to the time when they first met.

*   *   *

Raven and Dane became lovers in 1989. They met at the Fireman's Ball in Tallahassee. He wore a starched and pressed uniform; she wore a sleeveless slip dress and yucca fiber moccasins. Once they laid eyes on each other, no one else existed for them.

During their torrid relationship from 1989 through 1990, Raven was beset with three episodes of very heavy female bleeding. She had always experienced erratic monthly cycles, but these three times were different. They began with strong abdominal cramps that precipitated profuse hemorrhaging, leaving Raven feverish, weak, and anemic.

Dane knew when each episode occurred, even when he was nowhere near. He could smell the blood. Dane was a clairscentrist, one who could smell things beyond the human ability to do so. That was his specialty in the elite Trackers Team, a group of Native American Indians who track criminals and missing persons using the specially developed psychic powers of their minds. Dane was called "the Bloodhound" because of his clairscent gift.

Raven and Dane never realized that the three incidences were not menstrual in nature; they were miscarriages. A trip to her gynecologist after the last occurrence confirmed that Raven had been pregnant three times, and each time, she had been carrying twins—something that ran in her father's family.

When she revealed the doctor's findings, Dane had been overwrought with grief and guilt. Believing they were being punished by God for their immoral behavior, he began attending the Church of Jesus Christ of Latter-day Saints with Lee Thistleseed. The sudden embracing of a Christian religion caused a rift to form between the lovers. Dane refused to have conjugal relations, and Raven felt rejected. And then, there was the fire.

After a particularly hurtful argument, Raven came to Dane's house to make up with him. She brought with her a bottle of wine as a token of her apology, but Dane refused to drink any. Mormons did not drink alcohol or smoke. Raven did both. After another bout of heated arguing, the two of them drifted off to sleep on the couch. Raven's half-finished cigarette fell on the floor and ignited the carpet. A passerby named John Silver saw the smoke and rushed into the burning house. Mr. Silver carried both Raven and Dane out before the house exploded, killing him in the blast.

Dane's remorse was so great that he couldn't even look at Raven, and so she left Tallahassee and moved to her mother's hometown of Prescott. Two years later, when she returned to Florida, Dane and Raven found that they could not continue living without each other, so they rekindled their romance, but with one exception. They vowed not to have sex again until they were married; however, that decision was not made until after they had that first night of reunion lovemaking, and that one night produced yet another pregnancy. Dane proposed almost immediately—the next morning, in fact—and it was not until they announced their engagement at the Thistleseed house that fall that even they suspected her condition.

In October of 1992, Raven was poisoned by her perfume.

A misguided man with terminal cancer dosed dozens of fragrances with a synthetic ecstasy drug. Several people were killed, and Raven nearly died.

The night Raven was rushed to the hospital, Dr. Anjul Vidjapore took Dane aside and told him that the baby (babies!) had not been injured, despite the ecstasy poisoning. Anxious for their family to be complete and start out in the right way, they consented to Fawn's suggestion that they marry as soon as Raven was well enough. It took little urging on Raven's part. She had always been ashamed of the fact that her parents were not married, though she never told Dane of it.

*   *   *

Sitting now in their temporary Prescott home, Raven's eyes are drawn to the small kachina figurines on the mantle. She gazes longingly at her special kachina, "Little *Gisak*." Next to the kachinas is a color picture of Raven's father, Falcon Looking Bird, glancing sidelong at the camera, his mouth open in a perpetual laugh, as was his nature. She misses him terribly to this day. Next to him stands a black and white photograph of her grandparents, Walter and Carolina Sauvakwaka, but they are no more than faces in a frame, relatives she has never known.

Bugle, the ever-present beagle, sits upright from his spot at Raven's feet, his thick tail beating a rhythm on the couch. He yawns and then slithers lazily onto the floor. A deep chesty cough draws Raven's attention to the door. Robin is home from cleaning Hunter's house. Raven takes in her mother's pallor and chapped lips. Despite the ruddiness from the frosty wind, Robin looks unwell. Too much smoking stopped much too late. Results from a recent trip to the doctor confirm her suspicions. Robin Looking Bird has emphysema.

"Fawn-tea, Mama. Hot in the crockpot. Will you bring me a cup, too?" Raven drinks a lot of her mother-in-law's special tea concoction. It was this blend of herbs that Fawn Lightfoot used to nurse Raven back to health and save this pregnancy.

Robin smiles weakly through a deep shiver. "I can use

some. Cold out there. Colder than I remember it ever being in March." She heads for the kitchen, Bugle on her heels, and dips out enough for two steaming cups. Robin smiles at their nickname for the beverage. *Fawn-tea. Thank the gods that the woman had the uncanny medical knowledge necessary to save my daughter's life.*

Because they drink Fawn-tea so often (they go through three pots a day), Dane came up with the idea of brewing it in large batches and freezing it in plastic Kool-Whip container. Its shape fits perfectly into the crockpot for thawing and warming. A quick pass under the hot water faucet releases the frozen tea from its container. And since the temperature up on the mountain has been below freezing for so long, they simply keep the tea "bricks" in a large plastic bag outside.

Robin brings the cups to the couches, and the mother and daughter sip quietly, each lost in her own thoughts, letting the soothing liquid heal them from the inside-out.

Robin coughs deeply, clapping a paper towel to her mouth, and Raven holds her breath.

"Get rid of it, Mama. That's the best thing you can do," Raven says.

"Who knew a person could have so much junk inside her lungs," Robin says.

"That's why you need to cough it all out. Less poison in your body."

"Yippie." Robin takes another large swallow of tea, and them she spits out more phlegm, just as a blast of cold air enters the room, along with a *"baroo"* from Bugle.

"In with the good, and out with the bad," Dane says from the front door. "You girls on your third pot of tea yet?" He kisses both women—Raven's lips, Robin's cheek—and then he shakes the snow from his head and begins piling the firewood he has just gathered onto the hearth.

"How was work today?" Raven asks, pulling the woolen blanket up around her chin.

"Super. Three space heater fires in Chino Valley. Believe it or not, they were within a mile of each other. Families can't get their houses warm enough, so they keep multiple heaters going. You can't plug two heaters into one outlet. They draw too much power. And would you believe that at one house, these two old folks had a wood burning fire pit right in the middle of the living room? It burned all the way through the floor! We took them to the shelter at the library."

He throws more wood into the blazing cavity of the huge flagstone fireplace, and then he flops onto the couch beside his wife. "Florida, where are you? I miss you, humidity. I've forgotten what it's like to sweat. You didn't tell me it was going to be this cold, Babe."

"I'll warm you up later." Raven smiles, reaches up, and rubs his thick black hair.

"Don't make promises you can't keep, Chubs," Dane says with a wink and a nod.

"Did you forget I was here, kids?" Robin says.

Dane laughs and blushes. "What I meant was … uh … I mean, your daughter has the coldest feet in the world, and she plants them right up against my backside."

Raven closes her hand and give the hair brushing past the collar of his jacket a playful tug. She recalls a time when it was long and flowing past his shoulders. That was before his trip to New York to locate the poison-laced perfume that threatened her life; the trip that also threatened his. She shivers, and Dane, thinking she is cold, snuggles closer, tucking the blanket in around her.

CHAPTER TWO

THE FALCON AND THE ROBIN

RAVEN'S FATHER WAS MARRIED BEFORE—more than once, in fact—and though he was very much in love with young Robin Sauvakwaka of the *Wikutepa*, or Granite Peak, Band of the Northeastern Yavapai tribe, he was forbidden to marry her.

His name was Falcon Nookatuwa of the Hopi tribe in Oraibi, Arizona, and he was the seventh child born in a family of four sets of twins. All the children were named after birds because that was their mother's clan. In order of birth they were: Lark and Sparrow, Jay and Rooster, Pigeon and Dove, Falcon and Hawk. In their Native American traditions, it was said that the seventh child of a seventh child was destined to have second sight— psychic gifts. Being the first one to emerge during birth, Falcon was the gifted one.

Not having had the benefit of a mentor like Liahona Thistleseed to train him, Falcon Nookatuwa's gift was rough, but it was a gift nonetheless. He could see great distances beyond other men's ability to sight objects. He became a seer/guide, a man the hunting parties used on point because he could spot the prey miles away. It was this gift that brought Robin Sauvakwaka into his line of sight as she sat beside her mother weaving baskets.

Falcon had been asked to visit the Yavapai on the Prescott Indian Reservation to lead a hunting expedition for small game up on nearby Thumb Butte Saddle. The Reservation was located on land formerly occupied by the Fort Whipple Military Reserve. At the time of its establishment, there were just 75 acres on which the tribe could live. Thirty-one years later, in 1956, the Government added 1,320 more acres. The additional acreage gave the people more opportunities for both agriculture and hunting for sustenance.

Returning from his successful hunting venture with the men, Falcon happened to glance through the settlement, and there she was. Her beauty stopped him in his tracks. Robin was 14; Falcon was 32, but he fell in love with her instantly. When he set about to woo her, however, Carolina Sauvakwaka objected.

The word *Yavapai* was usually translated as "people of the sun," but another meaning was "mouthy, talkative people." Carolina embodied the latter. She was quick to tell him, in no uncertain terms, that her daughter was not available to be his wife. In the first place, Robin was still a child. Furthermore, he was much too old and had already married and divorced two other wives—thankfully, without children from either. Finally, and most importantly, the two were related to each other.

Falcon's mother had been Lucy Yapatisvo before she married Bob Nookatuwa. *Yapatisvo* was the Hopi word for "a little gray bird who imitates the sounds of other birds." The Yapatisvo people were members of the *Galyum* Clan of Hopi Indians—Small Bird Clan.

Robin's mother was married to Walter *Sauvakwaka*, which was the Yavapai word for "white deer." But, before her marriage, she had been Carolina Sakiye of the *Yavapé. Sakiye* meant "white head eagle"—also Bird Clan. Tradition dictated that children traced their ancestral roots through the mothers, and even though Falcon and Robin were from different tribes, their matrilineal roots still came from the same *pai* or people.

To marry someone of the same clan was considered incest, taboo, and completely forbidden. So, Falcon was rebuffed by the mother. But that did not quench his desire for the daughter, nor did it hinder Robin from falling in love with him. One night, Falcon Nookatuwa and Robin Sauvakwaka simply disappeared from Prescott.

Falcon had been discussing the purchase of a horse from Walter Sauvakwaka. Robin remained out of sight, listening and waiting for just the right moment. As Falcon started up his battered Chevrolet truck, Robin rushed outside clutching Falcon's pocketknife.

"Mr. Nookatuwa! Wait! You left your pocketknife." She sailed past her surprised father and mother. Before either one could voice a protest, Robin Sauvakwaka clambered into the bed of the truck, and the lovers vanished in a cloud of dust.

The couple traveled across the Painted Desert northeast of Flagstaff, Arizona, to the small village of *Paaqavi,* known as Bacabi, the Third Mesa on the Hopi Reservation. Falcon's sisters had relocated from Oraibi to Bacabi years before, and the couple was able to occupy a small house nearby. They lived there happily for many years among the Hopi Indians as man and wife.

Naming conventions among the Hopi were not strict. Many people, to fit in with white society, changed their lengthy Hopi names to the English forms. *Nooka* and *tuwa* were both Hopi words for "see," so Falcon and Robin Anglicized it and, rebelliously acknowledging their shared clan, gave themselves the last name of Looking Bird.

The name *Hopi* was a shortened version of *Hopituh Shi-mu-mu.* It meant "the peaceful people" or "peaceful little ones." Like the Yavapai, social and political structures were divided into powerful kinship groups of clans, and membership was traced through the mothers. Clan members fiercely guarded their ritual knowledge, shielding it from "outsiders" who could not fully comprehend their feelings about race, religion, language, traditions, historical experiences, and values.

Because she was Yavapai, Robin was an outsider, but Falcon ensured she was accepted by fabricating a matrilineal lineage with a Hopi family he had helped on a game hunt. For her part, Robin was diligent in her efforts to assimilate into the Hopi culture, so nobody was the wiser.

Robin became a well-known weaver of baskets, clothing, coiled plaques, and yucca moccasins. Basketry, in Robin's Yavapai culture, was performed under the protection that the men gave the women, so the women could practice and perfect their art form. Robin's mother taught her well, and her weaving arts conformed to the Hopi ideals.

The ceremonies surrounding the *Katsinam* were another aspect of Hopi life that were rarely shared with non-Hopi people. A *Katsina* dancer's sacred role was to represent a *Katsina* spirit in the ceremonial dances. Though primarily a male activity, women also had their part to play in the community ceremonies and dances.

Because she was so accomplished at such a young age, Robin's woven goods were highly sought after. She was invited to be initiated into the *Lakon* society and participate in the *O'waqölt*. It was an honor exclusive to Hopi women, which everyone assumed she was. The Basket Dance, like many of the women's ceremonies, was meant to express the concept of healthy impregnation—something Robin and her husband greatly desired.

Falcon's long-range seeing gift quickly became known around the territory, and he benefited the tribe on many hunts for *sikwi*, wild game meat. The family was regularly gifted with food, furs, and other useful items. Life was good in Bacabi Village for the Looking Birds.

The one area in which they had difficulty was with enlarging their family. Falcon had no children from his other short marriages, and they desperately wanted a baby, but Robin could not conceive. She was given many herbal concoctions by the medicine man, including a Hopi "cure-all" of greenthread tea, which was made from the flowers of a perennial aster plant called *hohoysi*. It calmed her queasy stomach, but since it was also used as a dye, it had the side effect of turning her tongue and lips yellow. It did not help with conception, however.

The couple also sought blessings from the *Katsinam*—the revered Hopi spirit beings. After fervent petitions and gifts of *beva* (tobacco) and *homa* (white corn meal) to KOKOPÖLÖ, the humpback *Katsina* of fertility, and *SIVUKATSINA*, the *Katsina* who promotes the procreation of life, Robin was finally able to get pregnant. Bringing the baby to term was another matter.

Robin suffered six miscarriages before she was able to bear a child. The birth was difficult, and Robin lost much blood. When the baby finally emerged from the birth canal, the placenta tore from the womb and was violently expelled. Though she was packed immediately with deer moss to staunch the flow of blood, Robin developed an infection. Many days later, after infusions of feverfew and hyssop tea and damp compresses of chamomile and purple coneflower, Robin's fever broke, and she was able to hold her baby for the first time, but she would never have another.

The child was beautiful beyond words. Her almond-shaped eyes were like the roasted nuts of the piñon tree, and her skin was smooth and flawless like unvarnished wood. Falcon kissed her pudgy little face and took to calling her his little *Qomi*—sweet corn flour dough. Though Robin laughed at his term of endearment, she emphatically stated she would not have her child named after food. She was unaware that twenty days would pass before her baby would receive a real name.

According to Hopi tradition, children were named by the female relatives of the father's clan. After twenty days passed, the women of Falcon's clan gathered for the naming ceremony. Each woman brought a gift for the child and a suggestion for a name. Falcon's mother had passed into the spirit world, but his four sisters were excited to give their ideas for the baby's new name, as were his several adopted "aunts" who were unrelated elderly women in the village.

Robin, the baby, the sisters, and the aunts met at the eastern edge of the mesa. Lark, as the oldest female relative, claimed the honor of giving the first blessing and naming. Holding an ear of white corn against the baby's chest, she raised the child aloft and spoke to the morning sun as it rose and brightened the horizon.

"This child is one of us. May she live long without sickness or evil in her life. I name this child *Tsosovi*. Bluebird."

Each woman in turn performed this same ritual and gave

the baby a name. Sparrow chose the name *Atokotiva,* Dancing Crane. Pigeon selected *Karocatori,* Parrot Spirit. Dove was the youngest sister, closest in age to Falcon, and his unspoken favorite. Because of the baby's pitch-black hair, she chose the name *Qomvitsiro,* Black Bird.

Among the various adopted aunts came their choices for names: *Pos Iwuu Hoomi,* Magpie Hair; *Lomahongava,* Beautiful Clouds Arising; *Zihmatotsa,* Spinning Hummingbird; and *Sihuqoto,* Head of Flowers. As each woman "named" her daughter, Robin smiled and nodded, all the while struggling not to laugh, wrinkle her nose, or show any sign of distaste.

With the naming completed, the women returned to Robin's home to present their gifts and share some food. Robin was looking forward to the meal because she had not been allowed to eat salted food throughout the twenty-day waiting period. The tradition of eating unsalted food was symbolic for periods of time when there might be droughts and starvation. It prepared the mother and the child to survive in the face of challenging conditions and to ensure each of them a long life.

First to eat, though, was the baby. Lark took the infant and fed her *pik'ami*—sweet pudding—made by combining sprouted wheat, cornmeal, boiling water, and sugar. The concoction had been baked in a special pudding pit for 24 hours. The cooled, semi-solid pudding was then dipped into a stew broth containing bits of *morivosi*—beans and vegetables—and fed to the baby on Lark's fingertips. It was her first food other than mother's milk, and the women laughed as she opened her eyes wide at the unfamiliar taste and feel.

After the first foods, the baby happily suckled on her mother while the others set their other presents out for Robin and her family. Though the gifts were simple, to Robin they seemed lavish and even decadent, especially the food items.

The older women had prepared various cooked foods, and the naming participants enjoyed eating, laughing, and sharing village news. Robin particularly liked the *somiviki*, a sweet tamale-shaped cake of blue corn that seemed to satisfy all her taste buds. The dish was made with ground blue corn, juniper ashes, honey, and boiling water. The mixture was carefully hand rolled, tied with thin strips of yucca plant, and then steamed.

One of her favorite food items was a huge basket of *piki,* which the aunts made on an outdoor cedar wood fire stove as she and the sisters watched. The traditional Hopi "paper bread" was made from a recipe passed down from mothers to daughters for generations. Falcon had told people that Robin's mother "died" before she taught her daughter the recipe, so the old women decided their gift would be to teach Robin how to make the bread.

Although *piki* took several days to make from scratch, the aunts hastened the process by pre-grinding the blue cornmeal to a fine powder and working together as a team. Like the other dishes, *piki* was made with few ingredients, the base of which was the blue cornmeal. One of the ladies mixed the meal with hot water in a large bowl. Then she added green juniper ash through a fine sieve. She continually added water to the sticky mush until the mixture became thin.

Another aunt brushed a coating of oil made from sheep brains across the flat cooking stone that rested atop the fire. After checking the stone's surface for sufficient heat, she hand-smeared a very thin layer of the batter onto the stone. If any holes appeared, she smoothed them away by adding more batter.

In a few moments, the sheet became dry enough to lift. Another woman carefully peeled away the cooked bread and transferred it a table. Working quickly to keep the bread from cooling and tearing, she folded it into a rectangular shape like a burrito. Then she laid the folded bread into the basket.

Robin watched the process with awe, committing to memory each step as the ladies made roll after roll of the paper-thin bread. When the batter was all gone, they presented the full basket of *piki* to her. Robin eagerly grabbed a roll. The aunts' combined expertise was evident. The bread melted in her mouth, and she smacked her lips loudly to everyone's delight. While she snacked on her treats, the sisters presented their gifts.

Lark brought two, carved wooden bowls full of sweet treats. The larger bowl held *maloni*—sweet musk melon like cantaloupe or honeydew. It was fragrant and juicy. A smaller matching bowl held pine nuts and *kwaani*—dried figs. Sparrow gave her a large lidded earthenware jar of freshly baked *tosi*—finely hand-ground sweet corn flour. Pigeon had gathered a bundle of *bacavi*—small, flexible reeds like bamboo that Robin could use for basket weaving. They were presented in a beautiful coiled basket she had fashioned herself. Dove's gift was a *naququsi*—prayer feathers. She had fashioned the small handmade fan from black raven feathers and tied it with a braided ribbon that had been dyed with yellow *hohoysi*. Robin loved it best of all.

The gifts were met with exclamations of "*Taah*," and "*He He Y*," by the ladies, for it was evident Robin was being greatly favored.

It was late afternoon by the time each guest had eaten her fill. Robin embraced every woman and thanked her by saying, "*Aus quali*." The naming party eventually departed, and Robin and her new baby were left alone to rest. Falcon came home soon afterward, and the parents settled down to the daunting task of selecting one of the names given to the child by the ladies.

While Falcon sampled the foods and examined all the gifts with approval, Robin was finally able to express herself about the names. Falcon laughed as she told him how solemnly the aunts had presented their choices. The couple immediately rejected Magpie Hair, Beautiful Clouds Arising, Head of Flowers, and Spinning Hummingbird. They both liked the sound of the names given by the sisters and agreed there had been more thought involved, so they deliberated on those names at great length.

Robin leaned toward *Tsosovi*, Bluebird. But Falcon had something else in mind. Dove was the sister of his heart, and he wanted to use her name suggestion, but *Qomvitsiro* was quite a mouthful for a delicate little girl, so he took his inspiration from Dove's gift, and Robin was delighted. Since the baby had a full head of hair, black as a raven's wings, they named her Raven.

By the time the sun set, Falcon had put the foods away and climbed into the bed beside his wife. With Robin lying in his arms and holding their beautiful daughter, Falcon was never happier. He took advantage of those peaceful moments to stroke

Robin's hair and tell her stories. That night, his story was all about the Raven.

"In Hopi stories, Raven is the same as Crow. Crow Mother is very important to us. Her name is ANGWUS-NUSOMTAQA. But that's way too much name for a little girl. I like Raven better, don't you?" Falcon said.

Robin nodded in agreement, drowsy from all the activities and food of the day, and because Falcon's voice was so soothing as he stroked her hair.

"I've heard many stories from many other tribes about Raven. She is the most intelligent of all the birds. She is a creature of transformation and change. She can deliver messages from the gods, heal the sick, and restore health and harmony. She is a keeper of secrets and can communicate deep mysteries. But, of all these things, the most important story I heard is that Raven is the bringer of light. She flew out from the dark womb at the creation of the world and brought the dawning of understanding for our people. They say, without Raven, the people would wander in darkness forever." Robin was still awake, so he continued.

"I'll tell you about the ritual of ANGWUSNUSOMTAQA KATSINA. Crow mother appears to the children at their initiation rites. She waits in the *kiva* with a WU KATSINA beside a large sand painting on the floor. She bears a yucca blade whip and hands it to the WU KATSINA as each candidate appears before them. The WU KATSINA delivers four swats on the child's backside. If the whip gets worn, Crow Mother gives the WU KATSINA a fresh one."

"Sounds kinda mean," Robin said with a yawn.

"Not really," Falcon said, "After the child is whipped, Crow Mother lifts up her skirts and gets the same whipping from the WU KATSINA. Then she gives the child gifts of prayer feathers— like the ones Dove made for you—and cornmeal."

"That's nice. What's good for the goose is good for the gander, huh?"

"Yes, it is. She comes in the winter and brings a basket of bean sprouts to coax the seeds to germinate. She embodies maternal leadership ... and compassion ...," he continued while taking the baby from the sleeping Robin's arms, "... and she's a guiding spirit for many people…as I hope you will be, my little Raven … my *Qomi* … my heart." He gently laid the baby in her crib and joined his beloved wife in peaceful slumber.

* * *

At age three, Raven demonstrated an amazing ability to draw. She toddled around the village with a thin stick perpetually clutched between her stubby fingers. When she saw something she liked, she simply squatted down and scratched the image on the ground with her stick. The people took pleasure in strolling from house to house, looking down at the ground and following an endless montage of little portraits of dogs, sunrises, lizards, mountains, birds, or what happened to catch Raven's attention.

Raven stubbornly refused to wear the traditional squash blossom hairdo of Hopi girls. Instead, Robin trimmed her hair in the style of young Yavapai girls—blunt cut below the chin with straight bangs. Raven preferred it, except for the inconvenience of the bangs when they grew long. But even the bangs did not diminish her artistic talents.

By the time she was five, she was able to draw human likenesses. She would sit hunched over on the ground with her legs splayed out, scratching in the dirt with one hand and holding her thick bangs out of her eyes with the other hand. When she straightened up, between her feet would be an image of Robin pounding corn, or Tessie White Tail stirring a pot over the fire, or Harry Rattler scolding his boy Wally.

To preserve the images she scratched into the ground, the people took to framing them with sticks or rocks, so they would not be walked over. But of all the things Raven drew, her favorite pictures were of the *Katsinam*.

Because the Hopi considered the images sacred, Raven was given a special place to create these pictures. A short walk from the village was a *wala*, which was a gap between mesas. Near the *wala* was a small cave with smooth walls which formed a perfect studio for her. A hole above the center of the cave was large enough for a man to enter by means of a ladder. It also provided natural light.

Raven, at six years old, was provided an array of pots with powdered colors from which to choose. A larger pot of clean water was placed in the center of the cave, along with smaller shallow pots in which she mixed her colors. Robin fashioned several short-tipped brushes out of stiff dog fur tied to sticks, one for each color of paint that Raven concocted.

Raven painted in her little cave studio during the day, moving to a different part of the wall as the sunlight shifted through the hole in the ceiling. Because of the presence of the painted gods, the elders called the place *Qomvitsiro Kivakatsina*—"little black bird's house of the gods."

A *kiva* was an underground ceremonial chamber and was a mystical holy place. Each Hopi *kiva* featured a *sipapu*, a small hole in the ground to simulate the opening from which the first people emerged. At night, the men would take their lanterns and candles inside Raven's *kiva* to sing and pray, surrounded by the images of their *Katsinam*.

Raven was believed to be blessed by the spirits of the *Katsinam*, for she had only to take one look at the beautifully carved cottonwood images or the masks of the ceremonial dancers, with their distinctive colors and patterns, to be able to replicate them on the walls of her studio. Her favorite was the Sun *Katsina*, *TAWA*, with the aureole of feathers around his head and his vibrant turquoise, red, and yellow costume, and his image appeared more than all the others on the walls.

Raven drew many pictures of the *Katsinam*, but she possessed only two kachina figurines. At birth, as with all newborns, she received a grandmother *Katsina* known as *HAHAI-I-WUUTI*. When she was a year old, the *Giver Katsina* dancer presented her with a *putsihu,* a small, flat cradle doll. It had been carved and painted especially for her of *TAWAKATSINA* holding a black raven in his hand. It was her most treasured possession until tragedy struck her young life on her seventh birthday.

The people of her village were primarily farmers, growing crops of maize, beans, and squash, which were called "the three sisters" by the Natives. But, they also supplemented their meals with wild game that they trapped or tracked. Falcon's skills were always in demand for these hunts, and he was happy to oblige.

During one such hunting expedition up on a very high mesa, several rabbits suddenly sprang from their burrow in a thicket, running right between the legs of the hunting party. Leonard Terrapin, 70 years old and normally sure of foot, lost his balance and toppled backwards, right into his son, Barley, who fell back against another man, who fell against yet another man, causing a domino effect that ended with Falcon.

The hunters watched in horror as their seer/guide disappeared over the edge of the cliff. Falcon made no sound as he fell, though he knew his fate. Later, when the hunters returned to the village, Barley Terrapin recounted how Falcon Looking Bird simply spread his arms wide and lifted his head to the sky.

They found him at the bottom of the arroyo in that same position. He had landed in the branches of a piñyon tree. The tree broke his fall, but it also broke his neck. The angle of descent and the spreading greenery spared his body from mutilation, and when they brought him down from the limbs, they found him clutching a small object in his right hand, as though shielding it from the effects of the fall.

Falcon had tried his hand at carving a *tihü*. The kachina was for Raven's birthday. At first glance it appeared to be *ANGWUSNUSOMTAQA*, Crow Mother, with her spreading black wings at either side of her head, but on the base, Falcon had written "Little *Gisak*," which Robin had told him was the Yavapai word for raven. So, that was the name the people gave Falcon's kachina. The wings on its left side broke off in Falcon's fall and were never found, but that only served to further endear the figurine to both Raven and the people. Some even referred to the kachina as "flight of the Falcon."

Robin stayed on the Reservation for six more years and made a decent wage off her weaving and basketry skills. Learning that Walter and Carolina Sauvakwaka had passed into the land of the spirits, Robin left Bacabi Village and went home to Prescott. There was no one family shame or dishonor her anymore. She held her head up proudly as Mrs. Robin Looking Bird, a respectable widow with a lovely thirteen-year-old daughter named Raven.

CHAPTER 3

COLD AND DARK

IT IS COLD AND DARK in the basement beneath his tiny cabin, and it is getting colder and darker by the day. He feels it, and they feel it. Despite his best efforts, they are unhappy. All of them. Day and night, he prays to them, sings to them, dances for them, but he feels so small and insignificant and entirely alone against their combined might.

Led by *Tawa*, the gods ignore his pleas. They stare at him from their specially prepared recesses in the walls around the makeshift *kiva*, his own sacred underground place of worship. He begs them for mercy and forgiveness, but they are silent and aloof. And the cold and dark become worse as the Sun god hides his warmth and light.

He has long since exhausted the last of his stored gasoline. The generator is bone dry, so his only source of heat and illumination comes from the pitiful fire which barely crackles in the circular fire pit. It produces no lasting heat, nor does it provide more than just a feeble glow. The adobe-covered walls and floors make the space claustrophobic and even colder and darker.

He moves closer to the fire and places his hands on the flat flagstones around it, trying to thaw his fingers, flexing them open and closed to ease the stiffness that keeps him from doing his task. If he cannot carve, he cannot appease them. If he cannot carve, he cannot make the exchange. If he cannot carve, he is doomed. The world is doomed.

He understands his skill is not equal to the greatness of the man who created the kachinas in the first place. "I didn't know it would be this way," he cries. "my master's exit was premature. I'm so, so sorry."

He acknowledges his shortcomings with profound regret and stares at the dying embers while his mind cruelly mocks him. *You knew the risk before the switch was made, but your pride made you blind.*

* * *

Jeffrey Wilson had been selected as the apprentice to Master Carver Frederick Kalyesvah, and he was eager to learn. The master would teach him, and the gods would adore him, but fate had another plan.

When Jeffrey returned from Utah in December, he was still riding the high he experienced with the successful rescue of the kachinas from the BYU Museum. Proud that Master Kalyesvah had entrusted the task to him, he anticipated a joyful reunion, complete with adoration and adulation. After all, it was Jeffrey's own plan to retrieve the carved gods.

He had visited the museum in Provo three times before, surreptitiously taking photographs of the selected pieces from every possible angle—front, back, above, below. It was necessary for his master to view the pictures to refresh his memory of each detail of the kachinas he had carved when he was a younger man, so Jeffrey had been diligent in documenting both the details of the figurines for his mentor and their placement in the display cases for himself.

Master Kalyesvah was pleased with his apprentice after each of the three visits and anxious for the fourth when the *Katsinam* would be rescued. The two men had a special bond which was forged in their talents as wood carvers. Their two-generation age difference had no bearing on their role as housemates. They were respectful of each other in the small cabin they shared and got along well. Frederick was the teacher and mentor; Jeffrey was the student and protégé. Frederick was strict, but kind; Jeffrey was eager, but deferential. They were both skilled carvers, and the relationship was symbiotic.

It took months to sculpt the duplicates, and the master carver labored long and hard at his worktable in the basement, while the apprentice honed his skills in the well-lit kitchen area of the cabin. Frederick preferred the firelight; Jeffrey preferred incandescence.

They had a carefully constructed system: the master entrusted the apprentice with each kachina as it was finished; the apprentice tediously compared the carving to the photos, making note of any deviation from the original piece. Finally, the first 23 pieces were completed. Master and apprentice rejoiced by ceremoniously singing, dancing, and praying to the *Katsinam* in their basement *kiva*.

They had packed the floors and walls of the basement during the preceding fall with local clay, dug from an area close to their remote cabin near Crown King Mine, some 55 miles southeast of Prescott. Because they wanted a fire pit in the center of the room, screen-covered pipes were installed near ground level to allow fresh air in and smoke out. Smooth river rocks lined the base of the pit, encircled by a ring of flagstone.

Four rows of cubbyholes with flat bottoms were carved into the walls at eye level. There were 28 nooks in all. Two walls held eight alcoves, one held seven, and the last held five. On either side of each niche was a candle holder. Then, the dried and hardened clay had been overlaid with sand to replicate the *kiva* where Master Kalyesvah had received his vision of restoring the gods to their rightful places in the womb of Mother Earth.

During the early 1970s, the *kiva* had been the "studio" of a young girl who was gifted with remarkable artistic ability. She had painted the images of the gods on the walls. The men of the mesa regularly prayed there at night, and the people of the village had been blessed with happiness and prosperity. Then, the young girl moved away.

In time, the neighboring white men enticed many of the villagers into other areas which were more suitable for agriculture. When the villagers relocated, the *kiva* fell to disuse. The non-water-resistant mineral and vegetable pigments of the little girl's paints were subjected to the elements, and the precious images on the walls did not survive.

Frederick Kalyesvah had been born and raised in Walpi, Arizona. There, he became a Master Carver of kachinas and embraced the traditional-style carving movement. Although the new kachinas were fancier and more anatomically correct, Frederick felt their spirit feeling was being lost. So, he went back to making kachinas the way they were sculpted in the 19th century, working with simple tools and the same hand-ground mineral and vegetable pigments later used by the little painter girl whose work he viewed several years after she moved away. The cottonwood effigies he created were blessed with the power of the masked spirits of their Hopi deities—the *Katsinam*.

The *Katsinam* were the spirits of gods and goddesses, natural elements, animals, or the deceased ancestors of the Hopi. Before every *Katsina* ceremony, the men of each village spent days making figurines in the likeness of the *Katsinam* which would be represented in that ceremony. The figurines were then handed out by the *Giver Katsina* during the ceremony to all the little girls of the village. After the ceremony, the kachina effigies were hung on the walls of the children's homes. Parents used them to teach their offspring the characteristics of those certain *Katsinam*. The kachinas were, therefore, a means of education, gifts at dance-time, decorative articles for the home, and constant reminders of the *Katsinam* to which they prayed for all their needs.

The Endangered Species Act and Migratory Bird Treaty banned the selling of kachina sculptures that carried any exotic bird feathers from birds, so Frederick dutifully refrained from using the traditional natural feathers of eagles or hawks. Instead, the feathers of his creations were artistically and realistically carved into the wood.

As early as 1900, other carvers had been selling their

kachinas to tourists, who called them "dolls." Although this commercial practice was frowned upon by the elders, consumer demand went up, and the prices of dolls rose significantly. Average prices ranged from $300 to $1,000. Occasionally, an authentic Hopi kachina carved from the traditional cottonwood root sold for as much as $12,000. Prices were comparable for Navajo or Zuni carvings, which were more anatomically correct; however, the Hopi considered these kachinas devoid of the *Katsinam's* spirits. Nevertheless, tourists were clamoring for kachinas, so many Hopi carvers resorted to mass producing and selling their kachinas to make ends meet.

Frederick Kalyesvah resisted the urge to sell his creations. Carving was, for him, a spiritual endeavor as each kachina was modeled on the masks and costumes of the ceremonial *Katsina* gods who embodied the Hopi religion. For this reason, he vowed never to let his kachinas fall into the hands of outsiders.

Unfortunately, life had a way of thwarting even an honest man's best-intentioned plans. One day, hungry and lost in thought, Frederick unintentionally drove home with an unpaid sack of groceries in his truck before a cashier could check him out. He was on his way back to the store to pay for the food when he was stopped by the local police and arrested for stealing.

Having no money for bail, Frederick spent several days in jail. The charges were finally dropped, and he returned home embarrassed but no longer hungry, thanks to the deliciously adequate meals served during his incarceration. When he arrived, he discovered his door was open, and his small cabin had been looted. Frederick did not have much in the way of possessions, but his greatest treasures—his kachinas and his carving knives— had been stolen. The theft was reported; an investigation was conducted, but neither the kachinas nor the knives had turned up. Heartbroken, Frederick Kalyesvah left his home and moved away to a small cabin about an hour from Prescott. He was eventually able to buy new knives, but he never stopped looking for his original kachinas.

In 1992, after years of searching, Frederick came upon a 1975 arts catalog published by The Heard Museum of the Barry

Goldwater collection of Hopi kachina dolls. Senator Goldwater had donated 437 kachina dolls to the Heard Museum in the mid-60s. After the 1975 catalogue went out of print, the museum acquired other historic pieces from a privately-owned fine arts collection. Part of the combined collection was on loan to the Brigham Young University Museum of Peoples and Cultures in Provo, Utah; the other part was housed in Prescott, Arizona.

Among the glossy color photographs of the kachinas at the BYU exhibit, Frederick Kalyesvah recognized 23 of his original carved creations and reverently spoke their names.

> "*ANGWUSNUSOMTAQA*, Crow Mother.
> *ANGWUSKATSINA*, Crow.
> *NATA'ASKA*, Big Mouth Ogre.
> *SO'YOKWUUTI*, Ogre Woman.
> *EWTOTO*, Chief.
> *AHÖLA*, Chief's Lieutenant.
> *LENANGTAQA*, Flute Player.
> *POLIIMANA*, Butterfly Maiden.
> *KWEWU*, Wolf.
> *SOWI'INGKATSINA*, Deer Dancer.
> *TSOPKATSINA*, Antelope.
> *SIKYAQOQLO*, Artist.
> *WUPAMOKATSINA*, Guard.
> *QALETAQA*, Warrior.
> *HEE'E'E*, Warrior Maiden.
> *KOYEMSI*, Mudhead Racer.
> *TUHAVI*, Paralyzed Brother.
> *KIISA*, Chicken Hawk Racer.
> *KWAHU*, Eagle.
> *KOKOPÖLÖ*, Humpback.
> *POOTAWIKKATSINA*, Coiled Plaque Carrier.
> *MUUYAWKATSINA*, Moon. *TAWA*, Sun."

In a photo of an exhibit in Prescott, he recognized the other five *Katsinam* he had given life and quietly addressed them.

"*MASAUWU*, Skeleton Man.
OMAWKATSINA, Cumulous Cloud.
AWANYU, Plumed Serpent.
SOOTUKWNANG, Star.
KOKYANWUHTI, Spider Woman."

Frederick slept fitfully that night. Images of his original stolen carvings appeared in his dreams. *TAWA* spoke to him from on high. *Carver rescue us. Carver reclaim us. Carver rehome us.*
When Frederick awoke, he had a plan.

He had recently taken a roommate, a young man named Jeffrey. The boy had talent and showed much promise as a carver. He was lean and hungry, but Frederick trusted him, so the next morning, he revealed the dream to his new apprentice. That day began months of careful planning which culminated in the theft of the 23 BYU kachinas and precipitated the recovery of the five kachinas on display in the Smoki Museum in Prescott.

*   *   *

When Jeffrey returned from Utah, he noticed the quiet first. Then, he noticed the darkness. He parked and then jumped out of the sturdy four-wheel drive Jeep Cherokee with oversized snow tires that allowed him to navigate the twisting path along the old Prescott and Eastern Railroad and past the abandoned mine. Moving moved around the corner of the cabin, he checked against the wall and counted seven full gas cans, just as he had left them. He frowned. *Frederick has let the generator run out, as usual.* He grabbed the nearest can and emptied it into the ancient generator, primed the bulb, and then he pulled the cord. With an asthmatic cough, the machine rumbled to life. The porch light flickered and lit, giving him a better view of the front drive.

He walked back to the vehicle, opened the back gate, and retrieved the duffle bag of carefully cushioned kachinas. Growing concerned about Frederick, he hurriedly entered the cabin and surveyed the interior. All the rooms appeared to be empty, so he made his way quickly to the kitchen. The entrance to the basement stared at him from the center of the floor like a dark eye.

"Master?" he called, "Master, are you in here?"

His unease increased as he descended the handmade rope and wooden pole ladder into the depths of the cavernous basement into their own homemade version of a Hopi *kiva*. He had expected his master to be working, but nobody worked in darkness. *Maybe he walked to the road and got a ride to town?*

Jeffrey blinked several times to adjust to the blackness and scanned the room, but it was impossible to see anything except the small rectangular area of the hole brightened by the kitchen lights. The fire pit in the center of the sandy floor was cold and devoid of any live embers.

"Frederick?" he called. No answer. A knot formed in his gut, and his heart pounded in his throat.

Setting the bag of kachina figures on the floor, Jeffrey flicked his lighter and ignited a pile of tinder in the pit. Blowing in short puffs, he was able to coax a small blaze from the added kindling. In the opposite corner of the room, he spotted the pale figure of the older man, sitting on his work bench, hunched over his carving table, which was littered with bits and pieces of wood. The apprentice rushed over to the table.

"Master ... Fred ... are you all right?" he asked.

When he placed his arms around the man, he knew Frederick was far from all right. His master was cold, so cold, yet he breathed. Jeffrey ripped his own heavy down coat off and wrapped the old man with it. Gathering Frederick into his arms like a child, he struggled to the base of the ladder. Changing his hold, he laid the man over his shoulder like a sack and climbed the ladder. As he ascended each rung, the ladder shook and creaked from the added weight. His mentor grunted and whined in Jeffrey's ear.

As soon as his head cleared the opening, he shifted Frederick onto the floor and climbed up beside him. In the light, he could see the ghostly pallor of his face. His dry and wrinkled lips were pulled back from his teeth in a grimace, his right eye was closed, and his left eye was rolled back revealing the white orb streaked with red. His right hand was clenched and drawn to his chest, still clutching a wood carving knife. *Stroke.*

Jeffrey carried the stricken man to the bed and covered him with several quilts. Rushing to the kitchen, he set a cast iron kettle of water on a wood burning stove and lit a fire in its belly. Then, he ran back to the room to check on his friend.

A bit of color seemed to be returning to the man's face. The apprentice stroked the wizened cheek of his master and rubbed his arms and hands through the quilts. In a few moments, the man's left eye rolled down, and he looked up. He attempted to speak, but no words came.

Jeffrey hurried to the kitchen and gingerly touched the side of the kettle. *Hot enough.* Removing it with a dish cloth, he poured the steaming water into a large black and white enamelware cup. He dropped a tea bag and a spoon filled with sugar into the cup, and then he rushed back to the bedroom.

Frederick lifted the left side of his mouth in a crooked smile. The right side of his mouth drooped, as did the rest of his face on that side. A single tear slid from the unaffected eye and disappeared into the pillow.

Jeffrey filled the spoon with tea, blew it, and tenderly put it to his mentor's lips. Some went in, but the rest went the course of the tear. He continued spooning liquid into the man's mouth until he could see a slight blush across the cheeks. All the while, the patient regarded his young nursemaid with a mixture of appreciation and sadness.

The apprentice ministered to his friend for the better part of the night until he, himself, finally succumbed to sleep. The next morning, Frederick Kalyesvah was dead.

The apprentice wrapped the master's frail body in the quilts, placed him over his shoulders, and climbed back down the ladder to the basement. He stoked the fire embers and got the fire blazing. Moving the carving table away from the wall, he dug a shallow grave and tenderly laid the old man into the ground. After praying and singing for two days, he covered Frederick's body with clay and pulled the carving table back over his mentor's resting place.

By the time he finished, the fire had begun to die.

Exhausted, Jeffrey climbed the ladder, closed the hatch, and went to his bedroom to mourn.

The kachinas remained packed and zipped in the duffle bag, on the floor of the *kiva*, in the cold and dark. Forgotten.

* * *

After many days and nights of mourning in the cabin, Jeffrey returns to the secret room. He glances at the carving table over his mentor's grave, and then he rests his eyes uneasily on the forgotten duffle bag of priceless kachinas. Wearily, he unzips the bag and begins to extract them.

In the cold and dark of the basement *kiva*, Jeffrey gazes at the gods staring back at him as he places each one in its assigned resting place along the walls. In his mind, he hears their constant repeated commands. *Carver, craft the duplicates. Carver rescue the others. Carver bring us the Mother of all that shall ever come.*

He also hears *TAWA's* unveiled threat. *Carver fail us, and we bring ruin.*

CHAPTER 4
POWERLESS

DANE AMBLES RESTLESSLY between the kitchen and adjoining dining room, stretching the coiled telephone cord dangerously thin as he talks quietly into the receiver.

"Yes, Hona. I've been trying, but nothing yet." He peeks out into the family room. Raven appears to be sleeping on the couch, and he does not want to wake her.

"Has Raven tracked at all?" Lee Thistleseed asks on the other end of the call.

"Nuh ... not lately, she hasn't," Dane replies. "At least, I don't think so. I haven't been able to beacon, so I'm not sure. She's got her pager, though. Haven't had an alert from Noah, so I suppose she's stayed put in her body."

Each of the Trackers carries a pager in case of emergency. Dane has two: one for alerts from the Chino Valley Fire Department; the other for contact with the members of his Trackers Team. Of all the members of the Team, Dane and Raven are the ones most likely to track spontaneously and without a beacon present. The others track in pairs. One person travels, while the second person listens for the word "home," the signal for the Beacon to send a homing light to bring the Tracker's mind back to its body.

It is a hard and fast rule that nobody ever tracks without a beacon. The mortality margin, as determined by Lee, is 55 minutes. If a tracking session is interrupted before the Beacon sends the signal, and the traveler's mind is not returned to its body in less than one hour, the person will become brain-dead, and the mind will forever be lost and wander in darkness until the body eventually dies. Dane knows all too well and remembers how, in the past—the very recent past, in fact—he, himself, was stranded without a beacon to bring him home.

In his sleep, he picked up the scent of a woman who died horribly after liberally dowsing herself with perfume poisoned by synthetic liquid ecstasy. The psychic scent triggered a tracking event, and Dane was without a beacon. Not having his pager in reach, he was saved only because Raven happened to be at his home and called Lee for help. A peculiarity of the symbiotic relationship between the Beacon and the Tracker is that the two must be in relatively close proximity to each other for the signal to be detected. Lee and Noah lived nearby and arrived in time to beacon him home. Dane can still almost smell that sickly aroma that launched him into an unintentional track.

He also recalls a couple of times during Raven's training that she lapsed into a track in her sleep. Fortunately, he was right there to bring her mind home. But, for safety, they both carry pagers that link directly to the other members of the Trackers Team in case one or the other happens to embark on an unplanned psychic journey.

When Raven and Dane married, it was planned that they could track and beacon together; however, with the loss of Dane's tracking and beaconing powers after he was attacked in New York, they can no longer be each other's safety net. Because they are so far away from the other members of the Team, Dane's and Raven's pagers now link directly to Dane's brother, Noah. Noah is the only Tracker able to beacon over great distances.

Lee is silent on the other end of the phone. He is remembering several tracks that both Dane and Raven have forgotten—tracks that the young Trackers will never, ever recall, but which Lee and Noah will never, ever forget.

* * *

Several years ago, an Outlaw Tracker with a powerful self-trained ability backtracked into the past—a practice forbidden to all Trackers because of its deadly repercussions. The Outlaw's purpose was selfish personal gain, and he achieved it through shapeshifting trickery and murder. His name was John Silver Eyes, and he was Noah Lightfoot's natural father.

John Silver Eyes seduced Dane's mother, Fawn, after causing her husband's death. Dane's father, Joe Lightfoot, was a Seminole *heles pocase*—medicine man. At that time, Dane was a small boy of ten and Joe Lightfoot's seventh son. Young Dane saw the silver-eyed man put a rattlesnake in the blankets of the family's open-sided *chickee* house. The snake struck Lightfoot, and Silver Eyes, a Creek *heles haya pocase*—doctor medicine man—hastened the man's death with powdered venom. Then, he "comforted" Fawn in the blankets ... and Dane saw it all.

Noah was born less than a year later. He was presented as the late Joe Lightfoot's eighth son. Only Fawn knew that Noah was the seventh son of John Silver Eyes, and he would also be gifted with second sight. Despite John's impassioned pleas and his declaration of love for her, she rebuffed his marriage proposal and took her two sons to live on Brighton Reservation with the Seminoles there.

Nearly 20 years later, in his quest for personal power and vengeance, John traveled back to the night Dane and Raven had the argument that resulted in the fire. To keep the adult Dane from spoiling his plans for political ascendance, he changed the past by allowing Dane to die in the burning house, but he saved Raven from death. He had plans for her.

When he returned to the present, he forced Raven to become his Beacon by playing on her guilt over Dane's death and by threatening to kill her mother. It was a fiendish plan that worked well until Noah happened to catch a psychic glimpse of one of their clandestine tracking sessions.

When Noah and Lee became aware of the changes

wrought by the Outlaw's trips to the past, they set about to stop him. The oldest and most experienced member of the Team, Lee tracked into the past with Noah as his beacon. Suddenly, Lee found himself alone and wandering in the darkness.

Noah had been rendered unconsciousness and kidnapped by Silver Eyes, who planned to backtrack and claim Fawn as his wife and Noah as his gifted son. During the track, Raven turned on the Outlaw and killed him. Noah waited silently, letting her think he was still unconscious. Once she left, Noah beaconed Lee safely home before the mortality margin reached its limit.

To align time on its natural course and restore balance to the present, Noah backtracked into the past. During his track, he encountered John Silver Eyes outside Dane's house and convinced him to save his brother. John carried Dane to safety, but Raven was left behind in the fire.

In one last track—meant to ensure the Outlaw could never use his powers again—Lee backtracked into the past. As a result of his trip. Dane and Raven were restored to life in the present, but John Silver Eyes was left in the house when it exploded. An unexpected side-effect of the trips into the past was that Lee and Noah, as the tracking participants, were the only ones aware of the changes. Neither Dane, nor Raven, nor any of the other Trackers ever knew that the present had been forever altered.

*   *   *

"Hona? You there?" Dane asks.

"Hm? Oh, yes. I'm sorry, son. Chenaniah was talking to me," Lee says.

"Kenny! How is he coming along in his training, Lee?"

"Wonderful! He's already beaconing, though I have to say I have never seen a light quite like it. It appears to be a shimmering purple with white flashes."

"No way!" Chenaniah "Kenny" Thistleseed is Lee's twelve-year-old seventh child. His powers manifested early just a few months ago when he began channeling the thoughts of a telepathic woman living somewhere south of the United States.

"Yes. I'm afraid it is 'way,' as you say. I still feel woefully inadequate to train him. I wish you were here to help me."

"Me too, Hona. I'm so dad-blamed cold here, and I miss my powers. I don't know if they'll ever return."

Since the trip to New York where he and Noah were mugged, and his long hair was chopped off, Dane has been completely powerless to use his psychic abilities. His valuable clairscent gift of smell seems to have disappeared.

"Ah, well, Dane … Chenaniah tells me you'll be fine once your hair grows."

"Kenny says, huh. What does Kenny know about it? Kenny's just a kid."

"Mmmm. Don't tell him that. He gets very huffy."

"Well, tell him I'm huffy, if that matters."

"Yes. It does matter. Quite a bit to all of us, I should say." Lee's voice holds a note of sadness. "Wait just a moment. Chenaniah wants to speak with you."

"Dane! What's happening?" Kenny's voice still tends to squeak when he gets excited.

"Kenny, my man! What's this hair thing you got going on in your mind?

"Dane. It's so, so simple. I don't know why we didn't think of it before. The Philistines took your power."

"The Philistines took my power. OK. Explain."

Dane takes a seat at the kitchen table as Kenny launches into a story. A history professor at Florida State University, Liahona Thistleseed has always held the Team a captive audience for his stories. Now, it seems young Chenaniah Thistleseed is following in his father's oratorical footsteps.

"OK. Now back in the early days there was a man named Samson. That means 'man of the sun.' He was one of the judges of the ancient Israelites. The last one, I believe. He was also a warrior, and he had incredible strength. And he was a Nazirite. A Nazirite's a guy who takes a vow to not drink or eat anything with grapes, or touch dead people, or cut his hair. But he liked to eat grasshoppers in honey! Strange, huh? So anyway, Samson had super long hair that made him strong. One time, he killed a lion with just his bare hands. And he mowed down a whole army of Philistines with an ass's jawbone."

"Chenaniah." Lee admonishes his son with a look.

"But, Dad. It's just another name for mule." Kenny is the picture of adolescent innocence.

"Then say 'mule,' please."

"OK. He killed 'em with the jawbone of a MULE. So, anyway, God told him not to cut his hair or he would lose his strength, and Samson agreed. But then, along came this lady named Delilah, and she was way beautiful. Pow! Samson fell in love with her. They spent lots of time together eating and drinking and who knows what, but he was really good about not eating those grapes or drinking wine or anything, even though she pushed it." Kenny pauses, and Dane hears him gulping something liquid.

"Gotcha so far, Ken. No wine, no grapes, no cut the hair, and then what?"

"Well, see, Delilah was not such a good lady, and she was tempting Samson, and she had these wicked Philistine friends who were trying to get her to sell him out. So, she started tricking him. She got him real sleepy, and while he was sleeping, she tied up his hands. Then she yelled, 'Samson, the Philistines are upon you.' Samson jumped up and busted outta his ropes, but there was nobody there. She did this a whole bunch of times, using different things to tie him up, and each time she did, he broke free." Kenny punctuates his story with hand motions.

"OK, so she keeps tying him up and he gets free. What happens then?"

"Delilah got frustrated because Samson was laughing at her every time, and her Philistine friends were getting annoyed. But one of them suggested that she cut all his hair off while he's sleeping, so she said, 'Hm. That's a twist. Let's try it.' Then she waited until he went to sleep, and she chopped off his hair, and tied him up again, and yelled, 'Samson, the Philistines are upon you.' And, guess what? He. Couldn't. Break. Free."

"Kenny, are you serious? She cuts his hair and he loses his powers?"

"YES! Don't you see? They cut off your hair, and you lost your powers!"

"But does he get them back?"

Kenny frowns. "Well … yeah … he did, but it was *not* a pretty sight. The Philistines captured him and poked out his eyes and chained him between the pillars of their temple while they drank and carried on."

"That's not very reassuring, Ken." Dane grimaces.

"Yeah, I know, but that's not the end of the story. After a long time, Samson's hair grew back. He was still blind, 'cause he didn't have any eyes, you know, but he got stronger and stronger every day his hair grew. One day, while the Philistines were partying in the temple all around him, he reached out and pushed the pillars of the temple apart. The whole temple came down and killed everybody in it. Delilah too, probably, I hope, because she deserved it. Anyway, Samson died, but so did all of them. Vengeance is mine, sayeth the Lord."

"I take it back, Kenny. That is reassuring. It makes a certain amount of sense. Maybe, when my hair grows back, I will regain my powers."

"No maybe about it, Dane. You will. When your hair grows, you will no longer be powerless. OK. Gotta go. Love ya," he says, hanging up the phone without returning it to his father.

Dane sits for a long time holding the phone. The shrill "off the hook" tone through the receiver startles him, and he replaces it in the cradle. He shakes his head, feeling the hair brush his ears and the back of his neck, and he smiles. *When my hair grows, I will no longer be powerless.*

CHAPTER 5
<u>SECRET SKETCHES</u>

RAVEN WAKES AND REACHES her hand to the pillow beside her. She rests it in the depression where her husband's head lay just a few hours before. She rolls to her back—a rare luxury, as her doctor has instructed her to remain on her side to avoid pressure on the fragile bodies of the babies she carries. She allows herself a leisurely stretch from her overhead arms to her outstretched toes, but a kick in her side prompts her to sit upright. The babies don't like the flatback position. She groans and swings her feet over the edge of the bed, scooting them around to locate her warm rabbit fur moccasins.

From the kitchen comes the sound of Robin humming while fixing breakfast. Raven is suddenly famished. Donning her fleece robe, she waddles toward the inviting smells wafting through the house. Her mouth waters in anticipation of bacon, eggs, home fried potatoes, and, of course, Fawn-tea. She is not disappointed when she rounds the corner. Her mother is preparing a typical breakfast feast. Raven gingerly sits in her chair at the table—the one with the thickly padded cushion. Robin smiles warmly at her.

"Hungry, *Qomi?*" she asks. Despite her proclamation that her child would not be named after food, Robin affectionately calls Raven the same endearment that her late husband did.

"Ravenous," Raven says, pronouncing it "Raven-us." Mother and daughter both giggle. This has been their special mealtime patter since Raven's father, Falcon, died.

Robin sets a heaping plate before Raven, along with a steaming mug of tea. She seats herself in the adjacent chair and sips her own mug of the delicious brew.

"No breakfast, Mom?" Raven asks.

"Actually, I ate with your hubby a couple of hours ago," Robins says.

"Did you dress him warmly and kiss him good-bye for me?"

Robin laughs, and then succumbs to a chest-rattling cough, followed by a spit into her napkin. Raven looks up questioningly. Robin shrugs and smiles apologetically.

"Sorry. Not so appetizing, huh?"

"No, I was just thinking that you sound better. Not so congested. Keep drinking your tea."

"I do feel better, you know? Maybe this Fawn-tea is really working," Robin says, taking a long swallow from her mug. "And to answer your question, yes. I dressed him warmly and made him wear a newly knitted cap. He was sweet about it, but I don't think the colors suited him. After all, I used the leftover yarn from the baby booties and blankets."

Raven lowers her brows and sends her mother a mock scowl. "I saw that hat, and I'm sure the guys at the firehouse are going to make fun of him. Powder blue, pink, lime green, and pale yellow are not very manly colors."

"Ha. You think you know him as well as I do? Think again. He snatched that hat off as soon as he got in the truck. But I guarantee you it will be on his head when he comes home tonight."

"Touché. You win. Well, what's on the agenda for today?" Raven forks the last few potato wedges and dredges them through the silky egg yolk on her plate.

"Wedding arrangements. WE are going to the Albertson house to make final plans for their daughter's wedding next week. I am going over the decorations and menu with Mrs. Albertson, and YOU are making sketches of the room as the background for their gift." They have decided to present the newlyweds with a portrait painted by Raven.

Raven smiles. *This will be new. It's been a while since I drew something for fun.* Sipping the last of her tea, she can feel the heat in her cheeks. It is not the tea making her flushed; it is guilt over the secret she keeps.

*　　*　　*

In January, after the family moved up the mountain, Raven began tracking. Not knowing when, or if, Dane would ever regain his powers, she convinced Noah to continue her training long distance. Since he was the only Tracker capable of long-range beaconing, and he was her brother-in-law, Noah reluctantly agreed. He also agreed to never divulge their training sessions with anyone else on the Team—least of all his big brother. Scheduling time for their sessions proved to be a minor miracle.

Dane left the house each morning at 6:30 AM. He worked at the firehouse in the valley Monday through Thursday, 7:00 AM to 3:30 PM, and Sunday, 12:00 PM to 7:00 PM. He always left at 10:30 AM so he could attend church in the hour preceding his Sunday shift.

Robin cleaned the residences every Monday and Thursday, usually from 11:00 AM to 3:00 PM. Noah had all-day classes at Florida State University every Monday, Wednesday, and Friday. This gave Raven a narrow window with which to practice her tracking skills.

Since Noah was on Eastern time zone, and she was on Mountain time zone—a difference of two hours—they arranged to meet over the telephone each Thursday from 1:00 PM to 2:30 PM her time. Noah had acquired a Nokia 121 cellular phone just for this purpose, and Raven sent him money to help cover its cost.

Noah designed the format of the sessions. At the appointed time, he called Raven and left the cellular phone on speaker mode, so he could hear her. She drew random pictures in her trance-like state, Noah sent a mental beacon, and then the two of them talked together to decipher the meaning of her psychic drawings.

The first session, however, was a disaster. Since her training had never been completed before she and Dane got married, she still tended to forget how to call her Beacon.

"Out! Come get me out!" she shouted.

Noah sent his mental beacon, and then he admonished her once she was out of her trance. "Raven … I've told you before. Say 'home.' That's all you need to do is say 'home,' and I will beacon. Try to remember."

"I know, I know. But I forgot," she admitted.

Noah laughed at her. "Well, at least you didn't sweat like you used to! I thought we were going to have to change the call word to '*bleep*' just for you."

"I hear you, smart-*bleep*."

"What's a smart-*bleep*?" Chenaniah's voice rang out in the background.

"Who's with you, Noah? Is that Kenny?" Raven asked.

"Yeah, he's sworn to secrecy. I've bribed him with colas and corn nuts," Noah said.

"But if he tells his dad, Lee will tell Dane."

"No, he won't. He promised."

"As long as you supply me with snacks, I'm good," Kenny said, "but if you run out … I may forget my promise." He gave Noah a raised eyebrow challenge, typical of pre-teenage boys.

Noah, though still a teen himself at 19, slowly leveled his head to the side and gave the younger boy a hard, non-blinking look of menace.

Kenny immediately assumed the posture of a beta-male in the presence of the alpha. "Just kidding," he mumbled.

Noah cuffed him on the head and grinned at Kenny, who laughed nervously. He took a long slug of his cola, followed by a loud belch, during which he tried to recite the entire alphabet.

"OK, Raven. Let's do another short exercise while we still have time. This time, I want you to draw Kenny," Noah said.

Raven took a deep breath and closed her eyes. Her hand rested on the sketch pad, a graphite pencil between her fingers. After a few moments, she began to draw furiously. She sketched and shaded with bold movements, and the image of Chenaniah Thistleseed sitting at Noah's kitchen table began to appear. The picture took shape quickly, and instead of a sketch, looked remarkably like a photograph.

The boy was sitting with his elbows propped on the table. His straight, glossy hair was parted in the middle, tucked behind his ears, and brushed the stretched-out neck of his t-shirt. Kenny's dark lashes fanned in semi-circles below his closed eyes. The picture detailed crumbs on his chin from the corn nuts and moisture from the cola on the barest trace of a mustache appearing on his upper lip.

While Raven drew, Noah sat with his eyes closed, breathing deeply, waiting for the word. Kenny, for his part, sat still and silent. He knew better than to interrupt when the Trackers were working. His own eyes were closed, and his head was cocked to the side as if listening.

"Come get … uh … HOME," Raven shouted. Her eyes flew open. "Oh, holy *bleep*, what was that?"

Noah's eyes flew open at the same time. He blinked a couple of times, and then whipped his head around and saw Kenny staring at him, a slight smirk on his face.

"Kenny! What did you do?" Noah demanded.

Kenny's expression faltered, and he lowered his head, black hair falling over his face. His lip trembled. "I just wanted to show you what I could do … you know, like you," he said.

"Noah, what was that purple light?" Raven asked.

"THAT … was Kenny," he said, "hang on a sec."

He scooted his chair closer to Kenny and put his arm around his shoulders. "Ken, I am so proud that you are learning to beacon, and your purple and white light is beyond awesome, but you can't do that ever again. It's really, really dangerous."

Kenny looked up at Noah with watery eyes. "I'm sorry. Don't be mad, Noah," he blubbered, "or you either, Raven. I'm just really, really stupid."

"No way. You are far from stupid. But there's a reason you are with me here while Raven and I practice. I need a responsible person … a trustworthy MAN to guard me while I am in the trance. If something happened to me, Raven could die. I could die. Do you understand? You are the lookout, and that's a very important job. You're up to it, aren't you? I picked you over anybody else because I believe in you, Ken," Noah said. He hugged the boy closer.

Kenny sniffed deeply and nodded his head. "I'm your guy, Noah. I'll always be your guy. Raven, I'm yours, too. Never happen again, OK? I promise. Y'all don't even have to bribe me with food," Kenny said.

"We love you, Kenny," Raven said over the phone's speaker, "no matter what."

"Love you, too," Kenny said.

Once the boundaries were established, the three of them made a good mini team. After that first dicey event, Raven and Noah began to get the knack of their long-distance tracking, and their symbiotic tracking and beaconing relationship grew quite strong. They did tracking sessions in which Noah designed more difficult parameters. He gave her targets to draw; she drew them; he beaconed her mind home; Kenny kept watch.

Following each session, Raven stashed her secret sketches in a shoebox labeled "summer mocs" at the bottom of her closet. Whenever she was left alone at the house, she pulled out the box and examined the papers inside, and then she carefully stowed them back in their hiding place beneath the other moccasin boxes.

For the past month, Raven had been drawing detailed pictures of locations and people upon which she and Noah had not previously arranged. Neither knew what the sketches meant, nor did they recognize the persons whose images Raven drew. The only things that held any meaning for them were the 28 kachinas she continued to produce, repeatedly.

After the first few drawings, she had added colors to the black and white images, as she remembered from her tracks. Knowing they were significant, Raven and Noah set about trying to identify the kachinas. Raven painstakingly described each kachina in detail, and Noah would scour the FSU library for books and magazines that held graphic representations of the figurines.

It was hit or miss. He would often think he had found the exact kachina, only to have Raven dismiss his find because of some aspect of its clothing or pose. Unperturbed, he continued to search.

Raven's remembrance of her early drawings of the *Katsinam* in the little *kiva* were yet vivid, and what ones were not, she would casually ask Robin about while they reminisced in front of the fire about the family's early days in Bacabi Village.

Last week, Noah struck gold. In the periodical section of the vast library, he happened upon a catalog from the 70s that someone had donated. The catalog had a long article about Senator Barry Goldwater's massive kachina collection, complete with color photographs. A good portion of the kachinas had been placed on loan at the Brigham Young University Museum of Peoples and Cultures. On a hunch, Noah called BYU and learned that almost two dozen of the figurines had been on display for nearly 20 years, and many more had been placed as permanent exhibits in other museums around the country.

He called Raven the same day. His description of the kachinas in the catalog exactly matched the ones Raven had drawn. Moreover, five of them were housed in the Smoki Museum, in Prescott, Arizona.

*   *   *

"What, Mama?" Raven asks.

"I said, 'get your hind end moving.' We need to leave soon to meet Mrs. Albertson and discuss the wedding plans. And don't forget to bring your sketch pad and colored pencils," Robin says.

Raven swallows the last of her tea and rises heavily. She is excited about drawing for fun, but in the back of her mind, she holds the image of the five kachinas just out of reach, down the mountain, in the town of Prescott.

She dresses as quickly as her ample shape allows, and then she reaches into the closet for her heavy moccasins. As she bends to grab them, her eyes travel to the box of summer mocs—the box which holds her secret sketches. She puts her hand toward them, and then pulls it back quickly. Now is not the time to look at them.

Though her tracking skills are getting much better, there is always the chance she may unintentionally lapse into a track. With Robin in the house, she doesn't want to reveal she has been tracking. Moreover, she certainly doesn't relish Robin telling Dane. He would be furious, and that's the last thing she wants.

She stuffs her feet into her rabbit fur mocs, grabs her sketch pad and pencils from the nightstand, and meets her mother at the front door.

* * *

Down in Tallahassee, Noah reflects on the close personal relationship he and Raven had before the backtracks that restored Dane's life, but Raven has no knowledge of that time. It has been forever erased from her memory, and neither Noah nor Lee will ever tell them what had occurred.

Raven had become a member of the Trackers Team after she painted a portrait of the police chief's wife. The woman had come to Raven's studio on three separate occasions, each time accompanied by a little blond-haired boy. Raven painted them in a tender embrace and was especially pleased with the quality of the portrait; however, when the family viewed it, they told her the child had died the year previously in a house fire. Chief Abernathy was acquainted with Lee Thistleseed, and his department had used the Trackers Team on other occasions, so he let his friend know about the woman's ability.

Raven and Dane had been an item a few years before, but they had kept their affair secret. Not even after the fire were any of the other Trackers aware of their relationship. Later, long after Dane perished in the blaze, Raven was recruited by Lee and Noah upon the recommendation by Chief Abernathy.

During the time the Outlaw was backtracking, Noah started spending more time with Raven, and he began to fall in love with her. For her part, she returned his affections because he reminded her of Dane.

Adding to Noah's confusion, he found he was also developing deep feelings for Maria Ramirez, the young daughter of Florida's Governor. The Trackers Team had been instrumental in locating and rescuing the Governor's seven-year-old granddaughter from a political mercenary hired by the Outlaw. During the ordeal, Lee and Noah discovered that Maria had some undeveloped psychic powers of her own.

Once Noah realized Raven was the Outlaw's Beacon, he

lost all romantic feelings for her. Thankfully, although it was painful at the time, the events left his heart free to be completely devoted to Maria, who was much closer to his own age.

During the backtracks Noah and Lee performed to set time back on its rightful course, Raven and Dane lost all memory of the events following the fire. They were both alive, but their lives were drastically changed. Dane and Raven split up, and she moved to Prescott. Ultimately, Raven returned to Tallahassee, and they renewed their love, got pregnant, got married, and temporarily relocated to Arizona to be with Raven's mother—in that order.

Raven never remembered her time with Noah, although he will never forget it. Now, because Raven has become his sister-in-law, and he loves her as such, he has agreed to be her secret Beacon. Just for good measure, he checks the signal on his Nokia phone and zippers it securely in the front pocket of his backpack. *Better safe than sorry when it concerns that woman.* He jumps in his Mustang and heads for the FSU campus. *Woe to us both if Dane or Lee finds out we've been tracking! I hope she hides those secret sketches well.*

CHAPTER 6
WHERE THERE'S SMOKE

DANE SITS IN THE BASKET of the fire truck's ladder extension, carefully cutting limbs from trees already so laden with snow and ice that they droop dangerously near the power lines. It has been a quiet morning, so far. No fires in the town or the surrounding valleys. It's the perfect time to do some preventative maintenance between Heritage Park Zoological Sanctuary and Embry-Riddle Aeronautical University-Prescott.

Heritage Park Zoological Sanctuary was established in 1983 and shelters nearly 200 native, exotic, and endangered animals. As animal lovers, Raven and Dane are contributors to the Sanctuary. Raven sponsors the peregrine falcon and an injured raven she donated when they first arrived. Dane sponsors a Mexican gray wolf and a Sonoran pronghorn. Whenever he has the chance, he checks on the facility.

Today's weather is clear and windless, for a change. He loves being outside, loves hearing the animals, loves the smell of the freshly cut timber. He does not love the cold.

Growing up in South Florida desensitized him to hot weather; however, it did not prepare him for the chill he feels in this harsh environment. Before he moved to Tallahassee, he lived with his mother, Fawn, and his brother, Noah, in an open-sided *chickee* house—much like a Tiki hut—in Seminole Village near Tampa where Fawn worked as a Museum artisan. Rarely did he ever wear long pants or shoes. He didn't even own a coat.

He wishes now that he had the presence of mind to grab his fleece toboggan cap off the dash of his truck. But he forgot it in his haste to remove the silly knit cap Robin forced on his head before reaching the firehouse. *Bless her.* He loves the woman, but what grown man in his right mind wants to wear a goofy multicolored knit cap ... except a hippie ... or perhaps a Jamaican cab driver in New York?

Dane smiles, thinking of the cabbie who saved both his and his brother's lives in the hostile city. He still has the single dreadlock that Jafee gave him before he and Noah boarded the flight back to Florida—pulled from beneath the cabbie's bright cap and unceremoniously sawed off with a pocketknife. Dane's own thick, long hair had been viciously hacked away during a mugging which was nearly a scalping. Jafee kept a handful in remembrance of the brothers. *When my hair grows, I will no longer be powerless.* Could it really be that simple?

His chopped-up locks had been carefully reshaped by Wren into a crew cut. Kenny considered his new look "very GQ," but Dane hated it, and he had been worried how his fiancé would react. Raven, though, saw only his heart ... not his hair.

That was October. Now, in March, his hair is way down past his collar, so it has grown quite a lot. *How long does it have to be to get my powers back?*

Suddenly, he smells smoke. Casting his eyes left and right, he hunts for the source. *A fireplace? Someone burning limbs in a 50-pound drum?* He doesn't see any smoke, so he turns around and scans the area in the distance behind him. He sees nothing. He lifts the chainsaw toward his face and sniffs near its blade. Sometimes the friction makes the sawdust smell as if burning. He detects sawdust, motor oil, and sap from the tree limbs, but no smoke.

Leaning over the basket, he tosses a small branch toward the cab of the truck. It hits the window, and the driver sticks his head out.

"Watch it, Lightfoot. That almost came in my window," Jimmy grumbles.

"Yeah, I know. Any calls?" Dane asks.

"Nuttin' honey," Jimmy responds with a chuckle.

"I smell smoke. Check the radio."

Jimmy pulls his head back in the window. Dane hears the squall of the radio. A moment later, Jimmy sticks his arm out the window and gives him a thumbs-down signal.

Dane straightens up and stands in the basket. Holding on to the sides, he makes a circular survey of the area. He sees nothing, but his nose burns with the smell of the smoke. It fills his nostrils and travels all the way to his sinuses, making his eyes water in the process. He sneezes violently twice. *I smell smoke.*

Forcing his index fingers up into his nostrils, he breathes through his mouth to clear the scent, and then he slowly removes first one finger, and then the other. The scent is still there, even stronger than before. He scans the horizon and sees not even the tiniest tendril of smoke wafting from the town. *There IS a fire. I know it. I smell it!*

Dane quickly presses the lever to lower the basket. Jimmy again sticks his head out the window.

"Hey, we're not done. You need a potty break or something?" Jimmy yells.

Dane hops out of the basket and runs to the passenger side of the truck. Climbing into the cab, he grabs the radio mic.

"This is unit 17. Smoke in the center of town. Responding now," Dane says.

"No smoke. No fire, Lightfoot," Jimmy says.

"Start the truck and get going," Dane says, "there IS a fire, and it'll soon be out of control."

"Where?" Jimmy shifts the fire engine into first gear.

"Somewhere east of town center. Let's get going, Jim.".

The radio crackles. "Nothing reported, 17. Do you have a location?" the dispatcher says.

"Southwest of the college, east of the courthouse, past the Gurley and Goodwin intersection," Dane responds.

"Whiskey Row?" Jimmy says.

"No, no. East of Whiskey Row, Jim."

Firetruck 17 roars toward the location Dane declared. The closer they get, the more he smells the smoke. At last they come to Arizona Avenue, to the Smoki Museum.

"Stop!" Dane yells, "This is it. The museum."

Jimmy stops the truck and looks toward the building. From inside, they hear a muffled *"whomp"* sound. Suddenly, Jimmy sees flames inside a window. He grabs the microphone.

"Unit 17 to base. Fire at Smoki Museum. 147 North Arizona Avenue. Repeat. Fire at 147 North Arizona Avenue. Smoki Museum. Request assistance," he calls.

"Acknowledged, 17. Sending assistance to Smoki Museum," the dispatcher replies.

Dane is already unrolling the hose when Jimmy exits the truck and spots a sign on the front door which reads "Back in 30 Minutes." The two men nod at each other and kick the locked door, which springs open. They send a heavy spray of water through the open door and into the interior floor of the building.

Jimmy is visibly upset. The Smoki Museum houses many treasured artifacts of southwest indigenous peoples, including some donated by his own family.

Dane glances at him. "I know, Jim, I know," he says. "Don't worry. We've got this contained already."

Jimmy nods, hearing the wail of another firetruck heading their way. "Good thing you smelled the smoke, Lightfoot," he says. But in the back of his mind, he thinks, *How did you smell smoke from so many miles away?*

Less than a quarter of an hour later, it is over. It was caught early. Dane and the other firefighters pore over the interior of the museum, searching for hot spots and assessing damage. The hoses wet a few paintings in the entrance, but these are commercially created pictures of little value which can be easily replaced. Thankfully, the exhibits are protected by thick glass cases, and they survived unharmed, albeit a little smoky smelling.

Jimmy claps Dane on the back. "You're unbelievable, Lightfoot! If not for your sensitive nose, my family would've lost part of our heritage," he says.

Dane smiles and nods, but his eyes are still scanning for anomalies. His past training as an arson investigator kicks in. Passing by a display case, he is struck by an unbalance of its contents. The items in the exhibit are not laid out evenly, as though someone has been rearranging them and has stopped before finishing. The kachina figurines themselves show no damage, they just seem to be disturbed. He makes a mental note to ask the curator later.

Adding to the curious nature of the exhibit is a flashpoint on the floor beneath the watercooler about five feet away. *The source of the blaze?* Dane sniffs and detects the odor of linseed oil—a highly flammable furniture polish—a scent he also smelled on the unevenly arranged display case. *This may not have been a natural fire; I think it was set.*

Dane is quiet and reflective on the ride back to the firehouse. Jimmy's incessant rehashing of the events of the fire are acknowledged, as always, with a nod of his head and an occasional, "uh-huh." He is vaguely aware of the driver's comments questioning how he was able to sniff out the fire from such a distance.

Dane's thoughts are not so much on the fire as on the detection of the fire and the reemergence of his gift. *Are my powers returning? Could Kenny's lady be right? And how does she know anyway?* That the mystery lady who has the telepathic link with Kenny can know what's happening in his life gives him an unsettled feeling. But, Lee and the rest of the Team seem to accept the relationship between Kenny and the lady, so it must be benign. Nevertheless, Dane can hardly wait to talk to them about it. And Raven. He must let her know soon.

As they pull into the station, their truck is met by Fire Chief Lenny Oatman. Chief Oatman rarely comes out to the garage, so his personal appearance there now suggests an event of some importance. Dane and Jimmy quickly disembark the cab of their firetruck.

"Lightfoot," Chief Oatman says, "I understand you had a rather successful morning."

"Me too," Jimmy says proudly, which is met with a scowl from his Chief.

"Yes sir," Dane says. "We were fortunate to catch it early before there was any damage."

"Fortunate to catch it early. I see. In my office, please." Oatman turns and pushes into the building, followed by Dane close upon his heels.

Chief Oatman settles into his leather desk chair and motions for Dane to sit in one of the chairs across from him.

"Good work today, Lightfoot, really good. Glad you were … fortunate to catch it early," he says.

Dane is not sure where this conversation is leading, so he simply smiles and nods. The two men sit in silence for a few moments, both nodding and smiling at each other.

"O.K. let's cut to it," Oatman says. "How did you catch it that early? Were you tipped off by someone?"

"What? No," Dane responds.

"Look, son. I've been in this town many a year, and I've been through a lot of junk. Did you know this fire station is the oldest in Arizona? Yep. Established in 1885. No, I was not around when it was started, but my ancestors in Prescott go way back before that. The Oatman family was attacked in 1851 by a Yavapai band and killed—all except for my great-grandfather Lorenzo. His sisters Mary Anne and Olive were sold as slaves to the Mojaves. I've seen this town and this fire station grow and develop into what they are today. We service a coverage area of almost 42 square miles. Prescott, Prescott Valley, Chino Valley, Dewey-Humboldt, and even out on the Reservation. This fire department has a spotless reputation. Spotless!"

Dane listens silently, nodding, puzzled. Chief Oatman abruptly leans forward, palms flat on the desk.

"Now, I want to know, and I want to know right now. How did you catch that fire?" he demands.

Dane stops himself from jerking backwards. He takes a calming breath. "I smelled smoke, sir."

Oatman presses his lips together and nods jerkily. "You smelled smoke." He backs into his chair. "That's what Jimmy told dispatch. 'Lightfoot smells smoke.' That's what the man said."

"Yes, sir."

"From miles and miles away. You smelled smoke. Didn't see it. Didn't see a smoke trail in the air. Smelled smoke before the fire even got started."

"Yes, sir."

"That. Is. Amazing." Oatman smiles with tight lips. "Never in my days have I heard of something so amazing. Smelled the smoke before the fire got going."

Dane is silent. This is not going well.

The chief slowly shakes his head, and his smile disappears. "No, sir. No, sir. That is not possible." He looks up at Dane and frowns. "I like you, Lightfoot. I really do. I got a great recommendation from your Tallahassee Department. They said you were a solid firefighter and an even better arson investigator."

"Thank you, sir."

"But I just can't buy this. It's too hinky. Please, tell me. Did someone tip you off? It's OK if that's what happened. Really, it is. You're an asset to this department. I don't want to lose you. I just want the truth."

Dane shrugs and takes a chance. "Sir, if you'd like to call and speak to my Chief in Tallahassee, he will tell you that they gave me a nickname. They called me 'the Bloodhound' because I have such a highly developed sense of smell. It's a kind of gift or talent. Honestly, I smelled that smoke."

Chief Oatman scrutinizes his firefighter for a couple of minutes, then comes to a decision. "OK, son. Wait outside my office. I'm going to make a call."

Dane rises, exits the office, and takes a seat in the hallway. He can hear Oatman talking on the phone. *Gee, what I wouldn't give to have Graham Skysong's clairaudience gift right now to hear what they're saying!*

Soon, Oatman opens the door and again ushers Dane into the office. His countenance is a bit different now—less hostile, more relaxed, somewhat in awe.

"You're a good man, Lightfoot. Your former chief says you have this knack for sniffing things out that other people can't smell. Called it 'hyperosmia' or something like that. He says I am lucky to have you, and if I don't want you to please send you back to him. I can't get a better recommendation than that," he says, the deep creases disappearing from his brow. "So ... you smelled the smoke, and where there's smoke, there's fire. Damn fine job, Lightfoot. Damn fine job. Take the rest of the day off. Tomorrow I'll need you fresh to help figure out how a fire started in the middle of the Smoki Museum during the curator's lunch hour."

Dane rises and shakes the hand offered by his Chief.

"Thank you, sir," he says.

"No. Thank YOU," Chief Oatman says.

CHAPTER 7

WEDDING PLANS

WHILE DANE IS SAVING the Smoki Museum from a premeditated fire, Robin and Raven are at the Albertson house making plans for an April third wedding the following week. Robin has her head together with Lois Albertson discussing flower arrangements, outside luminaries (if the weather permits), finger foods, and champagne. Raven, on the other hand, sits comfortably on a brocade sofa admiring the view out the back windows.

This house, like the one in which her family is staying, is high up on the crest of the Bradshaw Mountains and overlooks the grounds of the Embry-Riddle Aeronautical University-Prescott campus in the valley below. The university owns the houses, and their use is at the discretion of President Johnathan Hunter. This house has been reserved for ERAU's Vice-President/Provost as the overseer of the Arizona campus.

Dr. Wil Albertson and his wife Lois live here, along with Lois's mother, Mrs. Millie Wayne, and her chocolate miniature poodle, Teddy Bear. They moved here a year ago from the Daytona Beach main campus, where Dr. Albertson had worked for many years. Formerly a Colonel in the Army, Albertson retired from the military and developed a program for ERAU in which military officers and aviators could further their careers while on active duty or after leaving the service and in which military pilots could receive comparable college credits for flying time served. The Continuing Education Department at the Daytona Beach, Florida, main campus was so successful President Hunter asked Albertson to relocate to Prescott, serve as its Vice President/Provost, and implement the program here in Arizona.

The Albertson's daughter, Shelley, moved from Daytona Beach at the same time; however, her musical talent and performing interests took her on to Los Angeles where she is active in Civic Light Opera and entertains on the West Coast, in Las Vegas, and overseas in Japan.

The Albertson's son, Lewis, is living and working as a videographer—a growing, up-and-coming field. After beginning his career at ERAU in the video arts department, he was offered a position overseas in Saudi Arabia. Raven overhears Lois telling Robin that his work in the Middle East prohibits his attendance at the wedding.

The wedding next week is to be a family affair for Shelley and her fiancé, Lee Stone, a working actor in Hollywood. Lee has already done several national commercials, film parts, and recurring television roles, and his career is quickly on the upswing. The couple is scheduled to fly in next week, along with all the groomsmen and their families, Lee's mother, grandmother, and his sister, Anna. Anna is one of the bridesmaids. The other bridesmaids are two of Shelly's cousins, and her maid of honor is her best friend from college, whose husband works as the Coordinator of Student Services for Mr. Albertson at the ERAU-Prescott campus.

Never having met either Shelley or Lee, Raven must depend on photographs provided by Lois Albertson to create their portrait. Fortunately, the wedding dress is pressed and ready and hanging in the guest bedroom. Raven has already made sketches of it—a floor-length, lace-covered A-line skirt with a bodice of beaded and embroidered damask and spaghetti straps. A sheer, ivory lace shawl overlays the bodice. The shawl is waist-length in the front and angles downward on the sides to meet in the back just above the hem of the skirt, forming its own train. It reminds Raven of her own wedding shawl, worn not so many months before. She permits herself a sigh, and then she reviews her sketch of the bride's outfit. A lace mantilla completes the ensemble. It is simple, but stunning.

Shelley's hair, as shown in the photographs, is a shiny, chestnut brown. She wears it in short ringlets around her pixie face, with baby's breath placed here and there. Her round eyes are of the darkest brown, with thick, black lashes under arched eyebrows. Raven's favorite feature is the pair of deep dimples on either side of the girl's mouth that perfectly match her father's.

For the groom and the groomsmen, Raven has the formalwear's brochure for reference. The tuxes are grey tails, with white shirts, grey striped ascots, and satin cummerbunds. Again, understated elegance is the theme of this wedding.

The photos of Shelley's fiancé reveal a strikingly handsome young man with green eyes, dark auburn hair, a smattering of freckles, and a brilliant smile. Raven is delighted to note that Lee has dimples, as well. She is sure, when they have children, they will all be dimpled darlings.

Robin and Lois are still discussing the flowers, so Raven sits sketching the cathedral ceiling wall of windows overlooking where the vows will take place. She can see the mountains on the horizon and knows that the sun will be setting in the front of the house, giving the background that gorgeous red, yellow, pink, and purple coloring she sees each evening in her own house. Mrs. Wayne's Teddy Bear lies beside her on the sofa, his little pink tongue sticking out of his adorable face. Raven pets him, loving the feel of the curly brown fur.

"Come on, Teddy Bear," Millie croons from the back door, "time to go tee-tee."

Raven's face breaks out into a broad smile. *Tee-tee. That's such an old Southern-style term.* Raven needs a stretch break, so she urges the little dog off the sofa and decides to walk out back with him.

The old woman takes her hand, and the two of them throw ponchos over their shoulders and step out on the patio to watch Teddy Bear do his business.

"He sure is cute, Mrs. Wayne," Raven says.

"Thank you, baby, but please call me Miss Millie," the old woman says.

"All right, Miss Millie. How do you like it in Arizona?"

"It's mighty cold, baby. I grew up in Georgia. My daddy had a small plantation. We grew cotton, and we had workers come help us pick it. They wasn't slaves. Daddy didn't have no slaves. But our help was the dark people from the Okefenoke Swamp. Indians, I believe. I weren't supposed to have much to do with them. But I weren't scared. I liked them."

Raven listens intently, as the old woman talks. *I thought Dane was old Southern. I had no idea!*

"One time, I picked cotton with them." Millie laughs. "Mr. Jim, he give me a croker sack and told me to fill it up."

"A croker sack?"

"It's a long burlap sack that you stuff with 'taters or cotton or such. I was real little, so I had to drag it behind me. One of the women showed me how to tie up my skirt 'tween my legs and make it into bloomers. That way I could straddle the sack as I went down the rows. Worked right good, baby. Mr. Jim, he was gonna pay me a quarter when I got it filled up, but Daddy saw me out there, and he got so mad. Mama took a switch to my legs when he told her."

Raven is enchanted. She is even more captivated when Miss Millie pulls a baby food jar out of her apron pocket and spits into it. She screws the lid back on the jar, returns it to her pocket, and wipes the brown snuff juice from the corner of her mouth. *Old Southern? Maybe even ancient Southern?*

As the two women stand on the cold patio, Raven notices a moving shadow on the ground. Looking upward, she sees the source of the shadow. A golden eagle circles overhead. Before she can say anything, the eagle darts and snatches the little dog up in its talons. Miss Millie screams, and out run Robin and Lois. All the women watch in horror as the eagle lifts the dog aloft and begins to fly away.

"Nooooo!" Raven shrieks at the giant bird. "Bring him back!" Suddenly, she feels a piercing cramp in her left side. It renders her breathless with its intensity. Panting through her open mouth, she watches as the eagle circles back towards the house. In a graceful, fluid motion, it swoops down and deposits the unharmed Teddy Bear back into the yard. It circles the yard again, and then it soars away over the valley. Abruptly, the pain in her side ceases.

Miss Millie gathers her dog into her arms and disappears into the house, along with her daughter, Lois. Robin, however, moves next to Raven and looks her in the face.

"What happened to you?" Robin asks.

"I don't know, Mom," Raven says. "I had a terrible pain, then the eagle came back, then my pain went away."

Robin puts her hand on Raven's belly for a moment, and then leads her shaken daughter back inside. "I think that's enough excitement for today, Mrs. Albertson. I better take Raven home. I'll be back tomorrow."

As Robin and Raven start for the front door, Miss Millie appears, still clutching Teddy Bear. She steps up to Raven and plants a tender, snuff stained kiss on her cheek.

"Thank you, baby," she says. "You saved my Teddy Bear. You called that eagle back."

Raven shakily walks to the car. Looking back, she thinks about the incident. *I didn't call the eagle ... but somebody did.*

Raven and Robin are quiet on the drive back to their house. They are surprised to see Dane's truck parked out front at this hour of the day. Raven lumbers inside, and Dane exits the kitchen with a huge sandwich clutched between his hands.

"Hey, Chubs! Where have you two been?" he asks.

"Wedding planning," Robin replies. "I hope you left enough for us to have sandwiches." She heads for the kitchen.

"Uh, yeah. There's some left. I left it out for you girls. And maybe you'd like some tea, too, huh?" he says.

"Make mine a double," Raven says. She seats herself in her section of the couch and welcomes Bugle up beside her, where he sniffs and looks reproachfully at her, as if to say, *you've been with another dog.* She lays her sketch pad on the coffee table, leaving an empty spot for a sandwich and mug of tea, which appear soon afterward. Dane snuggles up next to her.

"So," he says, "how was your day?"

"Interesting," she says. "I'll tell you more after I get some of this sandwich and tea in me. Meantime, how'd you get home so early? Did you get canned or something?"

He shrugs. "Well, I thought I was going to, but instead I think I got a bit of a promotion."

She looks at him in surprise. "Spill the beans, Bucko. Tell me what happened."

"I smelled smoke." He can't contain his smile.

"Big deal. You smell smoke every day." She replies matter-of-factly, chewing her sandwich with gusto.

"Yeah...but not from ten miles away."

"What? What are you saying?" Raven jerks her head, food dropping onto her chest.

"We were over by the Sanctuary, and I smelled smoke ... from town. And there was no fire or smoke anywhere to be seen."

"Nah-AH! You did not!" She punches his arm with her fist.

"I did, Raven. I smelled the smoke, and I knew where it was coming from, and we hightailed it over there and put the fire out, and my boss didn't believe me and thought somebody tipped me off, so I had him call my supervisor in Tallahassee ... who gave me a glowing compliment, by the way ... and then Oatman says, 'Damn fine job, Lightfoot,' and gives me the rest of the day off!"

Raven squeals with delight and claps her hands. "He's back, he's back, the Bloodhound is back."

"Well, don't get too excited. I don't think I have my powers back completely, but this is a great start. Kenny was right."

"Huh? What does Kenny have to do with it?" She frowns.

"You know Kenny and his mind-link lady. He told me a long story about Samson who lost his powers when his hair got cut off, and he told me 'when your hair grows, you will no longer be powerless.' So, no more haircuts for me ... ever!"

"I'm thrilled for you, Dane," Robin calls from the kitchen. "Where was the fire"

"The Smoki Museum," he says.

Robin rushes into the room holding a slice of bread and a knife loaded with mayonnaise. "Dane! Some of my best pieces are on display at the Smoki."

"Don't worry, Robin, "I did a quick walk through and nothing seems to have been damaged."

Robin sits back against the sofa. "That's a relief." She closes her eyes and releases the breath she was holding.

Dane nods. "Yeah, the only thing amiss was one display case near the back. It seems to have been the target of the fire."

"Arson? Really?" Raven asks.

"Yeah. Pretty sure. Looks like somebody was trying to burn up the case of kachina dolls," he says.

This time Raven turns pale. "The kachinas? Were the kachinas damaged?".

"No. But it looks like somebody was messing with them. I'll know more tomorrow. Never fear, ladies. I am on top of it!"

Dane puts his hands on either side of Raven's face and gives her a long, enthusiastic kiss. Raven pulls herself together and beams at him. He kisses her again on the cheek. Then, he wrinkles his nose and licks his lips thoughtfully.

"Babe," he says, "when did you start dipping snuff?"

Raven laughs and rolls her eyes. "Miss Millie and her snuff. Well, Bucko, do I have a story for you!"

Dane is absolutely transfixed as Raven recounts the events of the day, and she spares no details. During the story, Robin brings in her own sandwich and tea. She sits on her couch and verifies the story about the eagle and the dog.

"What made the eagle bring back the dog?" Dane asks.

"Miss Millie thought it was because I yelled for it to come back, but it wasn't me. I don't have that kind of power. I … I think it was one of the babies," she admits.

The three of them sit quietly, absorbing that thought. *Could one of the babies be gifted?* Dane does a little mental arithmetic and shrugs.

"Well, technically it could be true. Given that the miscarriages were all twins, then these babies would be your seventh and eighth children."

"Even if those pregnancies never came to term? Would that be true?"

"I had six miscarriages before I had you, honey," Robin

says, "and you have the second sight."

"My church teachings tell me that the spirits waiting in Heaven to be born are just waiting for bodies. I believe that life begins at conception. There's a heartbeat in that itty-bitty body, so it IS alive. And, therefore, even if it is just a few days or weeks old, a baby has life, and the spirit can have a body," Dane says, holding her hand.

"So, you're both saying that one of these babies can have the gift?" Raven asks.

Dane and Robin look at each other and nod. "That's what we're saying," Robin says smiling.

Raven is a bit overcome by this revelation. She rises from the couch and makes her way toward the bathroom. "I think I need to tee-tee," she announces.

Dane and Robin look at each other in confusion as she leaves. "Tee-tee?" they say.

CHAPTER 8

SMOKI

PRESCOTT BOASTS TWO FINE MUSEUMS: Sharlot Hall Museum, which contains pioneer artifacts and preserves the spirit of the Old West; and Smoki Museum, which is a repository for all things relative to Southwest Indian culture.

Dane and Raven toured the Sharlot Hall Museum with Robin when they first got to Prescott. Named after a pioneer girl who arrived by wagon in 1882 at the age of 12, the exhibits feature artifacts from the 18th and 19th centuries, with memorabilia from saloons, general stores, mining companies, ranches, farms, and the everyday life of the pioneers. Sharlot was the territory's first known historian, and she collected stories and oral histories of Prescott citizens and heroes, Fort Whipple military life, and neighboring Yavapai Reservation life while traveling the primitive roads throughout Arizona. She founded the museum at the age of 57 to house her assortment of transcribed stories and original poems.

The Lightfoot family did not have the chance to visit the Smoki Museum. Because of the pregnancy and the high altitude, Raven's feet and ankles were already becoming swollen and painful just a week after their arrival. She spent most of her time in Robin's sitting room with her feet up, kicked back in the recliner, being content to leaf through pamphlets that Dane brought back for her from different places around town. Two weeks later, they moved up the mountain, so the scenes and sights of Prescott were put on hold until the spring thaw.

Strolling this morning through the Smoki Museum, Dane is not in tourist mode. His intent is to find the source of the fire, and then determine if the fire was, indeed, arson.

Remembering his mother-in-law's concern about her precious museum pieces, Dane first checks among the tribal collections of the Apache, Hualapai, Havasupai, and Yavapai. Robin's basket weaving handiwork is featured prominently in the exhibit "The Baskets Talk: The Woven Story of the Yavapai-Prescott Indian Tribe"—an exhibit that divides its time between the Smoki Museum and the Sharlot Hall Museum. Robin also has several baskets and yucca fiber moccasins featured in a Contemporary Tribes Handiwork exhibit at the Smoki. Dane is relieved to see Robin's pieces are not compromised in either exhibit. Likewise, unharmed are the displays of ancient pottery and stone tools excavated from prehistoric pit houses in Chino Valley.

Moving back to the entry, where the firehoses were trained, Dane examines the Kate Cory sketches and paintings of Hopi life in the early 1900s. He and Jimmy were careful to aim the water jets to the floor to avoid affecting any of the artwork, and their caution paid off. Finding no water damage, he moves counter-clockwise to investigate all parts of the pueblo-style stone building.

On the corn-grinding station at the children's touch table, he detects a rich aroma of both smoky and damp corn, the latter more likely from sweaty little hands than water from the hoses. He smiles. *Before long, I will have two contributions to those sweaty little hands.* He also notes the other items on the table: small adobe bricks, sand and water in sealed containers, molds to form the bricks, pine cones, a sealed container of pine nuts, a sealed container of pine needles, wooden mortars and pestles, and an array of spatulas and spoons. Judging from the crudely constructed adobe huts on the table and the miniature baskets filled with tiny fruits, nuts, and crushed corn, as well as an equal amount of sand, bricks, pine needles, and other items beneath the table, this is a popular local daytime play area.

The next display, safeguarded behind closed glass cabinet doors, showcases fine Indian jewelry crafted from all types of materials—seed beads, porcupine quills, turquoise, locally mined silver and gold, shells, painted and stained wood, braided animal fur, polished pebbles and raw gemstones, tanned leather, and plant fibers. He admires the silver discs with intricate designs etched into them, elaborately carved shells, gleaming green Malachite fashioned into necklaces and earrings, and bracelets of polished turquoise set into wide silver cuffs. He thinks of his mother Fawn and the beautiful seed bead jewelry she makes in the Seminole Indian Village down in South Florida. Dane leans closer to the case. Not only are these items artistically lovely, they are commercially valuable. *If someone wanted to rob the museum, surely this would have been a tempting place to begin.* Nothing seems out of place, so he moves on to the next exhibit.

This display has a diorama of Native American dancers. Reading the placard beside the case, Dane notes that the dancers are, in fact, Anglo Americans who organized themselves into the Smoki "tribe" in 1921. The members performed Native American rituals and dances to raise funds for the community's annual Frontier Days Rodeo. The placard stated it was not unusual for a cast and crew of hundreds to be recruited for the elaborate presentations. The monies received paid for the establishment of the present museum, hence the name "Smoki." According to the sign, the dancers came under criticism because they were non-natives performing sacred ceremonials, so the presentations were discontinued in 1990, but the name was kept for the museum.

The next diorama features historical scenes from early Yavapia life. Figures of people are depicted with several types of dwellings, including brush shelters called *whamboonayvas*, closed huts of ocotillo branches covered with animal skins, dirt, bark, and grass called *uwas* for the winter months, and summertime lean-tos without walls, which remind Dane of the open-sided *chickees* in which he grew up.

In the center of the display is a maize plant which seems to grow from Montezuma Well, the location the Yavapai believe was the origin of their people's entry into the world.

Around the corner from the diorama, Dane comes to the kachina display. Donated by former Senator Barry Goldwater from his private collection, these figurines are all created by master carvers from the Hopi tribe. A kachina, as explained on the accompanying sign, is a spirit that brings life to the Hopi people and can be represented by a dancer with a mask and costume or a *tihü*, a doll-like figurine that depicts a masked dancer. Both symbolize the spirit of the kachina.

The word "kachina" means "spirit/life father." Dane recalls that Raven told him the correct word for kachina is *Katsina* and comes from *katsi*, which means spirit or life, and *na*, which means father. The spirit fathers in this case are arranged by type. One group follows the usual form of animals, birds, and insects. Another grouping depicts elements of nature, such as clouds and rain. A third section features kachinas holding seeds and plants. The last cluster of figures represents ideas like birth and death and people such as hunters with weapons.

Unlike the rest of the exhibits which are meticulously arranged to balance display space with void, the kachina collection seems haphazard. Dane wonders if perhaps the curator had been in the process of rearranging the dolls before taking lunch break. He will be sure to discuss it with the man when he comes to the museum later.

The familiar tickling sensation in Dane's nose alerts him to a smell of burnt cloth, pine resin, and linseed oil. Squatting down on his haunches, he duck-walks until he locates the strongest scent. He finds the source in the remains of a box underneath the water fountain on a wall a few feet from the exhibit. He traces a definite line of the scents directly back to the kachina case.

He stands up and walks back to the front counter. The museum is still closed, and the curator is not due for another hour, so Dane makes himself comfortable in the receptionist chair. Running his fingers through his collar-length hair, Dane decides to take a risk he would not normally take. He pulls his pager from his pocket and punches in the number listed on the museum's phone. He offers up a silent prayer. *Lord, please let Kenny be right.*

Holding his hand over the button that connects to Noah's number, Dane closes his eyes, and tracks.

* * *

The man came in through the back door. Sweat. Body odor. Linseed oil. The odors comingled with each other. They were putrid. They were like death. The man moved stealthily through the museum. His clothing stank. His breath was fetid. He smelled like panic. He touched the cases as he moved past them, leaving his scent on each one like an animal marking its territory with urine. Urine. Yes, that smell was also present in the mélange.

He moved directly to the kachinas. Hands on the glass cabinet doors. Musty air escaped when the doors slid open. The man sucked in the air and let it escape his lips. Sour breath. Beer. Raw onions. Moldy bread.

The man reached into the cabinet. Carelessly touched a figure holding a bowl of seeds. Pushed it aside. Disturbed the musty air. Mildew invaded the open cabinet. It was an old man smell, but Dane was certain he was not an old man.

Fabric. Duck cloth. Metal. A zipper on a canvas bag. He dropped it to the floor, where it stirred up the earthiness of the dust. He kicked it with his boot. Sweaty feet. Rank.

There was more disturbance in the cabinet. Other figures were moved from their places. Some were removed, and they permeated the air with the sour smell of cottonwood and vegetable-based paints. The aroma disappeared as they were wrapped in a plastic material and placed in the canvas bag.

A different smell. New wood. Recently cut. Paint, fresher than that of the other figures. The air was again displaced as these newer items were set inside.

The doors were closed, and the musty air smell dissipated abruptly. Metallic teeth met in with a sharp tang as the zipper was closed. Dust kicked up again.

Linseed oil. Pungent. Cloying. He soaked a rag with it. Pine resin, no ... pinecones. From the children's touch table. The scent strengthened as he pulled them apart to expose the pitchy interior.

The hot smell of electricity emanated from down low, near the floor. A cotton fabric of some type, maybe a candle wick, was probably pushed into the electrical outlet. It smelled singed.

Suddenly, there was a sweet candy-like fragrance. It was sharp. A children's song erupted from his memory. *I'm a lonely little petunia in an onion field, an onion field, an onion field.* The sweet treat became corrupted as it entered the man's mouth. Gum. Chewing gum. Yes, he had seen it in the drain of the water cooler when he was here yesterday. Thought a kid had done it.

Then he detected the acrid smell of electricity again. Dane was now sure how the fire was triggered. The foil cover of the gum was pressed into the outlet with a wire, maybe a paper clip. The fuse. It sparked and ignited, lit the cotton wick. The wick burned slowly, allowing time for the man to exit the way he entered.

The candle wick reached the rags which were soaked in linseed oil. They blazed up and lit the pinecones which exploded with a *"whomp,"* and the fire was live.

*   *   *

Dane jerks, and his hand closes over the pager, depressing the "send" button. "Home," he says aloud, his eyes still closed.

Within seconds, the desk phone rings. Dane blindly grabs it as he opens his eyes.

"Dane!" Noah says. "Hey, bro. I sent you a beacon light. what's going on?"

"I. Am. Back!" Dane's shout is joyous.

"Back … as in your powers are back? You just tracked, didn't you?"

"I did, Noah, I did, and I'm as strong as I ever was!"

"No way!" Noah's excitement can be heard in his voice.

"Yes, way. My first case investigating a fire here. It feels awesome. I am a complete man again."

"You were always a complete man, you doofus. You just don't act like one."

"Ha. But now I have it all back, Noah."

"Where are you calling from?"

"I'm at a local museum in town. It's called Smoki, of all thing. Ain't that a hoot?"

"I've heard stranger things," Noah's answer is subdued.

"We both have, little brother."

"How'd it happen?"

"The fire or my powers?"

"Tell me about your powers first."

"I smelled smoke yesterday, from miles away. I was in the truck basket, and I couldn't see any smoke, but I knew, Noah, *I knew* there was a fire somewhere. Then, it was as if I had never lost my gift at all. I could sense the location over in the middle of town. We hightailed it over here and extinguished the blaze right after it became live. It was such a high! And afterward, the Chief said, 'damn fine job, Lightfoot' and sorta promoted me to something like my fire marshal position in Tallahassee."

"Wow. You couldn't have told me anything I enjoyed more. How about the arsonist?"

"This guy reeked worse than any B.O. I have ever had the displeasure to smell. Gag. He tried to burn up a kachina doll exhibit. Go figure."

"Did he now? People are weird, Dane. Hey, man, I am so glad you have your powers back. That's the best news I've heard in months," Noah says, keeping his apprehension hidden.

"I agree. Thanks for the light, bro."

"Anytime, anytime. Do you want to talk it out some more?"

"I do, Noah, but not now. I'm on the hunt for more arson evidence. Call you later. OK?"

"Sure, Dane. I'm so happy for you. Wait'll that wife of yours hears. She'll have a fit."

"You better believe it. Don't tell her, though. Let me. I can't wait to see her face."

"Good deal. Later," Noah says as he disconnects.

Dane replaces the receiver and sits quietly for a few minutes, just breathing heavily. Then, he bows his head, and offers thanks to God for the return of his gift, thanks for his gifted brother, and thanks for Kenny and his telepathic friend. He takes a deep breath and checks his watch. It is nearly time for the curator to arrive. He will probably be here investigating for several more hours. Afterward, though, he will make a direct beeline to his home and his wife. He laughs aloud and thinks: *Wait until Raven hears.*

CHAPTER 9

KATSINAM

WHILE DANE IS INVESTIGATING the Smoki Museum, Raven messages Noah on his cell phone for a brainstorming pow-wow. She is caught off guard when she hears the feminine voice that calls her back.

"Hello? Raven?" Maria Ramirez says.

"Uh … yes … Maria? Why are you … I mean … uh … is Noah there?" Raven stammers.

"Yeah. He's brushing his teeth. He handed me the phone. How are you doing? I bet you're ready to have those babies, huh?"

"You have no idea. I thought you were at college."

"Spring break!" Maria squeals. "I am so ready for it, too. In case you're wondering, I know the arrangement … with you and Noah tracking, I mean."

"You do?"

"Yeah. Noah's been working with me and Kenny. I've been here for your last couple of sessions. I'm kinda the backup, you know, watching to make sure nothing happens to y'all while you're tracking. Don't be mad. I told Noah he should've let you know. But don't worry. I keep secrets very well."

"Well, that's a load off my mind," Raven says, the sarcasm

apparent in her tone of voice.

About that time Raven hears Noah enter the room.

"Ahhhh," Noah says. "Now I'm minty fresh and perfect for a kiss from my little *Mia*!" He smacks Maria loudly on the mouth with a wet kiss.

Raven groans. "Please stop. I'm going to throw up."

"Sorry Raven," Noah says. "Spring fever. Love is in the air. Whatcha gonna do?"

Raven responds with a loud retching sound, much to the amusement of Noah and Maria.

"OK. OK. This is an unexpected call, Raven. What's wrong?" Noah says in a more serious tone.

"Somebody tried to burn up the kachina exhibit in Prescott last night. It was the exhibit that has those five figures that I drew. Dane smelled the fire and got there in time to keep it from destroying everything."

"I kno …," Noah says. He stops abruptly and adds "Way!" Hoping he has covered well enough to keep from giving himself away he continues, "Wait. Back up a sec … did you say that Dane *smelled* the fire? He has his powers back?"

"Yeah. I guess Kenny was right about the hair thing. Where is Kenny, by the way?"

"Still at school. They don't break until next week. So now, let me see if I got this. Dane has his clairscent powers back, and he smelled a fire at the very place those kachina dolls are at? What're the odds of that?"

"Yeah. So now I'm wondering … what is the significance of me drawing those figures? The exact same ones. And who's trying to get rid of them?"

"I don't know." Noah shrugs. "I really don't know."

"Hey, I've got that book from the library," Maria says in the background. "Why don't y'all use it to figure out what all these dolls have in common?"

Raven makes a noncommittal *humph* sound. "That sounds like a plan, Maria. Good thing you're the brains of the outfit."

Noah is quiet. For once, he has no retort. Instead, he smiles at Maria and accepts the book she offers. The two of them sit on the couch with the large Heard Museum catalog opened on the coffee table.

"All righty, Raven. So, how about you give us some schooling on these kachina dolls?" Noah says.

Raven spreads out her drawings on her own coffee table and begins to form a connection between the images she has drawn.

"First of all," she says, "they are not dolls. They are effigies of Hopi gods and goddesses, carved from the water-seeking roots of the cottonwood tree. Only these particular roots are used, and the carvers have to be very careful with the pieces because they are special and are in short supply. That's one thing that makes the kachinas valuable. The cottonwood root is full of *wuya,* or spirit power, that it has sucked up from Mother Earth. Hopi believe that once a carver begins to create a kachina, it acquires a soul and becomes a repository for the living spirit of that *Katsina.* To burn it would be to kill it."

Noah and Maria sit quietly, transfixed as Raven continues.

"A Hopi kachina is a one-of-a-kind item. And it is always hand-made. They can't be mass-produced because of the scarcity of the roots. That, and the fact that the root is not always straight. If it's bent or crooked, the carver makes the *Katsina* to fit the bend. You can tell if it's an original because each artist signs the base with his name or initials.

"Each *Katsina* figure has a Hopi name and an English name, but it isn't just the name that identifies the kachina. The figurines have painted or carved costumes that represent what is worn by the actual *Katsina* dancers. Some carry weapons, and some carry food, depending on their function. But the most important details are the colors and the faces. The face and paint colors let you know which spirit the figure is supposed to represent." Raven stops a minute, remembering with discomfort her drawing of *TAWA* with his ominous, inverted mouth. She wonders. *Could that have been a portent of this fierce winter? Truly, the sun has rarely shone in the past several months.*

"So, you're saying we need to separate them by color and face," Maria says.

"Yes, that's a pretty good idea. Also, by the role the masked and costumed dancer plays that the kachina is representing," Raven says.

Maria hops up and runs to the other room. She comes back with a wad of papers and a pen, which she deposits next to the book.

"OK. I'm ready. I'll make a list and we can find the corresponding picture in the book," she says.

Noah stares at her with a broad smile covering his face. There's no question anymore that his heart has no trace of room left for Raven; it's all full of Maria.

"All right, let's see. We have several categories. People. Birds and Animals. Elements and Unearthlies. That'll do for starters," Raven says.

As Raven names off the kachinas, Maria writes the names in the corresponding columns.

Under the people category, she lists:

EWTOTO—Chief.

AHÖLA—Chief's Lieutenant.

LENANGTAQA—Flute Player.

SIKYAQOQLO—Artist.

WUPAMOKATSINA—Guard.

QALETAQA—Warrior.

HEE'E'E—Warrior Maiden.

TUHAVI—Paralyzed Brother.

POOTAWIKKATSINA—Coiled Plaque Carrier

Under the birds and animals category, she lists:

ANGWUSKATSINA—Crow

ANGWUSNUSOMTAQA—Crow Mother.

POLIIMANA—Butterfly Maiden.

KWEWU—Wolf.

SOWI'INGKATSINA—Deer Dancer

TSOPKATSINA—Antelope

KIISA—Chicken Hawk Racer

KWAHU—Eagle.

Under the elements and unearthlies category, she lists

NATA'ASKA—Big Mouth Ogre.
SO'YOKWUUTI—Ogre Woman.
KOYEMSI—Mudhead Racer.
KOKOPÖLÖ—Humpback.
MUUYAWKATSINA—Moon.
TAWA—Sun.
MASAUWU—Skeleton Man, or Death.
AWANYU—Plumed Serpent.
OMAWKATSINA—Cumulous Cloud.
SOOTUKWNANG—Star.
KOKYANWUUTI—Spider Woman.

Maria and Noah study the list as Raven goes on to describe the colors, costumes, and facial features of each kachina. Suddenly, Maria sees a pattern. She takes her pen and circles some of the names, linking them to each other.

"Hey, some of these are paired up, like Crow and Crow Mother, Chief and Chief's Lieutenant, Warrior and Warrior Maiden, Big Mouth Ogre and Ogre Woman, um ... Artist and Flute Player ..." she says.

"Those don't match, Mia," Noah says.

"Yeah, they kinda do. They're both artists," she says.

"That makes sense, but the Flute Player accompanies the Butterfly Dancer, and the Artist matches up with Coiled Plaque Carrier," Raven says, "and there are some others who appear in dances together, like Paralyzed Brother and Mudhead."

"And what about combining Deer and Antelope, and maybe Eagle and Chicken Hawk Racer can go together. Aren't they pretty much the same thing?" Maria says.

"Not at all," Raven says. "A deer is like what people hunt in Florida. An antelope is more like a pronghorn. Bigger, sturdier, and almost as fast as a cheetah. An eagle is quite large and can be a bald eagle, like our national bird, or a golden. I saw one just yesterday, as a matter of fact. And the chicken hawk is smaller, but it's not what the name implies. It's really a prairie falcon." Raven suddenly gets a cramp. She sucks in her breath and holds it for a count of three before slowly and quietly letting it out.

"Hmmm, that leaves a bunch without partners. What about Sun and Moon?" Maria offers.

"*TAWA*, the Sun god, matches with *KOKYANWUUTI*, the Spider Woman," Raven says.

"How so?" Maria asks.

"The Hopi creation story tells that, in the beginning, there were only two great gods: Sun god and Spider Woman. These two great gods divided themselves to make all the other gods. They created all except for *MASAUWU*, the Skeleton Man, who is also known as Death, god of the Fourth World. He came into being on his own and was considered an evil god.

"Afterwards the two great gods shared a united thought, which was to make the Earth fill the place of Endless Waters between the Above and the Below. So, Spider Woman also became known as the Earth goddess.

"The two great gods saw that the Earth was lonely, so they shared another thought, which was to fill the Earth with living things. They sang, one to another:

> "*TAWA* sang, *'I am Light.'*
> *KOKYANWUUTI* sang, *'I receive Light.'*
> *TAWA* sang, *'I am Life.'*
> *KOKYANWUUTI* sang, *'I nourish Life.'*
> *TAWA* sang, *'I am the Father of all that shall ever come.'*
> *KOKYANWUUTI* sang, *'I am the Mother of all that shall ever come.'*

"Together, Sun god and Spider Woman shaped clay from the Earth they created into the forms of birds, animals, fish, and people. Then they covered their creations with a magic woven blanket. *KOKYANWUUTI* cradled the inert forms within the blanket while she and *TAWA* sang a Song of Life together. The forms in her arms took breaths and became alive. Then, the living things were divided into clans, each to their own kind, and set along their own paths into the World.

"The two great gods told the living things not to fear, that they would always be watched over, and then *KOKYANWUUTI*, the Spider Woman, disappeared into the Earth. But *TAWA*, the Sun god, rises each day from the east and watches over us all until he descends into his western *kiva*."

As Raven ends the tale, Maria claps her hands excitedly.

"*Bueno. Bueno.* That is a very good story!" she says.

"Everybody's starting to sound more and more like Professor Thistleseed with his stories," Noah remarks.

"Yeah, well. All stories aside, I'm afraid we've hit a dead-end with the pair-ups," Raven says.

"Girls, I think you've overlooked the one most important thing that connects all these kachinas," Noah says. He waits for a couple of seconds. When nobody responds, he continues his observation. "In the back of this guide, there's a listing of each kachina in the collection, along with page number, catalog number, height, weight, date, and ..." He pauses, waiting for someone to finish his thought.

"And what?" Raven asks.

"Carver," he says. "All of these kachinas were carved by either F.K. or F. Kalyesvah. Now my pea-sized man-brain tells me that F.K. *is* F. Kalyesvah. Ipso facto, they were all carved by the same guy."

"I can't believe I'm saying this, but you are a genius," Raven says.

"Thank you. Thank you. It just makes sense, that's all," Noah says.

"So, can you track this Kalyesvah guy?" Raven asks.

"I don't know. I really don't have enough information. I think it would work better to track the kachinas, but I don't know if the ones in this book are the same kachinas you drew. There are hundreds of them. I don't want to go off on a wild-kachina chase."

"I know what you can do," Maria says. "Track Raven's pictures! Can't you remotely view her drawings? And with your photographic memory, you can track just those specific kachinas."

"I take it back, Noah. She's the genius," Raven says.

"That's a great idea, but I don't think Mia is ready to

beacon for me. She's learning, but she's early in her training, and …" Noah says, pausing.

"And … what?" Raven says.

"And I haven't asked Lee if I can train her yet," he says.

"Didn't know that," Raven says.

"Now you do," Noah responds.

"You're such a rule-breaker, Noah!" Raven says.

"Yeah, yeah. I'm a rebel, for sure. But that doesn't change the fact that I can't track without a beacon … and YOU surely can't beacon for me! I need Kenny!" he says.

"At your service. It's nice to be needed. What do you need me for?" Kenny says as he walks through the front door.

"What? You must be psychic or something. Hey, wait. What are you doing here?" Noah says.

"Half day today. Bus driver dropped me off. What do you need me to do?" Kenny says with a huge smile.

"Ken. This is serious business. I need you to beacon for me. Are you up to it?"

"Are you kidding? I'm more up than you are! Are you the lookout, Mimi?"

"I am, I am," Maria says.

"My gosh, you guys. Can't you even use her real name?" Raven says.

"Sure," Kenny says, "But it's more fun to invent different nicknames. Keeps the mind sharp."

"Yeah, and it's way better than Bucko and Chubs, which is nauseating," Noah says.

"Got a point there," Raven concedes. "OK. Do it."

Kenny slides over beside Noah on the couch. Maria keeps her place on the other side of Noah. Both of them look at him intently. Noah closes his eyes, and Kenny does the same.

In just a few short minutes, Noah breathes the word, "Home." Kenny lifts his head and sucks in a breath. Noah immediately scoots back against the cushions, eyes wide open, eyebrows raised, mouth agape.

"Ken. We *gotta* work on your intensity. I feel like I just saw a nuclear explosion," Noah says.

"Sorry. I'll do better next time," Kenny says with a smile.

Noah shakes his head, and then he focuses on the red "training" thumbtack he has pushed into the far wall.

"The images are black and white, with primary colors shading the faces and bodies. They are nearly three-dimensional representations of the original carvings. There are 28 total figures arranged around all the four edges of the paper. Each figure seems to be enclosed in some type of display box with candles between each box. I have seen their duplicates in the book. And that's it," Noah relates.

"Wow. That's so impressive." Maria giggles.

Noah shrugs and grins, and then he claps his hand on Kenny's shoulder. With his other hand, he rubs his knuckles against the top of the boy's head.

"And you! You crazy animal. You get a great big noogie for doing such a super beaconing job!" he says.

Kenny laughs and slaps his hand away, and then he jumps up from the couch and heads for the kitchen. "And so, I think I deserve snacks," he says.

Noah stands, pulls Maria up, and follows Kenny into the kitchen. "We all do, buddy. We all do," he says, leaving Raven hanging on the telephone line.

"Hello? Thanks, guys. You're welcome, Raven. OK, fine. Goodbye, guys," she says.

CHAPTER 10
<u>CROSSING THE ROPE</u>

KENNY SITS SWAYING GENTLY in Noah's front porch swing, enjoying the beautiful spring day. A breeze blows his straight black hair around his face, bringing with it the smell of wild onions and gardenias. After having an impromptu lunch, Noah and Maria go out for a drive to see what's blooming around town, and Kenny takes the opportunity to spend the rest of his half-day off in silence until they return. He relishes this rare bit of solitude. Going to his own home means enduring cacophony, with his many siblings immersed in their various conversations.

After the successful tracking session in which he, Kenny Thistleseed, was the beacon extraordinaire, he basks in his accomplishment. He is confident in his beaconing ability, now that he has officially used it for a legitimate tracking session. Soon he will be able to beacon for the rest of the Team ... as soon as Noah clears it with Kenny's dad.

Kenny sits daydreaming of his future as a member of the elite Trackers Team. The prospect it exciting; he will be equal to the grown-ups. He knows he is the youngest Tracker to have beaconed, and that makes him feel special and unique. It's hard to be special and unique in a family of ten.

Until now, his father was the youngest Tracker at 15. Noah was 16, Dane was 18, and Graham was 19. Raven was in her 20s, and Maria, whenever she finishes her training, will be at least 17, probably 18. He has a birthday coming up next month, so that means he will be 13 when he becomes a full-fledged Tracker, but he will still have the record as the youngest. He smiles, pushing his foot against the porch rail to rock the swing.

The motion of the swing is relaxing, and Kenny closes his eyes. After a while, the rhythm of the swing becomes slower. To the casual passer-by on the street, it looks as though he is just an ordinary young boy, catnapping in a porch swing. But in all reality, Kenny Thistleseed is deep in a trance having a meeting of the minds with his telepathic friend.

She usually comes to him unannounced, at her choosing, and often when his conscious mind is engaged in something mundane. Some of the time, she has instructions for him to carry out. But at other times, she brings a warning specific to the Trackers. Today is the latter. Her message is full of warning.

Kenny listens as his telepathic friend speaks. It is an odd feeling, having someone in your head. It's like wearing headphones and listening to a book on tape as the narrator reads the text of the story. But there is no rewind button, so it's important to listen carefully to the message. There is never any back and forth; no dialogue between the two of them. She speaks; he listens. He doesn't even know her name, but she knows his. She calls him by his given name, Chenaniah.

The girl has a strange accent and a peculiar way of stringing her words together, as though English is not her first language. Kenny doesn't know where she lives (for, indeed, she is a living person instead of a spirit), but he is sure it is somewhere in Central America. He recognizes the slight accent the girl gives to many of her words, much like his electives teacher, who is Hispanic.

A propensity for speaking and understanding languages is developing as Kenny's second-sighted gift, along with his telepathic channeling. Though he is enrolled in Spanish at his middle school, he has already finished the entire set of lesson books for the first, second, and third *Digame en Español* series. His school does not offer a fourth-year course of Spanish study, and he is not allowed to take the French series until next year. He spends his classroom time delighting his teacher by eagerly helping the students who are struggling with the language. While the others are busy doing their seatwork, Kenny gets to have real conversation with the teacher.

Kenny also detects another element of the girl's dialect that is more like that of Noah and Dane when they talk in their native Muskogee Creek language. He has listened to them often enough to understand much of what they say when they're carrying on a conversation they don't want others to hear. He must keep a poker face when they talk so he doesn't give himself away.

The telepathic girl often uses unusual or put-together terms for common things. She told him once he needed a "healer and a shearer." His oldest sister Shine is a vet tech, so he figured she was like a healer. He had to ask her what a shearer was. He associated it with someone who cut sheep's hair; he was pretty close on that one. The girl meant they needed someone, who turned out to be Kenny's mom, to trim Dane's hair after the muggers hacked it off.

She also told him to "send your father to the large bird building to get the brothers." That one he understood well enough. Dad was to pick up Dane and Noah from the airport. Clearly, this girl has never been to an airport, let alone seen an actual plane, but she knew that it was something that flew and landed in a big place.

None of these idiosyncrasies strike Kenny as unusual. After all, he has been around second-sighted people his whole young life. That a telepath communicates to him in his mind is just a matter of course. And since the Trackers are all from different Native tribes, he is already mastering the nuances of all their dialects.

Today, however, the girl's message is more than scary. She feels fear for the artist woman and her children. That, of course, means Raven and the babies. Raven is the portrait clairvoyant, and they all know she is expecting twins. When he has heard from the girl before, she did not exhibit fear. She simply delivered the messages and instructions, and then she faded away. The fact that she is now afraid sends an ominous chill through Kenny, making his stomach lurch.

He tries to man-up, but the very idea that a 12-year-old can do a man's job is more than overwhelming. The earlier euphoria he experienced is dissipating. *What if I am not up to the task? What if I can't help them?* He desperately fights to retain composure. It is this raw emotion rising from deep in his gut that finally breaks through the mental barrier between him and the girl.

What can I do?" he whines aloud.

I will help you. We are strong together.

"You … did you hear me?"

Yes, Chenaniah. We have now crossed over a rope. She sounds cheerful in his mind

"A rope? What do you mean by a rope?"

She is silent, and Kenny panics, thinking she has broken the mental link.

"A rope to where?"

A rope over agua grande.

"A rope over big water. Oh! A bridge!"

Si, si. A bridge. We have crossed over a bridge.

In his mind, Kenny hears her laugh. It is a wonderful sound, like a wind chime echoing in an empty room. He cocks his head, trying to memorize it. In a small way, he has a crush on her. Though he doesn't know her age, she sounds a lot like Maria, so he chooses to think she is a teenager, too.

Thank you, Chenaniah, I care for you, too.

Kenny opens his mouth to deny his feelings, but he knows it is useless. She knows his every thought. She must know how her message terrifies him down to his very toes.

I do, Chenaniah. I sense your unrest. I, too, have a fearful stomach to my toes. I want to tell you to be at peace, but I cannot. I do not know the outcome. I have yet to see it. I only feel there is great danger for my sister and my nephews.

"Sister? Nephews? Wait! Are you telling me that you are Raven's sister?"

Si. Now that she is my brother's wife, I am her hermana.

"What? So, you're saying that you are *Dane's* sister?"

I am. And I am Noah's sister.

"Wow! Is Fawn your mother?"

No. My mother is here with me. She is Susannah. She has been with me since the beginning. We live here together.

"Then you must have the same father ... Joe Lightfoot." He wonders how Mr. Lightfoot met the mother of this woman from Central America.

I ... I do not know that, Chenaniah. My mother does not speak of my father or how they were together. There was some wrongness with him, something long ago that happened. I do not know more. She does not tell me this thing.

"I'm totally blown away by this news."

How are you blown away? Is it a strong wind?

Kenny laughs aloud. He must remember that she is very literal in her understanding and expression of things. He rephrases his statement. "I have much surprise and many questions," he says.

Enkv. OK. Comprendo. I understand. But we must speak of the danger, Chenaniah. I have much to tell you, so now you must listen and not question.

Kenny nods his head, fully aware that she knows he is agreeing. He listens, and her words fill him with dread.

* * *

When Noah and Maria return home sometime later, Kenny is inside the house, eating another cheese sandwich and drinking his third can of cola. He wants desperately to tell Noah about his sister, but the girl swore him to silence. She told him, *"Your knowing is all that can be. The knowing of others will bring many bad things. You must not tell my brothers yet. They have danger around them if you do."* Kenny just stares at him uncomfortably.

"What's up, Ken?" Noah asks.

"Nothing," Kenny snaps. "Nothing's up. Just need to go home. Can you take me home?"

"Sure thing. But do you want to help me track these kachinas first?"

"No, I need to go home."

"Right now?"

"Yes, right now." Kenny insists, stuffing the remainder of

the sandwich in his mouth and washing it down with the rest of his cola. "Right now, please."

Noah and Maria exchange puzzled looks, then they make an about-face and head for the car. Kenny rushes ahead of them and jumps in the back seat of the Mustang. Noah and Maria again exchange looks. Usually, Kenny petitions to ride "shotgun" in the front passenger seat. His behavior is decidedly odd, but then again, Kenny is 12, and most "tweens" are decidedly odd at times.

Kenny is silent on the drive over, even though Noah and Maria both try to engage him in conversation. When they reach the Thistleseed house, he jumps out and runs inside, throwing a wave over his shoulder. Shrugging their shoulders, the lovebirds back out of the driveway and leave.

His father's truck is parked in the carport, but the rest of the family has gone out. Kenny goes to his room, throws his books on his desk, and falls backwards on his bed. He puts his arms behind his head and thinks about his conversation with the girl.

The message had several parts: An old man dies before completing an important work; a younger man makes fire in a building; gods are mad and hold back spring; and the cold kills many people. But most importantly, she told him that Raven and her babies get lost and can die.

Despite her reassurance that the outcome can be different, Kenny is distraught. He rolls over on his stomach and begins to cry.

Passing into the foyer, Lee hears his son sobbing upstairs. He ascends the stairs and knocks tentatively on the door.

"Chenaniah? Are you all right?" he asks.

"Yes, I'm fine," Kenny replies in a muffled voice.

"Are you sure, son. You sound upset."

"No, I'm fine, Dad," Kenny says, sniffing loudly.

"Do you wish to talk?"

"No, I'm fine. OK?" Kenny's voice cracks, betraying the depth of his despair.

"As you wish, but should you need me, I am here for you."

The bedsprings creak, and a puffy face, red-eyed boy stares at Lee from the doorway. Without another word, Lee steps toward the room, and Kenny falls into his arms, weeping. Lee moves him forward, and then he closes the door behind them, away from curious siblings, should they happen to come home. He does not speak; he simply lets Kenny cry it all out. When it seems Kenny has exhausted his tears, Lee leads him to the bed and sits beside him. He has learned from two older sons that boys reveal more when they sit side-by-side, rather than being confronted face-to-face.

"Chenaniah. I am here," Lee says, gently patting his back.

"I know, Dad. I know. You are always here for me, and I really, really need you right now." Kenny sniffs.

"Are you in some trouble?"

"No. Yes. We're all in trouble, Dad. Big trouble." *I'm sorry, Luna. I have to tell my Dad,* he thinks.

He feels her nodding in his mind.

Yes, Chenaniah. It right to tell him. He is the one who can cross the rope for the others.

The boy shudders, then he squares his shoulders, sits upright, lifts his head, and looks straight ahead.

"I've spoken with Luna, and there is terrible danger coming," Kenny says.

Lee nods his head. "Luna?"

"Luna. My telepathic friend. That's her name. She came to me today, and I spoke with her for the first time."

"That … that is quite a breakthrough."

"That's not all, Dad. I beaconed for Noah today on a real important track." Kenny shifts his eyes, looking for Lee's response.

Lee lifts his eyebrows but does not comment. He has been expecting this. Noah and Kenny are very close, and they spend a great deal of time together, especially lately. It was bound to happen. In a way, Lee is relieved. He trusts Noah with his life; he trusts him with his son's life.

Kenny takes silence as a good sign and continues talking. "You have to keep all this a secret, Dad. I don't know why it's important, but Luna says it is a matter of life and death."

"That you beaconed for Noah?"

"Nah, not that. That's not the secret. That was actually pretty neat, by the way. The secret is what I'm about to tell you. But it's just between us, OK? You can't let anybody else know. Get ready for the biggest shock of your life."

Liahona Thistleseed could never have anticipated the words that come from his young son. But the more he considers them, the more they make sense. Knowing what he does of past events, he is surprised he didn't guess sooner that Luna—Kenny's telepath—is in some way related to someone on the Trackers Team. He sits quietly without commenting as Kenny continues his message: An old man dies before completing an important work; a younger man makes fire in a building; gods are mad and hold back spring; and the cold kills many people ... and Raven and her babies get lost and can die.

Liahona Thistleseed hugs his gifted son close and considers the words of the telepathic girl—Luna—sister to Dane and Noah Lightfoot. *I will help you. We are strong together.*

It is time for the entire Trackers Team to work this case. *We are strong together.*

CHAPTER 11

WEDDING DAY

APRIL THIRD ARRIVES with all the excitement of a special Hollywood-style wedding in the mountains. Out of town guests have flown in, and the unoccupied University house is filled with groomsmen and their families. Lee Stone's family—mother, grandmother, sister, aunt, and uncle—are the guests of President Hunter in the big house. The Albertson household is augmented by five of their extended family members.

In the morning, Robin and Raven carefully traverse the four driveways in the Explorer, with Raven at the wheel, and Robin holding the layered wedding cake steady in the cargo area. The large portrait of Shelley and Lee is wrapped and safely stowed behind the front seats.

All the hustle and bustle of the occasion is exciting, and Raven's mind wanders. Just as they arrive at the Albertson residence, a coyote runs in front of the car. Jolted out of her daydreaming, Raven hits the brakes, forgetting the rule of snow and ice driving: don't jam on the brakes. Fortunately, the driveway has been liberally salted, so she does not slide. Robin does slide, but she has a death grip on the cake, so no damage is done, other than the words which tumble from her mouth that Raven has never before heard her say.

"Mama!" Raven says, appalled, but also amused.

"Well, I'm sorry. We almost lost the cake," Robin says.

"It's been a while since I've driven. I feel like a beginner."

"Then you better take some refresher training from your husband after those babies are born. I won't have you endangering my only grandchildren."

Lois Albertson appears at the front door, along with her husband. She is a comical vision. She is wearing her high heels with a purple zip-front velour robe, and her hair is wound with toilet paper like a paper turban. Raven's eyes widen at the sight.

Wil Albertson wears blue jeans, an ERAU sweatshirt, and a stained barbeque apron. They certainly do not look as though a wedding is to take place in just a couple of hours. Lois waves and dispatches Wil to retrieve the cake, and then she turns on her heel and disappears back into the house.

Mr. Albertson is an intense man with a happy face, if such a thing is possible. His eyes reflect great intelligence, and his jaw pulses from the clenching of his teeth. That is his thinking expression. The look Raven knows, however, is entirely different. His eyes seem to twinkle—what you can see of them—because his round apple cheeks nearly obscure them when he laughs, which is often. When he grins, he usually sticks his tongue out. Of course, there are those deep dimples that he has passed on to his daughter.

Raven's feelings for Mr. Will (as he likes to be called) are conflicted and a little sad. She does not know him well at all, but he feels fatherly to her. Oddly enough, when she calls up images of her own father, Falcon, she sometimes sees the face of Mr. Will. *You would have liked each other,* she thinks.

Albertson helps Raven inside first, and then he goes back for Robin, the cake, and the wrapped portrait they have brought as their wedding gift. Raven begins to sit in one of the maple high-back chairs, but then she remembers her size and instead selects a wider, sturdier club chair. She knows Miss Lois is very particular about her high-back chairs.

Raven stretches out her legs and watches the lady of the house fussing about, making sure every little detail is exactly right.

This is an especially big day for her, and she expects nothing less than perfection. She has a whole crew of Mr. Wil's friends jumping. Raven laughs aloud.

Her laugh is cut short by another cramp in her side. She puffs out a ragged breath. *Yes, babies, yes. I know it's getting close. Patience, please. You will come into your own soon.*

Her attention is caught by a young woman who comes toward her, holding a steaming cup of tea. This is Shelley Albertson, the bride-to-be.

"Hi, Raven. I'm Shelley. I have some tea for you. It came from your house. Your mom called it 'Fawn-tea' and said you would probably need some," she says.

Raven accepts the tea gratefully and smiles at the girl. She is struck by the depth of her dark brown eyes. They seem to be all pupil. Then Shelley smiles, and Raven sees Mr. Wil in her face, especially those dimples.

"Thank you, Shelly," Raven says.

"Let me know if you need anything else. I got nothing to do except wait and stay out of my mother's way." Shelley laughs, purposely sitting on a "forbidden" high-back chair.

They are close in age, and Raven feels as though she has met a kindred spirit, only this one acts on her desires instead of repressing them. *How refreshing.*

"So, tell me, how did you call that eagle?" Shelley's eyes twinkle mischievously.

Raven almost chokes on her tea. "I ... don't think I did. It just ... uh ... came back. Maybe I screamed and scared it a bit."

"Ha! Like I believe your scream scared an eagle?"

Having no response, Raven takes a sip of tea to give her mouth something to do.

Shelley looks from side to side, and then she leans in closer and whispers. "I know what happened. Don't worry. I won't tell anybody. It's our secret."

"I don't know what you mean." Raven feigns innocence.

"Lookit. My grandfather was from the Georgia swamps. His family hid out there. My Mawmaw said he was one of the dark people, but he wasn't a black person. You know what I mean. She married him when she was just a little girl of 13.

"My Pawpaw had some special skills, if you understand what I'm saying. He could play any instrument he picked up He could design a house in his head and build it, piece by piece, without any plans. Animals and children were drawn to him.

"He could take a car apart and put it back together, even though nobody ever taught him how. His favorite place was his garage, and that was my playhouse. I spent my time with nuts and bolts and greasy tools while my cousin was playing with baby dolls. And while I 'worked,' my Pawpaw and I sang songs and built stuff from scraps of wood.

"His job was overseeing a junk yard. Mawmaw couldn't drive, so she and I would walk several miles to the yard each day with sandwiches and jars of sweet tea. He taught me how to drive in those junked cars. He would sit beside me and tell me 'Turn left. Go down this street. Mash on the brakes so you don't hit that nanny goat. Step on the clutch now, and back up.' I will never, ever forget that time with him.

"I'm like my Pawpaw in lots of ways. I don't have all of his special skills, and I don't have yours, but we know when we meet someone else like us, don't we?" she says.

Raven just stares. This is nothing she ever expected.

Shelley sits back against the chair and graces Raven with a radiant smile, just as Lois bursts into the room.

"Shelley, you better practice your song for the wedding, and please stop sitting in that chair," she says on her way out.

"Yes, Ma'am," Shelley says, rolling her eyes. She jumps up and starts into the living room where the piano is set up. She turns back abruptly.

"Don't go anywhere, Raven. I want you to hear the song I wrote for my wedding vows."

"I'd love to hear your song, but I'm not going anywhere. '

"Yes … you are," Shelley says before disappearing into the adjacent room.

Raven sits, somewhat dazed, as she hears the piano being skillfully played. After the intro, Shelley's clear mezzo-soprano voice rings out.

"Will you walk with me down beside the sea,
Where the mist makes diamonds in my hair?
Will you hold my hand and beside me stand,
Never mind the others walking there?
Will you touch my lips with fingertips
As you grace me with a smile?
Will you stroke my cheek as you softly speak?
And I'll be in Heaven for a while."

Listening to Shelley sing, Raven is instantly transported back to her own wedding just a few months before. Shelley's voice is reminiscent of Maria's, but it is more mature. Her vibrato is like the rhythmic beating of a dove's wings, whereas Maria's is faster like a hummingbird's. She sings as one who clearly knows she has talent and understands well how to use it. The wedding will be spectacular. Raven is sorry she will miss it.

It is not until this very moment Raven realizes she is, indeed, going somewhere. Shelley's song continues.

"Will you walk with me down beside the sea,
With the white birds winging to and fro?
Will you lay me down on the sandy ground
In the dunes where morning glories grow?
Will you plan the ways and count the days
As we journey mile by mile?
All the things we'll do—just me and you—
And I'll be in Heaven for a while.
I'll be in Heaven for a while, I'll be in Heaven for a while.
And no matter where, as long as you are there,
I will be in Heaven for a while."

As soon as the song finishes, Shelley comes back into the room. She sees Raven sitting with tears in her eyes and rushes over to sit by her.

"I see you liked the song. I'm really glad you got to hear it. Gotta go, Raven. Please be safe," she says. She gives Raven a warm hug, and then she pats her on the belly. "Happy Birthday, little fellas. I hope to meet you one day."

Shelley Albertson bounces down the hall, leaving Raven sitting with an empty teacup and an open mouth. But the girl's comments have stirred Raven to action. Now that she had made up her mind she is leaving, she gets to her feet and searches for her mother. Finding her in the kitchen with Mrs. Albertson and Miss Millie, Raven makes her excuses.

"I am so very sorry, Miss Lois, but I'm not feeling well. I'm having some Braxton-Hicks cramps, so I'm going to drive home and rest. Please apologize to Shelley and Lee for me. I hate that I'll miss the ceremony. I hope they like the portrait I painted for them," Raven says.

Lois is gracious, providing motherly advice to keep her feet up, stay hydrated, and get plenty of rest. Miss Millie fixes Raven two plates of food to take home with her and gives her another snuff kiss. Robin walks her daughter to the car.

"Be careful, *Qomi*. And don't worry about me. I will get a ride home from Mr. Wil or one of the others," Robin says.

"I'll be fine, Mama. Enjoy yourself." Raven squeezes into the driver's seat. She watches Robin go inside the house, and then she drives home.

When she gets to the house, she sets the plates of food on the table for Dane to eat when he comes home, and then she heads straight for the bedroom closet. She changes into her rabbit fur moccasins and grabs a hot-pink down jacket. She quickly pulls her sketches from the summer moccasin box and heads back out the front door. Even though she has drawn these pictures a dozen times, she wants to take them with her for comparison, if necessary. Setting the drawings and the jacket in the passenger seat, she wedges herself behind the steering wheel, buckles her seatbelt beneath her bulging stomach, and puts the car in gear.

*   *   *

By the time she gets to the base of the mountain, Raven is stiff and light-headed, and her hands are cramped from holding so tightly to the wheel. She knows she is being foolishly careless by driving down the steep incline, even though it has been salted and sanded to make it easier for the wedding guests to ascend, but she is compelled to examine these kachinas.

Raven feels a sense of empowerment that she may be able to do something to solve the mystery of the drawings and the fire. She only hopes she doesn't run into Dane. He will be furious. But he has planned to be out of the city limits until at least dusk, and she is sure she will be able to get back up to the house long before he discovers her gone.

Taking her time and being very careful with her driving, she navigates her way to the Smoki Museum. Even though it is closed for clean-up, she knows the curator will be there. She spots the adobe building and pulls into a parking spot right out front.

As she enters the museum, she can smell the scent of the smoke beneath the cleaning soap and air fresheners. Several workers are busily scrubbing, sweeping, and polishing. The people are methodical and almost reverent in their tasks, and Raven notices that they are all Yavapai. Cleaning up the museum is not a chore; it is an honor and a duty for them as caretakers of their Native history. And, of course, the museum is probably warmer than many of their homes.

A slight, middle-aged man with round glasses spots her and comes over.

"I'm sorry, but the museum is not open now," he says.

"Oh, I know. I am Mrs. Lightfoot. My husband put out the fire and is investigating," she says.

"Oh! Mr. Lightfoot! We are so thankful for him. He has saved many precious and irreplaceable historical items." He gives her a broad, toothy smile.

"Yes, I know. He ... um ... he asked me to come check on a couple of things ... because he had to be out of town today. Is that all right?"

"Of course, of course. How can I help you?"

"I want ... he wants me to look at the *Katsinam* in the display case."

"Ah, you know the correct name."

"Yes. I was born in *Paaqavi* and raised as Hopi, but I moved here with my mother when I was a teenager. She's Robin Looking Bird. She has some baskets and coiled plaques in your museum."

"Yes! I know Mrs. Looking Bird. She is such a talented woman, your mother. I hope she is well."

"Yes, she is doing well. Thanks for asking." When the man doesn't move, she adds, "Can I see the *Katsinam?*"

"Oh yes. Please, come this way. Do you know that someone tried to burn them up? Can you imagine? Tried to kill them!" His hands flutter around his face.

"What is wrong with people?" Raven asks shrugging.

The curator simply shakes his head. Raven reaches her hand toward the glass doors. "May I?" she asks.

"Yes, yes. Anything you need," he says obligingly before moving away to speak with a worker.

Raven scans the arrangement of figurines until her eyes stop on one she recognizes. She reaches in and carefully removes it. "*Sootukwnang.* Star."

Raven examines the kachina. The first thing she notices is its roughness. It has not been sanded properly. Next, she sees that the paint is a little too bright. A figure this old should be more subdued in color. Finally, she inverts the image and looks at the base. There are no initials. She puts it back in the case.

Scanning the next shelf, she finds two more. "*Awanyu,* Plumed Serpent. *Omawkatsina.* Cumulous Cloud."

Like the other kachina, these two are not finished well. She looks at the base. Blank. She replaces them.

On the bottom shelf, Raven sees the last two kachinas. She takes them out. "*Masauwu,* Skeleton Man. *Kokyanwuuti,* Spider Woman," she says. Again, these are not expertly crafted, nor do they have the carver's identification under the base. As she puts them back in the case, the curator returns to her side.

"Is everything all right, Mrs. Lightfoot?" he asks.

"Oh, yes. This is a fine collection. I can tell you take very good care of the spirit fathers, and they are fortunate to have you as their guardian," she says.

The little man beams proudly. "And there is no damage?"

"No, no. You had them well protected. I will be sure to let Mr. Lightfoot know. Thank you so much for allowing me to view them." She smiles, turns, and exits the front door.

Sitting inside her car, Raven consults her drawings. She is sure that the five pieces in this museum are counterfeit. They are not of the quality she saw in her mind and put to paper. And they were obviously the reason for the fire. Someone is trying to cover up the theft of these five kachinas. And if that is true, then there is a good possibility that the other 23 that are in the Provo museum are copies, as well. If not, they soon will be.

Raven sighs heavily. She will have to tell Dane. He will be angry, but it is easier to ask forgiveness than it is to ask permission. He will get over it. She puts the car in gear and begins the perilous drive home.

CHAPTER 12

BIRTH DAY

AS RAVEN LEAVES THE SMOKI MUSEUM, she is lost in thought. Assembling the pieces of this mystery in her mind is like working a giant jigsaw puzzle, but without having the picture of the box for reference. From her perspective, she only knows a portion of the overall design. She thinks about how the Trackers would use all this information. They would put things in their logical order. Since she is on her own, for the moment, she tries to do the same thing. She numbers each point off in her head as she drives.

One. She has been drawing pictures of specific kachinas. During her short tracking sessions with Noah, she has drawn the same figures over and over. Each time she draws them, a little more detail emerges. In the beginning, they were images all around the paper. Now, they have color and shading and seem to be displayed in some manner in a particular order.

Two. All the kachinas have come from the collection of Senator Barry Goldwater. The senator was an avid collector, amassing over 400 figurines in his lifetime. Raven only draws 28 of them. Therefore, these 28 are significant in some way.

Three. Twenty-three of them are on display in Provo, in the Museum of Peoples and Cultures at Brigham Young University.

That collection is quite large, but again, she only draws 23 of them from the exhibit.

Four. The other five of the *Katsinam* she draws are ... *were* ... in the Smoki Museum, in Prescott, Arizona. Goldwater was from Arizona. What made these pieces more suited to the Smoki? *MASAUWU,* Skeleton Man. *SOOTUKWNANG,* Star. *AWANYU,* Plumed Serpent. *OMAWKATSINA,* Cumulous Cloud. *KOKYANWUUTI,* Spider Woman. She sees a connection. These *Katsinam* carry greater spirit power than any of the others. Of all the *Katsinam, Tawa,* Sun god, has the greatest position and power, and his kachina is grouped with the largest of the figurines, perhaps to rule them, perhaps to protect them.

Five. All the pieces were carved by someone named F. Kalyesvah. Who is he? Where is he? He is the link between all the drawings. He is the carver. He created the receptacles for the lives of the gods.

Six. Someone carved forgeries and replaced the original figurines in the museum. Was it F. Kalyesvah or someone else? Maybe the carver wanted his pieces back. Maybe Goldwater didn't have his permission to buy them. This Kalyesvah is important, so he needs to be located.

Seven. Someone—probably that same someone—tried to cover his deception by attempting to burn the evidence. He (and Raven somehow knows it is a *he*) deliberately set the fire to destroy the kachina exhibit. The only reason he would do that is to get rid of the fact that the four pieces were not Kalyesvah's work. But why didn't he torch the BYU Museum? Maybe that's next on the list?

While Raven's mind takes over and tries to piece together the mystery, her driving becomes automatic. But her concentration is compromised, and she misses her turn. In her desire to solve the puzzle herself, she has made a fatal error and taken a route that leads her away from the carefully salted and sanded road. She is on a spur that winds around the back of the mountain, and it is slick and hazardous.

By the time Raven realizes her mistake, she is committed to the route; there is no way to turn around. She fights her momentary panic and puts her full focus into safely navigating the narrow path that is leading her, inexorably, higher up the mountain. Her only hope is for the road to level out and send her around the back of the mountain to the fork that leads to the safety of the President's Residences.

To make matters worse, it is now past noon. The skies are overcast, and daylight fades quickly these days. Soon she will be fighting the shadows of the setting sun, the oncoming dusk, and the pitch-black night. There are no streetlights here, there are no houses, and the weather is freezing.

Raven keeps a steady foot on the accelerator, neither increasing nor decreasing her speed, keeping her foot away from the brakes despite the twistiness of the road. And all the while, she is going upward, higher and higher, and everything looks the same … white.

She is not religious, but fear and desperation create many believers. She prays to *TAWA*; she prays to *KOKYANWUUTI*; she even prays to Dane's Jesus. She hopes one of them will help.

Suddenly, Raven hits a patch of black ice. There is no way to prepare for the effect of that deadliest of winter hazards. It causes the Explorer to spin. She is careful not to brake. *Turn into the slide,* she remembers. She tries to twist the wheel in that direction, but the bulk of her pregnant belly keeps her from executing the maneuver. The car slides closer and closer to the side of the road. She panics. Beyond the edge is air and free-fall.

Raven holds her breath, fearing the worst. The bumper strikes a mound of snow, and the car ricochets off in the other direction. She is powerless to do anything to stop it. She is helpless inside a deathtrap, and her babies will never be born.

Without warning, the car comes to an abrupt halt, and Raven hits her head painfully against the window, leaving a splatter of blood from a split in her scalp. She looks out the front windshield and sees absolutely nothing. Looking in the rear-view mirror she realizes the car has wedged itself across the road. She exhales raggedly, but her relief is short-lived. The car begins to slide sideways down the incline.

In her terror, she grasps the door handle, and the door pops open. She releases the seatbelt and finds herself halfway out of the car. Her body is inches above the road as she clings for her life to the door handle. The wind catches the bundle of drawings, and they fly out into the snow. Raven wonders idly if they will be ruined.

As if things could get no worse, she feels a spreading wetness between her legs. *Did I just tee-tee?* She thinks. Then, she has a fully formed contraction. *My water just broke,* she realizes, *and this is not Braxton-Hicks.*

Raven screams long and loud, and the sound echoes all around her, long after her scream stops. She looks up and sees, improbably, a large bird perched on the top of the door. Raven recognizes it. Prairie falcon. It regards her for a moment, and then it screeches again. When she doesn't move, it continues screeching, flapping its wings and scooting its talons across the door, closer and closer to her.

It's going to attack me, she thinks. Indeed, the bird is aggressively threatening her. She grasps the door frame and pulls herself out of the vehicle, landing heavily on her back. She throws her hands over her face as the falcon flaps over top of her. But it doesn't attack; it disappears inside the vehicle. Raven is amazed to see it emerge with her pink down jacket in its talons.

Raven is slipping down the icy road just a few feet above the sliding car. She turns to her side and claws her way over to the side of the road, grabbing hold of the slender trunk of a tiny tree. She glances at the car just in time to see it slam through the snow drift and slide completely over the side of the mountain. She screams again as another contraction rips through her.

In her tormented mind, there are few outcomes to her situation. Below her and beside her are certain death. To release the tree means she will either fall over the edge where the car disappeared or, at the very least, be battered to death on the way down the road. Above her is snow, only snow, and snow-covered trees higher up into the mountain. All ways lead to destruction, for she cannot possibly climb this incline in her condition, and to stay tethered to this tree means freezing to death.

The colorful knit tunic Robin made her for the wedding has slid up above her waist, exposing her bare skin, which is scraped and bleeding. Her matching tights are torn on the knees, and she has lost one of her rabbit moccasins. Her teeth chatter from the cold and from the terror of her situation.

The falcon screeches at her again, dropping the jacket near her head. She clutches it with her other hand and pulls it closer, instinctively knowing she will need it if she is to survive the night. Maybe the Trackers will look for her. Maybe Dane will come for her. Maybe Noah will see her. Maybe, maybe, maybe.

Raven is just about to give in to despair when she hears a pounding sound nearby, followed by the heat of a heavy blowing breath. She looks up and sees two deer. No, not deer. These are antelope. Sonoran pronghorns. She remembers seeing one at the Heritage Park Zoological Sanctuary. They are a pair—a buck and a doe. The buck's thick two-pronged antlers protrude from his head above his round, black eyes. His mate paws the ground.

They come closer, and the buck leans his head down toward her, pushing one antler against her hand. The doe moves to the opposite side and stares at her intently. It is almost as though they are trying to communicate with her.

Raven pushes her free arm through one sleeve of the jacket and reaches out, touching the doe tentatively. The animal kneels and allows her to grab onto the fur at the back of its neck. The buck pushes her hand again, forcing her to release the tree.

She begins to slide down, but the buck thrusts his antler into her open hand. She clutches it tightly in her fist, and he raises his head, pulling her up with him. The doe, likewise, pulls her up, and they flank the woman between them.

Raven wraps her arm as far around the doe's neck as she can, while still holding tightly to the buck's antler. The pronghorns begin climbing the mountain, pulling the pregnant woman along. They climb harder, moving faster and faster until they are nearly running, and Raven's feet are dragging, dancing over the snow.

The trio of figures rises higher and higher, farther up the mountain—two brown ones with a flapping pink one in between. Puffs of vapor escape their mouths. They weave in and out between sparse, and then dense, snow-covered trees. Just when it seems they can go no further, Raven spots an especially large pine tree. The antelopes come to a stop at the edge of its spreading branches.

Underneath is a relatively thick blanket of pine needles and very little snow. This is the destination.

Raven releases her hold on the animals and sinks to her scraped knees. She scrabbles toward the base of the tree, pine needles painfully sticking into her legs, and props up against it, breathing heavily.

She has lost her other moccasin, and her lower legs are covered with snow. Though she wears just a long tunic sweater, she knows she has exerted herself, and putting on the down jacket now will make her sweat. Sweating will, in turn, make her colder, so she forces herself to warm her feet first. She kicks her legs together to brush off as much excess snow as she can and throws the down jacket over her shins, pushing it awkwardly to wrap around her icy feet and ankles.

After a few minutes, she pulls the jacket back up and puts it on backwards, thrusting her arms through the sleeves and covering her front. She is thankful that the falcon happened to snag it from the car. Inside the pocket she finds a pair of colorful knit gloves. She struggles to pull her legs up and does her best to stretch a glove over each foot. Not the best fashion statement, but they will give her feet some protection.

Now that she is safe from falling to her death, she realizes she is literally not out of the woods yet. She is hit with another powerful contraction. *I am going to have my babies in the wilderness, and we will all die of exposure.* She lifts her bottom and pushes down her maternity tights over her belly, thankful that the heavy fabric is loose and stretchy. And now, finally, as the shock sets in, she begins to cry.

While she weeps, she is unaware of the activity around her. When she settles down, she notices there is quite an assemblage of small creatures under this tree. She sees several mice, a few rabbits, some large Albert squirrels, smaller ground squirrels, a couple of racoons, and even a fox, in addition to the two pronghorns who seem to be standing guard. Above her, in the branches of the tree, are little birds, a great-horned owl, and the prairie falcon.

They are watching her intently, turning their heads this way and that, creeping closer, yet keeping their distance. She is in active labor now, and her babies will soon be born. Raven accepts this fact and stops her tears. Her thoughts are only about her children. She must protect them and give them every chance.

Remembering her mother's stories of how her people used to give birth, Raven scoots up against the tree trunk until her back is flat against it. Putting her feet beneath her, she pushes up into a crouch and pants. When a contraction comes, she screams. It feels as though she does this for an eternity.

Finally, when it seems she has no physical reserves left, she knows it is time. She pushes up into her crouch, reaching above and behind her to grab the tree trunk. When the contraction comes, she bears down as hard as she can, screaming louder and longer than she has up to now. Again and again she does this until she experiences a feeling of euphoria. She has delivered a baby. No, she has delivered both babies.

Sitting on her haunches, she sees the infants. They are both boys, and their tiny arms are wrapped tightly around each other in an embrace. Their faces are cheek to cheek, and their legs are entwined. They were born simultaneously. They are seventh sons of two seventh children—destined to be gifted.

Raven scoops them into her arms and wipes their faces with her sleeve. She does not clean their bodies, nor does she tie or cut the umbilical cords. The sticky, cheesy substance that covers their skin will protect them and keep them warmer. The blood that will continue to flow from the placenta for a while will make them stronger. These are the old ways her mother has taught her. She whispers a silent *thank you* to Robin for preparing her.

She clears their tiny mouths and noses with her fingers and blows forcefully into their faces. They cry, and it is the most beautiful sound she has ever heard. She puts the babies on her stomach and covers them with her sweater. Unbuttoning the first few buttons, she pushes the infants higher onto her chest, until their heads rest just beneath her chin, and then she buttons the tunic back over their tiny bodies. She pulls her tights back up, thankful that they are made of wool, which will stay warm even when wet. Exhausted, she rights the down jacket and zips it closed. She folds her arms beneath her boys, and she and her little ones fall asleep.

While they sleep, the animals advance. The two pronghorns again flank her, moving up close and lying against her side, transferring their body heat to her. The squirrels and mice and other small bodies cover her legs and feet, adding their warmth to the family, as well. A large white hare scoots his back up between her open, outstretched legs, effectively acting as living cotton packing to staunch the bleeding. The great-horned owl and the prairie falcon keep watch from the tree above. The snowy forest is quiet again as night falls.

CHAPTER 13

TRACKING RAVEN

ABOUT THE TIME RAVEN MISSES HER TURN, Dane arrives at home. Seeing that Robin's SUV is not in the driveway, he surmises that the ladies are busy enjoying the wedding festivities. Weddings are not his thing, unless it happens to be his own, so he is looking forward to some quiet time in front of the fireplace.

As he enters the kitchen, he spies the covered plates on the counter. Peeking under the tin foil, he is delighted to find all manner of delicious treats, both sweet and savory. Raven or Robin must have brought the food home just for him. If not, then it doesn't matter. He's still going to eat it.

He grabs both the plates and a fork, pours himself a brimming glass of iced tea (Dane prefers it cold and sweet as syrup) and makes his way back to the sofa. Setting his feast on the coffee table, he removes his heavy boots, snatches the fleece cap off his head, and shakes out his hair. He smiles and thinks, *Ahhh. It is so good to have hair AND psychic powers again.*

Dane removes the foil and digs into his treats: crudités with dipping sauce, homemade chicken salad, barbequed cocktail weenies, and rumake (chicken livers and water chestnuts are not his favorite, but he's a man, and he's hungry). For the main course, he devours the tender roast beef, scalloped potatoes, and bacon-wrapped asparagus. This is food he never gets around this house. Raven can't cook, and Robin has a westerner's taste buds. He misses Wren's pot roast.

After polishing off the savory plate, he uncovers the sweet samplings. There is no wedding cake (as it is not cut until after the ceremony), but there are other delights: apple pie with a flakey crisscross lattice crust, thick and gooey peach cobbler, and generous squares of velvety chocolate fudge. Dane leaves no crumbs and even licks the plate. He laughs at himself. *It's a good thing the girls are gone. They'd shame me.*

Ever the good husband and son, he takes his empty plates to the kitchen and dutifully sets them in the sink for somebody else to wash. Before leaving, he refills his tea glass and carries it out to the sofa.

A piece of paper catches his eye, and he reaches down to retrieve it, thinking he has dropped his napkin. It is a drawing. He recognizes the paper from Raven's sketch book. He sits down and examines it.

The drawing is indicative of her earlier haphazard tracking attempts. Large and small images cover the page, sometimes overlapping one another. The subject of the drawing is evident. These are kachinas, like the ones she drew after she got the kachina book from her mother ... exactly like the ones he recently saw in the Smoki Museum.

He sits up straighter and takes a closer look. Yes, he can identify four of the figures from the display case—the display case that was targeted by the arsonist.

"Huh," he says aloud. "You've been tracking, haven't you, my dear little wife?" He begins to smile, and then he is hit with a terrible thought. *She's been tracking without a beacon.* He sits back, and when he does, his hand brushes against his pager. *Or maybe she HAS been using a beacon!*

He strides into the kitchen, picks up the phone, and dials Noah, who answers on the first ring.

"Dane!" Noah says.

"Yes, I am," Dane says.

"Yeah, I'm just going into Lee's house right now. What do you know?"

"I know my wife has been tracking, and you've been her beacon, haven't you?"

"Well, yeah. So, she finally told you, huh?"

"No. She did *not* tell me. I found one of her drawings."

"Ruh-roh. She shoulda told you, bro."

"You shoulda told me … bro."

"Hey, man. You oughtta know your wife by now. A little headstrong, don'tcha think? She made me promise not to."

"I believe that, Noah, but it's so dangerous for her. She's not exactly thinking with a clear head lately. I really wish you'd told me before ya'll went and did this."

"I bet she's giving you quite a look right now, huh?"

"She's not here. She's at a wedding."

"Oh, she's at a wedding? Fun, fun. Don't be too hard on her when she gets … wait. What's that, Ken?"

Kenny is standing in front of Noah, face pale, eyes huge. "She's not at a wedding, Noah," Kenny says.

"What?" Noah says. He quickly puts the phone in speaker mode so Dane can hear.

"What is it?" Dane says.

"Hold on, Dane. Just a sec. Now Kenny, what do you mean she's *not* at a wedding?" Noah says.

Kenny looks near tears. "Raven's not at the wedding. Raven's lost," he says.

"WHAT?" Dane shouts.

"She's lost. That's why everybody's here. Raven's lost, and you guys have to find her," Kenny says.

"Kenny are you sure?" Noah asks.

Kenny bites his lip and nods vigorously, just as his father enters the room.

"Noah, Chenaniah, please come into the family room. Now," Lee says.

"I've got Dane on the phone," Noah says.

Lee is quiet for exactly three beats. "Bring the phone. He needs to hear," Lee says.

Dane's legs turn to jelly, and he sits heavily in Raven's padded kitchen chair, holding the phone to his ear, the delicious meal he just consumed like a rock in his belly.

"Lee ... what ... tell me what's happening," he says.

"Chenaniah relayed a message to me that he received from his telepath. She says that Raven and the babies are in danger. I have Noah and Graham, here ... and my son. We are going to track Raven. It is good you called. I understand your gift has returned. We will need your help, as well," Lee explains.

The men sit in a huddle around the central cedar stump coffee table in the family room, while the women and younger children watch and listen from the kitchen table. Everyone is quiet, waiting for Lee to direct the proceedings.

"Maria, Shinehah, Wren. You ladies are the lookouts. Be sure nothing interrupts us. Children. Do not utter a word, please. Raven's life is at stake." He looks in the direction of the kitchen at the stricken faces of his kids.

"Noah, I want you to track first. See what you can about her surroundings. Chenaniah, you beacon for him. Go now," Lee says. Kenny moves next to Noah on the loveseat, and the two of them close their eyes as Noah begins to track.

Dane's jaw drops. *Kenny is going to beacon for Noah?* He remains quiet. Lee is the boss; he knows what he is doing.

"Graham, you will take your ears and listen. See what you can hear of her situation. I will beacon. Dane, get pencil and paper. I will be going when Graham returns, and you must decipher my words," he says.

"Yes, Hona," Dane says. He reaches over to the counter, grabs the notebook and pen next to the phone ... and waits.

In a short while, Noah returns from his journey. "Home," he whispers. Kenny's eyes snap open seconds later.

Noah looks at Kenny beside him. "Much better, Ken. Good job," he says, giving the smiling boy a thumbs-up.

"Noah," Dane says, "Did you find her?"

"She's in the car, Dane. There is snow everywhere. I only saw snow out every single car window. She's OK, but she is lost for sure. Wait, here comes Graham."

Graham and Lee open their eyes simultaneously. Lee glances at the big man and is unnerved to see Graham sitting with his mouth agape, eyes wide in shock.

"Graham," he says. "What did you hear?"

Graham begins panting like a dog, his voice punctuated with little staccato bursts of "oh-oh-oh" and moans. Shinehah jumps up from the table and grasps the doorframe, watching.

Suddenly, Graham emits an ear-splitting scream .. in Raven's voice. The Thistleseed children scream. The Trackers are frozen in place. Graham again pants quickly.

Wren turns to her brood and motions for them to go upstairs. "Out, children, out. Quickly and quietly. Stay in your rooms until I come for you," she whispers. They file out through the dining room and run up the stairs. The second-floor bedroom doors close firmly, and then there is silence.

Graham screeches again, but this sound is more like metal against metal or nails on a blackboard. "*Kree-kree-kree-kree,*" he shrieks, his voice high and jarring.

Graham's breathing becomes ragged and hoarse. He continues to pant and utter nonsense syllables of someone who is clearly terrified. In between non-words, he makes a sound like horses running through beach sand. All the while, his Raven-voice pants and grunts.

Then, he again makes the sound of a woman screaming in pain. And again. And again. The screams are more frequent.

Shine begins to cry. Kenny begins to cry. All the men are sitting with clenched teeth.

"Raven! Raven! Something is hurting her. She's being attacked," Shine wails.

Wren steps up beside her daughter and speaks to the men in the room. "She is in labor," she states.

The next sound they hear is a deeper cry from Dane. "Raaaveeeen!" They have forgotten the man on the phone. Lee takes charge quickly.

"Graham. Stop. That is enough. I must locate her. All of you, pay close attention. I don't know where this will lead, but Dane will have to physically go find her. Noah, you are my light. Let's go now," he says, closing his eyes and sitting straight in Wren's patchwork chair. Noah lifts his head, closes his eyes, and listens as Lee's monotone voice fills the room.

"The lone explorer departs the house of smoke. The black bird travels to the north along the white trail of cotton. There is no salt, there is no sand, there is only the white blanket over the broad, flat snake.

"Black bird passes the creatures of the land: a hornet, an antelope, a dragonfly; she runs past a cactus and a sundog. The water of Watson is far to her left. Her nest is farther that way. She moves into the Eastern Storm, and the trees become her sentries; the forest is at her service.

"The lone explorer falls back from the snake. It jumps into the air and sails away, caught in the outstretched arms of the piñon people. But the black bird with pink wings flies to the north. Her companions are her hooved feet; the feathered one leads the way.

"Grandfather Ponderosa spreads his arms and offers needled shelter. Father Sun departs his daytime home, his coat of red and yellow and orange trailing behind. The trio rests with furry friends. Their journey now is done. And the Tracker must come home." Lee opens his eyes and looks around. The others are furiously scribbling notes.

This is the most important track. Lee is the one who pinpoints the location. But his track is always in poetic metaphor, and the Trackers work together to decipher it.

"The lone explorer. That's Robins SUV," Dane says. "She took her mother's vehicle. The house of smoke. That's the Smoki Museum. She went to the museum."

"Yes. We found out that they had some kachinas that were from a certain collection, all carved by the same guy. It's why somebody tried to torch the exhibit. They were counterfeit duplicates," Noah says.

"Yeah. Found one of her drawings tonight."

"Black bird. That's obviously Raven. She's going north. No salt. No sand. White trail of cotton, white blanket, long flat snake. That'll be a slick road covered with snow. I thought you guys treated the roadways up there," Graham says.

"We do. Especially today because there was a wedding up here. So why is her road untreated?" Dane says.

"She took a wrong turn," Kenny says. "That's how she got lost." They accept his assessment. He knows how this works, and even though he is young, his opinion is as good as anyone else's.

About this time, Dane hears the front door close. Robin enters the kitchen and sees him talking on the phone.

"Dane, you're home," she says, smiling brightly. Then she looks puzzled. "Where's my car?"

He covers the receiver with his hand and gives her a very sobering look. "Raven took the car, went into town. Now she's taken a wrong turn and is lost. We're looking for her," he says.

Robin turns pale, but she doesn't question him. She also knows how this tracking works. She deposits her coat and purse on the table, dips herself a steaming cup of Fawn-tea, and takes a seat next to Dane. She looks at the notes he has written.

"Hornet, antelope, dragonfly cactus, sundog. The water of Watson?" she says frowning. "Dane, those are roads. And Watson is a lake east of here on the other side of the mountain."

"Did you guys hear that? She's on the opposite side of Bradshaw Mountain," Dane says.

"OK. We've got a general direction, but let's finish before you go off half-cocked," Noah says.

"And Eastern Storm. That's a road, too. East Storm," Robin points out.

"You're right, Robin. Very wooded up there," Dane says.

"The forest is at her service. The forest is at her service. Why does that sound familiar?"

Dane sits upright suddenly. "Forest Service Road. Of course. The fire department uses that road, when it's not iced over like it is now." He stops and looks at Robin, who is thinking the same thing. *The road is iced over.*

"The lone explorer falls back from the snake. It jumps into the air and sails away, caught in the outstretched arms of the piñon people." Lee reads from his son's notes. His voice quivers just a bit, and he looks shaken.

"The car went over the edge and landed in the trees," Kenny

says. "But she didn't go with it. Dad. She's still going north. And now she has pink wings?"

They all look at each other in confusion. Robin's voice comes across the phone speaker. "She has a pink down jacket. Maybe she took it with her," she says.

"Bingo! You got it, Mrs. Looking Bird," Noah says.

"I don't know how to interpret her hooved feet. What animals have hooved feet that live up there?" Graham says.

"Deer, antelope, moose, horses," Shine says from the doorway. "And the feathered one, that's obviously a bird. My guess is it's a hawk."

"Why do you say that Shinehah?" Lee asks.

"When Gray was screeching once, it was not like a woman but was more like a hawk. '*kree-kree-kree-kree.*' That's what I think," she says.

"Beautiful and smart," Graham says, gracing his beloved with a tender smile.

"And later on, Lee said she rests with furry friends. There must be lots of animals around," Dane says.

"Lee said *'the trio'* rests with furry friends. Trio. Three of them. She's had the babies," Noah says.

Robin draws in a quick breath and lets out a small sound of "oh!" Dane reaches over and takes her hand, squeezing it.

"Grandfather Ponderosa. That's a big ole Ponderosa Pine tree. Spreads his arms. She's beneath it," Graham says.

"Offers needed shelter," Kenny says.

"No, Ken. He said 'needled' shelter. She's under a huge pine tree on a bed of pine needles," Noah says.

"And the sun is setting," Graham says.

"That's right," Lee says. "The sun is setting, and the night will be cold and dark. Dane now is the time for you to go. Call your firefighting friends and get to her as quickly as you can. Notify Mrs. Looking Bird when you find her. We will wait for word. In the meantime, Noah and Chenaniah, take another trip and assess her condition. You should be able to see her in the waning light. Go now, boys. I mean … men."

Dane hangs up the phone and immediately calls his

firehouse. Then, he laces up his heavy boots, grabs his parka, and heads out the front door, leaving Robin minding the phone.

At the Thistleseed house, Noah returns from his second track and relates what he has seen.

"It's getting pretty dark, but I was able to see Raven beneath the tree. She's wrapped in a fluffy pink jacket. There are multicolored gloves on her feet. She appears to be sleeping and is in no distress. But, y'all. It's the dangedest thing I have ever seen. She is covered head to toe with small animals. Head to toe! And beside her are two humongous deer, one of them with two huge straight antlers," he says.

Kenny throws his arms around Noah in a big bear hug.

"What's that for?" Noah asks.

"Luna says she will be all right," Kenny smiles.

"Aw. That's great, Ken." Then Noah frowns and pulls away, looking at Kenny. "Who's Luna?"

CHAPTER 14

PRONGHORN AND PRAIRIE FALCON

THE HARE HOPS THROUGH THE SNOW. It is on a special mission, sent by the new human—the cub. Its fur, normally white as survival camouflage to save it from being seen by large predators, is no longer white. It is rusty red from the blood on the female human's legs. It wants to be seen; it needs to be seen; it must be seen. That is its mission.

At the same time, the prairie falcon scans the ground many feet below its vantage point in the overcast sky. It is also on a special mission, sent by the other new human—the fledgling. Its call is loud and piercing, "*kree-kree-kree-kree*." It wants to be heard; it needs to be heard; it must be heard. That is its mission.

The female human slept through the night. Even the little ones slept, until early this morning. Now, they are awake. Their cries are as different as their looks. One howls like a wolf's cub; the other squawks like a bird. The mother human feeds them together, and they are quiet, content, confident in the instructions they imparted to the hare and the falcon.

All through the night, the guardian creatures heard the frantic sounds of the searchers. They were near, but they were not near enough. Despite their calls, the female human did not wake;

she was spent from her birthing ordeal. Afterwards, she was warm and drowsy from the bodies of all the guardians. It was good; she needed rest, as did the little ones.

Now, the daylight is breaking and gives warmth and color to the morning. The snow glitters where the sun struggles to peek through the clouds. The forest creatures have done what they can for the female and her young. It is time for the searchers to come and rescue them. While the others continue to provide their life-giving heat, the hare and the falcon are dispatched by the tiny ones. They have a great work to carry out. They must alert the searchers to the whereabouts of the human family.

Dane and a crew of police and firefighters continue looking for Raven. They have been scouring the side roads and paths on the mountain all night, calling her name, shining powerful flashlights, checking beneath every tree. After all these hours, even with the benefit of Lee's directions, they have not yet found her, and Dane is beside himself with worry.

Dane recalls the anguish in Graham's voice as he relayed Raven's screams. Childbirth always carries with it an element of risk, even with one infant. Raven was carrying twins, and she had already miscarried so many times. So much could go wrong: if they were turned wrong, if the cord wrapped around their little necks, if she simply gave out from the combination of exhaustion and the elements. His mind went to scenarios he dreaded, yet he was unable to stop thinking of what grave danger she ... they ... were in. *What if we can't find them in time?* he wonders.

A shout commands his attention. He looks in the direction of the activity and sees a group of men staring over the edge of the mountain. They have found the wreckage of the Ford Explorer in the branches of a strand of piñon trees. Dane watches as Jimmy cinches up a harness and rappels down into the trees to examine the vehicle.

When Jimmy reaches the vehicle, he sees that the driver's side door is open. He notices blood on the window and some wicked scratches on the top of the door. He does not tell Dane that he thinks his wife may have been thrown from the car and could be lying broken and mangled farther down below.

Dane turns away. He is not so concerned about the car. He knows from Lee's track last night that Raven was not in the vehicle when it went over the side. She continued upward. He heads off in that direction.

Beside the road, Dane spots a splash of color. He hurries over to that area and bends down. Brushing the light dusting of snow away, he picks up a handful of Raven's sketches. She was here. He stuffs the pictures in his pocket and keeps going up. Lee said she kept going north.

Even though the sun has risen, it is still fiercely cold. Dane pulls his knit cap farther down on his head. It is the multicolored monstrosity that Robin knitted from the scraps of baby clothes yarn. He wants to think it will bring him good fortune. It is freezing outside, and even though she has a down jacket, the elements are brutal. He worries about the babies.

He scans desperately for footprints. There are none. There was a light snow during the night that obliterated any evidence of tracks. Looking to the white expanse above the road, he sees a lone rabbit sticking up in the snow. *Poor little creature. Frozen solid.* He looks closer. *That's not a rabbit. That's a rabbit fur moccasin!*

"Here," he calls. "She was here!" He begins frantically scaling the incline on this side of the road, clutching the frozen slipper in his hand.

He stumbles and his foot sinks into a depression in the snow. Stepping back, he examines the depression more closely. There are six depressions—four outer ones, two inner ones. The inner depressions are like sled runner tracks leading up the mountain. The outer ones are deeper and broken, making the impressions resemble Morse code. Hooves. Hooves on either side of her, pulling her, dragging her. It makes sense.

Dane struggles to follow in the tracks left by the unknown animals and his wife. "She's on this side," he calls to his colleagues. "She's up the mountain."

Dane continues to ascend the slope, and behind him follow Jimmy and Chief Oatman, who personally organized the rescue efforts. The forest gets denser up here, and Dane must zig and zag around trees as he follows the tracks, but he is doggedly following.

They are like breadcrumbs from a fairy tale he remembers of two children lost in the woods. He also has two children lost in the woods, and a wife of incalculable value.

A screeching prairie falcon overhead draws Danes attention farther up the mountain. It compels him forward. He takes off, running as best he can up the slippery slope. The falcon continues calling, urging him onward. Dane steps into a particularly deep drift and almost loses his footing. The falcon swoops and snatches the multicolored cap off his head, freeing his hair. It whips around his face like a black bird taking wing.

Dane lifts his head and takes a deep breath. Underneath the fresh smell of the snow and the tang of the pine trees, he detects the scent of damp animal fur and old blood, like prey that has been left after the initial feast. He shivers, and then the wind carries the improbable aroma of vanilla. It is fresh and heady, and it fills his nostrils with its sweetness. It is Raven's signature fragrance. He can smell her; he can smell his children. He twists around and shouts. "She's up here!"

Up the slope, Chief Oatman spots a large hare covered in blood, behaving strangely, coming down the mountain. Every few feet it rolls as if trying to wipe off the blood.

"Lightfoot," Oatman shouts, "Look at that rabbit. What's wrong with that rabbit?"

Dane sees the hare, smells the blood, and runs toward the animal. He sees it has left a trail of bloody smudges in the snow. *My wife's blood,* he realizes.

Adrenaline pumping, Dane continues scaling the incline, grasping limbs and pulling himself upward. Jimmy and the Chief fall far behind, unable to keep up. But Dane will not stop. The love of his life is up here ... and his children.

Just up ahead, Dane sees a huge pine tree. The falcon circles the tree, screeching at him. Dane runs, falling, stumbling, making his way to the tree. As he gets within sight of its spreading branches, he sees a bizarre sight. Against the trunk, atop a hot pink down jacket, are animals of all kinds. Beneath them, covered nearly head to toe with squirrels, mice, rabbits, and even a coyote, is his wife. Dane stops his forward motion and stands still, not believing his eyes. He is terrified. *Is she dead?*

Coming up behind him, Jimmy raises his gun in the air to scare them off, but Dane stops him. The small animals gaze at Dane, their hot breath leaving little puffs of vapor in the air. One by one, they carefully move away from the woman, but two huge Sonoran pronghorns remain steadfast on either side of her.

Her face exposed to the sudden coldness of the air, Raven wakes, opens her eyes, and sees him. "Dane." She cries silently.

Dane's feet move of their own accord and take him directly to her beneath the tree. The pronghorns rise to their feet and back up to let him near. He drops down on his knees and takes his wife in his arms, weeping.

Chief Oatman arrives and stands with Jimmy, looking at the scene in awe. "I feared the worst," he says.

"So did I," Jimmy says.

"But have you ever seen …?" Oatman says.

"Never. Never in my life," Jimmy replies.

Dane and Raven break their embrace and she opens the top of her jacket. Dane sees his children for the first time. He looks at her quizzically. "Boys," she says smiling.

Oatman calls for the rescue team to bring the stretcher sled. He and Jimmy stand together, shaking their heads in disbelief.

"A woman gives birth to twins and stays the night in the wilderness," Jimmy says. "What a woman!"

"What a woman, indeed, Jim," Oatman says. "Damn fine woman, I'd say."

The stretcher arrives, and the medics help Raven into it, covering her and the babies with several warm blankets. Only after they have secured her in the stretcher do the pronghorns move completely away.

As the rescuers descend the mountain with Raven and the infants safely strapped into the stretcher, Dane looks back at the tree. It is deserted now; all the animals have disappeared. He silently whispers a grateful prayer to God and to all the creatures that kept his little family safe.

Dane keeps one hand on the stretcher all the way down the slope to the rescue vehicle. Sitting beside her as they drive down the road (which has now been salted and sanded), he gazes as his little boys. They are fraternal twins, not identical. He marvels at the differences in their looks at less than a day old.

"They don't look like twins, do they?" he says.

"No. They are each unique. But they were born together," she says.

"What do you mean?"

"Their arms and legs were entwined, and they were cheek to cheek, holding each other. These little boys wanted to be born at exactly the same time."

"So that means …" Dane says.

"Both of them. But they will be different, Dane. Even now I know it. Their cries are completely unlike each other, too."

"Raven, what about those animals? How did that happen?"

"The boys. They already have some abilities. One called the mammals; one called the birds. In utero, Dane. *Before* they were even born."

Dane shakes his head, looking at his sons in a completely new light. *And Hona thought he was unprepared for Kenny? What in the world will I do with these guys?* He thinks.

"I've named them," Raven says.

"Why am I not surprised? Want to let me know what to call them?" Dane asks.

"I have named them after your mother and my father."

Dane grimaces. "Fawn and Falcon?"

Raven laughs. She pulls the blanket off one baby's head. He has a shock of black hair that sticks up atop his head like a feather headdress. He opens his eyes, and Dane wonders if he can see yet. Even through the blueish tint, he can tell his son's eyes will be soft brown and almond-shaped, like his mother's.

"This one is *Kiisa.* He will be as sharp-eyed as a prairie falcon, just like my father."

"*Kiisa,*" says Dane, shrugging.

She uncovers the other baby. His hair is straight and fine, like his daddy's. His eyes are also open, staring back at his father with interest. They are barely blue, and Dane sees they will be large and round and black.

"This one is *Tsop*. He will be a strong, fast runner, like a deer or antelope."

"*Tsop?*" says Dane, a curious look on his face.

Raven laughs again, and Dane falls in love with her all over again. She snuggles the boys lying on her chest.

"Chubs. I hate to say it, but we gotta work on those names. I appreciate the thought ... but *Kiisa* and *Tsop?*"

"Don't worry about it, Bucko. I wouldn't do that to them. Those are their spirit names. Mortal versions of the *Katsinam*."

Dane rolls his eyes to the sky. "Woman, you are gonna kill me yet." He brings his lips to her mouth.

Raven smiles sweetly at him and nudges the babies awake again. Holding their little heads up a bit, she kisses each one's cheek. She lovingly meets her husband's eyes as he reaches forward and places a large hand on top of each little boy's head.

"Meet your sons, Dane Lightfoot. This is *Kiisa* and *Tsop*, but we will call them Perry and Buck."

CHAPTER 15

SPIRITS, GHOSTS, AND THE LIVING

IN THE BASEMENT *KIVA*, Jeffrey fits the final *Katsina* into its carved-out resting place. The *kiva* is completed. He sighs and wipes his forehead with his shirt sleeve. *Finished at last, but I wish Frederick could be here.*

He has followed Frederick's vision to the very last detail. The niches surround the walls at eye level. Each *Katsina* has its own home, carved from the adobe-covered walls, its recess designed to fit each god comfortably. *It is good,* Jeffrey decides.

A fire blazes in the central flagstone pit, warming Jeffrey's body. He scans the room, its corners cloaked in darkness. The firelight flickers and casts shadows on the walls, making him imagine the spirit fathers are moving from within their niches.

He walks to the ladder and climbs upstairs to the kitchen, taking the canvas bag and the protective wrapping with him, careful to leave no debris in the *kiva*.

After depositing the bag on the floor, he walks to the table. He navigates by the light which spills from the opening in the floor. There has been no gas for the generator since he returned after rescuing the *Katsinam* from the museum earlier in the week. No generator also means no power for the well, but there is plenty of snow. He pours himself a glass of water from the tin coffee pot he previously filled with snow and melted on the pot-bellied stove.

A cast-iron pot on top of the stove sends tendrils of steam up to the ceiling. Jeffrey removes the pot with a heavy towel and sets it on the table. Then, removing all his clothing, he dips a rag into the pot and begins to bathe.

Once he has cleansed himself, Jeffrey paints his entire body red, yellow, brown, and blue. He paints with his hands in the ancient, traditional way. Though he did not grow up Hopi, he has been learning from his mentor for the past couple of years. He knows that a spiritual essence exists in every part of life, and it is important to acknowledge that essence. Spirit lives in the seasons, the elements, the outer reaches of the universe, the two- and four-legged creatures, the winged ones, the insects, the trees, the plants, and even the rocks.

Jeffrey then takes a special *homamoki* bag down from atop the cabinet. It contains ground corn meal and has been resting in the kitchen until such a time as the *Katsinam* are returned. Holding the bag carefully, he descends the ladder into the *kiva.*

The *kiva* is the central area of life and is the most sacred Hopi ceremonial space. The underground chamber and the *sipapu* hole represent the Below, the world from which all Hopi people emerged, symbolic of the womb of Mother Earth.

Jeffrey places the bag on the floor which he has meticulously swept. Climbing back up the ladder, he closes the hatch into the kitchen and locks it from the inside. After a deep, shuddering sigh, he climbs down to the floor, removes the ladder, and dismantles it.

He takes the pieces of the ladder to the fire pit and arranges them according to size beside the flagstones. He digs a small hole with a trowel and places the metal bolts and nuts into it. He removes the handle from the trowel and tosses it into the fire, along with the cords that bound the ladder together. Then, he buries the metal shovel part in the hole with the other metal objects, patting down the earth smoothly.

Opening the *homamoki* bag, he removes a simple *paho*—a single downy eagle feather tied with a cotton string. Frederick had ritually smoked and prayed over this feather, blessing it before placing it in the bag with the blessed corn meal, to be used for the return of the gods. He ties it in his hair.

Reaching into the bag, Jeffrey takes a fistful of corn meal and spreads it on the floor beneath the hatch where the ladder once stood. This will prevent any living creatures from coming into the *kiva*. He lifts another handful of corn meal over his head and sprinkles it liberally onto his naked, painted body.

He moves about the room, casting corn meal along the base of each wall, into the corners, and beneath the carving table which covers the grave of his mentor. A tear escapes his eye as he regards the carving implements Frederick cherished, the hand-mixed paints, the brushes of all sizes and textures, and the newly created grave which contains the remaining unused cottonwood roots. *Master, I will try to do you proud tonight,* he vows to his friend.

He returns to the fire, feeds it with some of the smaller pieces of ladder, and waits for it to blaze up. Then, taking a slender piece of kindling, he walks to the first wall of *Katsinam* which extends from the left of the carving table.

This wall holds a group of five niches with a candle set in a holder in the wall beside each cubbyhole. He lights each candle and reverently addresses the god it illuminates.

"*SIKYAQOQLO*. Artist, who endowed my master with your talents, and who resides beside his resting place. I welcome you to your home.

POLIIMANA. Butterfly Maiden, whose beauty graces the dances. I welcome you to your home.

LENANGTAQA. Flute Player, whose music makes the Butterflies dance. I welcome you to your home.

POOTAWIKKATSINA. Coiled Plaque Carrier, whose woven gifts bring pleasure to the people. I welcome you to your home.

KOKOPÖLÖ. Humpback, who blesses the people with fertility and increases the clans. I welcome you to your home."

Jeffrey walks to the adjacent wall in which eight gods stand in their carved niches.

"*KWAHU*. Great Eagle, who soars the skies and bestows your sacred feathers. I welcome you to your home.

KIISA. Chicken Hawk Racer, who whips the opponents you catch in the races. I welcome you to your home.

TSOPKATSINA. Antelope, who dances for successful hunting. I welcome you to your home.

SOWI'INGKATSINA. Deer Dancer, who brings increase in game animals. I welcome you to your home.

KWEWU. Wolf, who guards the animal dancers. I welcome you to your home.

ANGWUSKATSINA. Crow, who enforces order with the yucca whip. I welcome you to your home.

ANGWUSNUSOMTAQA. Crow Mother, who instructs new initiates. I welcome you to your home.

WUPAMOKATSINA. Long Mouth Whipper Guard, who supervises the security forces of the *WHIPPER Katsinam*. I welcome you to your home."

He moves clockwise to the next wall of eight gods and continues the ritual.

"*KOYEMSI*. Mudhead Racer, who carried your crippled brother on your shoulders into battle. I welcome you to your home.

TUHAVI. Paralyzed Brother, who rode on your blind brother's shoulders into battle. I welcome you to your home.

AHÖLA. Chief's Lieutenant, *Katsina* priest who is the right hand of the Chief. I welcome you to your home.

EWTOTO. Chief, who is leader and spiritual father of the people. I welcome you to your home.

QALETAQA. Warrior, who protects the sacred rituals from interruption. I welcome you to your home.

HEE'E'E. Warrior Woman, who leads the fierce *WHIPPER Katsinam* into the village. I welcome you to your home.

NATA'ASKA. Big Mouth Ogre, who frightens children into good behavior. I welcome you to your home.

SO'YOKWUUTI. Ogre Woman, who disciplines naughty

children. I welcome you to your home."

Jeffrey moves to the last group of seven gods—the most powerful group of all. He lights their candles.

"*OMAWKATSINA.* Cumulous Cloud, who brings life-giving rain. I welcome you to your home.

SOOTUKWNANG. Star, who maintains balance and manages the movement of the universe. I welcome you to your home.

MUUYAWKATSINA. Moon, who guards the people at night and provides messages from afar. I welcome you to your home.

Tawa. Sun, who rules the Above and watches over the people by day. I welcome you to your home.

KOKYANWUUTI. Spider Woman, who created the Between and all life with the Sun. I welcome you to your home.

AWANYU. Plumed Serpent, guardian of flowing water. I welcome you to your home.

MASAUWU. Death, Skeleton Man, god of the Fourth World, who guards my master's resting place and cares for us in the Afterlife. I welcome you to your home."

With all the candles lit, Jeffrey returns to stand in front of Frederick's carving table. He scans the room and watches the gods as the flickering candlelight in the semi-darkness makes them seem to dance within their alcoves.

He removes the prayer feather from his hair, holds it aloft in his hand, and addresses the *Katsinam* as a unit.

"Great ones. Spirit Fathers and Mothers. This carver has done his best to bring you home. This carver has worked to restore balance. Reward this Apprentice, Jeffrey Wilson, and the Master, Frederick Kalyesvah, who first created the bodies in which your spirit now lives. Grant that we may return to this world as rain clouds, as spring showers or summer storms or winter rain, that we may nourish the world Between and bring forth life in our death. If you find us worthy, may our endeavors be rewarded with life reincarnate." He prays fervently, his voice ragged with emotion.

After the prayer, Jeffrey Wilson feeds the remainder of the

ladder into the fire. His face is shiny with sweat from the heat, and he backs away, sitting stiffly on the bench in front of the carving table. As if in answer to his prayer, he hears a loud explosive thunderclap from above, and then the staccato of heavy rain beating on the tin roof of the cabin.

He sits there on the bench watching the fire burn itself down to embers, watching the shadows creep into the corners of the room, watching the *Katsinam* moving from side to side, watching the candles growing smaller and finally winking out, watching the world turn to darkness within the *kiva*.

* * *

Jeffrey opens his eyes to the sound of someone calling his name in the darkness.

"Jeffrey, wake up," the voice says.

"Who is there?" Jeffrey asks.

"Wake up, Jeffrey. They are waiting."

Jeffrey's eyes register light coming from the center of the room. It is dim at first, and then it brightens. The fire crackles and burns, but it gives off no heat. But neither is there a sensation of coldness. Jeffrey looks around, blinking. A hand touches his shoulder, and he turns his head to see a young man standing in front of him, much the same age as himself, his face shadowed by the backlit fire.

"Who are you? And how did you get down here?" Jeffrey asks the man.

"I was already here. I came before you," the man replies.

Jeffrey is confused, and he rises to move forward and get a better look at the man. He is vaguely familiar, but he cannot entirely place his face. He has a feeling he should know this guy.

"Do I know you?"

The young man turns his face toward the fire, and suddenly Jeffrey recognizes him.

"Frederick?"

"I am he who was your master," Frederick says.

"But how ... what ... I'm confused."

"We are who we were when we were the best version of ourselves. We will remain as we are now."

"Are … are we dead? Are we ghosts?"

"We live as spirits, so we are not dead, in that respect. We are in another realm. You can call us ghosts, if you wish. We simply are as we are."

Jeffrey nods his head and looks around. "And this place?"

"This place is our place. This is where we will be."

"I thought we would be rain clouds."

Frederick laughs. "I suppose the gods have a better use for us. We are to be their keepers, their subjects, their people in this place." He sweeps his arm towards the walls.

Jeffrey looks at the four walls, expecting to see the *Katsinam* in their cubbies. Instead, he sees an assemblage of men and women in full masks and costumes. The gods nod to him in greeting. He returns the gesture. Frederick takes his arm and leads him back to the bench, sitting beside him.

"What now?" Jeffrey asks.

"Now, we wait, and we watch," his friend says.

One by one, the *Katsinam* dance around the fire. Some of them tell stories, some of them race each other, some of them sing. The two young men watch, and listen, and join in the songs and dances, while outside, the world succumbs to spring rains.

* * *

Robin Looking Bird struggles with the umbrella as she stuffs the last of her packed suitcases into the back of Dane's new Chevy Tahoe. It is loaded up to the ceiling with everything the family could possibly fit inside. She makes one last look at the house that has been their home for these past several months, and then she climbs into the back, stowing the wet umbrella at her feet. She buckles up beside the baby seat holding one of her new grandsons, Perry Lightfoot.

The other baby seat is secured next to this one so Robin can easily reach both infants. Taking up a place next to the other door is Bugle, his tail held tightly in the grip of Buck Lightfoot.

Raven is already in the front seat, and once Robin gets in, she hands her a diaper bag laden with bottles, wipe cloths, pacifiers, and various toys to entertain the little boys. Robin takes a tiny pillow stuffed with down feathers and puts it beside Perry's head. He snuggles against it contentedly.

Raven gazes at her sons. They are perfect, in her eyes. Two gifted children: one who communes with animals, and one who communes with birds. What a homecoming they will get in Florida where there are plenty of adoring family and friends to spoil them. She can hardly wait to get started. She reaches over to the wheel and honks the horn.

"Get a move on, Bucko. I need to get out of Arizona," she calls through the partially open window. The sound of the horn sends Bugle into a *"baroo,"* and Buck cackles, beating the captive tail against the baby seat.

Dane appears at the door. He shakes his head at her impatience, but he is every bit as ready to leave this mountain and get home to heat, humidity, and home. It will be May, the edge of summer, when they return. He looks forward to short pants, flip-flops, and t-shirts. He can almost smell the newly cut grass. Raven honks the horn again, disrupting his daydream.

He locks the door, sets the key under the mat, and strides to the car, not minding the pouring rain that plasters his long hair to his head. When he gets into the car, he makes a big deal of shaking his wet hair, causing the women to scream and the babies to chortle with delight. He turns the key and exits the driveway, navigating the wet road carefully.

Thus begins a long, but happy trip for the family of five. In roughly two days' time (30 hours as the crow flies), they will be back in Tallahassee. Arrangements have already been made for Robin to take over Raven's apartment and her car. The second bedroom of Raven and Dane's house will be converted to the boys' room, and Dane even has the offer of his old job back as a fire marshal.

The case of the missing kachinas is still ongoing, but only for the Trackers. Nobody could find a record of an F. Kalyesvah anywhere in Prescott. There was a Frederick Kalyesvah—a master kachina carver—who lived for a time in Walpi, but his whereabouts were never discovered after he left that area.

Fingerprints on the display case at the Smoki came back as unidentified. Neither Dane nor Raven ever disclosed the revelation that certain kachinas in the case were forgeries. It would be best if the authorities never knew.

Noah tracked the kachinas he had seen in Raven's drawings, and though he saw them as figurines in carved-out niches the first time, the second time he tracked, they were gone. Their alcoves were empty, the room was dark, and all he could see were some ghostly, spectral images. He chalked this up to being tired and didn't give it much more thought.

The night after Raven was recovered from the mountain, there was an earsplitting thunderclap, and then the rain began pouring in torrents. It continued for days, melting all the snow and causing many incidents of mudslides in all the mountainous areas around Prescott.

Several small cabins were engulfed in the mudslides, including one that housed an underground *kiva* filled with 28 precious *Katsinam* and two dead bodies. The remains of the cabin would not be discovered for many months, and even then, nobody would think of digging down beneath the rubble.

To this day, visitors to that area—especially overnight campers—swear that they hear singing and laughter and feet pounding like dancing, but the mountain can play tricks on people. Most likely, they hear the sounds of a screeching prairie falcon as it circles above a tall ponderosa pine tree and the hooves of a pair of Sonoran pronghorns running through the forest.

EPILOGUE
THE KEEPER

I FINISH COLLECTING RAVEN'S STORY—the Snapshot's. It is late in the evening, and Mother is there, as usual, to bring me home. I drop my flute, and I hear her pick it up. I am exhausted. This journey has been a difficult one. For the first time, I did not know how it would end.

"Luna," Mother says, "*Enkv?* OK? *¿Que Pasa, mi amor?* How are you, my love?"

I am used to the odd mixture of Spanish, English, and Muskogee in her conversation.

"Yes, mother. I am just tired," I whisper.

"You traveled long, my daughter. I will help you home," she says, taking my hands and pulling me to my feet.

"Yes. I don't think I can walk by myself," I say.

Mother puts her arm around my waist and walks slowly beside me, stopping every few steps to allow me to catch my breath. She is always here for me.

"Your sister? Is she well?" she asks.

"She is well, but I had much fear for her," I say.

"And her children? Are they well?" she asks.

I smile through my weariness. "Yes, they are all well. I have two fine new nephews, and they are special," I say.

"All children are special, Luna," Mother says. Her voice has an odd tone to it.

Sometimes Mother is sad, and I do not know why.

"You hide something from me, Mother," I say.

She is quiet for a few moments. "I ... I am also tired, daughter," she says.

We keep walking, but I know my mother well. For 19 years she has kept a secret, but I am sure she will reveal it when the time is right. Now is not that time.

"Yes. You must be. You have stayed with me the whole time. *Gracias*," I say.

"*De nada*. It is nothing," she says.

We walk a little farther, and Mother stops. "Tell me of your nephews," she says.

"They are perfect ... and they are gifted," I say.

"Both of them?" she asks, surprise evident in her voice.

"Born at the same time in a loving embrace," I say.

"Do you know their gifts?" she asks.

"Yes. One speaks with the animals, and one speaks with the winged ones," I say.

"*Mvdo*. It is good," she says. Then, seeing my frown, she asks, "But what is wrong?"

"My friend, the boy Chenaniah. The one I speak with His sister and her man who will be her husband within a day. Their family has heartbreak and much danger coming," I say.

"Do not worry, Luna. You are a *hecetv*—a seer. You will see the danger and keep them safe," she says, "but first you will rest, my daughter."

I nod my head and bite my lower lip, for I know they will experience great sadness and much pain, and I cannot stop it But Mother is right. I *will* keep them safe.

APPENDIX

LANGUAGE TRANSLATIONS

Muskogee Creek Language

The Muskogee Creek language is spoken extensively on the reservations in Oklahoma; however, in the Southeast, there are relatively few native speakers. In the tri-state region of Florida, Georgia, and Alabama, language classes are held in an effort to keep the language from becoming extinct.

The vowels are pronounced as follows:

A=w_A_tch	E=_I_tch	E=s_EE_
I=s_AY_	O=m_OA_n	U=b_OO_k
V=_U_nder	EU=_U_se	UE=b_OY_
VO=n_OW_	Note: vowels are voiced with partially closed, tight mouth.	

Consonants are sounded as follows:

C=ri_CH_	C= ca_TS_	C=_J_am
F=_F_air	H=_H_air	K=bi_K_e
K= _G_o	L=_L_ike	M=_M_an
N=ma_N_	P=_P_ie	P= _B_uy
R=_TLH_ or _HL_ (There is no English equivalent. The sound is much like an attempt to bring forth phlegm)		
S=_S_ee	S= _Z_oo	SK=wi_SH_
SS=wi_SH_	T=_T_ea	T=_D_ie
W=_W_et	Y=_Y_et	
Note: Consonants are voiced with tight mouths, far back in the throat. The sounds are almost "swallowed."		

Muskogee Words, Phrases, and their Meanings
(in order of appearance)

Hvresse Torwv—Moon Eyes

Chickees—open-sided houses

Heles pocase—medicine man

Heles Haya Pocase—doctor medicine man

Mvdo—It is good

Hecetv—a seer

Spanish Language

Conversational Spanish, in its many forms and dialects, is one of the most widely spoken languages in the world and is prevalent throughout Mexico, Central America, and the United States. Though it varies slightly by regions, it is generally consistent in its pronunciation.

The vowels are pronounced as follows:

A=w_A_tch	E= b_E_d	I =s_EE_
O=m_OA_n	U=b_OO_k	Y =s_EE_
Note: vowels are voiced with open, relaxed mouth.		

Consonants are sounded as follows:

B =_B_ed	C=_C_ow	C=_S_ow
D=_Th_ink	F=_F_un	G=_G_un
H=silent	J=_Ch_ew	K=_K_ick
L=_L_ick	LL=_Y_ard	M=_M_an
N=_N_ow	Ñ=can_Y_on	P=_P_ark
Q/QU=_K_ick	R=ca_RR_y	RR=as _R_, but trilled
T=_T_ake	V=_B_ed	W=_W_ater
X=e_X_cuse	Y=_Y_es	Z=pin_TS_
Note: consonants are voiced with open, relaxed mouth. Hard consonants are explosively voiced.		

Spanish Words, Phrases, and their Meanings
(in order of appearance)

Ojos del Luna – Eyes of the Moon (proper name)
Bueno—good
Digame en Español—Tell me in Spanish
Agua grande—big water
Hermana—sister
Comprendo—I understand
¿Que Pasa, mi amor?—How are you, my love?

Gracias—Thank you
De nada—It is nothing

Hopi Language

Hopi is a Havasupai language with several locational dialects spoken by about 5,000 of the Hopi people of northeastern Arizona. It is a difficult language with very long compound words and is related to the Aztec language. The Third Mesa dialect is used in this book.

The vowels are pronounced as follows:

A=w_Atch_	E= b_E_d	I =s_EE_
AA=w_A_tch (drawn out)	EE= b_E_d (drawn out)	II =s_EE_ (drawn out)
O=m_OA_n	Ö=w_O_rd	U=p_U_t
OO=m_OA_n (drawn out)	Ö Ö =w_O_rd (drawn out)	UU=p_U_t (drawn out)

Dipthongs are sounded as follows

AW or AU=c_OW_	AY=h_YE_na	EW=Oh_IO_
EY =h_AY_	IW=p_EW_	IY=s_EE_
OW=sh_OW_	OY=b_OY_	UW=t_OO_
There is no English equivalent for these dipthongs		
ÖW=Ö ending with a W sound	ÖY=Ö ending with a Y sound	UY=U ending with a Y sound
Note: vowels are voiced with open, relaxed mouth.		

Consonants are sounded as follows:

H =_H_ay	K=s_K_y	KW=_QU_ick
L=_L_ick	M=_M_an	N=_N_ow
NG=si_NG_	P=s_P_y	Q=_K_ick

QW=_QUart_ (voiced farther back in the throat)		
There is no English equivalent for these consonants		
NGW=_riNGWorm_ _(ng+w)_	NGY=_like_ _Spanish N_ _in piÑon_	R=_like GE_ _in garaGE_
S=_See_	T=_sTar_	TS=_caTS_ or _CHop_
V=ca_Ve_	W=_Way_	Y=_Yes_
' = _pause or glottal stop like – in uh-oh_		

Hopi (Havasupai) Words, Phrases, and their Meanings
(in order of appearance)

Angwuskatsina—Crow _Katsina_

Angwusnusomtaqa—Crow Mother _Katsina_

Nata'aska—Big Mouth Ogre _Katsina_

So'yokwuuti—Ogre Woman _Katsina_

Ewtoto—Chief _Katsina_

Ahöla—Chief's Lieutenant _Katsina_

Lenangtaqa—Flute Player _Katsina_

Poliimana—Butterfly Maiden _Katsina_

Kwewu—Wolf _Katsina_

Sowi'ingkatsina—Deer Dancer _Katsina_

Tsopkatsina—Antelope _Katsina_

Sikyaqoqlo—Artist _Katsina_

Wupamokatsina—Guard _Katsina_

Qaletaqa—Warrior _Katsina_

Hee'e'e—Warrior Maiden _Katsina_

Koyemsi—Mudhead Racer _Katsina_

Tuhavi—Paralyzed Brother _Katsina_

Kiisa—Chicken Hawk Racer _Katsina_

Kwahu—Eagle _Katsina_

Kokopölö—Humpback _Katsina_

Pootawikkatsina—Coiled Plaque Carrier _Katsina_

Muuyawkatsina—Moon _Katsina_

Tawa—Sun _Katsina_

Katsinam—_more than one Katsina_

Katsina— from *katsi*—spirit or life + *na*—father.

Nookatuwa—*Nooka* + *tuwa*—to see

Yapatisvo—little gray bird who imitates the sounds of other birds

Galyum Clan—Small Bird Clan

Pai —people

Paaqavi—Bacabi, the Third Mesa on the Hopi Reservation.

O'waqölt—Basket Dance

Lakon—an exclusive women's society of basket weavers

Sikwi—wild game meat

Hohoysi—greenthread tea

Beva—tobacco

Homa—white corn meal used for prayers and ceremonies

Sivukatsina—fertility *Katsina* who promotes procreation

Qomi—sweet corn flour dough

Tsosovi—Bluebird

Atokotiva—Dancing Crane

Karocatori—Parrot Spirit

Qomvitsiro—Black Bird

Pos Iwuu Hoomi—Magpie Hair

Lomahongava—Beautiful Clouds Arising

Zihmatotsa—Spinning Hummingbird

Sihuqoto—Head of Flowers

Pik'ami—sweet pudding

Morivosi—beans and vegetables

Somiviki—a sweet tamale-shaped cake of blue corn

Piki—traditional Hopi "paper bread"

Maloni—sweet musk melon

Kwaani—dried figs

Tosi—finely hand-ground sweet corn flour

Bacavi—small, flexible reeds like bamboo

Naququsi—prayer feathers

Taah—a surprised exclamation

He He Y—a joyful exclamation

Aus quali—thank you (feminine form)

Wu Katsina—Whipper Katsina

Wala—a small gap between two mesas

Qomvitsiro Kivakatsina—little black bird's house of the gods

Kiva—underground place of worship, sacred to the Hopi

Sipapu—small hole in the floor of a kiva through which the first people emerged

Hahai-i-Wuhti—grandmother *Katsina*

Putsihu—small, flat cradle doll

Masauwu—Skeleton Man, or Death.

Omawkatsina—Cumulous Cloud.

Awanyu—Plumed Serpent.

Sootukwnang—Star.

Kokyanwuhti—Spider Woman

Tihü—a doll-like figurine that depicts a masked dance

Wuya—spirit power

Homamoki—special bag for holding white corn meal for prayers

Yavapai Language

Yavapai is an Upland Yuman language with several locational dialects spoken by the Yavapé people near present-day Prescott, Arizona. It is similar in some ways to the Hopi/Havasupai dialects and is also a difficult language with very long compound words related to the Aztec language.

Yavapai Words, Phrases, and their Meaning
(in order of appearance)

Sauvakwaka—white + deer

Yavapai or Yavapé—people of the sun or mouthy, talkative people

Gisak'—raven

Sakiye—white head eagle

Whamboonayvas—brush shelters

Uwas—closed huts of ocotillo branches covered with animal skins, dirt, bark, and grass

ACKNOWLEDGMENTS

I want to thank those who had a part in the inspiration and completion of <u>The Trackers Series</u> books (in alphabetical order):

Andrew R., Angie J., Ann C., Bryan C., Carol J., Cheri H., Guy P., Helen S., Jackie T., Jan V., Jennifer K., Katie M., Lisa B., Margaret K., Mark K., Matt B., Matt K., Micki C., Mike C., Robert N., Stephen N., Steve N., Tonna B., Wayne B., my editors, my publisher, and especially my family.

ABOUT THE AUTHOR

MICKEY MORNINGGLORY's diverse background includes the *American Federation of Television and Radio Artists (AFTRA)*, *Apalachicola Band of Eastern Creek Indians*, theater, civic light opera, and ethnomusicology. She writes for all ages under the pen names of Mickey Middleton, M.M. Busby, and Michelle Busby and is a member of *Women's Fiction Writers Association (WFWA)*, *Sisters in Crime (SinC)*, *American Copy Editors Society (ACES)*, *National Association of Independent Writers and Editors (NAIWE)*, and *Society of Children's Book Writers and Illustrators (SCBWI)*.

Ms. MorningGlory's involvement with indigenous Native tribes has made her *"a friend of many fires."* She crafts The Trackers Series multicultural paranormal mystery books in her writing studio in Northwest Florida.

Readers can visit her at www.patentprintbooks.com.

www.ingramcontent.com/pod-product-compliance
Lightning Source LLC
Chambersburg PA
CBHW021841010726
47493CB00005B/1500